THE BOOK NOOK
A PAPERBACK
CADILLAC, MI 49601
(231) 775-8171

HE'D FOUND A VIRTUAL EPIDEMIC OF NARROW MINDS AMONG HIS FELLOW PHYSICIANS

Initiative had been bred out of his generation of doctors, thought Kramer, leaving them distressingly conformist, and passive to the point of inertia. What did his former colleagues know of innovation, of dedication, of risk-taking? Of original thought?

"Fools."

Kramer turned from the window, his gaze coming to rest upon the massive refrigeration unit across the room. Made of reinforced glass two inches thick in a stainless steel frame, its shelves held dozens of quarter-liter bottles of a clear gold liquid that reminded him of white blood cells that had undergone pheresis.

He'd named the substance Affinity, and if it fulfilled the promise of his initial findings, it was every bit as precious as its golden hue might suggest.

Were it not for the parochial attitude of by-the-book doctors and scientists — and the cumbersome bureaucracy of the Food and Drug Administration, whatever their claims of having speeded up the process of drug approval — he would have been able to introduce his discovery to the world.

Instead, he had to confine his treatment to the desperate few who would make their way to this isolated corner of Nevada.

They would be the lucky ones. A n

Prepare Yourself for

PATRICIA WALLACE

LULLABYE   (2917, $3.95/$4.95)
Eight-year-old Bronwyn knew she wasn't like other girls. She didn't
have a mother. At least, not a real one. Her mother had been in a
coma at the hospital for as long as Bronwyn could remember. She
couldn't feel any pain, her father said. But when Bronwyn sat with
her mother, she knew her mother was angry—angry at the nurses and
doctors, and her own helplessness. Soon, she would show them all the
true meaning of suffering . . .

MONDAY'S CHILD   (2760, $3.95/$4.95)
Jill Baker was such a pretty little girl, with long, honey-blond hair
and haunting gray-green eyes. Just one look at her angelic features
could dispel all the nasty rumors that had been spreading around
town. There were all those terrible accidents that had begun to plague
the community, too. But the fact that each accident occurred after
little Jill had been angered had to be coincidence . . .

SEE NO EVIL   (2429, $3.95/$4.95)
For young Caryn Dearborn, the cornea operation enabled her to see
more than light and shadow for the first time. For Todd Reynolds, it
was his chance to run and play like other little boys. For these two
children, the sudden death of another child had been the miracle they
had been waiting for. But with their eyesight came another kind of
vision—of evil, horror, destruction. They could see into other
people's minds, their worst fears and deepest terrors. And they could
see the gruesome deaths that awaited the unwary . . .

THRILL   (3142, $4.50/$5.50)
It was an amusement park like no other in the world. A tri-level mar-
vel of modern technology enhanced by the special effects wizardry of
holograms, lasers, and advanced robotics. Nothing could go wrong—
until it did. As the crowds swarmed through the gates on Opening
Day, they were unprepared for the disaster about to strike. Rich and
poor, young and old would be taken for the ride of their lives, trapped
in a game of epic proportions where only the winners survived . . .

*Available wherever paperbacks are sold, or order direct from the
Publisher. Send cover price plus 50¢ per copy for mailing and
handling to Zebra Books, Dept. 3747, 475 Park Avenue South,
New York, N.Y. 10016. Residents of New York and Tennessee
must include sales tax. DO NOT SEND CASH. For a free Zebra/
Pinnacle catalog please write to the above address.*

PATRICIA WALLACE
FATAL OUTCOME

ZEBRA BOOKS
KENSINGTON PUBLISHING CORP.

For Andy
and
In Loving Memory of
Robert Curtis Cook

ZEBRA BOOKS

are published by

Kensington Publishing Corp.
475 Park Avenue South
New York, NY 10016

Copyright © 1992 by Patricia Wallace Estrada

All rights reserved. No part of this book may be reproduced in any form or by any means without the prior written consent of the Publisher, excepting brief quotes used in reviews.

If you purchased this book without a cover you should be aware that this book is stolen property. It was reported as "unsold and destroyed" to the Publisher and neither the Author nor the Publisher has received any payment for this "stripped book."

First printing: May, 1992

Printed in the United States of America

Show him death, and he'll be content with fever.

— Persian proverb

Part One

April 1992

Chapter One

Blood flooded the operative field, shocking, bright red blood, which pooled with the saline solution used to irrigate the surgical wound . . .

"Dr. Kramer," the anesthesiologist said, "the patient's blood pressure is ninety over sixty and falling."

The blood billowed, forming liquid clouds in the abdominal cavity, pulsing clouds that matched an increasingly erratic heartbeat. His hand shook, fingers gripping the scalpel tightly.

"It's eighty over fifty, and still falling." There was alarm in the anesthesiologist's voice now. "Dr. Kramer? Dr. Kramer?"

"Dr. Kramer?" Footsteps sounded behind him, echoing along the hallway. "Excuse me, Dr. Kramer?"

Alan Kramer continued walking until he reached the laboratory door, then stopped and turned abruptly. He didn't recognize the young man striding toward him, but that was no surprise. With the clinic only a week away from completion, carpenters, electricians, plumbers, and painters were swarming through the building like so many worker bees in a hive.

"What is it?" Kramer asked, not bothering to hide his impatience.

"I'm Marty Lebowitz," the young man said, "from Tower and Price."

The rising inflection in Lebowitz's voice made it sound more like a question than a statement of fact. Tower and Price were the architects Kramer had hired to design the clinic, and though they had made themselves personally scarce since the ground-breaking—which evidently coincided with the check-cashing—he'd heard rumors that a junior partner had been sighted on the premises.

"And?"

"I'm here to run interference for you with the county building inspector. He's due this afternoon."

"I see."

Lebowitz smiled uncertainly. "This particular building inspector is into molehill enhancement, and I thought, that is, Mr. Price thought—"

"Molehill enhancement?"

"As in making mountains out of . . . you know."

"I see," Kramer said again. "And this requires that you interrupt my work?"

"I . . . I . . . I didn't mean to—"

"But you have, haven't you? In less than a month, Mr. Lebowitz, this will be an operational medical facility. Lives will be at stake. I have more urgent matters at hand than a building inspector, whatever his inclination toward molehills."

"I'm sorry, I—"

Kramer turned and ran his ID card through the access reader. The laboratory door slid open. "I haven't time for this," he said, and stepped inside.

The door closed behind him and he listened to the series of metallic clicks that signaled the activation of the lock mechanisms. Next to the door, an LED displayed the date and time of entry. Above that, an indicator light panel—configured like a traffic signal—switched rapidly from green to yellow to red.

Secure.

Automatically, the master computer that controlled

10

the laboratory environment raised the lights from dim, turned on the air filtration and conditioning unit, and engaged the remote closed-circuit camera system.

A few seconds later, soft strains of the Andante from Mozart's Piano Concerto no. 21 drifted soothingly from hidden speakers. Kramer nodded in satisfaction and started across the room, pausing to adjust the clear plastic cover on the Zeiss microscope.

The laboratory had been the first section of the clinic to be completed — at his insistence — and it alone was exempt from the noisy intrusion of the workmen. The lab had become his sanctuary, in more ways than one.

Although he felt the pressure of time — the Alternative Therapy Clinic would admit its first five patients in a scant few weeks — he found himself drawn to the smoked-glass windows that overlooked the Nevada high desert.

Odd country, he thought, but strangely beautiful. Wind-sculpted clouds saved the seemingly endless expanse of blue sky from monotony, and cast curious shadows on the sun-browned hills. Beyond the hills, to the west, he could see the higher, blue-green peaks of the Sierra Nevada.

Off to the north, three miles distant, was the town of Idle Springs. According to a bullet-riddled sign he'd seen, the town's population hovered at an anemic and probably stagnant 180.

He recalled a favorite saying of his father's: "The smaller the town, the narrower the mind." Having grown up in a town not much larger than Idle Springs, he knew it to be the truth.

Then again, small towns had no corner on that market; he'd found a virtual epidemic of narrow minds among his fellow physicians. They prided themselves on being bold and progressive in pursuit of medical advances, but in truth they were timid, cowering in fear of malpractice suits and million-dol-

11

lar judgments.

Initiative had been bred out of his generation of doctors, leaving them distressingly conformist, and passive to the point of inertia.

Medicine had to be practiced within certain boundaries, delineated by conventional treatment plans and short-sighted protocols. His former colleagues not only accepted such limitations, they had embraced them.

What did they know of innovation, of dedication, of risk-taking?

Of original thought?

"Fools."

Kramer turned from the window, his gaze coming to rest upon the massive refrigeration unit across the room. Made of reinforced glass two inches thick in a stainless steel frame, its shelves held dozens of quarter-liter bottles of a clear gold liquid that reminded him of white blood cells that had undergone pheresis.

He'd named the substance Affinity, and if it fulfilled the promise of his initial findings, it was every bit as precious as its golden hue might suggest.

Were it not for the parochial attitude of by-the-book doctors and scientists — and the cumbersome bureaucracy of the Food and Drug Administration, whatever their claims of having speeded up the process of drug approval — he would have been able to introduce his discovery to the world.

Instead, he had to confine his treatment to the desperate few who would make their way to this isolated corner of Nevada.

They would be the lucky ones.

Chapter Two

Boston

Honor Matheson tore off several six-inch lengths of tape and stuck them in a neat row on the IV pole, then turned to the procedure table and selected an 18-gauge intracath from the tray.

"Okay, Mr. Rinaldi," she said, opening the sterile package, "this is going to sting."

Mr. Rinaldi's mouth worked furiously, forming tiny bubbles of spittle, but if there were words compelling his reaction they failed to make themselves heard. Of course, at only twenty-two hours post-op, pumped full of Demerol, and with a nasogastric tube still in place, that was to be expected.

Honor repositioned his arm and tightened the tourniquet slightly, noting with approval the resulting prominence of his veins. She swabbed the area above the antecubital vein with alcohol, and quickly pierced Mr. Rinaldi's skin with the needle.

There was a hint of resistance at the vein wall and then a yielding, indicating that she was in. A fat drop of dark red blood welled from the needle shaft, confirming it. She carefully pushed the intracath a couple of millimeters further in, then reached up with her left hand to release the tourniquet.

She'd already hung the lactated Ringer's solution, and had attached the tubing to the liter bag, running

13

fluid through the line to clear it of air. Now she connected the intracath to the tubing and opened the stopcock.

"There you go, Mr. Rinaldi," Honor said, reaching for a length of tape to secure the needle. "Drinks are on the house."

His response was a gentle snore; at some point in the process, Mr. Rinaldi had fallen asleep.

She took that as a compliment to her technique.

Out of consideration for the old man's tissue-paper-thin skin, she gently tucked folded gauze between his forearm and the tubing. Beneath her fingers, she could feel his flesh cool as the Ringer's lactate infused.

This patient had a history of pulling out his IVs when agitated — he'd yanked out three of them since his arrival in the Surgical Intensive Care Unit — and so she fit him with one of the new ComfortPlus armboards. With any luck, its wide Velcro straps would hold well enough to withstand his next assault.

One last adjustment to the IV flow rate, and she began to clear away the mess.

"So this is where you're hiding," a voice said from the doorway.

Honor smiled and shook her head, but didn't look up. "I'm working."

"On your last day? Get real. Anyway, it's one minute past three; you could've left that for the P.M. crew. Give them something else to bitch about."

"As tempting as that is, I'd rather they remember me kindly when I'm gone."

"Fat chance."

Honor dumped the IV wrappings in the trash, stripped off her latex gloves and tossed them too, and retrieved her bandage scissors from the procedure tray. Only then did she glance toward the door.

Patti Cummings grinned, holding out a child's party hat similar to the one perched on her tight red curls. "It's party time."

14

"I told you I didn't want a going-away party," Honor said, walking slowly toward her friend. "As a matter of fact, I distinctly recall having told you 'no party' at least twice a day since I gave notice. Which comes to some forty-odd times."

"Must have slipped my mind."

"Patti, I—"

"Don't be a spoilsport. Everyone's in the Conference Room, waiting to help you celebrate your getaway." Patti plunked the hat on her head, and snapped the thin elastic band under her chin.

"I'm not up for this," she warned. She'd spent the previous evening finishing her packing, and then, feeling restless, had wandered through the apartment until the early morning hours.

"That's too bad, because everyone else is." Patti tucked an arm in hers. "And we'd better get in there and join them before the smell of chocolate cake incites a feeding frenzy."

"All right, but I'm going under protest—"

"Duly noted."

"—and I reserve the right to sneak out if it goes on too long." Last year Dr. Stewart's farewell party had turned into a marathon event, involving all three shifts before it broke up a day and a half later.

Or so she'd heard.

"If it goes on too long," Patti said, wrinkling her nose, "you can run out screaming for all I care . . . right behind me."

"Our loss is definitely Nevada's gain," Patti said, when her turn had finally come to give a toast. She lifted a plastic cup decorated with Christmas poinsettias and filled with pink champagne. "To Honor, one of the best damned nurses ever to work her fanny off for almost no recognition and, God knows, even less money."

Honor wasn't convinced that she could, or should,

drink another drop — champagne had never been a favorite of hers, even when it wasn't lukewarm and flat — but she did, upending the glass.

"Ever the agitator, Patti," the nursing supervisor observed, stepping forward. She handed Honor a gift-wrapped box, its long thin shape familiar to any student nurse or pre-med hopeful. "It's a stethoscope. Traditional, but also practical."

"So is a bonus," a voice called out.

The supervisor permitted herself a tight-lipped smile amid the laughter that followed. "Seriously . . . what I will remember most fondly about Honor Matheson is that she always volunteered to work holidays and weekends, and never called in sick on the first warm day in the spring—"

There were groans all around.

"Get a life, Matheson," someone stage-whispered, and again laughter rippled through the room.

"Or rent one . . ."

Honor wasn't at all sure that the comments were being made in jest — she knew her reputation at Physician's & Surgeon's Hospital was as the straightest of arrows — and she felt the color begin to rise in her face.

"Enough with the lamebrained witticisms," Patti said. "Who's for cake?"

The mention of food had the desired effect; Pavlov's dogs had never drooled so responsively.

Honor smiled her appreciation to Patti for the distraction and began to work her way from the back of the room toward the front. Weaving through the crowd, she headed for the double doors, which stood open invitingly. Moving against the flow of traffic, she made slow but steady progress.

Fragments of conversation reached her, and she listened unwillingly.

"— the man is a certified megalomaniac. He may even be dangerous—"

"— hiding from the medical community, which tells

16

you straight out that his all important work can't bear the light of day—"

"—but what do you suppose her motives are? You wouldn't catch me uprooting myself for someone else's pipe dream—"

"—no better than a charlatan, feeding off the fears of the terminally ill—"

Had she suddenly become invisible, she wondered, that they were saying these awful things? Or, knowing her loyalties and her aversion to confrontation, did they want her to hear?

"—brilliant, erratic . . . a surgeon to the bone. If only he had the grace to retire—"

"—next in line for charge nurse in SICU, from what I heard."

"You're kidding, charge nurse? Shit, maybe the meek *will* inherit the earth."

"—in love with him?"

Honor was seething with anger by the time she made it to the doorway. She passed between a respiratory therapist and an X-ray technician, neither of whom seemed aware of her as they shoveled cake and spit crumbs.

Starting to shake now from repressed rage, she went first to the nurses' station to get her purse, then hurried down the hall toward the time clock to punch out for the last time.

"Honor," Patti called after her. "Wait a second, will you?"

Her instinct was to go on, to get out of this place and away from these people and get on with her life. But Patti had been a good friend, maybe even her only true friend. She stopped and turned to wait, leaning against the wall for support.

"Damn, girl, I've left a few parties early before, but you may have set a new world's and Olympic record. We'll have to call Guinness and check. Granted, there weren't many bubbles in the—"

Honor couldn't restrain herself for a moment

longer. "Did you hear what they were saying?"

"I'm sorry, what?"

"How could they be so vicious? I—"

"Hold it, who was vicious?" Patti's expression sobered. "Who do you mean?"

"Who? Who? Everybody! These are the people I've worked closely with for eight years, *eight long years,* and this is how they talk?"

"About you?"

She nodded, but couldn't bring herself to repeat what she'd overheard, saying instead: "There isn't one of them fit to speak his name."

Awareness dawned in Patti's eyes. "So that's what this is about. Dr. Kramer."

The 'again' went unsaid.

"You'd think they would have compassion for him, for what he's been through."

"Well, yes, but it *is* a little difficult to feel sympathy for a surgeon who knowingly puts his patients at risk—"

"I won't listen to any more." Honor pressed her hands over her ears, feeling absurdly like a five year old being teased in a school yard.

It was every bit as ineffectual now as it had been against her classmates' taunts; she could hear the intercom paging a Code Blue to the Emergency Department, as well as the hacking cough of a patient across the hall.

"Okay, okay. I don't know what Alan Kramer ever did to earn your loyalty—"

"No one understands."

"Then let's consider the subject closed." Patti consulted her watch and nodded in the direction of the elevators. "It's not quite three-thirty, but what the hell, it isn't every day you can make a break for it . . . let's get out of here."

Later, though, alone in her apartment for her final

18

night in Boston, Honor had no choice but to listen to the thoughts echoing in her head. Words and phrases tormented her, but what was worse was that for the first time she felt stirrings of doubt.

Doubt . . . and a sense of foreboding.

Chapter Three

Los Angeles

On a subliminal level, Shea Novak was aware of silence descending over the office. The drone of voices faded, and the phones rang less frequently until they finally fell quiet. The low hum of computers and laser printers in the background grew steadily softer as the machines were turned off, one by one.

A typist punctuated the stillness with staccato bursts of productivity that ended abruptly when a car pulled into the gravel driveway and honked.

Even the distant sirens that were the city's heartbeat had ceased, if only momentarily.

Shea sat in the firm's law library, paging through volume after volume of California Appellate Reports and Supreme Court Reports, searching for judicial rulings relevant to her case.

It wasn't the kind of reading that usually allowed for scanning, but time was running out; somehow it had gotten to be Friday, and The State of California versus Ernesto Juarez Sanchez was on the Superior Court docket for Monday morning at ten A.M.

Her first felony case as attorney of record, and it had been unceremoniously dumped on her this past Tuesday. Since she'd been routinely putting in fourteen-hour days this month searching for "father-friendly" judgments in child custody disputes for an associate, she hadn't done much more than review the file.

The charge was burglary and the state's case was pretty straightforward: Mr. Juarez had been discovered inside a dry cleaner's at 3:17 A.M. one clear January morning by patrol officers responding to a silent alarm. He had located the canvas bank bag with the previous day's profits where the owner, fearful of being robbed at the night deposit box, had hidden it in a supply room, among cartons of cleaning solvents.

How her client had known to look for the bank bag there remained unclear. The police suspected an accomplice working on the inside, a scenario Mr. Juarez denied. Individually and collectively, the employees likewise denied ever having seen or heard of Mr. Juarez before.

Regardless of how he'd come to find the hidden money, if he had taken it and run he most likely would have gotten away, the solved burglary rate being what it was. But a powder-blue tuxedo caught his eye on the way out and, planning ahead to a cousin's summer wedding, he stopped to try on the jacket.

The police arrived to find him struggling with the red cummerbund, the bank bag at his feet.

It was a toss-up who was the most surprised: the cops catching him in the act, or Mr. Juarez on being caught. And the owner of the blue tuxedo in which Mr. Juarez was hustled off to jail probably rated an honorable mention in the competition.

In most instances, Mr. Juarez would have been represented by a public defender, who would've pled him out to breaking and entering and accepted a few months in County Jail. But as luck would have it, his family had put some money aside for *un día de escasez* — a rainy day — and they were adamant that he not be found guilty.

The factual evidence in the case appeared to have escaped the family, or at least was considered by them to be of no consequence.

21

What they were looking for was a technicality—a much sought-after quirk of law or procedure that of itself often set miscreants free—and they felt the chance of discovering one was better with a "real lawyer" from a private law firm. So far, though, the legal pad on which she had planned to cite case law and outline her strategy was depressingly blank.

So was her mind. Blank and aching. She rubbed her eyes and winced at the pain. The afternoon sun, slanting through the venetian blinds, seemed inordinately bright for this late in the day.

Aspirin, that's what she needed. Or rather, more aspirin; she'd taken three only a couple of hours ago. And those tablets had been all that was left in the bottle she kept in her desk.

I just bought that bottle.

There was a small market within walking distance, a block or so away, but even though Stojanovich, Kincaid and Wheeler was a prestigious law firm, the neighborhood in which their offices were located was not. Joseph Stojanovich's near-legendary loathing for high-rise buildings accounted for that, although the old man might not have anticipated how quickly the city would decay around them when he'd opted for this particular site.

With walking so unappealing, the next obvious choice was to drive, but she strongly suspected that once she was in the car, the urge to go home would assert itself and she'd be disinclined to return to work. And she *had* to work; she couldn't risk going into court unprepared.

Another alternative existed. Ardath McHenry stocked a virtual mini-pharmacy in one of her desk drawers. Ardath was the firm's Office Manager, as well as Private Executive Secretary and Senior Administrative Assistant to old man Stojanovich . . . and a world-class hypochondriac in her spare time.

Ardath had never met a pill or potion she didn't like; the office wags joked that her inventory was the envy of the Colombians. She stockpiled drugs, squirreling them away as if in fear that the pharmaceutical industry was on the verge of going belly-up.

Shea rested her head in her hands, closed her eyes and used her index fingers to apply pressure to both eyelids, massaging gently. It didn't help. Maybe aspirin wouldn't help either, but it was worth a try.

Her vision was blurred when she opened her eyes. She blinked rapidly, trying to focus. Nausea accompanied a wave of dizziness when she raised her head.

Could she be coming down with something? A nasty strain of flu had been working its way through the office staff in recent weeks, prompting a spate of jokes from the attorneys—those so far unaffected—as to the immunity conferred by BMW ownership.

Less than a year out of law school, she had yet to acquire that exclusive status.

Whatever it was, flu or simple exhaustion, she was feeling sicker by the moment. Getting to her feet, she left the library to look for aspirin and maybe something to ease the growing queasiness of her stomach.

A hush had settled over the office with the dimming of daylight. Shadows pooled in recesses and hollows, transforming the familiar into indistinct—and slightly menacing—shapes.

It would be night before long.

Turning the corner into the reception area for the executive suites, Shea was startled to see a figure standing in the gloom, near one of the huge, leafy potted plants that Joseph Stojanovich insisted sweetened the air.

"Ardath," she said, recognizing the woman's rigid bearing, "you scared the hell out of me . . . I thought everyone had left."

Ardath glanced at her but continued watering. "Everyone has."

Shea interpreted that to mean that no one of importance—specifically, none of the partners—was on the premises. "Well, I'm glad you're still here. I've got

23

a killer of a headache, and I was wondering if you might have something I could take for it."

Even in the limited light, she could detect the spark of interest in Ardath McHenry's eyes.

"A headache?"

"I've been taking aspirin, but—"

"Aspirin!" There was scorn in her voice. "A lot of good that'll do."

"Oh, it helps a little, although I need at least three or four to make a dent in the pain." Shea rubbed her temple gingerly. "And then it doesn't last."

"How long has this been going on?"

"I don't know. A couple of days, I guess." In fact, now that she thought of it, she couldn't recall a recent day when she hadn't had a headache. At the back of her mind, a memory surfaced. Wasn't that how it had begun? . . . but no. It couldn't be.

Shea felt Ardath watching her, and wondered if her alarm showed. "I've been under a lot of stress."

"I have something that will help you, but you'll need to go home before you take it. You can't be out driving afterward."

"But my work—"

"—will have to wait." Ardath set the watering can down and motioned for Shea to follow her into the inner offices.

As bad as she felt, she had little choice but to comply, rationalizing that if the headache went away, she could get a good night's sleep, and would be fresh in the morning, better able to concentrate.

All else being equal, she'd settle for just losing the headache.

"Let's see what we have here," Ardath McHenry said, and turned on a desk lamp.

The light hurt, and instinctively Shea raised her hand to shade her eyes.

"Sensitive to light, are we?"

24

"A little."

Ardath pursed her lips. "That isn't good, Ms. Novak. It isn't good at all."

Shea didn't want or need to hear that, and she was in a hurry. With any of the other secretarial staff she might have tried to pull rank at this point, but she'd bet a month's salary that a first-year attorney had absolutely no standing as far as Ardath McHenry was concerned.

"It isn't," she agreed and, trying to be tactful, added, "But I think you're right about going home."

"I'd see a doctor if I were you."

"If the headaches continue, I will. But for tonight . . . could I please have the pills?"

"Hmm." Ardath used a key to open the deep bottom drawer of her desk and began to rummage around. "It could be a tumor, you know. Or an aneurysm."

Shea could feel her pulse throbbing inside her skull. "I'm sure it's nothing quite so dramatic. I've had bad headaches before; after I took the bar exam, I was in bed for two days—"

"Have you any allergies? To medication, I mean."

"No, none."

Ardath selected a clear vial with perhaps a dozen yellow tablets inside and handed it to Shea. "These should take care of your headache, but they may upset your stomach. I find that lying down helps."

There was no identifying label on the vial, and no instructions as to the dosage. "How many do I—"

"One will do, every six hours. They're pretty strong . . . you could even take half a tablet at first and see what that does. They're scored, so they break easily."

"Half a tablet?" That didn't sound right, and she squinted, trying unsuccessfully to read the name stamped on the pills. "What is this?"

"Percodan."

She blinked, surprised. "Isn't that a prescription drug?"

25

"Yes, and I have a prescription for it. Besides, I doubt that anything you could buy over the counter would do any good."

"But it isn't legal—"

Ardath McHenry sighed. "Lawyers. I might have expected you'd worry about that."

"It's not that I'm worried, exactly—"

"It isn't the worst thing you could ever do."

"But—"

"Take the pills, Ms. Novak." Ardath closed and locked her desk drawer. "They'll get you through the weekend, and that's what you want, isn't it?"

There was no arguing with that. Shea closed her fingers around the vial. "Thanks."

When Shea got home, she took half a Percodan and went straight to bed. Forty-five minutes later, still in pain, she swallowed the second half.

Eventually she drifted off to sleep, only to wake during the night in even more pain. Her skull felt as if it were on the verge of shattering.

This time she took a tablet and a half. Her hands were shaking so badly that instead of bringing the pills up to her mouth, she had to lower her head and lick them out of her sweating palm.

Curled up in a fetal position, she had to fight to keep from whimpering as she waited for the medication to take hold.

Relief, when it came, was blessed.

Chapter Four

La Jolla, California

Tiffany Stratton didn't wait for the chauffeur to get out and come around the side, as was customary. Instead, as soon as the limousine came to a stop, she reached over to the control console, released the lock, opened the door, and slid out of the seat.

"Now Miss Tiffany, you know you aren't allowed to play with that—"

It would be rude, she supposed, to shut the door on Juliet's near-constant recital of things she really shouldn't do, and so she simply walked away.

The path to the doctor's office passed by a clover-shaped pond, and she hesitated there for just a second, searching for the fat white and gold koi that often hid beneath the water lilies. The surface of the pond, though, was mirror smooth, and Tiffany understood that without skimmers or other insects to attract it, the fish would remain out of sight.

That caution ensured the koi's survival, which she also understood, very well.

Behind her she could hear Juliet coming, muttering under her breath.

Tiffany went ahead to the doctor's, glancing over her shoulder when she reached the door; her mother's social secretary didn't look any too pleased. But then, Juliet never did when asked to see to "the child."

Once, Tiffany had overheard Juliet complain to the gardener that she hadn't taken the job to become wet nurse to a spoiled, pampered brat. She wasn't sure exactly what a wet nurse did, but she wasn't at all fond of being called a brat.

She entered Dr. Langston's office and, feeling contrary the way a brat might, she locked the door. The waiting room was empty — she guessed the doctor didn't see many patients on Saturdays — and it smelled of perfume instead of medicine. She crossed to the reception window and rapped on the frosted glass.

"Here you are," the nurse said, sliding the window open just as the door began to rattle. "Now what on earth is that?"

Tiffany widened her eyes innocently. "What?"

"Someone's at the door." The nurse gave her a quizzical look. "Did you — oh, never mind."

Never mind. Adults were always saying that to her, that or forget it. Either one would do.

The nurse was shaking her head as she came through the inner office door. She was dressed in street clothes rather than the usual white uniform, and her heels kept sinking into the thick carpet as she hurried to the door. Juliet had begun to knock.

"I'm sorry," the nurse said, "I don't know how that happened."

One look at Juliet's face and Tiffany could tell that *she* knew.

Without further comment, the nurse ushered them from the waiting area and along the hallway to an examining room, where she switched on the lights. A pale yellow gown lay folded on the padded table.

Tiffany remained for a moment in the open doorway, watching with dread as the nurse raised the head of the examination table and pulled out the built-in step at its end.

"You'll need to undress, hon. Take off everything but your panties."

"I know." She came in reluctantly and stood next to

28

the table, fingering the soft material of the gown. "I can do it myself, okay?"

"I'm sure you can, a big girl like you, but the doctor has to leave for the hospital in a little bit, and maybe it would be faster if your—"

"She isn't my mother," Tiffany said, "and I don't want her here."

That earned a frown from both of them. Juliet, though, recovered first. "But I am here. The doctor will ask a lot of questions, Miss Tiffany, about what's been ailing you, and—"

"What could *you* tell him? You don't know anything about me."

"—your mother has questions for him." Juliet dug into her shoulder bag and brought out a mocha-colored envelope as proof. This year the initials on the wax seal were P.T.G., at least until the divorce was final.

Tiffany ignored her, turning instead to the nurse. "I want to see the doctor alone."

"Well." The nurse and Juliet exchanged a look. "I guess it won't do any harm. All right, then . . . Dr. Langston will be with you in a few minutes."

She waited until the door had closed behind them before she went to the alcove at the back of the room and began to unbutton her blouse, starting with the three small pearl buttons on each sleeve. There were hooks on the wall behind a wicker privacy screen, and she hung the blouse on one, then unfastened the snap of her jeans. Her panties had snagged in the zipper—she'd rushed to get dressed before anyone could come into her bedroom—and it took a bit of doing to release them.

Tiffany kicked off her shoes and stepped out of her jeans, which she folded and left on the chair. In her stockinged feet, she returned to the exam table and slipped into the gown. She could only reach to tie the top of the gown.

Then she climbed up, using the step, and sat down

29

to wait, the gown pulled over her knees, with ankles crossed and hands folded primly in her lap.

Out in the hall, she could hear that they were talking, but their voices were muffled, their words unclear.

"Tiffany," Dr. Langston said when he came in, "they tell me you've been causing a fuss."

She didn't say anything—it was true, after all—but watched as he warmed the stethoscope between his big freckled hands. She liked Dr. Langston more than the doctors in any of the other places they lived.

"And I also heard that you haven't been eating well lately. Only had soup for dinner yesterday and didn't have breakfast this morning?"

The cook must have told her mother; she'd been alone for both meals. "I wasn't hungry."

When he came near, Tiffany could smell the soap he always used to wash his hands. For some reason, that smell made her feel safe.

"Not hungry, huh?" Dr. Langston lifted her hair off her neck—his fingers were cool—and untied the gown, easing it from her shoulders.

Tiffany closed her eyes, intending to keep them closed. Any second now . . .

"Where'd you get these bruises, honey?"

Her breath caught in her throat; the secret she'd kept for weeks was out. But because she liked him, she answered honestly: "I don't know."

"Have you been playing on the monkey bars?"

The doctor's touch was feathery, and kind of tickled, as his fingers found and traced the many bruises on her chest, back and legs.

Tiffany shook her head. "My mother thinks monkey bars are common."

Dr. Langston made a sound that might have been a laugh. "Common!"

"That's why our limousines are all Mercedes; she

30

thinks Cadillac limousines are common."

This time there was no mistaking the laughter. "God, yes, any poor schmuck can own one."

Beguiled into looking at him, she saw the smile tugging at the corners of his mouth, and smiled back until she saw that it was only his mouth smiling. His eyes were full of concern.

Dr. Langston touched the angry red and purple bruise on her collarbone. "You haven't injured yourself, then, playing, or . . ."

"I don't play much," she confided. As far back as she could remember, she'd spent most of her time with adults who expected her to be a proper young lady. A couple of months shy of her eighth birthday, she knew no other way to act; although she'd watched other kids, she didn't really know *how* to play.

He took her hand and turned her arm gently so that he could see the rash-like bruising near the crook of her elbow. "Your mother's note mentions that you've been complaining of being tired lately?"

"I guess so." In fact, she'd been napping again frequently, and not always voluntarily. More than once she'd fallen asleep in the limo, driving to or from her ballet, riding, or French lessons.

"Lie back for a second," he instructed, lowering the head of the exam table so it was flat.

Tiffany did as she was told, watching his face as his fingers probed the left side of her abdomen, which hurt a little, and then her neck, which didn't. His eyes narrowed, and the skin beneath them seemed to crinkle, as though he'd looked directly into the sun.

"Have you had any fever?"

"I don't remember."

"What about pain? What hurts you?"

"Sometimes . . . it hurts to breathe."

The doctor stroked his chin; he hadn't shaved, and it made a raspy sound. "Well, we're going to have to do some blood tests."

Tiffany had had a blood test before, to check if she

was — what was the word? She couldn't remember. But he said tests. More than one. "A fingerstick?"

"I'm afraid not, honey." He patted her hand. "We'll need more blood than that."

She pulled her hand away from him. "I don't like needles."

"I'm not too crazy about them myself, but it's got to be, sweet pea."

Tiffany squeezed her eyes shut, trying not to cry. Getting jabbed in the finger was bad enough, but at least it was quick. Having a needle in her arm for longer than a second or two . . . ugh. Besides the fact that being stuck just plain hurt, even the thought of a needle made her feel woozy.

"Be a big girl now."

"Will you do it?" she asked, covering her eyes with her left hand.

"If it'll make you feel better, I will."

The nurse had come in to assist, and Tiffany peeked through her fingers to make sure it wasn't the nurse sticking her. Dr. Langston, catching her peeking, gave her a little wink.

Feeling the sharp sting of the needle, she lay very still, not wanting to move her arm for fear that the needle would break. The doctor had told her to make a fist and her fingernails were digging, *hard,* into her palm. Any harder, she thought, and they could've collected the blood from her hand.

"So," Dr. Langston said, "I know the baseball year's barely started, but who do you like in the World Series this year?"

Tiffany lifted her hand from her eyes and wrinkled her nose at him. "What?"

"You're not a baseball fan, I take it. Too common for you?"

"I guess." Out of the corner of her eye, she saw the doctor hand the nurse a glass vial. Her blood.

Swallowing hard, she looked away.

A minute later, she felt the needle being withdrawn and looked over to see a cotton ball being taped over the hole. Dr. Langston bent her arm upward at the elbow while gently easing her fingers open. "That wasn't so bad, was it, kiddo?"

"Yes."

The doctor smiled and shook his head. "Doesn't say much for my charming bedside manner."

Tiffany tucked her blouse into her jeans and sat down to put on her shoes. When she came out from behind the wicker screen, she saw that they'd left the door slightly ajar. Curiosity drew her forward.

" — able to reach the mother?" she heard Dr. Langston ask.

"No, not yet," the nurse said. "Evidently she's out on the family yacht."

"I find it hard to believe that would put her out of touch. What about ship-to-shore radio? Or a cellular phone, for crying out loud!"

"I would suggest," Juliet said, "that if she's out of touch, it's by choice. Mrs. Gray has been . . . entertaining . . . a male friend this week."

"I'll send the frigging Coast Guard after her if I have to."

Tiffany had never heard Dr. Langston angry before, and she inched the door open a little wider so she could look through. His back was to her, but she could see both women's faces.

"I want you" — Dr. Langston pointed a finger at the nurse — "to run these slides over to Memorial, and get a hematologist to look at them immediately."

"I'll do my best, but it *is* Saturday — "

"No excuses, period. And you" — his finger seemed to freeze Juliet in her tracks — "chase down Pamela by whatever means it takes. Because if she's not at the hospital within the hour, I'll get a court order naming

33

a guardian for Tiffany so the child can be admitted."

"A court order!"

Juliet's eyebrows shot up, the way Yosemite Sam's did before his face turned red and fire shot out his ears, but somehow Tiffany didn't feel like laughing.

"Really, Dr. Langston, is such an extreme measure necessary? Mrs. Gray will certainly be back at the house by this evening."

Tiffany had begun to back away from the door — they were scaring her — but she heard the doctor's reply.

"We haven't got till this evening," he said, sounding very different from when he'd joked with her a few minutes before. "We may not have much time at all."

Chapter Five

Near Stateline, Nevada

Lassiter had parked a good fifty feet off the east-bound side of Interstate 15, but the big rigs heading for Las Vegas and points beyond were hauling ass and making time, and their slipstreams rocked the van as they roared past. If it wasn't so damned blistering hot out, he'd welcome the blasts of air that whistled around the corners of the side windows — their rubber seals were in the final stages of disintegration — but each gust of diesel-flavored road wind was dustier and hotter than the last.

When he bought the van, a few years back, he'd paid a bootleg customizer a hundred bucks to apply a mirror-glaze to all the glass except the windshield, both to keep the interior cool and to keep folks from looking inside. The glaze was worthless as a sun screen — if anything it attracted heat — and had started to flake almost immediately, but what remained, plus a hundred thousand miles of road grime, provided at least the illusion of seclusion, hiding him from prying eyes as he attended to business.

Perspiration beaded on his forehead and trickled down the sides of his face and the bridge of his nose. He could actually *feel* the sweat growing heavier as the drops merged and gathered at the tip of his nose, where they defied gravity for a few seconds before splashing into the blue enamel wash basin in front of him.

He'd squirted a fair amount of lemon-scented dish soap into the basin, but it hadn't sudsed up much, maybe because he'd accidentally bought distilled water to wash up in. Whatever the reason, the water remained clear enough so that he could see every last detail of the bone-handled knife at the bottom, from the nicks on the blade to individual streaks of blood.

It had been about an hour since he'd tossed the knife in back of the van, in a hurry to put distance between himself and California. In the arid desert heat, an hour was plenty of time for the blood to cake and dry.

And contrary to those commercials where the exact same dish soap dissolved globs of coagulated grease from pots and pans, so far the blood was sticking to the stainless steel like glue.

Scrubbing would dull the knife's edge, but he trusted that a good soaking would be sufficient. The abortive six months he'd spent in nursing school back in 1978 had taught him that.

Among other things.

He turned his attention to the nylon sportsbag beside him, reaching inside to withdraw several three-foot lengths of heavy-duty clothesline. He examined them, looking for blood stains or strands of blond hair that might have become entwined around the cord. He found nothing incriminating, but in these days of high-tech crime labs, he had to consider microscopic fibers and whatnot.

On the other hand, clothesline was cheap, and plentiful to the point that it was probably impossible to trace, so why worry? He put the ligatures aside, intending to burn them later.

Next he pulled out his tools: a pair of vise-grips,

36

a ball-peen hammer, a set of needlenose pliers, a hacksaw with spare blades, and, his sentimental favorite, an eight-inch pipe wrench that cracked walnuts or finger joints with equal ease.

Looking at them laid out ceremoniously on the brown shag carpet, he felt a sense of satisfaction, a feeling he supposed he shared with every master craftsman. Over the years he'd narrowed his choice of equipment to this efficient minimum, at the same time refining his technique and polishing his execution into a precision dance of torture and death . . .

Unfortunately, today he hadn't had the luxury of time in which to utilize any of his tools. He'd barely unsheathed the knife when some fuckface off-road enthusiasts started barreling across the desert toward the van. The clouds of dust churned up by their four-wheelers was both a warning and a threat. Even though they were miles off and could just as easily miss him as not, he obeyed his gut instinct to cut and run.

Problem was, by then he'd gone too far to stop. No way he could turn the girl loose and have her play show and tell with the cops. As a result, he'd had to hurry through the essentials and forego the niceties.

It was a hell of a thing when a man couldn't find a few minutes of privacy in the middle of a damned wasteland like the Mojave Desert in which to pursue his constitutional right to the pursuit of happiness.

Rather than let this outrage fester, though, he tried to be philosophical about it. There was no lack of young talent working the byways, and the next one would be that much sweeter for the wait.

Lassiter continued to rummage in the sportsbag, pulling out four rolls of duct tape and one of U.S. Postal Service-approved reinforced packing tape, the latter of which was all but gone. A good product, that. The bother of having to cut it instead of simply tearing a piece off was more than made up for by its strength. He'd add a couple of rolls to his shopping list when he hit Vegas.

Gardening gloves, spirits of ammonia for the fainters-he wanted them to *know* what was happening to them—and his rattlesnake bite kit.

Check and double-check. So much for tools and supplies; all that remained in the sportsbag were the items of jewelry he'd removed from the girl's body.

A few years ago, the police had identified the skeletal remains of a body found near Baker, California by a hand-crafted turquoise ring on a disarticulated finger bone. It was one of a kind, and photographs and an artistic rendering of the ring were faxed to police stations across the country. Within a week, the cops had a match with the "last seen wearing" description of a Riverside runaway.

Besides positively establishing the victim's identity, that ring had eventually led to the arrest and conviction of the murderer, a gas station attendant who'd been overheard admiring the ring while coming on to the fifteen-year-old wearing it.

It didn't take a rocket scientist to catch *that* drift; the removal of jewelry might save him a shit-load of trouble down the road.

Not that anything he'd culled from this outing was as memorable; he'd never come across a sorrier lot of costume trash in his life. He'd found better in a box of Cracker Jacks.

The girl had been wearing five earrings, three studs on her left ear and two hoops on her right. Any pretense of gold- or silver-plating had been worn off all five. The stones in the studs would never even be mistaken for that Cubic crap, much less the diamond, sapphire and emerald they imitated.

There were half a dozen necklaces, most of the dime-store variety, with colored glass or ceramic beads. One had a broken clasp and was being held together by a rusting safety pin. And he counted thirty-three thin metal hoop bracelets, which had jingled and clanged so annoyingly on the girl's bony wrists.

Despite her other excesses, she'd worn only one ring, on the little finger of her right hand. To him, it looked like a baby ring, so small that he couldn't fit it over the tip of his pinkie. Silver, with a narrow band widening to an oval top, on which the date *10-12-75* was amateurishly engraved. Her birthdate, he figured, which would've made her sixteen.

She looked younger, particularly when it dawned on her what was going to happen and she started to cry. Sniffled like a broken-hearted three-year-old whose ice cream fell off the cone.

Lassiter reached for the hacksaw to cut up the ring—custom-made or not, the birthdate had to go—and felt a sudden wrenching pain in his abdomen, as though someone had snagged his innards with a grappling hook. In an instant the heat receded as he was bathed in an icy sweat.

He leaned against the padded interior of the van, swallowing air and belching to relieve the pressure in his belly. It had worked before—his stomach had been bothering him off and on for years—but not this time.

Saliva flooded his mouth. He clenched his jaw, fighting a violent nausea, but was startled a second later when fluid spurted without warning from his nostrils. He scrambled forward in time to keep what followed from splattering all over the place.

Face inches from the basin, shuddering uncontrollably, he vomited a bitter greenish substance that he took to be bile.

His sinuses burned and his lungs were stinging from inhaling when he shouldn't have. His throat felt raw, seared by the caustic stuff.

He expected to feel better after puking, but the pressure in his stomach hadn't eased a whit. Instead it seemed to be moving upward, causing pain to radiate through his chest.

A heart attack? Was he having a heart attack?

In his mind's eye he saw flickering images of smiling dead faces, gratified by his distress.

He had a notion of something swelling within him, as though a balloon were being inflated in his gullet, forcing its way up his throat and threatening to suffocate him by blocking his airway. Deliberately he lowered his face again until it was only inches from the basin, hoping that the smell of lemon soap and bile would induce his stomach to spasm and expel the mass.

Eyes tearing, he could barely distinguish the outline of the knife in the now-turbid water. Strange that at this moment he could recall with clarity the ripping sound the knife had made as he'd opened the girl from sternum to pubis to make the pickings that much easier for the desert scavengers . . .

Lassiter began to pant, his breath making ripples in the water. A sign that his windpipe wasn't as obstructed as it felt?

Straightening slightly, he clenched his hands in a double fist and drove them into his upper abdomen. The first blow seemed to loosen something, so he did it again and again.

A thick, coppery odor invaded his nostrils and triggered his gag reflex. A surge rose from the pit of his stomach and he vomited again forcefully, the effort nearly making him pass out.

"Shit," he rasped when it was over, blinking and wiping away tears. He collapsed onto his side, exhausted, and lay staring up at the broken plastic cover on the dome light. The muscles of his body quivered and quaked, for the moment leaving him unable to move.

Out on the Interstate, tires squealed and a horn blared, but there was no sound of impact. A near miss, then, like he'd just had.

Another near miss in the desert, with those off-roaders bearing down on him.

Lassiter wasn't superstitious, and didn't believe in omens, but it crossed his mind that maybe today wasn't his day.

After wiping his nose and mouth, he drew back his hand and realized there was no maybe about it.

Dark, purplish, clotted blood. And granulated, as if someone had mixed sand into it. Blood that had come from his stomach! God, that meant he was, or had been, bleeding internally, and people died of that.

He had to get to Vegas and a hospital.

A less disciplined man would have flagged down help on the Interstate fifty yards away. A trucker with an eye on the clock might not stop, but would most likely summon aid on the old CB.

Aid in a trooper hat, sporting a shoulder patch reading Nevada Highway Patrol. Aid who'd have himself a look in the van and get to wondering . . .

No, that wouldn't do.

He had to finish cleaning up. Empty the basin and start over, make sure the knife was spotless. Wipe down his tools even though he hadn't used them. Hide the sportsbag in its usual place in the tirewell. Maybe he'd come across one of those portable chemical toilets the road crews used, and he could dump the rope in there. And he could dispose of the jewelry by tossing it out the window a piece at a time as he drove.

With a grunt, Lassiter sat upright. Averting his eyes from the contents of the basin, he got to work.

"Lassiter," the Emergency admitting clerk said. "Is that with—"

41

"Two esses, one tee."

The nurse, a ripe Georgia peach of a woman, released the valve on the blood pressure cuff to deflate it. "Are you on any medication, Mr. Lassiter?"

"No, I—"

"First name?" The clerk again.

He had to think on that a moment, putting names together in his mind, looking for a fit. He'd been using aliases for so long, it was hard to keep them straight.

"Morgan," he said finally. "No middle name."

Chapter Six

Seattle

It was with some confusion that Naoka Tanaka opened her eyes and found that she was still alive. Her dreams had been of death and darkness, of hands drawing a shroud over her powdered face, of jasmine incense burning to mask the aura of decay.

So real not to be true.

In David's bedroom at the rear of the house, the clock-radio came on.

Six-thirty A.M.

Naoka glanced at the window. It had rained all yesterday and well into the night. Outside the morning was gray, and she could feel the chill coming off the water-streaked glass. With some reluctance, she pushed aside the covers and sat up, reaching for the blue fleece robe the boys had given her for Christmas.

"It will keep you warm, Mama," David had said. "Better than silk."

The robe had been made for someone much taller than she, and only her fingertips showed at the end of each sleeve, but as a gift she treasured every fluffy inch. She drew it snug around her and tied the belt, tucking the ends in a pocket to keep them out of the way.

43

The smell of coffee greeted her in the hall, and she wrinkled her nose. Kenichi no longer shared her morning tea, having declared his preference for a dark, pungent blend of three kinds of coffee beans he had specially ground at a shop near his office.

When she'd prepared the automatic coffee maker and set the timer last evening, she had noticed the one-pound bag was almost empty. It was rare than her husband would let his supply run so low . . .

In the kitchen, she put the kettle on, placed her grandmother's *Tokoname* teapot and a solitary cup on the counter, then went to the cupboard to get a canister of good *sencha* tea. Standing on tip-toe, she hesitated in mid-reach to listen, straining to hear and place an unfamiliar sound that she thought had come from the family room. The sliding glass door?

Naoka walked to the entryway that led to the dining room and beyond. From there she could see the door, which was shut. Outside on the patio four pairs of *geta*—traditional Japanese footwear—were lined up neatly beneath a low bench, protected from the rain.

Her imagination supplied the distinctive sound of wood clattering on the brick pathways, and, less clearly, that of a child's laughter.

She blinked slowly, then turned away.

Naoka moved aside delicately flowered rice bowls and *chawan mushi* cups, reaching to the back of the shelf where the plain white plates Kenichi preferred for everyday use were kept. Stacked next to the plates were the deep bowls that had come with them, which made her think of the dish she'd seen a neighbor put out for a dog.

Very unappealing, she thought, taking a bowl from the stack. But as a good wife, she obeyed her husband's wishes in this and all matters. Knives, forks and spoons instead of chopsticks. Quilted mats in place of the black lacquered trays that, if somewhat formal, were traditional in her family.

Besides the presentation of the food, breakfast itself had changed since the boys had started school; their friends did not eat steamed vegetables or *tsukemono* or soup or even rice at the morning meal. Now David wanted toaster waffles or microwave pancakes with boysenberry syrup, while Mark experimented with one cereal after another, even though it seemed his main interest was collecting the small toys in the boxes.

Kenichi's work was demanding, leaving him little time for breakfast, but on his way out he would almost always take with him a fresh cinnamon roll. Because the rolls were sticky and messy, every morning she laid out a moist towel by his coffee mug; in the evening she would retrieve the used towel from the car.

Despite the fact that she baked the rolls with loving care, she did not believe that sweets were good for her husband, who tended to gain weight, so every morning she also fixed what he called his American breakfast: a sunny-side-up egg served cold, peeled grapefruit sections, and dry wheat toast. Just in case he had time to eat it.

Most days, he did not.

None of her family cared for the fish and rice that she'd grown up eating—Kenichi was second generation and had lived all his life in this country, and their sons had been born here—but rather than make a separate meal for herself, she had tea.

Tea.

The kettle was whistling vigorously. Naoka realized that she had been standing there, unaware, holding two of the white plates and a bowl in her hands. For how long, she did not know, but the water which she had meant only to heat had boiled, and now would be too hot to make proper tea. Shaking her head at her foolishness, she hurried to the stove and turned the gas off.

The whistling became less shrill, then stopped altogether.

She sat at the table, hands folded in her lap, and watched the shadows move across the hardwood floor. The sun had come out, off and on as the morning passed, but had not asserted itself, allowing the drizzling clouds to absorb its heat.

Naoka regretted that; even in the fleece robe, she couldn't get warm.

She thought of returning to bed. The sheets would be cold and damp at first, but if she wore the robe beneath the covers and bundled up, it wouldn't take more than a few minutes to grow warm. And once she was comfortable, she could doze off.

Escape into dreams.

The fragrance of jasmine beckoned, and Naoka looked toward the hallway, feeling the lure of the oblivion of sleep. Balancing that desire was shame at her failure to overcome it.

Still, after a moment of indecision, she stood up, ready to succumb to her weakness.

The doorbell rang before she'd taken a step. Her heartbeat quickened. Who would come to her home unannounced? With the exception of a few of Kenichi's coworkers, whom she'd been introduced to at a company picnic last summer, and her sons' teachers, she knew no one here.

The bell rang again, three times in rapid succession, conveying a sense of urgency that left her no choice but to answer.

She did not immediately recognize the man standing at her door. Tall and slim, black hair glistening from the rain, his dark blue eyes held a familiar sorrow, one she'd seen too often.

"Mrs. Tanaka, hello."

Naoka bowed her head slightly. "Yes?"

"Do you remember me? Father Quincy?"

She noticed then the priest's clerical collar, and saw that he held a well-worn bible in his hands. Although they were not Catholic, the boys attended a parochial school, and she had a vague memory of having met a Father Quincy at the Christmas pageant last year. He had come in with a group of the older boys after playing a noisy and exuberant game of basketball in the near-freezing rain.

"I am sorry, of course I remember." She stepped aside and welcomed him in.

"I've been meaning to come by for several weeks now, but I didn't want to impose."

"It is no imposition," she demurred.

Naoka closed the door behind him, then turned and looked at the house as if with his eyes. Many days of unopened mail had collected on the entry table. The air felt thick and stale, bereft of oxygen. A film of dust covered the teak furnishings. And while there was no real disorder, neither was there harmony.

"I haven't come at an inconvenient time, then?"

Greeting a caller in her robe was an unforgivable lapse of etiquette, and normally she would be humiliated, but she heard genuine kindness in the priest's voice, which set her at ease.

"No time is better than another," she said matter-of-factly. "Come, please."

Naoka led him to the living room. When they passed the dining room, she heard his footsteps falter behind her, and knew he had seen the table set for four, the food she'd prepared untouched.

His expression was troubled when he sat down.

Naoka remained standing, as required by her duty as hostess. "May I offer you tea?"

"No, thank you."

"You prefer coffee? Or—"

"I'm fine, really." His smile seemed tentative. "Please, Mrs. Tanaka, sit down."

She did, if reluctantly. Although she had not invited him, it was important that she extend every hospitality to the priest, even if they were of different faiths.

"I don't know if you were aware of it, but I knew Mr. Tanaka . . . Ken."

"Kenichi." Naoka did not care for the Americanization of her husband's name.

"Kenichi, yes. Perhaps he mentioned me? We were on a fund-raising committee together last year. For the United Way?"

She had no knowledge of any committee, but she nodded. In this country men told their wives such things, and she didn't want Father Quincy to think less of Kenichi because he hadn't.

"We were on the same schedule, got to know each other fairly well. When I heard about the accident, I felt as though I'd lost a friend."

There was nothing to say. She nodded again.

"And the boys . . ." The priest's eyes filled. "The loss of a child is the cruelest blow. To lose two in an instant is a devastating tragedy most of us would be unable to comprehend."

48

Naoka sat perfectly still. She had done her grieving in private, and would continue to do so. The ache in her heart would not be relieved by a public display, nor could words comfort her.

"I realize," Father Quincy went on, "that it's only been six weeks since it happened—"

She wasn't used to answering the phone at night. But Kenichi had taken David and Mark with him when he went out for cigarettes. The boys would beg him to stop for ice cream or some other treat, and he would indulge them, a doting father when he had time.

"—and I empathize with you in your loss."

That was why they had been gone so long. David was very much like his father and would make a decision quickly as to what he wanted. But Mark needed to consider every possibility with equal diligence. A hot fudge sundae or a banana split, or maybe a chocolate chip brownie with a scoop of strawberry ice cream?

"I respect your need for privacy, and hope you won't think I'm interfering—"

That was why they were late. Kenichi had yet to put down his foot with Mark. He treated his sons alike, but in his secret heart, Naoka thought, Kenichi favored their youngest, who'd been sickly as a newborn, and whom they'd almost lost.

"—but quite frankly I'm concerned about you." He reached out as if to touch her, but drew back when she flinched.

When the phone rang, she'd answered it, expecting to take a message from an associate of her husband's, or, though the hour was late, perhaps from a classmate of David's asking about a homework assignment.

"I know from what Ken told me that you haven't any family here."

49

The voice on the phone was brusque, impatient, asking for Sergeant Wagner. A wrong number. Not to be alarmed. Except for another voice in the background, which said. "The first victim was Kenichi Tanaka, adult male, age thirty-eight, dead on arrival at County General . . ."

"That's why I've come, Mrs. Tanaka. To be a friend to you."

She had stopped breathing, waiting to hear what more the second voice would say, the words "first victim" echoing in her head. At the same time, someone knocked on the door. Her fate awaited.

"Your neighbors have noticed that you don't look well. They tell me you haven't gone out since the day of the funerals."

She'd rushed to the door, desperately hoping that her ears had heard wrong. All it took was one look at the sergeant's face, and she knew that no one would be coming home that evening, or ever again.

"I want to help you, Naoka."

The use of her given name recaptured her attention, and she looked at him.

Father Quincy reached out, and this time he did touch her, one hand covering hers. He nodded toward the portrait above the fireplace. "I can see for myself that you're thinner."

Naoka glanced at the photograph, but it wasn't her face that she saw. David had wedged his tongue in the space between his missing teeth, and an unruly lock of Mark's hair was sticking straight up.

Her fingers remembered the coarse, bristly texture of her youngest's hair, and she closed her hand into a fist. How could it be that she'd never caress him again? Could God be that cruel?

"You haven't been eating, have you?"

50

Naoka said nothing.

"But you're still preparing meals for your family," the priest said.

There wasn't a trace of shock or pity or chastisement in his voice, and that gave her the courage to answer truthfully. "Yes."

He was silent for a moment, his blue eyes thoughtful. "Naoka . . . you mustn't allow grief to become the only thing in your life."

"My life," Naoka said quietly, "is over."

Chapter Seven

Idle Springs, Nevada

The screen door slammed behind Joshua Reid as he jumped off the porch, disdaining the stairs and ignoring the tingle that ran up his spine. As pissed as he was, he didn't care whether he reinjured his back. What difference did it make if he hurt himself?

Wasn't he the once-and-forever disposable kid?

Joshua kicked at a partially buried rock with the toe of his Nikes, dislodging it and a shower of dirt. The effort, minor as it was, reminded him of the growing numbness in his thigh.

Across the road, old lady Metzger peered through the gap in her lace curtains. A busybody from the word go, she had some kind of snoop sonar that tipped her off every time he set foot out of his grandpa's door.

A variety of hand gestures ran through his mind, but he resisted the urge to escalate what had thus far been only a war of dirty looks. Old lady Metzger was vocal in her dislike for teenagers, not that there were many around. At thirteen he barely qualified, but somehow or other he'd climbed to the top of her hit parade.

Probably because he lived within boom box distance. Was it his fault she had no taste in music?

"I don't like me living here any more than you do," he muttered, starting off down the road. Knowing that she was watching after him, he tried to put a little funk in his walk, the way he'd seen the black kids do back home in San Francisco. He wasn't very good at it—he felt, and probably looked, like an epileptic on the verge of a fit—but *she* sure as hell wouldn't know that.

Out here, a million miles from civilization, no one knew much of anything. He'd been surprised to find that they had phones, much less satellite TV.

Talk about casting pearls before swine! These were "Green Acres" type of folks, with a dash of "Beverly Hillbillies" thrown in. He couldn't begin to guess what they'd make of his favorite shows, "Crossfire," "The McLaughlin Group," and the hard-core science episodes of "Nova."

As for the telephone in Idle Springs it was a weapon of sorts, with gossip as the ammunition. Even now, the old biddy from across the street was most likely engaged in a delirium of dialing, spreading word of his insolent behavior, lack of respect toward his elders, and latent criminal tendencies.

And the first person she'd call would be his grandfather, who happened to be chief of this backwater's four-man police force.

"Garrett Reid," she'd say indignantly, "that no-account grandson of yours is sashaying down the road like he owns it. Blood kin or not, the boy is up to nothing but trouble if you ask me."

Joshua could hear the nasal twang of her voice so clearly that he turned halfway around to see if she was coming after him. She wasn't, of course; even her house was out of view.

His imagination was getting the better of him again, but he couldn't refrain from talking back: "No one asked you, you old bitch."

He kicked the dirt again, stirring up a platoon of the red ants that were native to the area. Entomology wasn't his thing, but he was kind of mesmerized by these muscle ants with their attitudes.

That didn't stop him from grinding a dozen into the ground. Power was power, after all.

Walking on, he soon arrived at the edge of town, discernable primarily in that there was now a solid white line painted down the middle of the road. As far as he could tell, the line was regarded by the locals as decoration; traffic lanes were a foreign concept here, and were seldom respected. Right of way was determined more by the gross weight of the vehicle and the reputation of the driver than by any rule of law.

He might be the only kid in town who wasn't frantic to learn to drive.

At the moment, though, the main street of Idle Springs was deserted. A line of dusty pick-ups were parked diagonal to the curb in front of Lucy's Diner.

These were Ford F-150s, Dodge Rams, and Chevy Blazers, along with one primer-coated Jeep. No foreign import would be welcome here, but especially none of the "toy trucks" that the locals associated with effeminate Californians.

No real man would buy a Tonka Toyota. Drive a mini-truck, the feeling went, and you might as well wear a mini-skirt.

Inside, Joshua knew, it would be standing room only as the real men in town had a mid-morning piece of Lucy's deep-dish apple pie, and coffee so strong it could almost strip the chewing-tobacco stains from their teeth.

Passing by, he made a point of looking elsewhere, a Californian still.

Next to the diner was the Mercantile, which sold groceries, items of clothing, and assorted hardware, besides serving as the post office. Through the store front window, he could see the owner using a feather duster on the canned goods.

He also caught sight of his own reflection, and was startled to see that he was walking hunched over like an arthritic old man, his right shoulder angled down and forward.

A shiver ran through him.

Could something like that be caused by pulled back muscles and a pinched nerve?

That's what the local doctor had said was the problem. Of course, the doctor had also said he'd be better by now, and he wasn't. Then again, what did he expect from someone who smelled faintly of booze and who had never once looked him in the eye?

His failure to get better was something else to be pissed about.

"Later," he said aloud, averting his eyes from the glass and hurrying along the uneven sidewalk. "One piss-off at a time."

He needed his anger to burn white and hot, or he'd never have the nerve to confront his grandfather. And he had to confront him, didn't he?

The Police Department was just ahead now. A perfect square, it sat low to the ground, its earth-colored walls a close match with the surrounding terrain.

A no-nonsense kind of building. Sturdy, solid, strictly no frills.

The same could be said of Garrett Reid.

The Idle Springs Police Department had two patrol cars, racy 5.0 liter Mustangs, and both were

55

parked in front. That meant his grandfather was in.

His stomach tightened. Maybe he wasn't as eager for a showdown as he thought. Maybe there'd be a better time and place. Maybe —

The door swung open, settling the matter as his grandfather stepped out into the sun. As usual, he was wearing dark aviator's glasses — Joshua wondered if they were part of the uniform — and chewing on an unlit wooden kitchen match.

In his police uniform, the old man looked forbidding. Joshua had seen photographs of his grandfather as a young deputy in Harris County, Texas, and his bearing now was every bit as straight.

His uniform shirt was blue, accented by darker blue pocket flaps and shoulder epaulets. The pants were dark gray with a black stripe down each leg. His trooper hat was also dark gray.

Add to that the wide leather belt sporting a Smith and Wesson .38 Chief's Special, and Joshua was face to face with Authority, in more ways than one.

"Josh," Garrett Reid said, "what brings you down this way on a Sunday morning?"

It would be so easy to make something up, to swallow his anger and forget the whole thing. It wouldn't be the first time in his life that he'd had to back down from an issue; he'd been doing that ever since he could remember.

This time, though, he couldn't.

"I need to talk to you" — he pulled a well-creased envelope from his hip pocket — "about this."

The dark glasses hid any response. With his tongue, grandfather shifted the matchstick to the other side of his mouth. "Where'd you find that?"

"In your desk."

56

"My desk."

"Yeah." Joshua's heart was thudding painfully, but he lifted his chin in defiance. "In the top drawer, to be exact."

"If memory serves, I keep that drawer locked," the old man said mildly as he took the envelope and turned it over in his raw-knuckled hands.

Joshua shrugged. "You could've told me. Make that you *should* have told me."

Garrett Reid frowned. "I was thinking on how to do just that."

"That letter was postmarked more than a month ago," he said, unable to keep the sarcasm out of his voice. "How long does it take to find a way to tell a kid that his so-called mother has decided not to come back for him?"

His grandfather put a hand on his shoulder and steered him around to the passenger side of the closest patrol car. "Get in."

"I want an answer."

"This is family business, by God, and I won't be discussing it here where anyone happening by can listen in. Get in the car."

Feeling himself near tears, Joshua got in, after shoving a clipboard off the seat onto the floor. He slammed the door emphatically.

"Josh," his grandfather said a moment later as he backed out of the lot, "I'm sorry. I know that's not much comfort, but it's the best I can do."

A monster lump had formed in his throat, and it hurt to talk around it, but he said, "It's not enough."

"I'll accept that, but you have to understand, I don't have a lot of practice at raising kids."

Joshua steeled himself to hear the family history, a frequent occurrence since the old man had taken him in. As if the fact that his grandparents

57

had gotten divorced and his father had grown up in a badly broken home was an explanation for every problem in Josh's life.

The Reid Domino Theory was how he thought of it, though he'd never dare tell the old man . . .

His grandfather picked up the radio mike and mumbled something into it. There followed a blast of static and a curt "10-4."

"The thing is, I wrote to both Jack and Claire, and was hoping to hear from one or t'other before discussing all this with you."

Joshua stared out of the window, unconvinced. As far as he could see, it was pretty straightforward. When he'd read Claire's letter, written in her childish hand, it seemed as if he could hear her speaking the words, the way it happened in the movies:

It will be better for me if this is a clean break. I can't pretend that I have feelings for Jack's boy or even Jack anymore. I wish I was a better person, and could keep my promise to your son, but you know he never kept his promises to me. I'm sorry.

He sat turned in the seat, watching the barren countryside pass by. Sagebrush and manzanita, scrubgrass and tumbleweed . . . what a pit.

"The letter I wrote to your stepmom came back with no forwarding address. As for your Dad, he's got another two years to serve at the very least."

Joshua felt a rising sense of hopelessness. "That long?"

"As I figure it, there's forty-four months left on his original sentence, which with time off for good behavior should work out to two years, give or take a few weeks. *If* he keeps his nose clean."

"Right," Joshua said, and snorted.

"What I'm trying to say is, I wasn't disregarding

your interests in keeping Claire's news to myself. I just wanted to determine what's what. I mean, the woman could've changed her mind. It's happened before."

"Shit."

His grandfather gave him a sideways glance. "Watch your mouth, now. I understand that you're upset, but using foul language won't help."

Neither would *not* swearing. He could say "please" and "sorry" and "pardon me" until he was hoarse, and it wouldn't matter a bit.

"Anyway, what's done is done. I can put feelers out and see if I can't track Claire down, but what with them not even being legally married, she's under no obligation to care for you."

Joshua pulled an imaginary handle and made a flushing sound. "Down the toilet, Reid."

"I don't want to hear you talking like that. Your life is just beginning." His grandfather used an index finger to lower the aviator glasses a couple of inches, revealing his hard blue eyes. "Now . . . it's up to us to go on from here. Am I right?"

Adults were like that, thinking things were settled because they wanted them to be. But he knew better than to argue, and so he nodded.

"Good. How about we sneak into Lucy's for an early lunch?"

"Sure," he said, without enthusiasm.

The patrol car made a sweeping U-turn; they were south of town, near the turnoff to what the other kids in town were calling the K.O. Clinic. K.O. stood for either Keep Out or Kill Off, depending on who you asked. Perched up on the rise, the building's dark tinted windows and sleek lines gave it a slightly malevolent air.

Joshua stared at it, intrigued. The only reason he could think of for a place like that to be built in a place like this was that someone—a mad scientist, for instance—had something to hide.

He twisted in the seat, wanting another look, and felt a shooting pain race up the length of his spine. He took a quick breath and sat back cautiously. A prickling sensation spread through his lower back and upper thighs, but it lasted only a few seconds before the numbness set in.

By the time they reached Lucy's, he couldn't move his legs to get out of the patrol car.

Chapter Eight

Alternative Therapy Clinic

"And this"—Honor Matheson held the door open and stood aside as the other nurses entered—"is Treatment Room One, or T-1, if you prefer."

"I prefer." As he'd been doing throughout the morning's orientation tour, Scott Hosfeldt made himself comfortable—and the center of attention—by flopping in the reclining patient chair in the middle of the room. "Does this thing vibrate, by any chance?"

Honor chose to ignore his juvenile posturing; she hadn't wanted a male R.N. on the staff for precisely this reason. If only she had been better able to articulate her objections to Dr. Kramer, and then had the self-confidence to stand her ground.

For once.

"There are," she said briskly, "four treatment rooms altogether, but for the first six months we'll only be using One and Two."

Judy Bettencourt, who hailed from, in her own words, "a stinky, dinky hick town in Tennessee" ran a hand along the marble countertop and then opened the cabinet doors, revealing shelves stocked with intravenous needles of every type and

61

gauge, cutdown trays, IV tubing, and other related supplies.

"Believe it or not," Judy said, sounding awed, "the *emergency* room I worked in back home wasn't anywhere near this well equipped."

"I believe it, I surely do," Scott said, rather cannily imitating her accent.

Judy appeared not to notice. "This is super, really. I'm so impressed."

"Dr. Kramer demands the very best."

Scott buffed his nails on his shirt, preening. "I'm living proof of that."

Again Honor chose not to respond, instead crossing the room to the wall directly behind the head of the chair. She pressed a metal plate and a recessed panel slid open. "Here you'll find the oxygen, with both mask and nasal cannula. Blood pressure cuff, sphygmomanometer—"

"God, I love a medical vocabulary," Scott said. "What a kick it is to watch a woman work her mouth around all those syllables."

Bree Patrick, the blonde pediatrics nurse from Southern California, laughed.

Another applicant she hadn't wanted to hire, if for different reasons. Luckily, both Bree and Scott were assigned to the late shift, working from eight in the evening to 8 A.M., and she should be able to avoid them, more or less.

Less in that they would be living at close quarters, at least part of the time. The employment contract they all had been required to sign on hiring specified that the nurses were to remain on the premises during their three duty days per week—she alone was working a five day week— staying in assigned efficiency apartments located in the private staff wing.

Some contact was inevitable.

"Oh goody," Judy said, coming up beside her, "you've got electronic thermometers. Heavens, but I hate those old glass ones. I'm always expecting someone to bite right through them, you know?"

"Actually, I—"

"Just the sound teeth make on glass is enough to give me fits. For my money, it's a hundred times worse than fingernails on a blackboard. And then you always have to worry, did you switch oral with rectal, if you know what I mean."

That brought a guffaw from Scott.

Honor tried to keep her expression neutral. "Yes, I think I do. Now, moving right along . . . there are also leads for the cardiac monitor, which prints out via telemetry located in the nurses station."

"What about a crash cart?" Restlessly retired after twenty years as an army nurse, Estelle Gunther was proving to be extraordinarily detail-oriented.

"Good question. It's in here." Honor indicated a side door which opened as she approached, revealing a six foot by eight foot alcove equipped with a stainless steel sink, glass-fronted linen closet, and the traditional red crash cart. "This also provides access to T-2, by the way."

Estelle made a beeline for the cart and began opening drawers. "Laryngoscope, endotracheal tube, Swan-Ganz catheter—"

"It's all there," Honor assured her. "If, heaven forbid, one of the patients should code, we have everything necessary for resuscitation."

Estelle nodded but continued her examination of the crash cart's contents, moving on to the medication drawer. "Atropine, epinephrine, sodium bicarb, lidocaine, quinidine, morphine sulfate, potassium chloride—"

"Yes, well." Honor glanced at her watch; they were an hour behind schedule, almost to the minute, bogged down by Estelle's meticulous tabulations and Scott's aren't-I-cute-and/or-clever distractions. What was needed, she knew, was for her to assert herself and take more control.

Although she'd interviewed the nursing candidates with Dr. Kramer—minus veto power—and would now be their direct supervisor, Honor felt uneasy at the prospect of being in charge. On an objective level, she knew she was the best qualified nurse among them, with a Master's degree in Nursing Administration and eight years of intensive care experience in a big city hospital. Her skills and training were top-notch by any standard. Somehow, though, knowing all that didn't translate into confidence.

But confident or not, she couldn't allow them to get any further behind schedule, or there wouldn't be time to review the treatment protocol for Affinity this afternoon. And Dr. Kramer had made it clear that he would be expecting them to have gotten through the fundamentals when he met with them tomorrow at eight A.M. Sharp.

Alan was relying on her.

Newly resolute, she walked by the recliner, pushing the lever that sat the chair upright, and was gratified by Scott's startled grunt. "Let's finish our tour of the facilities, shall we?"

Later that afternoon, having made up the time, Honor felt a sense of achievement as she circled the oak conference table handing gold-colored binders to each of the nurses. On resuming her place at the head of the table, she looked at each of them in turn, and began:

"The Alternative Therapy Clinic is exactly what the name implies: a clinic offering non-traditional forms of therapy or treatment for terminal patients."

"Ah, yes," Scott said, affecting a sepulchral tone, "the dead and dying."

Honor wished a thousand curses on whoever had first mistakenly told Scott Hosfeldt that he was even slightly amusing. "The clinic's treatment plan includes biofeedback, hypnosis, imaging therapy—sometimes erroneously called visualization—and meditation, but the primary modality will be nutrient therapy."

She removed a quarter-liter bottle from an insulated container filled with chemical ice packs. "This solution, which is called Affinity, will be the principal nutrient formula, and will be given in the appropriate therapeutic doses at Dr. Kramer's direction."

Estelle leaned forward with a frown, adjusting her bifocals for a better look. "This isn't some new form of laetrile, is it?"

"Not at all—"

"Because I had an aunt die from that. True, she wasn't in the best of shape, being weak from the cancer and all, but they think there was an impurity in the laetrile, some kind of contaminant."

"What?" Scott murmured. "Cyanide?"

"Mold spore comes to mind." Estelle glared at him.

"Just asking."

"I don't know all of the details, since it happened down in Mexico, at a clinic in Tijuana I believe, but it killed her"—she snapped her fingers—"like that."

"How . . . unfortunate." It was, she knew, an inadequate response, but it was the best she could do, considering the day she'd had.

"Pardon me, but I don't agree. I'd rather go quick," Scott said. "Who the hell wants to linger on as a human entree for the big C?"

"I hope you go quick, too," Judy said in her softly accented voice.

Hiding a smile, Honor busied herself putting away the bottle of Affinity, which had to be kept cool. Too bad maintaining her own decorum couldn't be accomplished by the application of ice packs.

Bree tapped a blood red nail on the table in a self-assured bid for the floor. "I've heard that Dr. Kramer makes it himself. Is that true?"

Heard where? she almost asked, but didn't. "It is. In addition to his medical degree, he has a doctorate in biochemistry. His interest in pharmacology goes back to his undergraduate days."

"Fascinating man, Alan Kramer."

There was something in Bree's expression Honor didn't like, but she could hardly argue. "Indeed. Now, if I might, I'd like to go over the treatment protocol for Affinity with you. If you'll turn to the first section of your procedures manual?"

She waited until they all had done so.

"You will note that the nutrient solution needs to be administered piggyback along with intravenous fluids, in this instance five percent dextrose in water." She glanced up from her notes. "The IV site of choice is either the cephalic or the median basilic vein . . . nothing different there. We expect the best results with an infusion rate of sixty to eighty drops per minute."

"On the slow side," Scott observed, with a shake of his head.

"Not necessarily, but if we err, we prefer that it's on the side of caution."

"I'm as cautious as the next person, but if the patient can tolerate a faster infusion rate, say a hundred and twenty drops per minute, that would cut the treatment time in half. And it's still a conservative rate. No one would mistake a hundred and twenty per for a bolus." He looked to the other nurses for confirmation.

Only Bree nodded.

"I don't think you understand: This is not a subject open for discussion. Dr. Kramer has already determined the optimum rate through his research, and he wrote the protocol accordingly."

"Hey, no problem. I just thought it'd save us all some time. Not to mention getting the needle out of the patients' arms a damn sight faster."

Staring hard at Scott, she wasn't convinced that he'd gotten the message that he was way out of line, but she had to go on if she wanted to finish by five P.M. Of course, it should be a moot point, since the protocol directed that the nutrient therapy be given early in the day, prior to other treatments and well before the time Scott would be reporting for duty.

"No problem," she echoed, hoping it was true. "Now . . . where were we?"

Estelle, who had evidently been tracking their progress against the first page in the manual, looked up and said, "Physiological side effects?"

"Right. The side effects of Affinity are relatively minor. The patient may exhibit a marginal dilation of the pupils, and a slowing of respiration. Of note is that the patient may experience a full body tremor . . ."

Chapter Nine

Los Angeles

After first verifying that her client had shown up, and then reporting in to the court clerk, Shea Novak found a quiet place near the back of the courtroom to sit down until her case was called — the judge was still in chambers. She took a deep breath and opened Ernesto Juarez Sanchez's file.

Trying to read caused the residual pain in her head to flare and brought on a recurrence of light-headedness, but she persevered. Compared to the pounding, grinding misery she'd endured over the weekend, this was little more than a twinge.

Even so, the ache in her head seemed to be affecting her ability to concentrate, and she had to read the complaint several times before the familiar wording sank in and made sense. The complaint asserted succinctly that one Ernesto Juarez Sanchez did willfully and unlawfully enter the commercial building occupied by the business of Fast Freddy's Dry Cleaners Incorporated with intent to commit larceny and/or any felony.

Larceny involved simply the taking of another person's property with the intention of depriving the owner of its use. In California, the law rarely got any more basic than that . . .

"Larceny," she said aloud, struck all at once by

the insidious sound of the word. Strange that she'd never noticed it before.

The sound of raucous laughter caught her attention. Glancing up from the file, she noticed that the assistant district attorney who'd been assigned to prosecute the Juarez case was standing near the clerk's desk with several male attorneys from the Public Defender's office. Judging by their naughty-boy expressions and the level of hilarity, the ADA was most probably holding forth with a few of his trademark dirty jokes.

How many lawyers does it take—

The twinge in her head blossomed abruptly into full-blown pain. It felt as though thin quills of bone had erupted outward from the center of her brain. The analgesic effects of the Percodan she'd taken disappeared in the blink of an eye.

"Here you are." Eugene Kincaid, the youngest and most gregarious of the partners, sat down beside her. "I hope I don't pass the company jinx on to you, but I wanted to wish you luck—"

Shea brought her hand slowly up to her face. The left side of her upper lip had gone numb. So had the tip of her nose. A rushing sound filled her ears, muffling the voices around her.

"—on your first case."

Something was very wrong. When she looked at Eugene Kincaid, his face reminded her of how a 3-D movie looked without the special glasses. Indistinct, and kind of fuzzy around the edges.

"*My* first case was a disaster," he said from a great distance, "although of course I had devised a brilliant defense."

Shea wanted to interrupt him, but when she opened her mouth the words wouldn't come.

"And I should have won. I'd established so

70

much reasonable doubt, we were up to our ears in the stuff. Needed hip waders to slosh through it."

A surge of dizziness swept through her and she had a sense of fading, as if her consciousness was pulling away from her body. Frightened, she tried to stand, but succeeded only in shuffling her feet ineffectually.

"The judge *had* to be senile, always nodding off during my cross. He wouldn't know reasonable doubt if it bit him in the ass."

Her left hand was still clutching the Juarez file, and she stared at the complaint, trying to ground herself in a reality that had begun to dim — except her mind couldn't grasp what her eyes were seeing.

"What's more, if it did bite him, and he was bleeding, he couldn't find his ass with both hands and a flashlight, not even to save his life."

Save my life? Someone had to help her. Although he was speaking to her, Eugene wasn't looking at her. If she dropped the case file, he would pick it up, and once she had his attention, maybe she could make him understand that she was in desperate trouble.

"They say losing your first time out builds character and humility, but I ask you, what have I got to be humble about?"

She could move only her thumb and index finger, and the effort it took to do even that nearly caused her to pass out. Darkness had begun to creep in around the edges of her field of vision, and she feared that she was in danger of losing what little control she still had.

The file slipped gently to the floor, the pages barely fluttering.

"Oops." Eugene leaned over to pick it up. "You must be nervous."

Help me.

Get a doctor.

Call an ambulance.

Dial 911.

All those phrases crossed her mind, but "Larceny," was what she said, and none too clearly.

Eugene, who could be cute in the way puppy dogs were cute, full of bounding energy and wet-nosed enthusiasm, put the file in her lap and smiled. "Well, sure, I'd have done my best to plea it down from Burglary, but who knows? Maybe you can beat it."

Shea felt the blood leave her head. Her eyes rolled, and darkness came.

She regained consciousness in the ambulance, roused by the siren's plaintive wail. There was an oxygen mask over her mouth and nose, and a blood pressure cuff was wrapped tightly around her upper left arm.

She saw that the medic's back was to her.

How many times had she heard or seen an ambulance and wondered, fleetingly, about the circumstances of the person inside? If she'd ever considered that one day she might be the one being rushed to a hospital, she'd dismissed the thought summarily.

She never would have believed that awakening to find herself strapped onto a stretcher would inspire such stark terror. Neither would she have expected to be frightened to tears.

It had been a long time since she'd cried, but she was crying now.

* * *

There was a clock set into the wall in the Emergency Department, and Shea watched the second hand sweep the dial as though hypnotized.

Strangely enough, she couldn't have said how long she'd been here, but it felt like hours. They'd taken her blood, obtained a urine sample, and x-rayed her head. They'd poked her with pins, shone a painfully bright light in her eyes, and checked her reflexes. They'd asked her questions about the day and date and month, and who did she think was President.

She'd answered their questions with only slight hesitation, and correctly, she thought. And with some relief that she had regained her ability to talk.

A very young doctor had informed her that they were calling a specialist to examine her. As he left, he'd warned her to lie still, although without saying why, commenting in an offhand manner that someone would "be down" to take her for further tests.

A nurse had come in shortly afterward with an injection of Valium because, she'd said, "Some people freak out in the scanner."

Seconds swept by, melting into minutes and, ultimately, hours.

The scanner proved to be a huge white machine with a circular opening into which a stretcher-sized platform moved. She was installed on the platform and her head was held motionless by a collar that supported her neck firmly.

Inside, her face was only inches from the

curved interior core, the upper half of her body contained within a metal cocoon.

Shea had never considered herself to be claustrophobic, but beneath the Valium haze she could feel tinglings of panic at being confined in such close quarters. No wonder people freaked out.

"How're you doing?" a disembodied female voice said near her ear.

"Okay, I guess."

"Great, I'm glad to hear it. We're ready to start, and if you hold real still, maybe we'll get it right on the first go-around."

Maybe they'd get it right?

"The machine hums and makes a clicking noise, so try not to be startled by it, okay?"

"Does it . . . take requests?"

The technician's laughter echoed in the chamber. "Not that I'm aware of, although that's not a bad idea. If you're ready, here we go."

There was a deep rumble, which Shea felt as a vibration rather than heard. A few seconds later, the clicking began, somewhat louder than she'd expected.

Forewarned, she remained perfectly still, motivated in part by her desire not to be entombed in this metal coffin for another "go-around."

After her brain scan, she was taken to a semiprivate room on the Neurological floor. The six o'clock news had begun before the specialist the Emergency Department doctor had referred to showed up.

"Miss Novak, I'm Dr. Timothy Wahl."

Wahl, at least, looked reassuringly mature with a close-clipped graying beard and laugh lines at

74

the corners of his eyes. Not that he was smiling now; his expression was somber, even grim.

"Dr. Wahl." Her mouth had gone dry and she licked her lips. "How am I?"

He didn't answer immediately, but crossed the room to get a chair from beside the vacant second bed. After he was seated, he folded his hands and pressed his thumbs together, aligning them just so. Then he shook his head. "I'm sorry, but . . . it isn't good."

Shea realized that that was what she'd expected him to say. "What is it?"

Wahl frowned. "Do you have family, Miss Novak? A close friend? Someone I could call for you?"

"Not . . . no, not really." Her hands were trembling, and she hid them beneath the covers. "In any case, I'd rather hear the news in private."

"As you wish," he said, and sighed. The pads of his thumbs had whitened from the pressure. He cleared his throat, looked down and then up again.

"It's a brain tumor, isn't it?" she asked, preempting him.

Wahl appeared to be relieved at not having to say the words. "Yes, I'm sorry, but it is."

Somehow, she'd known.

Outside in the hall, aides were collecting dinner trays. She hadn't been allowed to eat, a fact for which she was now grateful.

"I noticed in reviewing your family history that your father died of a malignant brain tumor. Do you happen to recall—"

"What kind it was?" Shea struggled with memories she'd rather have left forgotten. "It was a glioblastoma multiforme. He died very quickly."

"They all do," Dr. Wahl said quietly. "Of that."

A cold rush of adrenaline chilled her heart at the tone of his voice. "Is that what I have?"

"Yes."

"You're sure?"

"I'm sure."

She closed her eyes momentarily, allowing the news to sink in. Strange, but after the initial surge of fear, she felt nothing in particular. She opened her eyes to find Wahl watching her.

"You might know," he said, "given your father's illness, that glioblastoma multiforme is a tumor found primarily in males, but we do see it in an occasional female."

"And I'm the lucky one."

Wahl shook his head. "Not very."

"It's inoperable?"

"There are surgeons who'll operate," Wahl said carefully, "but with limited success. They might postpone matters for a couple of weeks, if that. Surgery, of course, has its own inherent risks."

"Yes, I know." Her father, confident that he'd lick brain cancer as he had every other challenge in his life, had gone under the knife. He'd been unable to speak afterward, and she would never forget the betrayed expression in his eyes.

Would she see that look in her mirror one day?

"Since you're familiar with the disease, you probably already know that the outcome for glioblastoma has been uniformly fatal. Particularly for a tumor of this size. To be honest, I'm not sure how you've managed to keep going for so long."

Shea tried to smile, and felt her lower lip quiver. "I had work to do."

"Could be as simple as that, I suppose." Wahl

stood up. "Are you sure I can't have the nurse call someone for you? A neighbor or . . . anyone?"

Unexpectedly, she thought of Steve, but quickly dismissed him. How much comfort could an ex-husband offer under these circumstances? They hadn't parted all that cordially, despite his oft-repeated vow to keep their divorce civil and remain friends.

So she said, "I don't think I could face anyone right now."

"The nurse can arrange for the hospital chaplain to stop by, if that would help."

"I'd really rather be alone for a while."

Wahl surprised her by coming to the bedside and patting her hand, still tucked under the sheet. "I'll be back in the morning to answer the questions you can't think to ask right now—"

Shea already knew the answers. A death warrant had been issued, and for this there would be no appeal.

"—and I have an idea for you, about where to go from here. Okay?"

All she could manage was a nod.

It was morning before she slept.

Chapter Ten

La Jolla, California

Tiffany waited until she was in the stairwell before sitting down and putting on her shoes. The cement step felt cold even through the fabric of her denim jeans, adding to her overall impression of the hospital as a place of little warmth.

In fact, she'd been chilled since the moment she'd arrived, late Saturday morning. In the past three days, her bones had begun to ache from the cold.

They'd given her a private room on the eighth floor, with a window that looked out on the Pacific, but the glass was thick and tinted, and even when she pressed her face against the smooth pane, the afternoon sun couldn't reach her through it.

Maybe she was just being silly, but she was beginning to understand how a Popsicle must feel.

That made her wonder if the cold was intentional, to keep her together, to keep her from melting away.

She gave an extra tug on her shoelaces to make sure they were tied securely, and stood up. Just being dressed in her own clothes made her feel better, stronger.

Tiffany started down the stairs, her fingers

skimming along the metal handrail. Afraid of attracting attention and at the same time feeling kind of weak, she proceeded slowly and cautiously, her footfalls nearly silent. The only sound was of her breathing, which seemed louder than normal in the confined space.

She might not have noticed the sound at all, if it wasn't for Saturday . . .

On Saturday afternoon, after she'd been admitted but before her mother had arrived, they'd taken her to Radiology in a wheelchair. No one had told her directly why she needed to have an X ray, but she figured that it had to do with all her bruises.

The transportation orderly had parked her in the waiting area and disappeared down a hallway, looking for someone to give the blue order slip to.

For a couple of minutes, Tiffany had amused herself by raising and lowering the leg rests on the wheelchair, which were operated by rubber-handled levers. Then she found the brake and unlocked the wheels.

Turning the wheels hesitantly, she made her way to the entrance of the waiting area, and looked in both directions down the hall. She saw no one, but heard a curious rasping sound from off to her right.

She really did know better than to go wandering off on her own, but for some reason, finding out what was making that peculiar noise seemed more important than obeying the rules.

A bit of maneuvering got her through the entrance into the hallway, where she made an awkward right turn, bumping into the kiwi-fruit-colored wall hard enough to leave a squiggly scuff mark.

At home, a stern-faced adult would have shown up at this point to scold her properly for her recklessness. Juliet, in particular, seemed to be forever lurking watchfully in the background, but if she was otherwise occupied, the cook or any one of the maids or other household help could step into the role.

Here there was only that rasping sound, and, Tiffany realized, an underlying murmur of voices.

She wheeled toward the source of both, heading further into the maze.

Maybe because it was the weekend, there weren't a lot of lights on. Tiffany passed several opened doors that revealed darkened, empty rooms. In one room she thought she saw the huddled shape of someone—a forgotten child?—on a table beneath a hulking cone-nosed machine, but a closer look revealed that it was only a pile of black leather sandbags, like the ones she'd noticed earlier in Emergency, while Juliet was getting directions to the Admissions Office.

At the next corner she turned right again and noticed two things. One was her own reflection in a round mirror mounted near the ceiling at the corner of the hall, and the other was a young girl lying on a table in the center of a well-lit room.

There were several nurses and at least two doctors crowded into the small room, talking in quiet but urgent voices as they tried not to get in each other's way. The orderly who'd brought her to Radiology was helping a nurse stick something that looked like a clear hose into a glass jar on the floor.

Tiffany eased the wheelchair back into the shadows.

Even at a distance, she could see that the girl, slightly older than herself, appeared terribly ill. Her skin was gray, except where it was smeared with purplish streaks of blood. There were needles in both her arms, and tubes coming from under the sheet that covered her from the waist down.

As Tiffany watched, a doctor in a white coat approached the girl's side. He held a pointed silver rod in his gloved left hand. With his right hand, he traced a line along her ribs.

A nurse stepped in and began to wash the girl's ribcage with a brownish liquid that, oddly, stained her skin orange. Tiffany thought she recognized the biting smell as that of iodine.

When the nurse had finished, she moved to the end of the table and held on to the girl's arms, which were extended, crucifix-style, above and to either side of her head. The girl's eyes were closed.

The doctor now held the rod in his right hand. With his left thumb and forefinger he stretched the skin tight between the girl's ribs. The pointed end of the rod touched her flesh.

Tiffany couldn't help but gasp when the doctor pushed the metal rod slowly *into* the side of the girl's chest. Blood began to trickle from around the wound, while a pinkish foam bubbled from the exposed end of the rod, which she could see now was hollow.

Only then, when the noise changed from that rasping, crackling cellophane sound into a more identifiable wheeze, did she understand that it had been the girl's tortured breathing that she'd heard.

81

Her view of the girl was blocked then, but a moment later, the jar on the floor began to fill with a bloody froth.

That had been only the first of many horrible things she'd seen.

There was a little kid, maybe four years old, whose face was swollen up like a puffer fish so that the features were stretched like letters on a balloon. The kid—Tiffany couldn't tell if it was a boy or a girl—sucked one thumb constantly while twisting the last few strands of hair on its head around the other.

There was a boy in the room across from her who was strapped into what an orderly told her was a circle bed, because of a broken neck. Bolts actually came out of his skull—his head had been shaved—and were connected to a frame around his head, which reminded her of a halo.

Another boy sat in a wheelchair near the nurses' station most of the day, chattering like a monkey and making about as much sense. His eyes were an awful blood red where they should be white. Beneath his eyes the skin was black and blue and purple.

It scared her to even look at him, but much worse was to have him look at her.

And there was an older girl, thirteen at least, Tiffany guessed, whose thin, pale arms were disfigured by something called a shunt. The shunt in her right arm had collapsed after becoming infected, and so they'd had to put another one in her left arm. The girl pushed the sleeves of her robe up past her elbows, inviting everyone's stares.

All this had convinced Tiffany that she wasn't

going to hang around and let them do those things—or worse—to her.

If she had to run away and hide for the rest of her life, she would do it. Luckily, she wasn't totally unprepared. Back near Valentine's Day, when her mother had told her about this latest divorce, she'd packed a suitcase, although then she'd thought she'd just be going to Palm Springs to stay with her Great-Aunt Mathilde, as she always did during her mother's break-ups, so she wouldn't be underfoot during the coming "unpleasantness."

All she had to do was sneak home for her suitcase, get the money she'd saved from her weekly allowance and hidden under her mattress, and disappear.

Of course they'd look for her in Palm Springs, so she couldn't go there or to any of her family's houses, but there were other towns. She'd traveled more than most kids her age, and although she'd always had a companion, she'd taken notice of other kids who were on their own. As long as a kid had a ticket and seemed to know where he or she was going, the adults paid them no mind.

So the first thing she had to do was call a taxi to take her home.

Tiffany found a row of pay phones near the hospital gift shop, one of which, intended for the handicapped, was at her height. There were dozens and dozens of taxi companies in the phone book, but she selected one from the middle of the listings and, using her mother's calling card number, which she'd memorized, started to punch out the number.

A hand came to rest on her shoulder.

"Tiffany?"

The voice belonged to Dr. Langston. She hung up the receiver and turned to face him. Already shaky from coming down eight flights of stairs, her legs threatened to give way, and she supported herself by half-sitting on the narrow shelf beneath the telephone.

"Hi," she said.

"I wondered where you'd disappeared to. Had to make an important call?"

"Sort of."

"The nurses were worried you might have run off, but I knew you wouldn't leave Dr. Bowman and me twiddling our respective thumbs."

"Dr. Bowman?"

"I told you about her the other night, remember? That she'd be coming in to see you? She's a specialist, a pediatric oncologist and hematologist."

Tiffany frowned and chewed at her lower lip. What she remembered was that the two "gist" words had to do with what was wrong with her. And today was the day they were going to tell her what was making her sick.

"Is she here?"

"Yes. She's waiting in your room. And your mother is on her way." Dr. Langston cupped her chin in his hand. "It will be all right, sweet pea."

Tiffany nodded, but she didn't believe him.

"Come on . . ."

She wanted badly to run, but she allowed herself to be ushered across the lobby to the elevators. When the doors closed, she felt trapped, and hopeless of doing anything about it.

Her mother arrived in a cloud of perfume that made the back of Tiffany's throat itch.

"I *am* sorry if I'm late," her mother said, coming to the bedside and brushing Tiffany's cheek with her usual hit-or-miss kiss. "Darling."

Tiffany watched for a second or two as her mother turned to offer a manicured hand to Dr. Langston, Dr. Bowman, and a third doctor, a child psychologist from India, whose complicated name she'd forgotten. Then she pulled the covers up and closed her eyes.

Listening to them this way, she could pretend they were talking about someone else, another little girl.

Another little girl.

"We have confirmed the diagnosis," Dr. Langston said. "Tiffany has ALL, acute lymphoblastic leukemia, the most common childhood leukemia."

Common again. In spite of how frightened she felt, Tiffany couldn't help but smile a little; her mother would hate that her disease wasn't the rarest kind.

All her mother said was, "Oh my. But aren't they . . . can't you cure that now?"

"The cure rate for leukemia in children is approximately seventy-three percent," Dr. Bowman said, "which is a vast improvement on the four percent they saved thirty years ago, but which still leaves twenty-seven percent who we can't make well."

"The problem is," Dr. Langston added, "that we're catching it late."

"Very late, I'm afraid." Dr. Bowman sounded angry. "In the majority of cases, ALL patients are treated both with radiation and an aggressive course of multidrug chemotherapy; but in instances of advanced disease, the only hope is often an immediate bone marrow transfusion."

Dr. Langston sounded winded, as if he'd run up the stairs. "I won't lie to you. The fact that Tiffany has a rare blood type is of grave concern—"

Tiffany moved her hands to her ears.

Another little girl.

Chapter Eleven

Las Vegas

Ice chips.

Damned frigging ice chips.

What did they think he was, a penguin? Did even penguins eat ice chips?

Lassiter lifted his head off the pillow and brought the paper cup to his mouth, tapping on the bottom of it to dislodge another few slivers of ice.

Pain slashed across his abdomen and he felt his stitches pull. It was easy to imagine the sutures tearing the edges of his skin, and his belly popping open like a gutted deer. "Shit."

Behind the inadequate privacy curtain to his left, a gruff male voice echoed the sentiment in triplicate: "Shit, shit, shit!"

"Shut the fuck up," Lassiter said. With the pain and all, he wasn't in the mood to put up with an Irish Rose drunk who'd been flirting off and on with a screamin' demon version of the d.t.'s.

It irked him that they'd put him in a six-bed ward for winos and bums, but since the taxpayers in Clark County would be footing the bill for his medical care he guessed that he fell in the beggar category, and couldn't—or shouldn't—be choosy.

Still, after what the doctors had told him the

day before yesterday, he felt entitled to at least *some* consideration.

Wasn't every day a man got the news that he was in a footrace with death.

The surgeon had laid it out for him plain and simple: when they opened him up in the O.R. they found him riddled with tumors, which had invaded virtually every one of his internal organs.

"I found," the surgeon had said, never once meeting his eyes, "a large nodular mass in the pancreas, with resultant necrosis. The liver was badly diseased, with a cluster of tumors blocking the flow of bile from the liver to the small intestine, which explains the clinical presentation of jaundice."

Jaundice. Well, he'd thought his skin had a yellow tinge to it lately.

"There were also metastases to the gall bladder, stomach, and spleen."

Lassiter had heard enough, thank you, but the surgeon had gone on at length, finally calling the disease "an advanced, galloping carcinoma in the end stage. Totally inoperable."

"What about chemotherapy?" he asked.

The surgeon seemed taken aback, as though Lassiter shouldn't know such terms. "That's not my field, but I'd doubt that chemo would accomplish anything, except to make your last days miserable. It'd probably do you more harm than good."

The internist who'd been the admitting doctor stood at the end of the bed, arms folded across his chest, -shaking his head now and then but saying nothing. The lack of sympathy on the man's face made Lassiter regret not having claimed a male victim when the opportunity presented itself.

88

Too late for that now, he supposed.

Or not?

"How many days are we talking about?" he asked. "How much time have I got?"

The surgeon scratched his nose. "It's difficult to estimate, really. There are so many variables—"

"Hey, I'm not gonna sue you if you're wrong, so give it your best shot."

"Six weeks, maybe . . . a couple of months if you can avoid other complications. Pneumonia is always a risk when you become bedridden."

Lassiter didn't care for the sound of that. Being slowly suffocated by pneumonia wasn't how he'd pictured himself dying—not that he'd spent a lot of time worrying about how to check out.

"About all we can do," the surgeon concluded, "is give you medication for the pain. And there will be a significant degree of pain."

"Huh." He couldn't think of what else to say.

The internist cleared his throat.

Lassiter wondered, was he choked up?

"I can give you a referral, Mr. Lassiter, if you're so inclined," the internist said. "There's a doctor up in the northern part of the state who has a program you might be interested in . . ."

He caught the quick look the doctors exchanged, filed it mentally for future reference, and listened to what might be his last chance at life.

This morning a social worker had shown up to advise him that he was to be discharged on Friday—they would need his bed for the weekend rush, she'd said—and that arrangements were being finalized to transfer him by private air ambulance to the Alternative Therapy Clinic up north, near a town called Idle Springs.

The only hitch was that the clinic wasn't accepting patients until Monday, and so he'd have to spend a couple of days in a hotel in Reno, under the watchful eye of a private duty nurse.

The bill for the ambulance, hotel, nurse, and other incidentals would be picked up by the clinic, at the directive of its founder, Dr. Alan Kramer.

All of which was fine and dandy, except Lassiter wasn't sure that when they lifted him off the bed, his guts wouldn't spill out onto the floor. Placing a hand experimentally on his bandaged midsection, he coughed and then watched for telltale spots of blood to appear on the pristine white dressing.

None did.

Behind the curtain, the sot in the next bed continued his increasingly sibilant chant of "shit."

The clatter of the dinner cart drew his attention, and he glanced toward the doorway. Working alongside the aide, a pretty young thing wearing a pink-striped tunic over a white culotte dress peeked under two or three serving lids before selecting a tray.

"Mr. Lassiter?" she said.

He raised a hand, index finger pointing heavenward. "Here."

She smiled as she crossed the room to his bedside, but Lassiter was busy watching the shift of her slender hips. He envied anyone with a view from behind.

The girl put the tray on the table and picked a yellow index card off the tray. "Let's see, for our first post-op dinner we've got defatted chicken broth, lime Jello, and ginger ale."

"Lucky us," he said absently, noticing the fine blond hair on her tanned arms.

"The nurses said you're not supposed to sit up yet, so I'm going to have to feed you—but exactly how we're going to manage, I don't know." She looked from the tray to him and back at the tray. "Nothing I can stick a fork in, that's for sure."

Delicate wrist bones, and nicely shaped hands with slim, long fingers. Her nails were short— God, but he was tired of the talons so many women wore!—and adorned with a pale rose-colored polish.

"I've got a straw for the ginger ale, maybe we could use it for the broth? Or maybe the spoon would be okay."

"Whatever works," he said, meeting her eyes.

"Right. My name is Holly, by the way, and I'm a volunteer, which explains why they don't fire me." She jockeyed the table around, pantomiming how to serve him from several different angles before settling on the most obvious one. "Well, here goes nothing."

His appetite whetted for other things, he obediently opened his mouth when the spoon approached. She might have been feeding him dishwater for all the flavor the broth had.

But he didn't care. Lassiter watched the way her lips parted as she fed him. He studied the lush fullness of her lower lip and wondered if anyone had ever bruised her mouth with a kiss.

Or held a hand roughly across her mouth to keep her quiet while tasting, nibbling, biting elsewhere. He caught a glimpse of the tip of her tongue, imagined it flicking in his ear, and swallowed a groan.

91

"How old are you, Holly?" he asked after the next spoonful.

"Sixteen." She wrinkled her nose. "Why, don't I look it?"

"All of," he assured her.

"Good." Tilting the soup bowl to get the last of the broth, she frowned. "There's not a speck of chicken in this, you know."

"I know."

Holly brought the spoon to his mouth. "I can appreciate that there's a difference between broth and soup, but what's the point of eating if you can't chew on something?"

Damn, but she was prime! The curved hollow at her throat looked tender, vulnerable.

"Now what are we going to do about this?" She held up a dish of inch-square cubes of green Jello. "You know, when I was a kid and had my tonsils out, I sucked my Jello through a straw—"

"No, you didn't."

"I did."

"A big piece like that?" he teased. "Nah, I don't believe it."

"You want me to show you?" A hint of a blush colored her cheeks.

"Go ahead."

The girl looked over her shoulder at the others in the ward—the aide had long since gone—then leaned toward him. Her wheat-blond hair brushed against the line of her jaw and it took every ounce of willpower in him not to reach up and touch the soft warmth of it. He could smell the clean scent of baby shampoo.

"The nurses would have kittens if they saw me doing this," Holly said, "but you asked for it."

And if I asked for something else?

Lassiter watched her intently as she stripped the paper wrapping off a white flexible straw. She jabbed the straw into a cube and lowered her head.

He didn't dare take a breath, fearing that she would hear it catch and know the cause.

Lips pursed, Holly sucked.

The straw turned green as the Jello was drawn up through it, and a hole appeared in the cube. Moving the straw back and forth, sucking noisily, within a minute she had gotten most of it.

She looked at him through silky lashes as she raised her head, and winked.

"Told you," she said.

Lassiter narrowed his eyes before closing them. He *knew* Holly would taste of soap. There was a freshness about her that none of the others could ever remotely approach. Her skin would be smooth to the touch, and warm.

There would be no dirt around her ankles from having walked along the road, thumbing rides. She didn't stink of cigarettes and beer, nor of cheap perfume applied over sweat in place of a bath.

The way the others had.

"Are you okay?"

Even her voice was different, lacking the streetwise edge and the suspicion which, though obvious in their eyes, never seemed to keep the road nymphs from going with him.

From a very early age, he'd known that equality was a myth. Some lives were simply worth more than others. In fact he preyed deliberately on those of lesser value, partly because he had easy access to them, but also because he trusted that their loss would not be so sorely felt.

93

It occurred to him now that he had never, and *would* never, possess a young woman who could in any way match Holly's worth.

"I'm okay," he said, when he trusted himself to speak, and he licked his dry lips.

"Do you want some Jello?"

Only if he could lick it out of her belly button. "I'd better not."

"Ginger ale?"

Her eyes were golden brown. There was a dusting of honeyed freckles across her nose. Everything about her was rich . . . creamy . . . silky . . .

Untouchable.

Beyond his reach.

Or not?

"No, but leave it; I might want it later." He found the nerve to touch her gently on the arm to keep her from taking the straw. "Leave that, too."

"But I—"

"I don't mind that you used it."

"I can get you a fresh one."

Never as fresh, he thought. "It's not worth the bother, Holly. Really, it'll be fine."

Chapter Twelve

Naoka Tanaka knelt on a *tatami,* a straw mat, next to David's futon to fold his shirts. Arranging the sleeves just so, she turned the shirt tails up a quarter-length, and then folded the garment in half.

Noticing a loose thread, she wound it around the button twice for luck, then broke off the remainder. After smoothing the material one final time, she placed the shirt in the cardboard box at her side.

Near the door was a similar box, taped shut, that was full of pants: slacks for school, jeans for play, and brand-new shorts bought for this coming summer. Shorts that she'd hemmed because David's legs were short, like his father's, and slightly bowed, like those of his grandfather—her father—Tetsuo Hirose. Her father, who had sought refuge from the disgrace of a business failure by taking his own life when Naoka was twelve.

Seppuku.

Ritual suicide. In Japan, it was an acceptable practice, in part because the brutal manner of death was not for cowards. And it was better than living with the shame of a flawed character.

Better than living without reason.

Naoka turned her mind from those thoughts and reached for the blue Seahawks shirt that had been a favorite of her eldest son. This time she did not allow her hands to linger over their chore.

Almost done, now. These boxes would join those from Mark's room which were stacked in the entryway, and even more boxes she had stacked by the entry table, filled with toys, games, and sports equipment.

This afternoon, a truck from a local charity was to come for them. Already today, the mother of one of David's classmates had come for the books that Naoka was donating to the school library and supplies—notebooks, paper, pens, and pencils—that would be given to a needy student.

"Excuse me, Mrs. Tanaka?" a soft voice said from the doorway.

Naoka hesitated for a moment, composing her face before turning her glance to the door. "Yes?"

The young woman who stood there had sharply arched eyebrows, which gave her a perpetually startled look. "Would you come and join us? Iris has fixed tea, and I baked my famous lemon cookies . . ."

She recognized the kindness in the young woman's voice, but that did not ease the awkwardness she felt at being treated as a guest in her own home. After she had come home from the hospital, Father Quincy had come to see her, and since then there had been someone from his church at her house every day.

There were almost always two of them, usually women, and they watched her every move with the diligence of a jealous lover.

More than that, they swept and mopped and

96

vacuumed and dusted and polished. They brought groceries, prepared meals, and filled her freezer with casseroles. And baked famous lemon cookies.

The weight of their good intentions was a heavy burden for her to bear.

"I haven't finished here," Naoka said.

"Won't you take a break?" The woman smiled, showing crooked teeth. "Please? I can't relax knowing you're hard at work."

"The work isn't hard." She folded the Seahawks shirt and put it in the box.

"Please?"

How could she refuse and not offend? With a sigh, she got to her feet and followed the young woman through the hall toward the dining room.

"Iris," the young woman called as they entered the room, "guess who's having tea?"

"Oh, Janine, how wonderful." Iris, an older, heavyset woman with the most curious blue hair, clapped her hands in what seemed to Naoka excessive delight. "I'm so glad you've decided to join us, Mrs. Tanaka."

Naoka gave a little bow, and took a seat at the table. Her legs trembled . . . from kneeling too long? Or perhaps she was exhausted from having to meet the ongoing expectations of others.

The doorbell rang as Iris began to pour the tea. Naoka started to rise, but Janine beat her to it, bolting from the room like a frightened rabbit.

Janine returned a moment later with Father Quincy.

As if by design, Iris and Janine recalled other things that they had to attend to, leaving her

97

alone with the Catholic priest.

This had been arranged, she suspected.

Father Quincy sat in Kenichi's place and reached across the table to clasp her left hand in both of his. "Naoka, I have some good news."

She waited, impassive, for him to continue.

"Do you remember that I told you about an old friend of mine who is a doctor?"

Naoka shook her head. "I am sorry."

"No?"

In truth, so many people had been talking to her, or *at* her, she'd given up listening. "No. I am sorry."

"It doesn't matter . . . anyway, I've been trying to reach him for several days, and this morning we finally connected." The priest squeezed her hand. "He's agreed to accept you as a patient at his new clinic."

"Patient? But I am not sick."

"Naoka—"

It was rude to interrupt, but she couldn't keep silent. "They sent me home from the hospital. They said there's nothing wrong with me."

"What they said is, they couldn't find out what is wrong with you."

"It is the same."

The priest frowned. "I know the doctors told you they wanted to perform more tests."

"Three days of tests is enough. They found nothing. I'm not ill."

"Not physically ill, but I'm afraid you will be, if something isn't done."

"I do not understand what you mean."

"When I was in college, Naoka, I worked summers at an orphanage. Helping the children was rewarding, and I learned a great deal about the

98

resiliency of the human soul. But there were a few children who did poorly, no matter what we tried. They seemed to take no nourishment from food, and . . . physically, the poor little things hardly took up an inch of space."

Naoka saw in the priest's expression that the memory moved him deeply, but she could not discern how any of this related to her.

"These kids had no appetite for life. They never smiled, never laughed. They didn't respond to the other kids around them."

"They were sad?"

"Sad, yes, but also empty. Looking into their eyes was like staring down into a bottomless well . . . the emptiness was horrible to see. They were like robots, going through the motions without purpose."

She felt a pang at that; David and Mark used to imitate robots. Hardly a Saturday passed that she wasn't told by the teacher at *juku* that they'd disrupted the study session with their antics, which usually included the crushing of entire cities beneath their sneakered feet.

"If you ever saw one of those kids, it would make you cry. There wasn't a light within them." He held her hand to his chest, over his heart.

Disturbed by this contact, Naoka said nothing.

"The orphanage physician had a name for what ailed them; he called it 'failure to thrive.' From what he told me, it was sometimes fatal."

Fatal she understood, although she could not believe that any death could be worse than the sudden wrenching terror of being in a head-on collision in the dark of night. Her dreams reverberated with the screams of her sons amid the grinding of metal and the breaking of glass. And then the lick of flames . . .

She couldn't bear to think beyond that.

"I'm worried, Naoka, that the same thing is happening to you."

Naoka drew back, but Father Quincy did not release her hand. She could feel his heartbeat beneath the rough fabric of his coat. The implied intimacy made her lower her eyes in embarrassment.

"Each time I come to see you, I find you more gaunt. Thinner," he added, as though she would not know the other word.

"I am eating," Naoka said in a whisper. It was wrong of her, but she felt resentful at having to defend herself. What business was it of his — or anyone's — whether or not she had a desire for food?

"Your wedding band is loose," he observed, his hands again cupped around hers.

"It always has been."

His smile was gentle but disbelieving. "You keep those fingers bent, so the ring won't fall off. But you don't look well."

"Why do I have to look well?" A hard knot of anger had formed in her chest. "Is it customary in this country for a wife to mourn her husband and a mother to mourn her children in robust health?"

Father Quincy took a quick breath, as if her question had driven the air from his lungs. "No, of course not. But neither is it customary for someone to stand by and do nothing when another is suffering."

She knew very well that this wasn't true, that every day on the streets of Seattle, people averted their gaze to keep from looking at those less fortunate than themselves, those whose suffering was highly visible. But invited or not, the priest was a guest in her house, and it would be impolite to suggest that his concern for her was not welcome.

And yet this intrusion into her private grief made her desperately homesick for Japan, for the town of Sapparo, where her widowed mother, Michiyo, lived and, without interference or reprimand, mourned her late father. For how many years now? Twenty-three.

It wasn't difficult to imagine living again in her mother's small, cluttered house, each a widow, and each tending to the shrine of their dead loved ones as the seasons passed in numbing, endless succession. And every year, on the deathday — the anniversary of death — they would observe the custom of *meinichi*. On those days, the living remembered the honored dead, who were thought to be present in spirit, if not in body.

Across time and distance, the smell of the jasmine incense that her mother burned at her father's shrine filled her nostrils. After so many years, the fragrance haunted her in unexpected ways.

The incense was so pervasive in her mother's house that each letter she got from home reeked of it, however many miles separated sender from recipient. Naoka often had to let the pages air for several days before she could bear to read them.

And even later, the scent of jasmine lingered, seeming to beckon her toward a final sleep . . .

It struck her, then — was that really what awaited her? A solitary life filled with incense and ceremony, an ocean away from where her beloved husband and adored sons had been laid to rest?

All at once, her resistance vanished. If the

priest thought a doctor could help her, she had nothing to lose by letting him try.

"This doctor," Naoka said, "can he stop dreams?"

Chapter Thirteen

Idle Springs, Nevada

Garrett Reid turned off the ignition, yanked out the key, set the parking brake, and got out of the patrol car more or less simultaneously. With precision borne of long practice, he shoved his baton through the holding ring on his Sam Browne belt without looking. With luck, that was where it'd stay.

Up on the porch, Dalton Purvis sat back in his rocking chair, his size thirteens propped on the railing, sipping from a bottle of orange soda and watching calmly as Reid approached.

Trying not to be obvious about it, Reid took a peek at those boots, hoping for a hint as to how bad things had gotten inside. He didn't see any blood on the pointed toes, but that wasn't much of a guarantee; in his younger days, Purvis had been known to improvise, doing some nasty damage with his heel.

"Purvis," he said, taking the three steps at an even, unhurried pace. As composed as the man appeared at present, it wouldn't do to rile him.

"Chief. I told her not to call you," Purvis said, and now his brow creased. "Ain't no need to keep bothering you with our troubles."

Reid kept his tone neutral. "It's no bother. Jenny inside?"

"I 'spect she's in the bedroom, bawling her damned eyes out."

"Well, I guess I'd better have a talk with her, and hear what she has to say."

"I can tell you what she'll say." Purvis picked at a scab on his elbow, frowning at the effort of working blind. Succeeding in peeling the scab, he flicked it off the porch. "She'll say that I don't appreciate her and don't treat her right. She'll say I'm not *sensitive* and don't respect her *feelings*."

"Uh huh."

Purvis pointed the bottle at him. "You know where she gets those notions from, don't you? All that damned daytime TV she watches."

"Could be," Reid allowed.

"I ought to sue those mealy-mouthed bastards for giving her *ideas*."

Spoken like a true redneck.

"Dumb bitch don't know which side her bread is buttered on."

Reid shook his head. He tried not to make an issue of it, but he'd always been bothered by rude or crude language, which seemed to him to betray a lack of imagination more than anything else.

But all he said was, "I wouldn't be running off at the mouth if I were you, my friend. You might come to regret it later."

In response, Purvis grunted.

Like the pig he was. Reid walked past him and pulled open the screen door. "I'll be back to get your side of things in a while, so don't be going and making yourself scarce."

"Hey, I'm planted," Purvis said, and took another swig of orange soda.

104

Given his other character flaws, Reid considered it a small blessing that Purvis wasn't a boozer. Dangerous sober, the man would be a bona fide menace to the community liquored up.

Passing through the living room, Reid noted battle-related changes in the decor. An ashtray lay in pieces by the fireplace, with cigarette butts and ashes scattered along the flight path and beneath the point of impact—a gouge in plasterboard. The coffee table had been upended so that the legs were sticking in the air, and one of them had been busted off, the new wood showing in long, jagged splinters.

Jenny had a fondness for bric-a-brac, which she displayed on curio shelves as well as virtually every flat surface in the house. The figurines were, she said, "remembrances of happy times." Evidently, they also made excellent projectiles; the ceramic remains of a cross-section of the animal kingdom crunched beneath his shoes as he headed for the hall and the bedrooms beyond.

As Purvis had predicted, Reid found Jenny sprawled face down on the chenille bedspread, sobbing as though her heart would break.

If he hadn't found her thus so many, *many* times before, he'd feel a tad more sympathetic.

As it was, the pattern the Purvises had settled on in their domestic life was a seesaw affair of heated arguments that occasionally escalated into physical abuse—having the larger vocabulary, she usually won the arguments, while he was undefeated in the fights—followed by idyllic "honeymoon" periods during which Jenny would steadfastly refuse to press charges against her old man.

Frustrating, to say the least, particularly today

when he had other things on his mind, Joshua being foremost among them.

"Jenny, it's Garrett Reid," he said, nudging the mattress with his knee to draw her attention. "Sit up and talk to me, gal."

It took her a minute, but finally she twisted around so that she was sitting, Indian-style, in the middle of the bed. She brushed a tangled mass of peroxided hair out of her face and looked at him, red-eyed. Mascara tracks ran all the way down to her neck.

Appealing, she was not, not even on her better days. Jenny Purvis had a pasty Irish complexion and one of those scrunched up faces where the nose and the chin seem straining to meet. She also sported a whisker or two above her upper lip.

As for actual damage, this time it appeared to be limited to a slight swelling on the left side of her face and a trickle of dried blood from her nose.

Was Purvis mellowing over the years? Or had Jenny's reflexes sharpened to the point where she could duck in time to avoid the worst of his blows?

Whichever, Reid was glad to see it. He'd grown tired of this particular civil war.

"So?"

"So the bastard hit me," she said, and sniffled. She touched her cheek and winced, then, seeing her reflection in the mirror opposite the bed, began to rub at the marks the bedspread had left on her face.

Having witnessed evidence of abuse and having been told that Purvis did it, he was required by Nevada law to take Purvis in. If Jenny refused to sign a complaint—and a disturbing number of women did—Reid could sign the complaint on a misdemeanor charge on behalf of the state, and hold Purvis in jail for a minimum of twelve hours.

But without a willing complainant to ensure that the case was prosecuted to the full extent of the law, all that arresting Purvis really amounted to was a monumental waste of time and effort.

"You gonna sign the complaint?" he asked, trying not to let his irritation show. "Or does Dalton step back through the revolving door?"

A nervous tic brought the corner of her eyelid down in an unwitting wink. "You *always* ask me that, and you know I don't know what to do."

"Come off it. You know."

Jenny shrugged. "Maybe. Maybe not. Tell me what good it would do if I did press charges?"

"I'd think that would be obvious; Purvis won't be beating on you."

"He's stopped now. Besides, the way I see it, the only ones who'll profit are the damned lawyers. And who's gonna pay—"

"The state will prosecute—"

"—our bills? If he's sitting in jail, he can't work come Monday. Then what do I do?"

Reid could only shake his head at her priorities. It seemed to him that having the phone and electric bills paid wasn't an adequate trade-off for being slapped around. But it wasn't for him to suggest that she get off her behind and earn her own living.

"Anyway, that old dog isn't gonna learn any new tricks. He'll never change."

She had him there. Of course, it took two to tango. Why should Purvis change, if Jenny put up with him the way he was? Men like Dalton Purvis seldom had to deal with the legal consequences of their actions, and more often than not, that pretty much amounted to year-round open season on the wives.

"Well, it's your call," Reid said. "What's it gonna be? You can do it, or I will."

"My call. Right. Just . . . you do it. Get him out of my sight."

"Sure enough." He turned to leave, stopped at the door, and glanced back. "What was it about this time, anyway? The fight."

Jenny flushed a bright pink and gave him what was probably meant as a coy look, except that she wasn't the kind of woman who could carry it off. "Oh, you know."

On his mental scorecard he made a check in the Kinky Sex column. About half of their fights resulted from Purvis wanting to try some perverted thing he'd seen and admired in his vast library of porno tapes. The other fifty percent had to do with money, or more accurately, he guessed, the lack thereof.

Maybe if Purvis spent less on tapes . . .

"All right, then. But don't be going out tonight and partying, because he'll be calling you early in the morning for a ride home."

"Can't you run him back like usual?"

"Nope. I've got other things to do."

A frustrating hour later, Reid pulled up in front of the Alternative Therapy Clinic. After notifying the dispatcher that he was 10-96 — not in service — he headed for the double doors.

There was no one in the small but elegant

lobby, and his mounting sense of urgency drove him into the hall, where he paused to listen for sounds of human habitation. His task was complicated by the sound of classical music being played over the intercom.

The clinic building was shaped essentially like a hyperextended V, and from where he stood at its apex, he could see down the full length of both wings. The hall to the right was the more promising, since several doors along it were open, letting in the sunlight.

Reid hadn't gone more than ten feet when a man in a white lab coat stepped out of a room just ahead, coming abruptly face to face with him and, judging by their mutual intake of air, startling them both.

Out of habit, Reid took the measure of the man. About five foot ten, with a slim build and dark hair beginning to gray at the temples. A keen intelligence shone in deep-set hazel eyes.

A woman given to making such observations might consider them bedroom eyes.

Reid knew instinctively that this had to be Dr. Alan Kramer.

Not at all what he'd expected, he realized. Younger, and there was a wariness about him that suggested . . . what? That the doctor had something to hide?

He couldn't define it, exactly. Nor was he sure that it wasn't directed at him, or at the uniform.

He stuck out his hand. "Dr. Kramer? I'm Garrett Reid, chief of the Idle Springs P.D."

After a brief hesitation, Kramer extended his own hand. "Is this an official call, Chief Reid? Is there a problem of some sort?"

It could be the uniform, at that; generally it

was those who had no use for cops who felt the need to determine if they should be on the alert.

"Yes and no." Seeing Kramer's continued caution, he amended, "Or make that, no and yes. It isn't official, but I do have a medical problem that I'd like to discuss with you. It's my grandson—"

A young woman in a white pantsuit came up to stand slightly behind and to the side of Kramer, her expression inexplicably guarded, even hostile. She reached out but didn't touch him, although the doctor reacted as if she had, glancing over his shoulder at her.

She said nothing.

Pretty, in a quiet and unassuming kind of way, with dark hair and even darker doe's eyes, if she was Igor to Kramer's Dr. Frankenstein, things were looking up on the medical front.

A gold name tag identified her as Honor Matheson, R.N., B.S.N., M.N.A., Head of Nursing.

Educated folks certainly were partial to initials. Distracted by trying to make sense of them, Reid hadn't let go of Kramer's hand and as he was about to do so, he belatedly noticed an unsteadiness in the doctor's grip, kind of like a palsy.

Kramer was frowning when their eyes met again. "What's the nature of your grandson's problem?"

"Is there somewhere we can talk? Alone?" He guessed that his request for privacy wouldn't endear him to Ms. Matheson, but he had a hunch that he could better assure Kramer's cooperation without her presence.

"My office," Kramer said.

"Doctor," the nurse said almost inaudibly, "you

110

have a staff meeting in fifteen minutes."

"It won't take but five." Even as he said it, Garrett Reid knew that *they* knew it wasn't true, but he absolutely had to force this meeting, if it was the last thing he ever did. Joshua's life might be at stake.

Kramer and Ms. Matheson exchanged a glance, and she nodded at whatever instruction she read in the doctor's eyes. Then she turned and left without another word.

No sizzle, he thought, watching her go, but definite heat.

The way they communicated without speaking was interesting, too, if kind of spooky.

"The office is this way." Kramer gestured in the direction of the other wing.

Well, this was the reason he was here — so why had his mouth suddenly gone dry?

Reid followed the doctor into the darker hall.

Chapter Fourteen

Dr. Alan Kramer listened attentively as the Idle Springs Police Chief described the classic symptoms of spinal cord compression, secondary to either a neoplasm, an epidural abscess, or, less likely, a hematoma.

The clinical signs included a sensory deficit in the boy's lower back and legs, tenderness of the spine, and the sudden onset of paraparesis — the partial paralysis of the legs.

"Joshua has been complaining of pains in his back for a while now," Reid said, "but, ashamed as I am to admit this, when he first mentioned it, I thought he was just using that as an excuse to get out of a camping trip I had planned for us."

An undercurrent of tension there, and not all that far from the surface. Kramer rubbed his right thumb back and forth across the tips of his fingers, reassured by the confirmation of his tactile sense. "I see. And how long is 'a while'?"

Reid didn't respond immediately, which reinforced his impression of the chief's deliberate nature. A careful man, Kramer judged, and not prone to making unconsidered statements.

"About a month."

"A month."

Reid looked uncomfortable, but he nodded. "This might sound like I'm making excuses for neglecting the boy, but whenever I'd ask him if the pain was getting worse, he'd tell me no, that he was fine."

"Which you didn't believe?"

Again that hesitation. "I didn't *dis*believe, maybe because I wanted him to be okay. It might have crossed my mind that he was acting up to get my attention, the way his dad did when he was young."

"What prompted you to finally take him to a doctor?"

"He started to walk funny, kind of hunched over. And then . . . I heard him crying at night." Reid closed his eyes as he massaged the bridge of his nose. "Lord knows, the boy has reasons to cry."

"What did the doctor say?"

"Doc Bevins had a look at him, and said Joshua had pulled a muscle in his back."

A marginal diagnosis. "How did the doctor explain the numbness?"

"The . . . oh, right. Doc figured that was from a pinched nerve."

A year ago, Kramer would have found it difficult, if not impossible, to contain his outrage at such incompetence—subacute spinal cord compression required prompt diagnosis and aggressive treatment, whatever the underlying cause—but his own condition had precipitated a tempering of his response to any and all stimuli.

Now he restricted himself to the slightest of frowns. "What did Dr. Bevins prescribe?"

"Well, a muscle relaxant—"

"Which one?"

"Let's see, I wrote it down." Reid reached into his shirt pocket and pulled out a piece of notebook paper, unfolding it and smoothing it on his

113

upper thigh. He ran his index finger slowly across the page. "Aah . . . wouldn't you know? I can't read my own handwriting here. Looks like maybe an F—"

As a result of his background in biochemistry and pharmacology, Kramer had near photographic recall where drugs were concerned. A quick search of his memory and he came up with Flexeril. It wouldn't have been his first choice, or, for that matter, his second choice, but who knew what a small-town doctor might prescribe.

"—or a P, or it could even be an R."

Which could mean Robaxin, Robaxisal, Paraflex, or even Parafon Forte. Kramer held out his hand. "May I see that?"

"Sure, sure." Reid passed the paper across the desk. "I guess this proves you doctors aren't the only ones with bad handwriting."

Assuming that the comment was meant to be amusing, Kramer smiled. "It looks to me like Robaxisal."

The police chief snapped his fingers. "Robaxisal, that's it."

"How old did you say Joshua is?"

"Thirteen. Why?"

"The drug isn't usually recommended for children under twelve," he said absently, reading on. He had no difficulty deciphering Reid's notes, which included a reference to the boy's complaints of nausea and drowsiness two hours after the first use of the drug.

Reid had also compiled a listing of various other medications—for the most part, standard anti-inflammatory corticosteroids—which he gathered had been given to the boy during his hospital stay.

114

"Why is that?"

"Excuse me?"

"Why would it not be recommended for a twelve year old but okay for the same kid a year—or a couple of months—later? "

"Actually, it has more to do with a lack of clinical data regarding its safety and efficacy in younger children than any known toxicity."

Reid leaned forward and jabbed a finger at the paper. "See where I wrote that it made him sick at his stomach? I mean, he's only just had his thirteenth birthday. Do you suppose—"

Cutting him off, Kramer said, "I'm not in the practice of supposing at all. And in any case, Robaxisal is not relevant to my main concern, which is your grandson's present condition."

Reid sat back. "Sorry. I didn't mean to go off half-cocked like that."

"Not at all. I'd like to take a minute and read this if you don't mind."

"Absolutely."

He glanced back at the paper in front of him. Individually, the remaining notations seemed rather abstract, but taken as a whole, the story they told was clear. After losing the feeling in his legs, the boy had been taken to a hospital two weeks ago.

There were multiple references to X rays, first to rule out spondylosis or a herniated nucleus pulposus, and later to establish whether the lesion had caused spinal erosion, fracture or subluxation.

The word "myelogram" appeared next, with no fewer than a dozen question marks after it, as well as a comment on the boy's complaint of nausea and a splitting headache following the exam.

Syringomyelia had been ruled out at that point.

Evidently an emergency surgical decompression had been performed on the third day of hospitalization, but apparently the procedure had not alleviated the symptoms to any significant degree.

At the bottom of the page was the diagnosis, printed in carefully formed block letters: PRIMARY INTRAMEDULLARY SPINAL GLIOMA, with evidence of SECONDARY SARCOMA.

Those words spelled out Joshua Reid's fate. In plain language, he had a double dose of cancer.

Kramer cleared his throat. "I assume the doctors who are caring for Joshua have told you that the prognosis is guarded, at best?"

"Yes."

He could see by the police chief's expression that they'd also told him the worst, that the boy's cancer was inoperable and inevitably fatal. Radiation therapy might shrink the tumors, but in fully half of those afflicted, it did not.

"Which is why you're here." He refolded the notebook paper and handed it back.

Reid tucked it away in his shirt pocket. "I owe Joshua a chance, Dr. Kramer. And myself, too; I didn't do such a great job of raising his father. I'd like to do better by Joshua."

As a surgeon, Kramer had often chosen to remain distant from the emotional aspect of patient care. That had to change now — and would change — but for the time being, he still felt uncomfortable confronting anything that couldn't be excised or resected with a scalpel.

"Is there a reason or reasons you aren't willing to proceed with the treatment your grandson has been receiving in Reno?"

Reid's eyes turned hard. "The doctors have

116

given up on him. They'd deny it if I were to ask them outright, but one thing a cop gets good at is reading people. They've written him off."

Kramer didn't doubt what Reid was saying. Hell, he'd probably been guilty of doing the same back in Boston, when he'd accomplished all he could surgically for a patient and nothing had helped.

"But why here?" he asked. "Why here, instead of Tijuana or the Bahamas or—"

"Does it matter?"

"It might." It hadn't escaped his notice that the FDA had been sniffing around a clinic in Reno that prescribed kelation therapy for every malady that was known to man and a few that weren't. He hated to be cynical, but for all he knew, Joshua Reid could be in the best of health.

Perhaps he was overly suspicious, but anyone could scribble a few medical terms and a diagnosis on a piece of paper. Even if the FDA wasn't behind this, the grandfather might be using the boy as a pawn in some law enforcement game.

Not that he had anything to hide, really, but he loathed being associated with the purveyors of coffee enemas and wheatgrass juice. A fledgling clinic like his might not be able to withstand the negative publicity of an investigation, whatever its merits; and no less importantly, his reputation was on the line.

Relying as he must on referrals from former colleagues, he could not risk a loss of credibility. "You have to understand my position—"

Garrett Reid slammed his hand on the desk. "No, *you'd* better understand mine! They tell me that my grandson will soon be permanently confined to a wheelchair."

117

"I obviously haven't examined the boy," he said pointedly, "but *if* the diagnosis is accurate, that would be my estimation as well."

"They say he'll lose control of his bodily functions any time now. He'll have to wear a *diaper.*" Garrett Reid's jaw muscles tightened. "And the pain will get worse."

Kramer inclined his head in agreement. Everyone's threshold of pain was different, but there would come a time when morphine wouldn't ease the boy's suffering, and they'd have to resort to heroin.

"They said," Reid's voice grew husky, "that he'll be dead within a year."

He sensed that Reid wanted him to disagree with the doctors' pronouncement, but he could not. "I'm sorry, but that's true. A year would be a generous estimate."

The police chief seemed to have reached a threshold of his own; his eyes were brimming with tears. "Joshua needs a miracle, Dr. Kramer, and you're going to produce one for him."

Hearing the thinly-veiled threat behind the demand, he hesitated. It didn't take much of an imagination to see that Reid could make trouble for him, if not with the FDA, then with the media.

Or worse. As isolated as they were out here, nothing was out of the question. Anything could happen, anytime. A fire, theft, vandalism, physical or emotional intimidation of his staff . . .

Kramer sighed, realizing that he had no choice but to agree. "The program lasts six days. The clinic opens on Monday. Bring him in then."

118

Part Two

May 1992

Chapter Fifteen

That morning when he arrived in Surgery, he found housekeeping mopping blood off the floor in OR-1. The two housekeepers, gowned and gloved in deference to blood's status as a potentially hazardous substance, waved him away from the door with warnings in Spanish. The smell of bleach was nearly overwhelming.

It was 5:30 A.M., well in advance of his Pneumonectomy and Exploratory Laparotomy, scheduled for 7:00. He stuck his head into OR-3 to say hello to the night nurses, who were finishing the instrument count following, they said, an emergency splenectomy on a motorcycle accident victim.

Preoccupied with his own pending procedure, he listened absently to the details behind the mess in 1 — an aortic aneurysm that had blown in spectacular fashion as the surgeon lifted aside the intestines to expose the aortic saddle — then headed off to the doctors' lounge at the rear of the department.

Someone had made coffee during the night and he poured an inch into a cup, It was probably decaf, since caffeine gave some surgeons the shakes, but just to be safe, he limited his consumption.

Two bitter swallows while he took a cursory glance at the latest issue of the Annals of Surgery, and he tossed the cup in the trash. He grabbed a set of greens from the linen cart and went into the locker-room to change.

But when he began to unbutton his shirt, his right hand refused to cooperate.

Holding his hand in front of his face, he tried to make a fist and found that he couldn't. The little finger twitched, keeping quarter time, while his index finger remained obstinately straight. He massaged one hand with the other, working his left thumb into the palm, with little change in sensation.

Numbness extended along the ulnar nerve and he tried to remember if he'd hit his elbow or, since he'd come to the hospital directly from bed, whether he'd slept on it wrong. This had happened several times before in recent weeks, but never to such an extreme.

Manipulating his fingers determinedly, he was reassured to find both feeling and dexterity gradually returning. The twitch in his little finger lessened, but didn't go completely away.

A transient neurological event, he diagnosed, brought on by sixteen-hour days and aggravated, damn it, by the amphetamines he sometimes took to get through them.

Watching the tremors ease, he swore that he'd stop the pills.

At seven sharp he stepped up to the operating table, which had been adjusted to his preferred height, and caught the anesthesiologist's eye.

"Keep him light," he said. This patient was particularly sensitive to medication, and shouldn't require heavy levels of anesthesia to keep him under.

Seated at the head of the table among various machines and monitors, and partially shielded behind a sterile drape, the anesthesiologist nodded. "He won't walk off the table, but I'll keep him light

122

as a feather."

The surgical residents had opened for him, cutting through layers of skin and muscle, and tying off bleeders with hemostats preparatory to what was known in the vernacular as, "throwing stitches." But they worked slowly, and the surgical site still bristled with silver-handled clips.

He knew he wasn't the most patient member of the teaching staff and so he made an effort to resist hurrying the residents, but each whoosh of the ventilator reminded him that time was seldom on their side.

"Let me give you a hand with that," he said finally. In a few minutes he had them all tied off.

He turned his attention to the exposed sternum. The scrub nurse wordlessly handed him the Gigli saw and he cut through the sternum from the jugular notch, down the mid-line and off to one side of the xiphoid process.

His own pulse quickened: the smell of bone dust was to him what roasted peanuts were to a baseball fan.

Using a set of stainless steel clippers, he snipped through the top of the sternum where the saw hadn't penetrated. He dabbed a little bone wax on either side of the split with a double-gloved finger.

Next, the scrub nurse gave him the sternal retractor. Inserting the retractor down into the sternum, he cranked the center-mounted handle. The gears turned, slowly spreading the patient's ribcage to expose the pleural membrane, which glistened under the lights.

Across the room, the circulating nurse dropped a tray of instruments with an ear-splitting clatter.

His right index finger jerked in response and—

Kramer sat up abruptly in bed.

Drenched in sweat, his heart pounding in his chest, he gulped air like a drowning man.

Throwing the covers aside, he got up and started to pace. But his feelings of anxiety couldn't be calmed so easily, and that sent him to the black bag that he kept on the top shelf of the closet.

Chapter Sixteen

Monday, 8 A.M.

"Isn't this exciting?"

Honor Matheson looked up from the medication audit sheet at Estelle, whose body language reminded her of a workhorse champing at the bit. And although she was more nervous than excited, she nodded. "Very."

"The patients should begin arriving any time now." Estelle pushed up the sleeves of the dark blue sweater she wore over her crisply starched uniform. Her nursing cap, a white pillbox affair with black velvet trim, added a formal touch.

"I can't wait to get started," Estelle said.

Honor finished counting ten 2-milliliter ampules of Valium and returned them to the box before answering. "It'll be a long enough day as it is, Estelle, without jumping the gun."

"Oh, I know, you're probably right." The older woman's expression resembled that of the faithful who peddled religion door to door. "And I may change my mind, say in ten hours when I realize that I've still got two hours of work to go, but I have to tell you, I've been looking forward to this day since I retired from the service."

Honor understood what Estelle wasn't saying: that work was the only way she'd found to combat loneliness. She felt a pang of sympathy . . . and recognition. In not so many years she might *be* Estelle, with no life of her own save for her career.

Impatient with the negative direction of her thoughts, Honor reached for a plastic tray of pre-filled disposable syringes of Atropine.

"Not to change the subject," she said, with exactly that in mind, "but have you come across the 30-ml vials of five percent Demerol?"

At eight-thirty A.M. the first patient arrived in a Mercedes Benz limousine.

Standing in the lobby near the double doors, Honor took a deep breath, feeling ill-prepared.

If only Alan were here.

There was no other description for the child who stepped out of the limo but exquisite. White-blond hair framed a delicate, heart-shaped face. Her complexion was pale, with a hint of color tracing high cheekbones. Her nose was just slightly upturned, the effect aristocratic and piquant rather than snobbish.

When the girl looked in her direction, Honor was astonished to find herself looking into malachite-green eyes. Until this moment, she would have sworn that no one had eyes that color . . .

The simplicity of the clothes the child wore—faded blue jeans and a plain, long-sleeved red blouse—accentuated her fragile beauty in a way that frills and lace could not have.

The source of the child's extraordinary appearance was soon apparent, as the chauffeur assisted a stylishly dressed woman from the car. But while their facial structure was essentially the same and their coloring similar, there was a petulance to the woman's mouth that the girl didn't have.

126

Honor knew the child had to be Tiffany Stratton, and the woman was her frequently married mother, Pamela Gray, née Tucker. While reviewing the child's medical records last evening, she'd come across a *People* magazine article—tucked in the back of the file—which outlined that branch of the family tree.

To the best of her recollection Hugh Gray, of the Philadelphia Main Line Banking Grays, was the fourth and, for now at least, current husband. Before Gray had come Texas-oil-wizard-cum-land-baron Stuart Healy, who himself had supplanted tobacco king Malcolm Powers. Or was it Powers who'd followed Healy?

One thing she was sure of was that Wade Stratton III, Tiffany's father and heir to a shipping fortune, had been the first to claim the fair Pamela's hand.

All four of Pamela's husbands, past and present, were obscenely wealthy from old family money. Doubtless, any future husband would be likewise endowed.

Honor pushed open the door as mother and daughter approached, the chauffeur following at a respectful distance. Pamela Gray, eyes hidden behind dark glasses, gave her a fractional nod.

"Mrs. Gray . . . and you must be Tiffany." She smiled at the child.

Tiffany, who had a curiously expectant expression on her face, glanced at her mother before favoring Honor with a disarmingly shy smile. "Hello."

"Welcome to the Alternative—"

"Dr. Kramer was supposed to meet us," Mrs. Gray said, her tone icy enough to warrant a National Weather Service freeze warning.

"He's been detained, but he'll be in to see Tiffany after she's settled."

"But I must speak to him. Where is he?"

Ordinarily, Honor believed that a direct question deserved a direct and honest answer. As a nurse, though, she was often required to be evasive in the course of following doctors' orders. Only once in a blue moon did she encounter someone she didn't mind stonewalling.

She wouldn't mind now. More to the point, she had to stonewall because she honestly didn't *know* where Dr. Kramer was.

"All I can tell you, Mrs. Gray, is that the doctor will be here"—she crossed her fingers mentally—"within the hour."

"But I won't," Pamela Gray snapped. "I have a flight to catch."

It was so out of left field, so difficult to comprehend that a mother would leave her child under these circumstances, that Honor could only repeat, "A flight?"

"Call him. At least I can speak to him before I have to leave."

Nonplussed, Honor glanced at the stone-faced chauffeur, and then at Tiffany. Obviously the child had prior knowledge of her mother's plans; she looked resigned but not in the least surprised.

"I don't have much time," Mrs. Gray added.

"Well, then, I'll show you to Tiffany's room and try to reach him for you from there."

She could not, of course, reach Dr. Kramer, and Pamela Gray, after a cursory inspection of the room, made kissing noises in Tiffany's general direction and swept out to catch her flight.

Tiffany crossed to the bed, unzipped her suitcase, and went about unpacking her clothes nonchalantly, as though this were summer camp and not a medical facility in which she would be fighting for her life.

"Tiffany . . ."

"Don't worry about it," the little girl said, her voice emotionless. "It happens all the time."

"But—"

"My mother has an appointment at Le Petite Hermitage in Beverly Hills . . . have you heard of it?"

Honor shook her head.

"It's very expensive. Rich people go there for plastic surgery. This time she's having the fat taken out of her thighs. You know how they do . . ."

"Liposuction?"

"Liposuction, right, and then she's flying on to Milan—she adores Gianni Versace—for final fittings of her summer wardrobe."

Somehow the child's calm acceptance seemed sadder than if she had broken into tears. "Is there anything I can do to help? With the unpacking or . . . anything?"

"Not really," Tiffany said. "I can pretty much take care of myself."

And she'd have to, Honor thought.

9:15 A.M.

The next arrival came by ambulance with a private duty nurse in attendance.

"Mr. Lassiter?" Honor read the name off the transfer sheet. "Morgan Lassiter?"

The man, whose gaunt face and graying hair made him look older than his stated age of thirty-eight, smiled, which curled his upper lip. His eyes were sunken deep into their sockets, and the skin beneath them was a sickly yellow-gray. "That's me."

129

Estelle had been hovering in the background, and now she came around the nurses' station counter and took the private nurse's place behind the wheelchair. "He's assigned to room five; I'll take him."

"If you'll wait a minute—" Honor began, but Estelle was already halfway down the hall. With a shrug, she continued signing the carbonless forms that the ambulance driver handed her, one after the other.

There were a lot of them.

When she'd finished, the driver pulled out a copy of each form and handed them to her with a flourish. "He's all yours. I'll just go and get our wheelchair, and then I'll leave you to your *voodoo spells.*"

Honor was acutely aware that any number of health care workers would assume the clinic was yet another medical hoax, but she wasn't about to take anything off a damned ambulance driver whose main qualification for the job was a driver's license. "I'll have you know that Dr. Kramer is eminently qualified—"

"Yeah, yeah. I've heard it before," he said, waving off her protestations and heading down the hall.

She had started to follow him when the private duty nurse touched her arm.

"Listen," the nurse said, "be careful with Lassiter, okay?"

Still stinging from the driver's snide remarks, Honor thought first, incredulous, that a fellow nurse believed that she would intentionally harm her patient. "Careful with him?"

"Keep an eye on him, I mean. I just spent two days with him and"—she tapped a finger to her temple—"he might be mental."

That gave her pause. "Does he have a history of

emotional problems?"

"Hon, he doesn't have a history, period. From what I was told by the Registry, he may as well have dropped out of thin air. He showed up in Emergency with an abdomen as hard as a chunk of granite, a racing, thready pulse, and coffee-ground emesis."

"Internal bleeding."

"No kidding. And that pretty much sums up all they know about him."

Vaguely, Honor remembered having seen a photocopy of the patient's admission sheet from the Las Vegas hospital. There had been a scarcity of information, or looking at it from another perspective, an abundance of noninformation, including a notation in regard to the nearest relative that there were "none living."

But that was the standard transient response; as a group, transients were high on secrecy about their pasts — one of the few areas of their lives that they could control.

Which didn't make him crazy. "Anything else you think I should know?"

The private duty nurse glanced down the hallway at the ambulance driver, who was whistling as he pushed the now empty and collapsed wheelchair toward them. "Only that if I were you, I'd do some serious thinking before I turned my back on the man."

11:35 A.M.

Honor opened the drapes, letting sunlight flood into the room. The sliding glass door opened onto a small private patio that overlooked the high desert hills.

Glancing out, she was distracted momentarily by the sky. Although it was blue to the north and blue to the south, overhead it appeared to be silver. Her logical side began to consider the cause—ice crystals in the upper atmosphere?—but she also felt a surge of pleasure at the unexpected beauty of a silver sky.

She was smiling when she turned from the view. "That's an improvement, isn't it?"

Naoka Tanaka, her pallor emphasized by her choice of black attire, hadn't moved from the doorway. A shade under five feet tall, and thin enough to raise the possibility of anorexia, she appeared dazed, as though she couldn't remember how she'd come to be here.

Worse, she had the distinctive, frantic look of someone who feels the bonds of consciousness slipping.

Honor went quickly to her side, took her by the elbow, and guided her across the room to a chair. After helping her patient to sit down, she took a pulse and found it strong but rapid.

Of the five patients chosen for the ATC program, Honor knew the least, medically, about Naoka Tanaka. The paperwork from Seattle had been delayed, then mislaid, and now was presumed lost. Her condition had been given over the phone, without elaboration, as probable Post-Traumatic Stress Disorder.

An emotional ailment, then, with physiological manifestations.

Without even a causal pathology, she wondered what therapy could accomplish, but she trusted that Dr. Kramer wouldn't have accepted the woman as a patient if he didn't believe that he could help her.

"Are you feeling sick, Mrs. Tanaka?"

"Not sick," the woman said in a soft voice, "just

132

. . . disconnected."

Uncertain what to make of that, Honor could only offer what she hoped was a reassuring smile. "Why don't you sit back and relax there for a minute, while I get you a glass of water."

"Please . . ."

Honor turned toward the door, and her breath caught audibly in her throat at the sight of a figure lurking in the hall. The play of sunlight and shadow obscured most of his face, but she knew by the mocking expression of his mouth that it was Morgan Lassiter.

He took a step backward and then executed a neat about-face. In a split second he was gone, silently, and Honor had the strangest feeling that he hadn't been there at all, that the private duty nurse's comments had primed her imagination to a hair-trigger response.

Nevertheless, when she crossed the hall to the utility room to get crushed ice for Mrs. Tanaka's water carafe, she went about her errand without once turning her back to the door.

12:10 P.M.

Honor returned to the nursing station and went to the counter to finish assembling the patients' charts. It was easier to do standing up, which was just as well, since she was finding it increasingly difficult to sit and wait to hear from Dr. Kramer.

Think of something else.

Estelle had yet to return from lunch, which was prepared in the clinic's tiny but well-appointed kitchen by Philippe, an honest-to-God master chef who had somehow been spirited away from Dakota's, one of the finer restaurants in Boston's Downtown Crossing.

Aside from Affinity, nourishment played a key part in recovery, since with any serious illness lack of appetite was a frequent and often intractable side effect. But Philippe's delectable cuisine, served in the charming glass-walled dining room, should be able to tempt even the smallest appetite. None of the clinic patients should suffer from malnutrition.

The aroma of garlic and onions was making her stomach growl, and she patted it comfortingly. "Your turn is coming."

"Smells good," someone said.

Maybe she was getting used to being startled, because this time she didn't even flinch. Honor looked up with a smile, her composure intact. "Doesn't it, though. What can I do for you?"

"That is certainly the question of the hour." The woman placed a leather briefcase on the counter, opened it, and began rummaging through a thick stack of legal-sized manila folders. "Somewhere in here I have a letter for Dr. Kramer from Dr. Wahl . . . I'm Shea Novak, by the way."

Was this was the attorney from Los Angeles?

Honor took note of the tailored navy skirt and jacket, the white silk establishment blouse, the low-heeled sensible shoes, all of which proclaimed "lawyer"—and tried to correlate that with thick chestnut hair drawn into a French braid, and long-lashed smoky blue eyes behind black thin-rimmed glasses.

Never mind the rest of her.

"It does not compute," Honor said. It was one of Patti's favorite sayings. That and "There ought to be a law."

"I'm sorry, did you—"

"Never mind me, I talk to myself a lot."

"Oh. I'm usually more organized than this"—her

134

smile revealed a solitary dimple, all the more engaging for its lack of a mate—"but last week was one hell of a rotten week."

"I can imagine." All at once, she felt contrite. Shea Novak was terminally ill with the most virulent form of brain cancer; when he'd referred her to the clinic, Timothy Wahl had expressed concern that she might not even survive the six-day ATC program.

Having seen the X rays, CAT and MRI scans Dr. Wahl had sent earlier by Federal Express, Honor judged his concern to be valid.

And yet here she was, briefcase in hand, looking remarkably well. Then again, that was the way of certain brutally efficient diseases, which struck without warning and showed no mercy.

"Oops, spoke too soon." The dimple flashed. "Here it is."

Honor accepted the thick envelope. "I'll make sure Dr. Kramer gets this as soon as he comes in. In the meantime, let me take you to your room."

3:00 P.M.

Honor rested her head in one hand, holding the phone to her ear with the other. She'd lost count of how many times the line had rung, not that it made any difference. She hung up, dropping the receiver into the cradle noisily.

"Where do you think he is?" Estelle asked.

"I wish I knew."

"You worked with him before. Is it like him to disappear this way?"

"No, it's not like him at all." At least, not like him the way he was in Boston, before everything went bad. . . . She pressed her fingertips to her

135

temples and felt the throbbing distension of the veins. "How about you? Are you having any luck contacting Garrett Reid? Joshua was supposed to have come in to be admitted hours ago."

"Well there's no answer at the home number, and hasn't been all afternoon. I contacted the Police Department, but the secretary or whatever she is keeps saying that he's on a call and can't be disturbed."

"Can't she give him a message?"

"Apparently not." Estelle drummed her fingers on the laminate counter. "So what do we do?"

"I'll be damned if I know." Irrational or not, she laughed at the absurdity of it all. "Call out the National Guard?"

The older woman scowled. "A fat lot of good those weekend warriors would do."

"You must be Army," a male voice said.

Honor glanced up quickly. Speak of the devil . . . Reid was pushing his grandson's wheelchair toward them. The boy, Joshua, looked pale and miserable.

"Twenty years," Estelle avowed. "And you?"

"I only lasted five, throwing my fool self out of airplanes until my 'chute tangled with a tree." After reaching the nursing station, Reid set the wheelchair brake. "Busted my nose and a couple of ribs, loosened some teeth, *and* nearly lost a kidney."

Frown lines creased Joshua Reid's young face. "If you're gonna tell war stories, spare me, okay? I'm in enough pain already."

Honor watched the muscles clench in the elder Reid's jaw, but he didn't respond to the boy's insolence otherwise. Instead he handed her a set of X rays still in their hospital jacket. "I apologize for being late; I hope we haven't thrown a wrench in the works. There was a situation in town that I had

136

to attend to."

The boy exhaled pointedly, the puff of air ruffling a forelock of sandy hair on his brow. "Damn right. Who can tell what torching widows might lead to, if the law doesn't draw the line?"

"Torching widows?" Honor wanted Joshua to look at her, but his restless gaze flitted away.

Reid pushed the rim of his trooper hat up with an index finger. "It's not what you think. What the kids do is go hunting black widow spiders. When they find 'em, they take a can of hair spray, aim it at the spiders and ignite the spray. It's kind of a jerry-rigged blowtorch."

Estelle tsked disapprovingly. "What won't they think of next?"

"Of course, anything flammable has the potential to explode, but it works pretty well," Reid continued. "Burns the nasty buggers to a crisp—"

"The fat ones pop," Joshua said, his expression revealing an internal battle between adult disgust and childlike fascination.

"—but since spiders favor storage sheds and other outbuildings, where the wood tends to be especially dry, every so often a youngster starts a fire. If the wind kicks in, things can easily get out of control. So the kids have to be stopped."

"Damn right," the boy said again. "We can't have an all-American community like Idle Springs going up in flames. What a hell of a waste of scorched earth that would be, eh, Grandpa?"

"Joshua, I'll remind you to watch your tongue."

An interesting dynamic between them, Honor thought. She'd noticed also that throughout their exchange, Joshua had been surreptitiously pinching the tender skin on the inside of his knees.

Making himself feel.

"Well, you're here now," Honor said into the vac-

137

uum that had formed between the elder and younger Reid. "Estelle, why don't you take Joshua to room two?"

"My pleasure." Estelle beamed at Garrett Reid. "Were you ever in Fort Benning?"

"Benning, yes, but mostly Hood," Reid said as they started off down the hall. "Ate enough Texas dust to qualify personally as a state . . ."

Looking after them, Honor shook her head. Something about the lawman bothered her, although she couldn't have specified what. Maybe it was that Alan didn't trust Garrett Reid. Or it could be the way Reid had of staring right through her . . .

But there were other things to think about. She reached for the phone.

Again, the line rang and rang, its cadence almost hypnotic, but no one answered at the other end.

"Where are you?" she whispered.

Chapter Seventeen

4:30 P.M.

Estelle Gunther breathed a sigh of relief. Honor's shift was finally at an end. She liked her supervisor well enough, at least as well as she could like someone that young who was her boss, but she was used to being in charge. And she had her own way of doing things.

The proper way.

From her perspective, there was a lack of orderliness to the clinic. She would run things differently, and in the three and a half hours until her relief showed up, she intended to do so.

Granted, some laxity might be permitted in running a clinic versus a true hospital, but structure and organization were essential to any medical facility. Schedules, when strictly followed, provided a measure of security to both patients and staff. Rules and regulations existed for a reason, after all.

For instance, why weren't the patients issued gowns? Oh, she supposed they might be more comfortable in their own nightwear, but utility and expedience had to be of equal concern.

Hospital gowns were designed for a nurse's convenience; the short sleeves allowed unrestricted access to the arms for IVs and blood tests, while the open backs facilitated injections and any other medical procedure that might be required.

Heaven help her if she had to start an IV stat and needed to fumble with the wrist-length sleeves on the Stratton child's flannel pajamas. *Then* they'd see that sleeping in comfort wasn't worth a hill of beans, clinically speaking. After all, how much comfort would there be in having their clothes cut off in an emergency?

Worse than pajamas at night, though, was the fact that during the day, the patients were going to be allowed to dress in civvies. For the life of her, Estelle couldn't figure what possible good that violation of standard medical routine could accomplish.

To be honest, she didn't believe that Dr. Kramer had thought all of this through clearly. But that didn't come as a shock; doctors weren't much into hands-on medicine, and consequently were often ignorant of the realities of the daily grind.

In recent years she'd become aware of the increasing reluctance of some physicians to actually *touch* their patients; she'd once worked with an army neuroimmunologist who she swore examined his patients by proxy, never even entering the room. Whether this squeamishness was attributable to the hysteria surrounding AIDS or not she couldn't have said, but medicine was changing, and not for the better.

More than ever before, doctors' visits involved rushing in, asking a few questions, doing the stethoscope shuffle, palpating this or that, and getting the hell out. Then they'd write their orders and let someone else do the dirty work.

"But," she said under her breath, "at least they showed up."

Kramer still hadn't.

What to make of that, she wondered? Honor

hadn't said so, but Estelle knew her young supervisor was worried about an accident on a seldom-traveled back road. There were a lot of back roads in Nevada, and as far as she could tell they were all seldom-traveled, and all led primarily to *other* back roads.

But of course, Honor wasn't entirely rational when it came to Dr. Kramer. That was painfully obvious. And it was just as obvious that Kramer wasn't aware of her, except as a nurse. No need to stop the presses for that bit of news.

She would never say Kramer was self-absorbed, but if she were to draw a caricature of him—a hobby of hers—she'd have him facing a mirror singing "I Only Have Eyes For You" to his reflection.

But she'd wasted enough time on idle speculation, and there was work to be done. Estelle pushed up the sleeves of her sweater and collected the patients' charts, placing them, opened, along the desk.

Starting with Stratton, she began to reorganize the voluminous reports that had already accumulated, filing them in chronological order and by category. Working methodically, she quickly brought the charts up to snuff, pausing only to scan an occasional laboratory report.

This was a sick bunch of people. Kramer had his work cut out for him.

After replacing the charts in their slots, she had crossed to the forty-drawer forms cabinet to replenish the desk stock of nursing continuation sheets when the call board buzzed and lit up.

Room five. She pressed the intercom button. "Yes, Mr. Lassiter. May I help you?"

"Uh . . . there's blood on my bandage."

"I'll be right in." Releasing the button before he

141

could respond, she went into the supply room. There she selected several of the larger sizes of sterile Telfa dressings, a roll of two-inch-width hypoallergenic tape, a pair of latex gloves, and a handful of foil packets of Betadine swabs.

Humming, she hurried down the hall, glancing into each room as she passed by.

The little girl, Tiffany, was lying on the bed in her Care Bears pj's, facing away from the door, and appeared to be asleep. Excellent; a nap would do her good.

Joshua was in his wheelchair near the sliding glass door, staring out blankly. A nice boy, she thought, although like most of his generation, he should show more respect for his elders.

In three, the lady lawyer had papers spread all over the small bedside table. Ms. Novak hadn't changed her clothes, but her shoes were off and she was massaging a nyloned foot while she read.

Naoka Tanaka had gone out to the patio in a humongous blue robe—easily a fourteen on her size-four body—where she stood, presumably admiring the view.

Estelle rapped on the open door to five, hesitating because she didn't see Lassiter inside. "Mr. Lassiter? I'm ready to change your dressing."

"One second."

His voice had come from the bathroom. She went to the bedside and started setting out her supplies. She opened the paper wrapping of the gloves and slipped her right hand into powdered latex.

Fingers gripped her shoulder, and she about jumped out of her skin. She hadn't heard the bathroom door open, nor sensed Lassiter coming up behind her. "Lord be merciful!" she said, a tad breathless.

"Oh, did I frighten you? I'm sorry." The corner

of his mouth twitched. "Are you all right?"

Estelle thumped her chest, reminding her heart of what a normal sinus rhythm was. "I am."

He leaned over and, moving rather stiffly, picked up the second glove, which she'd dropped. Handing it to her, he grimaced. "That didn't feel too good."

Try as she might, she couldn't muster much sympathy for him after he'd scared her nearly into tachycardia. "How many days post-op are you? Nine? You can't be in that much pain."

"I shouldn't be bleeding, either."

He had a point. "You might have pulled a stitch out. Lie down and let me take a look."

Lassiter did as he was told, stretching out on the bed and opening his shirt.

The bandage reached from his ribcage to the lower right quadrant of his abdomen, and from left of the midline around to his right side. There were spots of blood at irregular intervals along the white gauze. Blood in the plural meant more than one stitch pulled.

Estelle frowned. "What have you been doing, Mr. Lassiter? Sit-ups?"

"Coughing," he said, and demonstrated.

"Well, stop it." She flexed her fingers in the gloves and then worked a corner of the bandage loose. "This'll hurt less if I do it fast."

"I—*ouch!*"

She'd yanked the tape before he could protest, pulling three quarters of the dressing free. His skin was colored brownish-orange from Betadine, but even so she could tell the edges of the incision were inflamed.

And indeed, she counted four stitches that had broken, tearing into soft infected flesh and making it bleed. Now, though, blood was merely seeping, and there appeared to be evidence of pus. She

143

traced her finger along the length of the wound, wondering why at nine days post-op it wasn't further along in the healing process.

"Is it bad?" Lassiter asked.

"Not bad," she said, "but not good, either. Your incision is infected and you've busted a few sutures. And this bleeding doesn't look that recent to me."

"I swear I just noticed the blood a few minutes ago, when I went in to take a shower."

"Hmm." She peeled the last of the tape off and tossed the soiled bandage in the trash. "Let me take a culture of the exudate, and then I'll clean it up as best I can. We can't resuture an infected wound, so I'll have to steri-strip it."

"How could it get infected? I've been taking antibiotics by the pound."

Estelle shook her head. "Not the right antibiotics. Some of these organisms are resistant to the usual drugs. But we'll find the magic bullet."

"Shouldn't the doctor take a look?"

"Absolutely," Kramer said from the doorway.

The doctor had finally arrived.

Estelle walked purposefully to the lab, holding the anaerobic culture swabs in their plastic transport vials. At the door, she slid her ID card through the access reader and, when the door *whoosh*ed open, went inside.

She located the slides for the Gram stain Dr. Kramer had requested and set to work, first igniting the burner. After labeling three slides, she carefully swabbed the purulent material on them and allowed them to air-dry for a moment, before passing the slides through the flame several times to heat-fix the samples.

Setting the slides on a rack to cool, Estelle began

opening cabinets, looking for the solutions with which to stain, decolorize, and counterstain the smear. She located the crystal violet, safranin, and Gram's iodine quickly, but not the ethanol/acetone mixture.

Wasn't that always the way? Seemed she was forever hunting for something, again attributable to a lack of organization.

Bending down to check the lower shelves, she noticed that an intravenous setup and tubing had been discarded in the trash.

Now that was a puzzle. Who would run an IV in the laboratory?

Estelle pulled the waste basket into the light. The intracath needle was missing, but otherwise the IV set was complete. Drops of clear fluid adhered to the inside of the tubing, which more or less verified that the setup had been used and not simply thrown out.

Beneath the coiled tubing, she saw an empty 500-ml bag that had contained D5W. And below that . . . Estelle pushed aside the IV leavings to reveal a quarter-liter bottle that had once been filled with Affinity.

She'd hate to jump to a wrong conclusion, but putting two and two together, there was a distinct possibility that Alan Kramer had infused himself with a dose of his own medicine. And recently.

Had he been in here all the time?

Chapter Eighteen

Lassiter grunted when the doctor pressed on his upper abdomen near the incision. "That hurts."

"I imagine it does."

"I imagine you're sorry." At Kramer's uncomprehending look, he added, "To cause me pain."

If he felt an iota of remorse, Kramer didn't show it. "You have a touch of lymphangitis. It's superficial, really—you haven't any of the systemic manifestations, no fever, chills, or tachycardia—but to be safe, we'll switch your antibiotic to something more specific."

Fourteen years since he'd bailed out of the nursing program, and he was gratified to find that he understood most of what the doctor was saying. Tachycardia, a singsong voice in his head recited, is an abnormally rapid heartbeat . . .

"The Gram stain will tell us if we're dealing with streptococci here, as I suspect. In the meantime, I'll have the nurse apply wet compresses to help alleviate the local discomfort."

"Yeah, well, if you'd stop poking me, that'd be a big help, too."

Dr. Kramer took a step back from the bed and began peeling off his disposable gloves. "How are you feeling otherwise?"

146

"How do you think I feel, carrying around a couple of pounds of tumors?"

The suggestion of a crease appeared between the doctor's eyebrows. "I'll do what I can for you, Mr. Lassiter, but you also have to help yourself. A positive attitude can work wonders."

"Hey, I'm positive I feel like shit," he said, with a sardonic laugh. He knew that as a patient, he was expected to be meek and subservient, continually kissing up to the almighty doctor, but he got a kick out of not playing by their rules.

Or any rules.

"You'll be feeling better soon," was all Kramer said as he left the room.

"I'd better be."

7:00 P.M.

After submitting to the prescribed treatment, administered efficiently by the nurse, he went along to dinner. He was still off his feed, but felt curious about his fellow sufferers.

A mixed bunch, even without counting him. He hadn't realized there would be children here. And the boy, who entered the dining area using an old lady's walker, was definitely still a child. Despite having attained Lassiter's own height of five foot six inches, the boy was far too thin, with slender, unmuscled arms, and a scrawny neck that Lassiter could have snapped like a pencil with his bare hands.

The effort of simply walking — although it really resembled more of a crablike shuffle — was evident in the beads of perspiration on the kid's face.

No threat there.

The little girl was a heartbreaker in training.

147

Clear-eyed, too pretty to be considered cute, she had many of the mannerisms of an adult without the cynicism that often came with precocious maturity.

And he ought to know; as a watcher, he was probably more in tune with human behavior than a truckload of hotshot psychiatrists.

Not that he was into prepubescents — he despised pedophiles as being beyond redemption — but give her a few years and she'd be fantasy material. Little white anklets and black patent leather shoes . . .

He forced himself to look away.

Moving on, he turned his attention to the Japanese woman, whose vacant expression made him instantly uneasy. She made him think of a mannequin, brought imperfectly to life.

He watched as she cut a spear of asparagus into even-sized pieces and arranged them into a flower pattern on her plate. This in addition to a starburst design made from carrots sliced lengthwise.

Weird.

The last to arrive for dinner was the lady lawyer, a neat piece of work, who took one look at them, seated as they were alone at separate tables, and went to sit with the little girl.

"Would you like to join us?" she asked the boy, but he quickly shook his head and averted his eyes.

In a flash of understanding, Lassiter realized that the kid was staying put in order not to have to resort to using the walker again.

He almost felt sorry for the punk.

Lassiter didn't take offense at not being invited in the kid's place. He could appreciate that his appearance was on the rough side; all his years on the road had exacted a heavy price. One of the

148

things he'd never done since being diagnosed was wonder "why me?"

He knew why.

He attributed his sickness to the type of life he'd been leading since the not-so-tender age of fifteen: wandering back and forth across the country, first hitching and then driving by night, and sleeping by day, often with the aid of rotgut gin.

There'd been countless greasy dinners eaten hastily in dingy, out-of-the-way cafes, washed down with far too much industrial-strength coffee, and accompanied by the occasional upper when he could score one.

Hard living, Lassiter thought, had caught up with him.

And of course there were the killings, the faceless victims he'd left in his wake, their bodies tossed like any other trash from his van.

Maybe the darkness that came over him at those times was organic. Maybe it had fed on the death-smell. He envisioned the darkness in his belly, a black growth that would kill him, now.

Feeding off its master.

What goes around, comes around, he thought philosophically. At least he hadn't lived someone else's version of life.

He'd done it his way. Him and Sinatra; only at the end, there'd be no one to stand and applaud *his* fading talents.

As he'd intended all along, Lassiter left the dining room after fifteen minutes. Assuming that the others would be occupied for a while—the nurse was feeding her face with the gusto of a longshoreman with tapeworm—he went on the prowl.

The first order of business took him to the

nurses' desk, where he copied items of personal information on the others from their charts. Names, addresses, phone numbers, dates of birth, social security numbers, next of kin, whatever he could find. Shea Novak was the only one gainfully employed; he added her employer's address and number to his list.

Never know what might be useful someday.

Searching quickly through the drawers, he came across a photocopy of the work schedule for the nurses, with phone numbers under each name. He folded it and stuck it in his pocket, trusting that its disappearance wouldn't be cause for concern. It was the kind of thing, he thought, that often got misplaced.

He went next to the first of the patient rooms. Knowing that it was the little girl's room, he didn't expect to find much; eight year olds weren't issued driver's licenses or credit cards. Still, he discovered that Tiffany had a padded leather portfolio containing a collection of house keys in neatly labeled slots.

Keys were handy things to have, but he chose instead to write down the corresponding addresses. He could always break in if need be; although it wasn't something he did a lot of, he was experienced enough to know that there weren't many burglar-proof houses.

The boy's room hadn't much of interest. There was a photograph of a man and woman taken on a cable car, presumably in San Francisco. It had to be Joshua's father, he guessed, but if the woman was the boy's mother he couldn't see the resemblance, what with the big black X drawn over her face.

In Shea Novak's room he found an open briefcase. Most of its contents appeared to be legal stuff, but he happened across a folder with checks paper-clipped to the assortment of bills inside. Most were for the usual, rent, electric, and auto insurance, but there was one check, for five hundred dollars, written for partial payment on a guaranteed student loan.

He'd seen the woman's diagnosis, and it figured that she *had* to be brain-damaged to be paying back a loan while she was camping on death's doorstep.

What did she think, that they had collection agencies in the afterlife?

In hell, maybe.

Anyway, it made him smile as he scribbled down the numbers of her personal checking account.

In room four, he hit the jackpot. Tucked into a side pocket of her suitcase he found a man's wallet, complete with a Washington State driver's license, American Express gold card, MasterCard, and Visa, plus a half dozen gasoline credit cards.

The wallet, practically new, was badly stained on one side. He brought it up to his nose, sniffing tentatively, but he couldn't identify the smell.

With a shrug, he tucked it in his pocket.

He doubted that he could pass himself off as Kenichi Tanaka, but the gas cards were coin of the realm, so to speak, and anything he couldn't use, he could sell to a guy he knew in Fresno.

Assuming he got out of the Alternative Therapy Clinic alive.

For now, though, he had a strong feeling that he'd better haul ass back to his own room before someone spotted him skulking around. He'd found most of what he'd been looking for, and there'd be plenty of time later tonight to hunt up the rest.

His instincts were running true to form; no sooner had he stepped out of Naoka Tanaka's room than the nurse exited the dining room, heading his way.

His luck held: she didn't see him as he moved along the shadowed wall and ducked into his room.

Things quieted down dramatically after midnight. The highbrow music that had been playing all fucking day long had finally been turned off, and the lights in the hallway were dimmed.

The evening nurse, a snooty little thing whose ego assets weren't secured by adequate collateral in her looks, had already come around to take his vital signs for the night. At his request she'd gotten him a sleeping pill, which he'd palmed for future use.

Lassiter stood just inside his door, looking down the darkened corridor toward the nursing station. The nurse was seated at the desk, her blond head bowed, as though she were reading.

So far, so good.

"Hey, bitch," he whispered, savoring the sibilance of the word.

The nurse did not look up.

Lassiter grinned.

He stepped into the hallway, flattening himself against the wall. After waiting a moment to see if the nurse would react, he crossed to the opposite side of the hall and headed for the supply room.

He hadn't had a chance to scout it out earlier, but he was hoping to find a weapon of some kind among the medical supplies. A disposable scalpel, or maybe scissors that he could convert to his own use.

Lassiter thought longingly of his six-inch, single-edged knife with the carved bone handle, hidden in his van back in Las Vegas.

He'd always preferred knives.

He'd take a knife over a gun any damn day. The main reason was, of course, the lethal silence of a blade. And if you lost a knife, it was far simpler to replace. Two minutes in a sporting-goods store, and you were back in business again.

In his entire life, he'd only used a firearm once. It had happened a few years ago, just outside Phoenix, and he could remember as if it were yesterday how startlingly loud the gun was.

He'd been on the Interstate, heading east, driving at night to escape the oppressive August heat. He had the windows down and was enjoying the balmy breeze, the peace, and especially the quiet, when a car approached from the rear.

He'd heard it before he saw it, because the stereo was blasting at roughly the decibel level of a jet lifting off. Looking in the side-view mirror, he squinted at the vehicle's high-beams and clenched his teeth to keep the silver fillings from being rattled loose from his molars.

A late-model Chevrolet Camaro passed leisurely on his right. The driver, a long-haired male, appeared to be alone. Steering with one hand, he was rapping his knuckles on the door panel, matching the beat.

Lassiter maintained a car length's distance between him and the Camaro, frowning at the noise. When the Camaro took an off-ramp a few miles later, he followed, reaching over to a folded newspaper, where he'd tucked the Smith & Wesson .44 Magnum, a Dirty Harry clone.

The Camaro glided to a stop at the end of the off-ramp, having caught a red. A garbage truck lumbered by, preventing the Camaro from making a right turn.

It only took seconds, although time seemed to move in slow motion. Lassiter pulled the van alongside the Camaro, slammed it into park, slid in a half-crouch over to the passenger's bucket seat, stuck the .44 out the window at a downward angle, and pulled the trigger.

Boom!

The recoil kicked his hand back violently, and fucking flames shot out from around the cylinder. Acrid smoke stung his eyes.

He had only a heartbeat to evaluate the result of his shot. His impression was that the driver's face had been all but blown away.

Returning to the wheel, he threw the van back into gear and drove across the road onto the on-ramp. He floored it, and the van reached sixty-five miles per hour before merging back onto the Interstate.

The throbbing bass of the Camaro's stereo faded as he put distance between it and him.

The only sympathy he felt was for the poor soul who'd have to stick his head into that rolling noise factory and turn off the damned stereo . . .

Looking back on it now, he had to admit the .44 had done a nice job, and for the way he'd used it that night, the gun was clearly the better choice. But he did most of his work in close quarters, and for that there was nothing that could match a finely-honed steel blade.

It took ten minutes or so, feeling around in the supply room and bringing what he found to the doorway to see what he had in the light, but eventually he located what he was looking for: a metal scalpel handle with two blades, sealed in a thick plastic pouch.

He shoved the pouch into his pants at the small of his back, then peeked down the hall.

The angle was wrong to see the nurse, but that was to his benefit, since it also meant she couldn't see him.

He listened for a moment and, hearing nothing, headed for his room.

Chapter Nineteen

Tuesday

Shea Novak closed her eyes and tried not to think about what the nurse was doing just out of sight. She'd been given a Valium with her breakfast that morning, the effects of which she felt as a vague lack of will or desire to act on her anxiety.

And she *was* anxious at some level; she hadn't totally convinced herself that she'd done the right thing by coming to the clinic. She'd made the final decision on the spur of the moment, and it wasn't resting easy with her. Having acted in haste, it didn't seem that she'd have the luxury of repenting at leisure.

"Okay, we're ready to go," the nurse said, her tone leaving little room for argument.

Shea looked up, watching as the nurse slipped a metal IV pole into a slot near the head of the recliner. A small glass container hung next to the larger polyvinyl bag on the stand. Clear intravenous tubing connected the two, via a blue plastic gizmo that allowed the fluids to mix.

Experienced in reading at odd angles—most attorneys were—she had no trouble determining that the bag held 500 milliliters of five percent Dextrose, and the bottle, Affinity.

Her pulse quickened.

The nurse tied a tourniquet an inch below her right elbow, snug but not tight. "Now, let's see what kind of veins you've got . . ."

"If they're anything like the rest of me," Shea said, "they're shaking in their boots."

"There's no reason to be nervous." The nurse wiped the inside of her arm briskly with an alcohol swab. "It'll take approximately two and a half hours to infuse the nutrient solution, and after that—"

"Good morning."

Dr. Kramer was standing in the doorway. Shea was struck at how much better he looked now than when she'd seen him last evening. So much better, in fact, that one would've thought he'd somehow squeezed a week's vacation into a single night of rest.

"Dr. Kramer, what a sur—" The nurse, sounding flustered, stopped herself between syllables and made a visible effort to regroup. "I didn't expect you in this morning."

The doctor merely smiled.

"You've been to see Tiffany?"

"I have, yes."

Shea knew that the eight year old was to have started her treatment earlier this morning; no one had said as much, but she gathered that they were being treated in order of the severity of their illnesses.

"Is she—"

"—tolerating the procedure very well. She's had nearly 200 milliliters."

The nurse's obvious relief at that bit of news did nothing to reassure Shea about her own upcoming ordeal. Was it too late to bow out gracefully?

"So . . . Shea. I'm sorry I didn't have more time

157

to talk to you earlier." He took a clipboard out of a wall-mounted file and came to stand at the foot of the recliner. "Are you still having pain?"

Last night she'd complained to him of a headache not unlike those she'd gotten as a child from eating ice cream too fast. "Less than yesterday."

"Visual disturbances?"

Shea glanced at the nurse, who was tearing open the IV needle packaging and laying the contents out on a cloth-draped silver tray. "Actually, today I see a kind of jagged flash, like a lightning bolt, in my left eye."

"Instead of the spots?"

"Yes. And it moves."

"When you say moves, do you mean it floats across your vision, or . . ."

"It vibrates."

"Interesting. Honor, would you get the ophthalmoscope and my loupe? And the tropicamide drops, zero point five percent."

"Yes, Doctor."

While he waited Dr. Kramer placed the clipboard on the counter and rolled a padded stool to the left side of the recliner. He sat down and adjusted the chair so that the head was tilted further back. When Honor returning he accepted the small metal basket the nurse handed him, took out a headband loupe, and put it on.

He shone the narrow beam of light from the ophthalmoscope on the palm of his hand—to test it, Shea guessed—and then leaned toward her.

"Open your eye as wide as you can," he instructed. "And look to your right, please."

She complied, trying not to blink when he put the eyedrops in, but unable to keep from wincing when the light flashed in her eye a moment later. Curiously, the lightning bolt acted as a prism, splintering the white beam into a spectrum of colors.

"Look at me, now."

When she did, the light rendered her momentarily blind. The pain flared.

"Well, there are no apparent lesions of the cornea or lens. No evidence of hemorrhage. The retina is also intact, which is very good news, since flashes of light across the visual field like you described are frequently associated with retinal detachment."

The doctor was close enough to her now that she felt his breath on her face, and although Shea couldn't see the nurse, Honor, she sensed a watchful stillness on the other woman's part.

"No vitreous opacities," Dr. Kramer continued, "and I don't detect any sign of abnormality on the optic nerve, either."

"It's my brain, then. Seeing things."

"So it would seem. A transient optical illusion. Nothing to worry about, considering."

Considering what, she didn't ask.

The light flicked off. Shea blinked at the red afterimage, both eyes tearing.

"Excuse me," the nurse said. "I need to get the IV running for her treatment, or we're going to fall behind schedule."

"I'll do it."

"But Dr. Kramer—"

"Honor, I'm fine."

Shea squinted at them, her eyesight still blurred. When her vision had cleared she saw that the doctor had taken the nurse's place on her right. He picked up the IV set the nurse had selected, and removed the shield from a rather wicked-looking needle.

Speak now or forever hold your peace.

"Excuse me, I—"

"Are you sure?" the nurse persisted, ignoring her.

"I'm fine." Meeting Shea's eyes, Dr. Kramer smiled. "I think I remember how to do this."

Indeed he did. With an economy of motion that could only come from natural skill, the doctor quickly put in the intravenous line. It amazed her that he'd caused no pain, that she hadn't even felt the needle's sting.

Good hands, she thought.

Dr. Kramer stepped back and allowed the nurse to finish up, taping a loop of tubing to her arm. "I'll leave you to it, then."

As he left, Shea noticed that Honor hesitated, watching after him in silence.

Then Honor turned to the IV stand, making an adjustment to the tubing coming from the bottle of Affinity. Using her thumb, the nurse advanced a dime-sized, sprocketed wheel within a white plastic casing.

Shea could see the liquid beyond the juncture of the tubes change from clear to the color of straw.

It would have been difficult to say exactly what she was expecting at this point, but it certainly wasn't a sudden rush of cold. It felt as if ice was forming in her veins, reminding her of time-lapse photography she'd seen in grade school of water freezing, sending delicate tendrils of crystals out from the frozen core.

A shudder passed through her, and a second later her body began to tingle, as though stimulated by a mild electric current.

The feeling wasn't entirely unpleasant, but because she had no control over it, she found it disturbing.

"Relax," Honor said.

Her heartbeat fluttered, then began to race.

The nurse was still at her side, taking her blood

160

pressure, but Shea felt a distance between them, a kind of separation from reality that made her doubt if they could communicate.

But that made no sense. No sense at all.

The tingling intensified, and now it was accompanied by a sudden warmth, which flooded her with an overwhelming feeling of well-being.

She shuddered again, violently, as heat spread like wildfire within her skull, and then she had the oddest thought, an impression really, that a dam was breaking somewhere inside . . .

Her breathing slowed.

"Better?"

"Yes," Shea said softly. "Better."

Chapter Twenty

In the privacy of her room, Tiffany picked at the edges of the bandage on the back of her hand. She wasn't happy about the puncture wound in her hand. She was even less happy that she had another hole in her arm, from the nurse's first try.

But she *did* feel better after the treatment, and that, she guessed, was worth being jabbed twice. The ache in her bones that had become a constant companion was all but gone. And if she didn't know it was impossible, she'd almost think that some of her bruises were beginning to disappear. So, as long as the wounds didn't pop open . . .

She peeked under the bandage to see if blood was still seeping.

"You shouldn't do that."

Tiffany looked up guiltily as the nurse came into the room pushing a cart.

"It itches."

"I can guarantee it'll itch a lot worse if it gets infected." The nurse wheeled the cart to the side of the bed, and after releasing three latches, lifted the lid. A computer, with screen and mini-keyboard, popped up like a jack-in-the-box.

Her curiosity drew her across the room. Closer, she could read BIO 2000 on a metal plate attached to the front of the cart. "What is that?"

"A biofeedback machine."

The nurse's answer wasn't at all helpful to h[er] since she didn't have a clue what biofeedback mig[ht] be, and could see for herself it was a machine; b[ut] she nodded politely. "Oh."

"Mind you, I've only trained on this here at th[e] clinic, so it may take me a minute to set up."

Tiffany said nothing, watching as the nurs[e] opened one of the two drawers on the front of th[e] cabinet and pulled out several sets of pencil-thin ca[-] bles in a variety of colors. It was with some relie[f] that she saw none of them had needles attached.

The nurse, whose name tag identified her as Es- telle Gunther, R.N., plugged the cables into the ma- chine—they were coded by color, Tiffany noted—and then plugged the BIO 2000 into the wall socket.

"On the bed with you, young lady," Nurse Gun- ther ordered, without looking up.

Tiffany climbed onto the bed and sat, Indian- style. It felt good not to become breathless from doing the slightest little thing.

Better than good.

Nurse Gunther opened the second drawer, from which she removed two plastic reclosable bags and a larger pouch made of a shiny silver material. These she opened, dumping their contents next to the cables.

Tiffany didn't know quite what to make of the strange contraptions collected there, but she saw that these, too, were color-coded.

Blue to blue, red to red, and green to green.

Pretty simple, she thought, but then what did she know? She was only a kid.

"Now, let's see . . ." After connecting the cables to the devices, the nurse selected the oddest looking of the group—which appeared to be the amputated

ti of two fingers of a rubber glove joined at the
ʁ by a short corkscrew tether—and turned to

ffany allowed the nurse to fit them onto her in-
ınd middle fingers. At a glance, she'd have sus-
d that they were too big and would fall right
ʾut the rubbery material clung to her skin.
ʾ wiggled her fingers experimentally. The tether
cted her movement, her fingers webbed to-
ʾr like a duck's foot.
ffany smiled.
ʾhis isn't a plaything," Nurse Gunther said
ıly, as she wrapped an inch-wide flexible band
ınd Tiffany's upper arm and fastened it.
he understood that as a command not to have
ı. "No ma'am."
The nurse's expression remained sour. "Unbutton
ur blouse."
Tiffany did as she was asked, using her free
ınds. She recognized the third device Nurse Gun-
ıer had; it was similar to what they used in hospi-
ıl on people having heart attacks.

That would have bothered her, except that she
knew that only old, sick people had heart attacks.
Which meant that there had to be another reason,
a less scary reason, for using them on kids.

The nurse peeled paper off of four circular pads,
and pressed them on the upper, lower, middle, and
left parts of Tiffany's chest, where they stuck as if
glued. Then she snapped wires—these were gray
and white, two of each color—into the center of
each pad.

"All right," the nurse said, turning to the machine and pushing a square button, "you are offi-
cially on-line with BIO 2000."

The computer screen lit up.

Tiffany could see that the screen was divided into

four sections of equal size. In the top left-hand corner, a green line made continual tracings in rhythm with her heartbeat, accompanied by a soft beep-*beep*. In the next panel, a slower-moving line, this one red, danced lazily across the screen.

It took her a few seconds to realize that the red line matched her breathing.

The lower left section featured several sets of electric-blue numbers, some of which changed as she looked at them. The numbers 99.8 flashed on and off.

In the final square, Tiffany read her own name, age, height, and weight. The date and time were also shown, down to the second, and beneath that, a question mark blinked insistently.

Nurse Gunther tapped something on the small keyboard, and new numbers appeared, chasing the question mark off the screen. A moment later, even *more* numbers lit up, these a vivid purple, next to the original ones.

Tiffany whistled through her teeth; the gardener had taught her how.

The nurse turned to her. "I'll second that . . . it's an eyeful, isn't it?"

Tiffany nodded.

"Well, it isn't as complicated as you think. It's designed to be quite simple, really."

"It doesn't look simple."

"No? I thought kids these days were computer-literate, what with Super Mario and—"

"I'm not allowed to play *games,*" Tiffany said, wrinkling her nose and copying her mother's tone of voice.

"Nevertheless, you'll get the hang of it. As a matter of fact, Dr. Kramer told us that children master biofeedback techniques much faster than adults."

Tiffany had her doubts, but she kept them to

herself, letting the quickened beep-*beep* of her heartbeat speak for her.

"Now, the idea is to match your pulse, respiration and temperature with the parameters—"

"The what?"

"The purple numbers."

"Oh."

"See, you've got a little temp, a degree and two-tenths. And you're breathing too fast, child."

Easy to fix that. Tiffany sucked air into her lungs and held it, as if she were trying to cure a stubborn case of hiccups.

"Ah! What are you doing? There's no need to asphyxiate yourself. What you want to do is concentrate on breathing slowly . . . and deeply."

Tiffany let the air out in a sigh.

"Listen, I want you to lie back and relax. Breathe slowly, deeply . . ."

"But I—"

"Relax. *Relax!* Do you feel warm, Tiffany? Can you feel the fever?"

The funny thing was, all of a sudden she did feel warm. Warm and sort of tingly inside. She felt heat across her cheekbones, like when she'd tasted the wine her mother was forever sipping. "Yes."

"Breathe slowly and deeply . . . good. Relax your body, let your muscles go limp, attagirl. And then work on lowering your temperature."

She had no trouble obeying the first two of the nurse's commands, but how could she satisfy the last?

"Look at the screen, Tiffany. See the numbers? Ninety-nine point eight. Bring it down to normal."

"I . . . I can't do that."

"Yes, you can."

Confused, she frowned. When she'd had a temperature before, Dr. Langston had given her aspirin, in spite of her mother's concerns over Reye's syndrome, whatever that was. "But how?"

"You're going to will it to change. *Think* your temperature lower. Can you imagine a cold, wet towel on your forehead?"

Tiffany imagined it so well that she could almost feel drops of water trickling down her scalp.

"In your mind, you see the numbers changing, down to the normal ninety-eight point six."

She closed her eyes, meaning to try doing it somehow, but the whole idea seemed so unlikely, so much like a game of pretend, that she gave up after a minute or so. "I can't."

"Sure you can."

How often had she heard fake encouragement from a grownup? Adults were always pushing her to do all kinds of things she couldn't do—or didn't *want* to do—and then telling her how important it was that she try.

They never seemed to care how bad it made her feel to try, and not be able to do what was asked of her.

"You can do it," Nurse Gunther said. "Come on, Tiffany, it's child's play."

Tiffany felt a pout coming on.

At the hospital in La Jolla, the nurses had left her alone whenever she said she was getting tired; the first thing she'd learned about having leukemia was that no one wanted to make her tired. But before she could get the warning out, the nurse gasped and, sounding strange, said, "Look at the screen if you don't believe me."

Incredibly, her temperature had fallen to ninety-nine degrees.

"But I—" she looked from the screen to the nurse "—I wasn't even trying."

Nurse Gunther didn't answer immediately. The

frown lines on her face deepened, and she blinked several times before shaking her head. "Well, I'll be damned . . ."

Glancing back at the computer screen, Tiffany saw that the numbers had changed again, this time to ninety-eight point six.

Normal.

Chapter Twenty-one

Idle Springs

Garrett Reid propped his feet up on the desk and hummed along with the music coming through the telephone receiver. He truly despised being put on hold, but since there was no way to avoid it, humming was how he stopped himself from being annoyed.

Life was far too short to waste his energies on minor aggravations. However, if raindrops kept falling on old B.J.'s head much longer, he might be prompted to make an exception to his own rule.

His office door opened and the dispatcher, Emily, bustled in. "You still here?"

"Apparently."

Emily, whom he couldn't remember ever seeing without pink foam curlers in her hair, crossed to the file cabinet and yanked open the middle case drawer. Pawing through folders, she said, "It's past five."

"I know. One of my qualifications for this job was the ability to tell time." The song playing now was Moon River; a wet theme was developing, here.

"Get through to Bakersfield?"

"Hmm . . . what are you looking for?"

"Miz Metzger's file."

His neighbor was a frequent and demanding caller, an irate taxpayer who expected a lot of bang for her buck. "Something up?"

Emily pulled a two-inch thick folder out of the drawer. "More of the same."

Which meant kids. Reid felt a curious mixture of relief that it couldn't be Joshua she was calling to complain about, and dread because of why it couldn't.

He wondered how Joshua was tolerating the treatment over at the clinic. He wasn't allowed to visit the boy until Friday, but by then there might be an indication, one way or the other . . .

Reid shook his head, trying to clear it of the doubt that tormented him when he let himself think. "Does she want to talk to me?"

"Pete can handle it."

Pete Chisolm was his salaried deputy; the other two were reserve officers, essentially volunteers with a modest uniform allowance. Among Pete's many fine attributes was a certain predictability, and an attachment to meticulous routine. Reid glanced at his watch. "Shouldn't he be at dinner?"

"Been and gone." Emily stopped paging through the file long enough to give him a significant look. "Joe Bob's slinging hash tonight."

"Ah." Joe Bob was the owner of Lucy's Diner—there'd never been a Lucy—and the overly protective father of Wanda, the seventeen-year-old waitress Pete had a yen for. Pete was counting the days until Wanda became legal, in the meantime keeping things between them light and flirtatious, but it would be suicidal to as much as wink at her under her Papa's keen gaze.

170

Too many knives in the kitchen.

As small a town as Idle Springs was, Reid felt it had, per capita, as many scandals and indiscretions as in any city, any day. Population density might intensify some aspects of human behavior—or rather, misbehavior—but life in the big city hadn't a corner on the market of crimes of passion.

"Well, then, I guess he can—"

Abruptly Emily held up a hand to silence him, at the same time raising her head, like a gundog on point. "Phone's ringing."

He hadn't heard it, what with Andy Williams and his Huckleberry friend.

Emily slammed the door behind her, rattling the hammered glass in its frame.

A revolving door might be in order, he thought idly. It could come in handy, allowing him to give unwelcome callers a little impetus on their way out.

"Chief," a voice thundered in his ear, "you still there?"

"I am." O'Callaghan had never grasped the miracle of fiber optics in transmitting sound. "I'm deaf now, but I'm here."

"Up yours. Listen, I hate to reward your patience with nothing, but that's what I've got."

Reid couldn't help but sigh; this had been his last resort. "She didn't go home, then?"

"Far as I can tell, Claire Elizabeth Morse, aka Claire Elizabeth Reid, hasn't set her dainty foot in Bakersfield since 1988. Which probably means she's smarter than you give her credit for."

"That'll be the day."

"*I* wouldn't be here if any other place had a use for my sorry ass. Not all of us can luck into

171

a cushy job like some sons of a bitch."

As if O'Callaghan had it rough as the owner of a private security firm. But he hadn't called his former partner to argue over who'd feathered their post-Texas-law-enforcement nest better, so he said agreeably, "You're right, not all of us can."

"Damned right I'm right."

He swung his feet off the desk and leaned forward, shuffling through his notes. "Listen, while I've got you on the phone, does the name—" he squinted at his handwriting "—Morgan Lassiter ring a bell?"

O'Callaghan grunted. "Which, pray tell, is the last name?"

"Lassiter. First name Morgan, no middle initial. White male, late thirties to early forties—"

"Oh yeah, there are only a few of those."

Reid ignored the sarcasm. "Hair is graying, brown eyes, below average height, say five seven or eight. On the skinny side, although that may be recent, due to illness."

"Why, you holding paper on him?"

"Nope, there are no wants, no warrants. I just happened across him the other day, and there was something about the man . . ." He left it at that, knowing O'Callaghan would understand.

If psychics had a sixth sense, a cop had to have at least seven.

"Did you run him through the computer?"

"You know I did. Nothing surfaced, but I figure the name has to be an alias."

"No prints?"

"Not a partial of a pinkie."

"Correct me if I'm wrong, but you've got nothing, and you expect *me* to ID him, pull a name out of thin fucking air?"

Reid frowned at the profanity, but let it pass. "Not really, but—"

"But! Why is there always a but?"

"I'm not the one always bragging on how I never forget a face," Reid said pointedly.

"Shit."

"Have you still got your collection of bad boys and girls?" Back in the old days in Harris County, O'Callaghan had amassed thousands upon thousands of wanted posters, most of them duplicates. He never hesitated to go even so far as to dig them out of the trash.

Faded, dog-eared, coffee-splattered or worse, it made no difference; O'Callaghan was a one-man salvaging crew. The last Reid had seen, there were at least three dozen thick binders, bulging with photographs.

"Yeah, I've got 'em."

Hearing the glum resignation in his ex-partner's voice, Reid laughed. "Anyone ever tell you, you're beautiful when you pout?"

"Only you, asshole, and I wish you'd stop."

"I call them as I see 'em, pal. Anyway, can I count on you?"

"Not so fast. I suppose I could have some minimum wage underling look through the gallery and pull out the possibles, but from the description you gave, that's gonna be a hell of a stack."

"I can live with that."

"I knew you were gonna say that." O'Callaghan paused. "And you need it yesterday, right?"

"Sounds good to me."

"You're gonna owe me."

"I always pay my debts."

His former partner sighed, sounding very much like a gale force wind over the phone line. "Consider it done, but it'd be simpler if you had prints."

"Maybe." The last time he'd sent prints to the FBI for matching—and granted, that had been four or five years ago, before the days of laser fingerprint scanning—it'd taken at least a month to get a response.

"There's no way you could—"

"I can't see myself serving him tea," Reid said dryly, "and bagging the cup for evidence."

O'Callaghan snorted. "I don't know why not. It works in the movies."

"Everything works in the movies. Anyway, as much as I enjoy trading insults and swapping lies, I'd better get back to work."

"Same here. When I've got something for you, I'll send it Federal Express."

"Gracias, mi amigo."

"Yeah, sure." O'Callaghan's tone was suddenly brusque. "Whatever."

On his way out, he checked the teletype, but the only thing new was a body—if bleached, scattered bones could qualify as such—found in the California desert, near Interstate 15.

The gruesome find had occurred far enough west of Las Vegas to keep it from being a Nevada concern, he thought. What with all the Silver State's budget woes, Nevada hadn't the resources to show more than a perfunctory interest in California's crimes.

As it was, too many of the bad guys evidently considered themselves Butch Cassidy, and Las Vegas their hole-in-the-wall hideaway. It seemed that every time he watched "America's Most Wanted" the law'd caught up to some desperado down south in Vegas.

A sorry state of affairs, indeed.

Reid put on his aviator's glasses before stepping outside. It was nearing seven P.M., and night was coming on fast, but at this altitude the sun seemed brightest just before it sank behind the mountains to the west.

He glanced to the south, toward the clinic, and wondered if Joshua would be watching this evening as twilight fell.

In the six months since Claire had dumped him off in Idle Springs, Joshua had never bothered to make a secret of his dislike for small-town life, but the boy couldn't deny that the sunsets up here could take your breath away. The sky had more color—from a pale gold to a warm rose to an unworldly shade of purple—and then there was the dramatic, chiseled silhouette of the mountains, no matter which direction you looked.

Hardly a day had gone by when Joshua didn't wind up out on the porch at dusk. Those were the only times that the tension in the boy's face seemed to fade.

It hurt to think that the kid might have only a year's worth of sunsets left to him.

Getting into the patrol car, Reid looked south again; the Alternative Therapy Clinic was little more than a dark blur on the hillside.

Chapter Twenty-two

Friday

Joshua turned over in bed, then lay staring at the ceiling.

He had the strangest sensation along his spine, a kind of prickling, as though someone were poking pins into bone. It didn't hurt, exactly, but he found the feeling unsettling, to put it mildly.

Restless-making, Claire would have called it. Claire had always been full of dumb sayings.

After a few minutes of squirming and twitching, trying to find a more comfortable position, Joshua gave up, sitting upright and reaching for the call button to ring for the nurse.

While he waited, he studied the play of reflected, dappled light coming through the window. There were only a few trees near the clinic building, and they were small evergreens, none of which looked to be over five feet tall, so he couldn't imagine what it was that was causing the shadows to flutter.

There was wildlife in the area, but the coyote and mule deer he'd seen hereabouts surely weren't as high as the pine and spruce trees.

Could someone be out there? The thought made the hair on the back of his neck stand to attention. He'd heard all kinds of stories about crazy old miners who combed the hills searching for abandoned mines.

Luckily, before he could frighten himself anymore, the night nurse, Scott, appeared in the doorway and turned on the recessed overhead light.

"Can't sleep?" Scott asked, crossing to the bedside.

"I feel . . . funny."

"Yeah? Tell me a joke."

Joshua made a face. Of all the nurses, Scott seemed to be the least regimented, an okay, regular guy, but sometimes his sense of humor got in the way.

"Not in the mood for frivolity, I see. So what's the problem tonight?"

"Well," Joshua began, and then paused as Scott took his wrist to check his pulse. He could see the second hand on the nurse's watch, and he waited until it made a full circle before repeating, this time questioningly, "Well?"

Scott shrugged. "Heart's beating."

In spite of his discomfiture, Joshua laughed. "News flash, right?"

"All kidding aside, your pulse is a little rapid, but I don't think it's anything to worry about. Now . . . what's up, doc?"

"My back," he said. "Do you remember that old Vincent Price movie about the Tingler?"

"Sure I remember, although I must say I'm surprised that you do." Scott wrapped the blood pressure cuff around Joshua's upper arm.

"My . . . uh, a friend of my dad's was a sucker for every hokey horror film ever made." The memory was surprisingly bittersweet. It seemed to him that he could smell the slightly scorched Jiffy

177

Pop that Claire always made for them, and taste the metallic flavor of Dr Pepper drunk from "his" blue aluminum tumbler.

Joshua cleared his throat. "When I was a kid, she'd wake me up at night to watch with her."

"Sounds like child abuse to me." Scott tucked the stethoscope under the cuff, pumped the cuff up—thankfully not enough to cut off circulation—and listened, eyes fixed on the column.

Joshua looked awkwardly over his shoulder, watching the mercury sink, hesitating once or twice on its way down. When it bottomed out, Scott removed the cuff and began to fold it. "So, you've got . . . the tingler."

"Or a reasonable facsimile thereof."

Scott grinned. "And here I thought you were a local. Not to say the locals are all brain-dead, but when I went to Idle *Things* the other day, I detected a definite scarcity of IQ points."

Since he'd often thought along similar lines, Joshua found it curious to hear himself defend the town, if halfheartedly. "It's not that bad."

"If you say so. How does a place that size exist, anyway? I mean, where's the tax base?"

That was yet another story Joshua had heard umpteen times. "Some prospector hit it rich and retired here. When he died, his estate went to the town. Some kind of a trust, I guess."

"Money down a rat-hole if you ask me, not that you did. Well, kiddo, your b.p. is slightly elevated, but it could be a matter of the spooks."

"What?"

"A case of the middle-of-the-night jitters. Nurses see it all the time. Death—" Scott grinned "—seems to slither a bit closer in the darkness."

"Except my back really is bugging me."

"The tingler, right. Dr. Kramer has standing orders on you. I can give you a Valium, or you can have an extra treatment of liquid gold."

"You mean Affinity?"

That brought a smirk to Scott's sharp-featured face. "Nutrient therapy, yes indeed. Otherwise known as the miracle elixir, the nectar of the gods. Which would you prefer? Or is that a silly question?"

Joshua felt a rush of warmth at even the thought. "Affinity."

"Coming up."

Five minutes later, Scott had finished setting up the IV apparatus and was pulling on a disposable glove, releasing it with a snap. "Which arm?"

Joshua raised his right hand. "It's the only side that works."

"You must be feeling like a pincushion by now," Scott observed, "with all these IVs."

"I guess."

Scott switched on a gooseneck lamp, adjusted the light, and then peered intently at Joshua's right arm. "Shit, it looks to me like your puncture wounds are healing up very well." Then he frowned. "You did say they stuck you on *this* arm last?"

Joshua nodded as he pointed. "Right there. You can see some of the adhesive from the bandage."

"Son of a gun. Talk about a case of accelerated healing."

"But that's good, isn't it?"

"Good and weird, my friend. But hey, healing's what you're here for."

179

Scott tore open a foil packet containing an alcohol swab. He started to wipe Joshua's inner arm, but then stopped. "You know, I'm gonna use the vein on the back of your hand . . . those needle wounds may be healed, but there's bound to be some soreness or tenderness in the surrounding tissue."

"Actually, it doesn't—"

"Don't disillusion me, Josh. I can only rationalize so much." Scott shook his head. "Now's the time to look away if you're so inclined."

Joshua wasn't and didn't; if anything, he was eager to watch the fluid drip into his veins. "What do you mean, rationalize? What about?"

Scott didn't answer immediately, concentrating on the needle as it pierced the skin. But after it was in, as he taped the butterfly-shaped needle guard in place, he said, "Basically, I have difficulty swallowing that this stuff is a frigging nutrient."

Anticipating that first wave of relief, Joshua said nothing, but tilted his head questioningly and waited for Scott to go on.

"I mean, there are plenty of substances that induce physiological effects—niacin is a good example—but there are effects, and then there are *effects* with a capital E. I've read all the charts, and this stuff . . . this stuff is something else entirely."

"Like what?"

"Obviously, it's some kind of a drug."

The prickly feeling in his spine had completely disappeared, as quickly as that. He felt a sense of incredible well-being. He was now in what he'd come to think of as the comfort zone.

"Not," Scott continued, reaching up and squeez-

180

ing the IV bag, "that I don't understand why Kramer is playing this game. Damn, but this is flowing at a snail's pace. What if I try this . . ."

Joshua looked up, watching the see-through plastic chamber through which the intravenous fluid dripped. The drops began falling noticeably faster.

"Anyway, just between the two of us, I think Kramer's smart to keep the FDA out of this."

Joshua couldn't recall ever feeling this good. When he was at the hospital in Reno, they'd gone through various medications, looking for something to ease his pain. He'd always asked what the drugs were, and usually the nurses would tell him. They'd started with Fiorinal, and tried Percocet and Darvon before settling on Demerol.

Nothing could hold a candle to Affinity.

What he liked best about it was that it didn't cloud his thinking the way the others had. On the contrary, it seemed to him that his thought processes were crystal-clear. It was as though all the doubt and confusion in his mind had been swept away.

"— you're up and running," Scott was saying. "How are you doing? Okay?"

"Fine."

"You know, maybe I shouldn't have said anything to you about Dr. Kramer."

"I won't tell."

"I'm already on thin ice with Her Honor for some reason. All I need is for her to find out I've been jacking my jaw, and I'll be out of a job."

"I would never —"

"Don't ask me why," Scott went on, as if Joshua hadn't spoken, "but Ms. Matheson took an instant, total dislike to me."

Joshua felt a mild disappointment that Scott, like most adults in his life, either didn't trust him, or couldn't be bothered even to listen to him.

The night nurse made another adjustment to the flow rate. "She'd dearly love to find an excuse to can me, so I'd better—"

Ask me if I care, Joshua thought petulantly.

His mouth snapped shut, and Scott blinked, then laughed, somewhat uncertainly. "I don't suppose you care about my problems, do you?"

Taken aback, Joshua didn't answer.

"Do you care?" Scott's expression had turned serious, his tone insistent, as though his future existence depended on receiving a reply. "Do you?"

Leave me alone.

Another change, this time bringing a dreamy look from the nurse. "I'll leave you alone now."

Joshua watched in amazed silence as Scott left the room.

What if I need anything?

Scott reappeared in the doorway. "If you need anything, just ring."

But Joshua, a quick study, had a hunch he wouldn't be needing a call button anymore.

Later that morning, Joshua had another treatment with nutrient therapy, prior to his regular scheduled hypnosis session.

With his silent assistance, the nurse, Judy Bettencourt, hit the vein on the first stick. Unusual for her. Then she increased the IV flow rate.

In session with Dr. Kramer, Joshua was careful, because he felt it possible that Kramer might be watching for any signs of increased mental capac-

182

ity. But he successfully resisted the doctor's attempts to deepen the level of his trance, which allowed him to deflect questions he didn't wish to answer.

What did his feelings of anger have to do with his cancer, anyway?

He didn't want anyone messing with his mind.

Chapter Twenty-three

Naoka Tanaka decided to forgo lunch, preferring instead to spend a few peaceful moments in the clinic's rock garden. Located between the building's outstretched wings, the garden offered privacy and solitude in fresh, pine-scented air.

Maybe *they* wouldn't find her here.

Maybe if she sat in the sunlight, she could chance falling asleep.

Maybe in daylight the dreams wouldn't come, the dreams that were becoming ever more vivid and, frighteningly, more real.

Naoka eased herself down onto a bench, its thin wooden slats warmed by the sun. The heated wood gave off a slight resiny fragrance that for some reason reminded her of home—home in this instance being Seattle, where her sons were buried.

Lately, Sapporo seemed much farther than an ocean away.

She leaned her head back and closed her eyes, listening to the stillness. In Seattle, during those empty, endless nights before she left, the wind had begun whispering her name. Here, the gentle wind caressed her, but so far kept its silence, leaving her to her grief.

Naoka knew that the silence wouldn't last. It was only a matter of time.

Just as she'd feared, when she dozed, the dreams came ... and brought the dead with them.

Somehow Naoka had come to be in the car, although she was not, of course, visible to anyone. Neither was she in her customary place at her husband's side, but rather found herself floating above and slightly behind him. David sat next to Kenichi in the front seat, while Mark was alone in the back.

The road glistened, wet and black in the drizzling rain. The car's headlights were swallowed up in the mist, allowing her to see only a short distance ahead.

Her husband was driving faster than normal. She knew that it was his practice to speed a little when she wasn't in the car to worry. It was the only matter in which Kenichi could be said to be reckless.

The road curved, rose, and then dipped. Water hissed angrily beneath the tires and beaded momentarily on the windshield before streaking up the glass. To the right, ghostly white fence posts stood like sentinels along the winding roadside.

Disoriented at first, she soon recognized the road as "the back way"—the short cut that really wasn't—from their house to her husband's workplace on the outskirts of the city. Kenichi must have forgotten an important paper or something, and was going to the office before running his other errands.

David breathed on the passenger window, then printed his first name in the fog he'd created. He sighed. "I'm bored. Can I please turn on the ra-

185

dio?" he asked his father, already reaching for the controls.

Kenichi glanced at their elder son. "Not rock and roll."

David slumped back in the seat, a study in dejection. With the elbow of his jacket, he wiped out his name. "My friends get to listen to whatever they want."

Giggling, Mark released his seat belt and wedged his wiry body into the space between the bucket seats. "Daddy, how about country and western?"

It was a family joke: her husband claimed to live in terror of being forced to endure "fiddle and banjo music." Kenichi made the expected expressions of fear and loathing, before turning suddenly, his eyes bulging in their sockets, and mimicking a scream only inches from Mark's delighted, if startled, face.

The child windmilled his arms as he fell backward, his legs kicking as his upper body slid down onto the carpeted floor of the car.

Seeing her youngest son in such a precarious position, Naoka could not enjoy their shared laughter. She saw instead, with a pounding heart, that Kenichi's attention had not returned to the road.

As only a spirit presence, Naoka was without a voice. She could neither save them nor warn them, could only watch and wait for what she knew to be inevitable.

David, whose love for his baby brother was often demonstrated by gruff, good-natured horseplay, reached between the seats and grabbed at Mark's exposed and ticklish belly.

Trying to defend himself, Mark kicked out, his

186

left foot hitting Kenichi's arm with a jolting blow.

The car swerved. Kenichi yanked at the wheel, over-correcting, which put the car into a spin.

Even as an observer, Naoka felt a sickening loss of equilibrium as outside points of reference blurred when the car began to shimmy.

An eternity passed.

She had an unbearable amount of time to see the laughter fade from her husband's face. His features went slack, his mouth fell open, his eyes widened in stunned awareness of their circumstances.

David's shoulder belt tightened, the strap pulling across the bare flesh on the right side of his neck. The nylon left a fabric burn on the boy's tender skin. The air was expelled from David's lungs.

If only that had been the worst of it . . .

Unsecured, Mark was buffeted by the force of the spin, arms and legs flailing. He bit his tongue, drawing blood that, mixed with saliva, flew in viscous strings from his mouth.

In the whirling darkness beyond, an ominous gray form appeared. As if by design, the car pulled out of the spin with a burst of acceleration, heading straight for that grayness.

Naoka was an unwilling, silent witness to the last moments of her loved ones' lives as the car slammed head-on into a concrete bridge abutment.

The violence of the impact pushed the engine into the passenger compartment. The steering wheel buckled as it crushed Kenichi's chest. An air bag, if there'd been one, would have been useless.

Skewed sideways, the engine pinned David's

fractured legs beneath his seat. The windshield exploded inward, but it was a piece of shorn metal from the hood that sliced into David's neck.

The back seat of the hatchback fell forward forcefully, striking the side of Mark's head, shattering delicate facial bones and knocking him unconscious.

There was an overpowering odor of gasoline, grease, and hot metal.

And there was blood everywhere.

Naoka had been told by the coroner that they all had survived the crash, although Kenichi had been very near death when the fire started.

There was a whoosh and a blue flash, and then a crackling sound. Thick black smoke began to fill the car's interior . . .

Naoka wrenched herself into wakefulness.

The sun had tightened her skin; her face felt like a mask to her fingers as she sought to wipe away the tears that had spilled from her eyes.

She was shaking badly.

Never in her life had she felt so adrift. Not after her father's suicide, nor thereafter when she and her mother had been forced to leave their home, nor even as a stranger in a new country when she'd arrived in the United States to attend college. Without Kenichi, who'd loved her in his own undemonstrative fashion, and without the sons she'd carried within her, near her heart, she no longer had a connection to the rhythms of daily living.

It was many months away yet, but Naoka could not begin to imagine how she would get through the New Year holiday season—*O-shogatsu*—without the boys. Who would accompany her on *Hatsu-mode,* the first and most meaningful temple visit of the year?

Could she stand alone at the shrine, and find the courage to listen to the sound of only her own hands clapping to call the attention of the gods? Was she expected to forget pressing coins into her sons' palms, that they might toss them into the offering bins?

What talisman would she find there to restore good fortune for the following year?

No, the festivities of *O-shogatsu* would be unbearable alone.

The wind sighed in sympathy, and then she heard a whisper: "You are not alone."

She did not bother to look and see who it was that had spoken to her, because she knew. *They* had followed her into the sunlight.

The dead.

They were becoming bolder as time passed.

In the beginning, she'd felt their nearness but not heard their voices. They made themselves known in other, more subtle ways. A door left slightly ajar would gently close. A light she'd switched off would be on when she looked again. A teacup forgotten on the dining room table would be found in the kitchen, rinsed and drying on a white towel near the sink.

Things her grandmother used to do.

Then she began to hear laughter, always at a distance, which stopped when she listened for it. Many times in the shower, she'd hear through the rush of water what sounded like her sons at play, but when she turned the faucets off, all that remained was silence.

And before long the voices had started, disguised at first as the wind, hiding amid the soughing of trees. They were indistinct, muffled, and she would wake from sleep only to hear the last syllable of whatever they were telling her.

Only lately had the words become clear.

Only since she'd been here in Nevada.

Only since Tuesday afternoon, when she'd had her first treatment.

And now they were taking form. Gathering substance. Disclosing their faces.

Revealing their intentions.

They wanted her to join them on the other side.

Chapter Twenty-four

Judy Bettencourt counted the 10-milligram pink and white capsules of Serax remaining in the blister-pack for the second time and came up with thirty-seven, the same number as before. She made a notation to that effect on the daily medication audit sheet, glanced at her watch, and added the time.

Four-thirty. Three and a half hours remaining of her twelve hour shift.

She closed the last pill drawer and hung the clipboard with the audit sheet on a hook above the locked narcotics cabinet. Honor would be by in a few minutes to verify her count and sign off the sheet.

Stepping out of the tiny drug room — it was roughly the size of four old-style telephone booths — Judy gratefully took a breath of fresher air. She'd never considered herself claustrophobic, but lately she'd become aware of a fear of being cornered in a tight space.

It seemed silly to her, since she'd grown up exploring caves and abandoned mine shafts with her spelunking brothers, but all the logic in the world couldn't change how she'd come to feel.

In fact, these days she was as jumpy as a toad on a white-hot, cast-iron griddle. And with no identifiable reason for it.

She locked the outer door of the drug room and went to sit at the desk.

Moving out West, she thought, away from her family and friends, and leaving Tennessee, where she'd lived all her life . . . well, sure, that kind of uprooting could throw a wrench into anyone's inner works. But she had never been a homebody in her heart *or* mind, and although she had to admit that she missed the taste of ripe persimmons picked off her Gram's tree, she could say with a straight face and a reasonably clear conscience that she wasn't homesick.

So it had to be something else.

Only what? She'd never seen a sky as wide and blue and endless as up here in these odd hills, and she couldn't fathom how such spaciousness could ever play host to a phobia such as she'd been experiencing.

Yesterday, she'd gone outside on her break to escape the seemingly narrowing walls, only to undergo a moment of blind panic when the van that delivered fresh produce pulled up to the rear of the building.

The sight of that van had set her heart pounding. And despite the fact that her knowledge of anatomy told her it just wasn't possible, she'd kept her mouth shut in order to keep her heart from leaping out of her throat.

Irrational in the extreme, perhaps, but damned if she hadn't believed it then. Gram always said she was the most "sensitive" of the kids—there was no telling if that was a compliment or a curse.

She wondered if she mightn't be suffering from altitude sickness. Maybe she ought to sneak into Dr. Kramer's office and take a gander at his

Merck Manual, or even *Bedside Diagnostic Examination,* to refresh herself in regard to the symptoms.

She'd done that exact thing last night, after going off shift, only then it had been to read up on bone marrow transplants.

A mighty peculiar turn of events when an eight-year-old child knew more about the subject than a nurse did. Of course, little Tiffany had a vested interest in information on the procedure, since a transplant had been in the offing had she not come to the clinic.

Then, too, where Judy was from, what with the tar-paper shacks and the kids who were splayfooted from growing up without proper shoes, medical advances were understandably slow to make the rounds.

Footsteps sounded along the hallway and Judy, startled from her reverie, looked in that direction, rubbing at the hair standing up on her arms. In the late afternoon, things were usually quiet while the patients rested, tired out from the day's treatments . . .

Honor emerged from the shadows carrying a phlebotomy tray.

Judy couldn't recall any new orders being written for blood work today. Maybe there had been a verbal order; Honor had spent several hours in the laboratory with the doctor this afternoon.

If she wasn't blessed with a pure and clean mind, she might wonder about that.

Honor reached the nursing station and put the collection tray on the counter. "I am *not* going to miss Mr. Lassiter when he's gone."

"What's he done?"

"Oh, you know. The rub."

She almost asked, "Is that all?", but held her tongue. How would she explain her dislike for the man, who hadn't done anything to her other than look at her with those flat, snake's eyes?

Besides, there wasn't a nurse living who hadn't been the victim of a supposedly accidental or incidental grope. Judy had worked with blue-haired grandmothers who were felt up more often than a D-cup teenybopper parked at Lover's Leap. It was an occupational hazard.

"Next time, jab him," she advised, and demonstrated with a ballpoint pen.

"I wouldn't give him the satisfaction of knowing that he's bothering me."

Judy shrugged. "Suit yourself, but I wouldn't let any vermin get his jollies off me."

"It's as much about power as—"

A distinctive *thump* caught their attention; one of the patients must have fallen. Without hesitation, they took off, running.

As fate would have it, it turned out to be Lassiter. He lay on the floor in the bathroom doorway. At a glance, Judy took in the water splashed on the tiles and the slick soles of his slippers, one of which had come off his foot and was balanced precariously on its toe, leaning against the shower stall.

Lassiter himself was turning a nasty, dusky shade of blue.

Honor, already on her knees beside him, first checked for a carotid pulse and then tilted his head back to open his airway.

"Is he—"

"He's got a pulse but he isn't breathing. Get Dr. Kramer in here, STAT," Honor ordered. "And bring the crash cart, just in case."

Judy complied, with one last glance over her shoulder to see Honor sticking ungloved fingers into the patient's mouth to clear it of whatever, prior to beginning artificial respiration.

Even as she ran to T-2 to get the crash cart — she'd save precious seconds and a few steps by calling the doctor from the phone in there — Judy couldn't help but be struck by the irony of Morgan Lassiter's fall. Here he'd been annoying Honor with his lascivious behavior, and yet she was going to save the man's life.

It was as if Mr. Lassiter was getting a taste of what was coming to him in payment for his sins, while at the same time experiencing the Lord's mercy at Honor's skilled hands.

Which was enough to make you wonder if Someone hadn't gone schizoid up there.

Thankfully, since her CPR skills were a tad rusty, Judy's contribution to the resuscitation effort was limited to handing things from the crash cart to Dr. Kramer and Honor when they asked for them.

Feeling woefully inadequate, Judy stood by, trying to stay out of the way.

"Is there an obstruction?"

Dr. Kramer, who was flashing a penlight over the tongue of the laryngoscope to look down the patient's throat, shook his head in the negative. "There doesn't appear to be. No edema of either the posterior pharyngeal wall or the epiglottis. And no sign of hemorrhage."

Without looking up the doctor held out his hand, into which Honor placed an endotracheal tube.

"He's becoming agitated," Dr. Kramer said. "Give him Pavulon, six milligrams IV."

Pavulon, Judy recalled, was a neuromuscular blocking agent that induced skeletal muscle relaxation, making it easier for a doctor to intubate. She found it in the medication drawer and handed it to Honor.

Honor quickly began to draw up the dose from a 5-milliliter ampule, but as she was tapping the syringe barrel to displace any air bubbles, Lassiter's chest heaved and his arms flailed out from his sides.

The patient gagged, expelling the laryngoscope, gasped, lurched partway off the floor, and vomited at least four hundred cc's of a clear, oily-looking liquid.

Honor, sitting on her heels near the patient's knees, got splattered before she could move out of the way, and ended up on her fanny on the floor. Judy avoided the worst of it by ducking behind the crash cart.

Wasn't that always the way, though? Never an emesis basin at hand when you needed one.

Mr. Lassiter, who had been slightly cyanotic till then, pinked as nicely as a newborn baby taking its first postumbilical breath.

Dr. Kramer raised his eyebrows. "Well, that saves me the trouble of—"

Without warning and faster than seemed humanly possible, Lassiter turned and lunged at Dr. Kramer, his right hand grasping the doctor's throat. His grip was tight enough that his knuckles were white.

Honor turned a similar shade. Judy could almost *see* a scream in the works as her body tensed and gathered, but none came.

196

As for Dr. Kramer, his reaction was remarkably subdued. He didn't attempt to knock the man's hand away and free himself, nor did he appear to be alarmed by this turn of events. Instead, he looked at Mr. Lassiter and, in a voice that sounded calm and only faintly constricted, said, "You're all right now."

He didn't *look* all right; his normally bloodshot eyes were open wide and bugged out, and the veins in his neck were distended.

"Everything is okay," Dr. Kramer soothed.

Judy glanced at Honor, who had all but frozen in place, hardly even breathing.

Maybe Judy herself ought to do something, like knock Mr. Lassiter upside the head with a waste basket. Old Flo Nightingale might not approve, but she couldn't stand by and watch the doctor get choked to death.

Only seconds had gone by, but it didn't take long to asphyxiate.

"Relax," Dr. Kramer said, sounding short of air. "You fell and hit your head—" he paused to draw whatever oxygen he could into his lungs "—and had a respiratory paroxysm, but there's no cause for concern."

Lassiter frowned.

"You're all right."

The message finally got through; Lassiter released his hold on the doctor's throat. The flesh was mottled, and there were several bloodied, crescent-shaped wounds where his nails had dug in.

"Damn." Mr. Lassiter wiped his mouth with the back of his hand.

Ninety-nine percent of the population would have gingerly checked their necks for damage, but

Dr. Kramer did nothing of the kind. Rather, he put on a stethoscope, placed the bell on the patient's heaving chest, and listened, Judy guessed, for adequate air exchange.

Honor got shakily to her feet.

Judy leaned over and picked up the syringe, which Honor had dropped in the confusion. It occurred to her that if she'd jabbed Mr. Lassiter the way she'd advised Honor to do, this entire episode would have been over in the blink of an eye.

As unobtrusively as possible, she found the blue plastic sheath and slipped it over the needle, then pocketed the syringe.

Before long, Honor would go off duty and Dr. Kramer would leave for his nearby home. There was no way she wanted to be on her lonesome here tonight, but since she hadn't a choice, at least she'd have protection.

Sometimes nursing could be dangerous.

Chapter Twenty-five

The Betadine stung when Honor swabbed it on the scratches on his throat.

"He wanted to kill you," she said. "I saw it in his face."

"That was his brain stem talking." The brain stem—the so-called lizard brain—was a classic illustration of the instinctive and involuntary versus the reasoning and intentional.

"That was *him*. He knew damned well what he was doing." She hesitated for a second to retie the cord at her waist, having changed from her stained uniform into a scrub suit, then added, "And to who."

Hoping to defuse the situation, he said, "Well, as long as Mr. Lassiter is showing no signs of increased intracranial pressure as a result of his fall, I think I can live with his primal instincts."

Honor removed a second Betadine swab from the foil packet. "I wouldn't be so sure."

Kramer didn't want to sound dismissive—of course he appreciated his nurse's concern—but neither did he want, tacitly or otherwise, to encourage an unnecessary uproar over an unfortunate and ultimately minor incident. "Let's forget about it, okay?"

"Lift your chin."

He obeyed. "Anyway, there was no harm done."

Honor didn't reply, but he knew by the brisk way she tended to him that she didn't agree with his assessment. He sighed. "That's good enough."

"Let me—"

Kramer pushed her hand aside, glanced at his reflection in the mirror above the sink, and then went around her into the office. He sat down at his desk and picked up the manila folder containing his consultation reports, back from the transcriber.

"Don't you want a bandage? It's bleeding."

"No." The transcriptionist had done a nice job, and he reached for a pen to begin signing them. "I've gotten worse from shaving."

"Dr. Kramer . . ."

"Honor," he laid the pen back down, "you know, after all the years we've worked together, it would be permissible for you to call me Alan."

Judging by her expression, he'd caught her off guard. The color rising across her cheekbones, flattering to her appearance as it was, suggested that he'd embarrassed her as well.

Once, as a boy, he'd found an injured baby squirrel in the woodpile behind the house. Holding it in his hands, he'd felt its heartbeat as a rapid quivering. He had the impression that if he were to go to her now, Honor would tremble likewise at his touch.

Not that he would do that—it would be a violation of his self-imposed rule against personal involvement with his staff.

He cleared his throat. "I have to finish up here, but why don't you run along?"

After making fleeting eye contact and blushing a deeper shade, she did as he suggested.

* * *

Upon dispensing with the paperwork, Kramer restored order to his desk, locked the patient file drawers, and went to the lab.

He'd already put an intravenous setup in his black medical bag, to which he added a half-liter of D5W and one quarter-liter bottle of Affinity. Closing the bag, he hesitated, tracing a finger across his initials, which were stamped in gold letters near the clasp.

The leather bag had been a gift; one was given to each of the young doctors in his class on attaining their medical degrees. The gift-giver had been a pharmaceutical company, currying favor, he supposed, with future prescribers of their products.

The last figure he'd heard was that it cost the pharmaceutical industry between eighty and a hundred million dollars to research and develop a new drug and bring it successfully to market. The time involved in R and D varied, but he thought five to seven years would be a good general estimate.

A great deal of time and an obscene amount of money were at stake.

What would they do, he wondered, if they found out about Affinity? But he already knew the answer to that: they'd descend on him like a swarm of ravenous locusts, destroying him and all he'd worked for in their insatiable hunger for profit.

If he had his way—and he certainly intended to—they would never know that his discovery was anything more than a nutritional supplement. They could run it through a High Performance Liquid Chromatograph every hour on the hour, for years on end, and they'd never get a fix on the essential substance, because the standard did not exist that would identify it.

He alone knew the source of Affinity. And he meant to keep it that way.

Approaching the nurses' station, Kramer noticed that Judy Bettencourt had the alert look of a sentry at the gate. Her gaze moved back and forth in a perimeter sweep of the hallway. When she saw that someone was coming, she tensed until she recognized him.

"Judy."

"Mercy me, Dr. Kramer, but you gave me quite a start," she said, sounding out of breath. "I thought you'd already left."

"Not yet. Have things quieted down?"

"Yes, it's . . . like a morgue." Her smile had a brittle quality, and there was a wariness about her that hadn't been there before.

Which meant the incident with Mr. Lassiter had upset her, too.

He came around the counter and sat down. He'd have to calm her before he left for the evening. The best way he knew to accomplish that was to focus on the routine of work. "How is Mr. Lassiter doing?"

"Fine, he's fine."

"Have you checked his vital signs?" He'd instructed her earlier to take the patient's pulse, respiration rate, and blood pressure at twenty-minute intervals.

Morgan Lassiter was in some danger of developing complications—primarily cerebral edema or hematoma with resultant nerve cell death due to hypoxia—after having hit his head on the bathroom floor. If that were to occur, their best chance of detecting the symptoms at an early stage was through frequent close monitoring and meticulous clinical observation.

"I checked him about five minutes ago," the young nurse affirmed.

"No complaints of a headache?"

"None."

"There've been no further episodes of vomiting? Or nausea?"

Judy Bettencourt smiled again, this time the genuine article. "He complained of being hungry and requested that I ask the cook to make him a sandwich, pastrami on rye if you can believe it."

"That's a good sign. If he truly likes pastrami." He doubtless needn't ask, but felt he had to, "You know what else to watch for?"

She ticked the signs off in rapid order. "Restlessness, changes in his level of consciousness, decreased pulse, slowed respiration or apnea, elevated blood pressure, weakness, or one-sided paralysis."

"And?"

Judy frowned and chewed on her lower lip. "What am I forgetting? Oh yes, irregular dilation of his pupils, possibly a low-grade fever, and—"

"Convulsions," he finished for her, nodding to show his approval. When he'd hired her, he hadn't been sure of the depth of her nursing knowledge, but she'd been recommended highly as a gifted caregiver, genuinely empathetic with her patients.

It was a skill he envied.

"I'll call you," she said, sounding confident now, "if Mr. Lassiter's condition changes."

* * *

When he reached the end of the clinic's private drive, he saw, parked and waiting like a vulture by the side of the road, an Idle Springs patrol car.

A shark in shallow waters, it seemed to him to be overkill.

The dome light was on, and between that and the last faint rays of daylight, he could see Garrett Reid give an all but imperceptible nod, then push his sunglasses further up on the bridge of his nose.

With no way to avoid the encounter, Kramer pulled up the Jaguar opposite the police cruiser and pressed the control to lower the driver's-side window. "I didn't expect to run into you twice in one day."

Reid reacted with what was either an emotional dyslexic's smile or a facial tic. Or perhaps he was simply a minimalist.

"I wanted to have a word with you about Joshua. A private word."

"I have an office for that purpose."

"I thought," Reid said, "maybe you'd like to follow me into town."

The question was, Kramer thought, was that an invitation or an order?

"We could have a cup of coffee at the diner. Or a beer, if that's your preference."

Why did it suddenly seem that this day would never end? He was mentally exhausted. He hadn't eaten since breakfast. A change in plans meant he'd have to call the clinic and let Judy know where she could reach him.

And he'd have to postpone his own treatment. With the tremor in his hand becoming more pronounced, that could prove problematic.

"Just thirty minutes of your time," Reid said. "Or even twenty . . . that's all I'm asking."

Some choices really weren't choices at all. He no longer believed that Garrett Reid had an ulterior motive for bringing Joshua to the clinic, but he knew there was little that escaped the lawman's notice. With no more than a glance, Reid had let him know that the fresh scratches on his throat had been noted, evaluated, and catalogued for future reference.

Feeling that scrutiny still focused on him, he nodded. "Coffee's fine."

"Glad to hear it."

On the way to Idle Springs Kramer had time to brace himself for an interrogation by Chief Reid, but once there, he got a temporary reprieve. For the first ten minutes after they were settled in at the diner he found himself listening as, one after the other, the townsfolk came by to greet the police chief. And perhaps, he suspected, to get a look at him.

Eventually, the parade ended. Reid pushed his coffee mug aside, folded his arms on the table, and leaned forward. "Tell me, how is Joshua?"

Unaccountably annoyed, Kramer shook his head. "You saw him this afternoon."

"I saw how he *looked*. What I'm asking, what I want to know, is how he *is*."

"You must understand, I'm not equipped at the clinic to do the kind of diagnostic examination that would answer that to any degree of medical certainty."

Reid's jaw clenched. "Still watching your back, are you?"

"Someone has to." In fact, it was simpler than that; he hated being put on the spot. But he knew Reid would not be denied an answer. "I'm sure you know from Joshua that there's been a significant lessening of the numbness in his legs and spine."

"I can't tell you how good it felt, seeing him walk without that contraption."

"He's made excellent progress. And he doesn't seem to be in any pain."

"Is he in remission?"

Kramer inclined his head, although remission wasn't how he thought of it. "I think so."

Something close to wonder showed in Reid's blue eyes. "Will the remission hold?"

"It's probably too early to tell for sure, but it looks good. Very good. Although Joshua will need to continue the nutrient therapy once a week for the next six weeks, on an outpatient basis."

"Is it over?" Garrett Reid persisted.

Feeling the pressure to say what he had previously only surmised, he said truthfully, "Yes, I do think it's over. I have reason to believe that when the scans are done, they'll find no remaining signs of the disease."

Reid closed his eyes and bowed his head. Earlier, he had made his hands into fists, but now he opened them, flexing and then spreading his fingers on the scarred wood tabletop.

Feeling that he was intruding, Kramer looked away. He was surprised to see that, with the exception of a waitress behind the counter, they were the only ones left in the diner.

He hadn't noticed the others leave.

Overhead, the ceiling fan revolved at slow speed, languidly stirring the warm, dry air. The fan motor hummed, the only sound in the stillness.

Finally, the police chief looked up. "You actually did it. You pulled off a miracle."

"I prefer to think of it as creative, innovative medicine."

"Call it what you will, you saved my grandson's life. And I thank you."

As a surgeon, he'd heard similar statements countless times before, but he couldn't imagine ever growing tired of hearing them. The gratitude of the families whose loved ones he'd healed invigorated him, a natural high.

Reid sat back, looking almost relaxed. "If there's ever anything I can do for you, Dr. Kramer, let me know. And I do mean anything."

"Joshua's a fine boy." It was unfamiliar territory, but he ventured in: "I hope the two of you can overcome the difficulties you've been having."

"Count on it. You've changed our lives, I guarantee it. And not just us, I'll wager; what you're doing out there at the clinic's gonna change a *lot* of lives."

Part Three

Mid-May 1992

Chapter Twenty-six

Malibu, California

Pamela Gray got out of bed, leaned over to adjust her black thigh-high stockings, and then pulled the top sheet off the bed, wrapping it loosely around her as she crossed to the open balcony that overlooked the beach.

"I hate that," a voice said behind her. "Why do women always steal the damned sheet?"

Pamela didn't answer. She found Nelson's carved ivory cigarette case on the black marble wall next to a champagne glass. Extracting a cigarette, she looked for the matching lighter, but it was nowhere in sight.

She only smoked after having sex, but then it was with an abiding passion.

Pamela heard the rustle of silk and a moment later a hand reached over her shoulder, proffering a light. She cupped Nelson's hand in hers, steadying it as she lowered her cigarette to the flame. She inhaled deeply, filling her lungs with smoke, and coughed. "Thanks."

"My pleasure." Nelson insinuated himself between her and the balcony wall, reaching beneath her sheet and working his fingers under the elastic top of one of her stockings. He stroked the inside of her thigh. "I can't tell you how sexy you are in these support hose."

She slapped his hand away. "You're a sick man, cousin dear."

"And you love it," he grinned.

"Besides, you know the doctor said I had to wear them after surgery, until the swelling goes down."

"Ah, yes. I forgot you were convalescing." Nelson sat on the wall, tucking the sides of his silk robe between his legs. "But did he mean while having sex?"

"I didn't ask him." Pamela blew smoke in her cousin's face. "I don't enjoy shocking people the way you do. Or being shocked."

"No?" Nelson arched his eyebrows. "Can you even *be* shocked, beloved? After all those husbands? After all those . . . others?"

"If you weren't family, I'd kick your ass out this very minute," Pamela said, with a tight smile.

"It's *my* villa, my sweet."

"You know what I mean."

"Cut me off?"

His laughter infuriated her, but she had long since mastered the icy exterior requisite to those of her station. "Both our mothers would freak if they knew we were intimate."

Nelson hooked his bare leg around her, pulling her toward him. An inch or two of her naked flesh made contact with the cold marble, and she shivered, at least as much from the chill as from his nearness.

"Intimate, what a civilized way of putting it." Nelson buried his face in her neck, nuzzling. "We're much more than that."

"Less, I think. I'm a convenience to you."

"If you say so."

His breath was like fire on her skin. "I say so. Keeping it in the family saves you from having to make an effort."

212

He pulled away from her, his expression incredulous. "Pamela my love, I've adored you all my life, but if you think being with you requires no effort on my part, you're sorely mistaken."

"You shouldn't bother, then. I'd hate to have you put yourself out on my account."

"Sensitive tonight, aren't we?" Nelson eased the tuck out of her sheet and let it drop to the floor, so that she stood nearly nude before him. "But you *are* beautiful."

"Hmm."

He ran his fingertips over her breasts. "We could have another go at it."

Pamela flicked her cigarette off the balcony. A shower of sparks marked its trajectory to the sand and rocks below. "Not tonight. Tiffany spent a few days in Palm Springs with Aunt Mathilde, and they're expecting me this evening. I have to go."

"How is Tiffany, by the way? I meant to ask earlier—" he leaned over and brushed his lips along her collar bone "—before you distracted me."

"The doctors tell me she's fine." She reached for the cigarette case again.

"I still don't understand why you didn't send her to Bethesda."

"It was Tiffany's choice to go to Nevada." This time she lit her own cigarette.

Her cousin drew back from her, shaking his head. "Why let an eight-year-old make a decision like that? From what I heard, the program at the Children's Inn is the best in the country."

"It's her life," Pamela said.

"Or death."

"You do have a flair for the dramatic," she said dryly. "Besides, she detests it back East. And I told you, the doctors say she's fine."

"Far be it from me to criticize, but sometimes

you treat the kid as if she's nothing more than a
. . . than an accessory to your life."

"I don't need criticism from you. If we're being
brutally honest — "

"The operative word being brutal."

" — wasn't it your analyst who concluded that
you're sitting out your own sweet life?"

"That's a cheap shot, Pamela, really beneath
you." He moved away from her, stopped after a few
steps, and turned. "Pardon me for caring."

"Nelson, don't be such an ass."

"Then don't be a bitch."

Pamela kissed the air in his direction. "You know
me better than anyone; it's in my genes."

"I suppose I know you, but I sure as hell don't
understand you. How can you be so indifferent?
About Tiffany, I mean."

"Oh? And did you visit her in the hospital? Jet
up for the day? Did you call her?"

"I sent flowers."

"God, Nelson, how . . . quaint." She bent down
to retrieve the sheet and was mildly disappointed
that Nelson made no attempt to stop her. In truth,
she would gladly have been coaxed to return to his
bed.

It was something of a mystery to her why she
lusted after her cousin, but fifteen years and four
husbands after their first awkward encounter, he
persisted as a fever in her blood.

And a pain in the neck. "I'm getting dressed,"
she announced.

Nelson shrugged.

Pamela stalked past him. In the bedroom, she located her clothes in various corners of the room,
and dressed slowly, waiting to be stopped.

She was stepping into her acid-washed jeans
when she became aware that Nelson was standing in

the doorway, leaning against the frame.

Looking at him, she wondered at the attraction. At thirty-two, he was only two years older than her, but he seemed to be aging prematurely. He had already the beginning of a pot belly, and his muscle tone was shot.

He also had an ugly scar on his forehead from a childhood accident, and although she'd given him the name of a superb dermatologist at Columbia Presbyterian who was performing miracles with scar abrasion, he refused to get himself fixed up.

The line of his chin was softening and there was a dissipated puffiness around his eyes. And his hairline was receding at an undistinguished pace.

Not exactly an Adonis, even in his prime. He was past that now, and didn't seem to care.

"What are you looking at?" he asked.

"You."

"You have a strong stomach for a woman." A smile pulled at the corners of his mouth.

Seeing that, she discarded her black see-through blouse and walked toward him deliberately. "Are you angry with me?"

He shook his head. "I guess I should mind my own affairs, and leave you to yours."

"Don't you dare." Only inches away from him, she reached to untie the belt of his robe.

Nelson didn't try to stop her. He was wearing polka-dot boxer shorts underneath.

Typical.

Pamela grabbed the lapels of his robe and, walking carefully backward, pulled him with her over to the bed. "Let me make it up to you, won't you, for calling you those awful names."

"Do you have time? I thought you had to be in Palm Springs."

"I do." Reaching the bed, she released him and

215

unzipped her jeans. With practiced grace, she stepped out of them and tossed them aside.

Ever the voyeur, Nelson watched as she lay back on the bed in her black lace underwear. "Shouldn't you at least call?"

"Mmm." She hooked her thumb under the waistband of her panties and tugged playfully, showing him her flat belly. "Later. Tiffany won't mind."

"Won't she?"

"She's used to it by now," Pamela said, and patted the mattress beside her.

Nelson didn't need convincing.

Later, she sat up and reached across to the bedside table for the telephone.

In the bathroom, the shower was running and Nelson was singing gamely, slaughtering the lyrics to *The Barber of Seville*.

Pamela punched out the area code and number of her aunt's desert estate. Listening to it ring, she had an urge to hang up and go get a cigarette instead.

She prayed that a maid would answer the phone, since Aunt Mathilde would demand an explanation for why she hadn't shown up. Coming up with enough details to impart a sense of authenticity to an excuse was always a chore.

Aunt Mathilde must have been reincarnated from the time of the Spanish Inquisition.

"A maid, the cook, the groundskeeper," she said under her breath, almost as a mantra, "the butler, the chauffeur, the—"

"Tucker residence."

Pamela recognized the voice. "Juliet, thank heavens. It's me."

"Mrs. Gray?"

"Yes, I—"

"Is everything all right, Mrs. Gray? They were expecting you hours ago, and everyone's been wondering where you are."

"I've been unavoidably detained." She opened the bedside-table drawer, hoping to find a cigarette. "Let me talk to Tiffany."

"Miss Tiffany has gone to bed. She was upset that you hadn't come and wanted to stay up to wait for you, but she finally fell asleep."

She frowned. "What time is it?"

"Nearly midnight."

"Damn, I had no idea it was that late. Listen, I'm not coming tonight. Tell Tiffany I'll be there for lunch, and we'll go riding." Her plastic surgeon would not be amused. "Or something."

"Very good."

"And have her packed, Juliet. We'll be leaving after dinner."

"May I ask—"

Voila! She found a solitary cigarette at the back of the drawer. "I don't know where we're going yet, we're just going."

"Very good."

The cigarette was a woman's brand, with a floral border around the filter. Unless Nelson had turned, and that wasn't bloody likely.

So it wasn't his thumbs he was twiddling, waiting for her to complete her divorce from Hugh. The rat. The pudgy, balding, two-timing rat.

"I'll see you tomorrow," she said, and hung up the phone.

The shower shut off.

Pamela collected a dozen pillows, reclined on a few of the fluffiest, and prepared to throw the rest.

Several minutes later the bathroom door opened and Nelson, wrapped in a towel and looking oddly

217

dazed, came out. He didn't even glance in her direction, but walked straight through the bedroom and onto the balcony.

Curious, Pamela leaned forward.

He stopped at the wall, took a step back, and then hoisted himself up on it.

"Nelson, what are you—"

His form was perfect. He bounced gently on the balls of his feet, raised his arms above his head, and dove off the balcony onto the rocks below.

She was so shocked that she couldn't even scream . . . until later, and then she couldn't stop.

Chapter Twenty-seven

Las Vegas

Holly Caughlin buttoned her candy-striped tunic and then went to the mirror in the volunteer's lounge to put on the new pink cap the Ladies' Auxiliary had provided. It took eight bobby pins to secure it, but she supposed that was better than having the stupid thing fall off every time she turned around.

It looked as though someone had smashed a pink Hostess Sno-Ball on her head.

Holly stuck her tongue out at her reflection; this was not cool. Turning from side to side, she searched for a better angle, but there wasn't any. So she removed six of the bobby pins.

Maybe it would be better for all concerned if the cap conveniently got lost.

Holly returned to her locker and hung her sweater up, dug through her shoulder bag looking for breath mints, and collected the change from her wallet to buy a Coke on her break.

Here all of five minutes, and already she was ready for a break.

Volunteering had been her mother's idea, so she'd know there was more to life than going to the mall, and that "no one lives forever."

Huh!

She worked at the hospital between six and eight

hours a week. Usually that meant two hours each evening on Tuesdays and Thursdays, and up to four hours on Sunday afternoons when all the Surgery patients were admitted. During the school year it was okay, it got her out of the house in the evenings, but with summer vacation coming, it meant two fewer nights to go hang out with her friends.

. On Tuesday, she'd politely asked the Volunteer Coordinator if there was some way she could change her hours for the summer, but the answer had been a stern "no," followed by a foaming-at-the-mouth lecture on what was wrong with kids these days.

As her English teacher, Mr. Murtaugh, would say, hoist by her own petard.

Whatever that meant.

Holly closed her locker and spun the dial on the combination lock. Out of habit, she yanked on it, then let it clatter when she let go.

She went to the Information Desk in the front lobby to get her assignment. She was hoping to get ICU-CCU, because that's where the best-looking doctors worked, including one who resembled that hunky Eldon on "Murphy Brown," but they sent her to Admitting instead.

There were only two scheduled late admissions, and they'd probably show after dinner—one less exposure to lethal if tasteless hospital food—so they sat her down with a short stack of undeliverable mail.

Sometimes a patient was discharged before his or her friends got around to sending a get well card, in which case she had to write the patient's home address on the envelope and send it on. She got that information from the five-by-eight "hard cards" that were kept on file for a month or so after discharge.

Other times, the patients had expired, and that pretty much eliminated any chance of successful forwarding. On that mail, she was supposed to write "Deceased" and stick it in the mail for return to sender.

An awful thing that must be, to get a card back in the mail with "Deceased" written all over it. What a burn! And wouldn't it be terrible if some old lady getting the news that way keeled over and expired, too.

But policy was policy, and she knew she had to follow it or else face the consequences. Whenever she came across a dead one, she took special care with her penmanship, so that whoever'd be getting their best wishes back would at least be spared eyestrain.

"Holly." An admitting clerk sat beside her. "Did you get your call?"

"What call?"

"Some guy called earlier wanting to know if you'd be working tonight."

"What guy?"

The clerk shook her head. "He wouldn't leave his name, but he hinted that he'd be seeing you later."

Holly made a face, wrinkling her nose. "The only guy who's ever called me here is my brother, and he *knows* I'm working. The little punk's probably in my room snooping through my stuff right now."

"Maybe you've got a secret admirer."

"None of the boys I know could keep a secret in solitary, like, confinement."

"Anyway, I thought you'd like to know someone's interested."

That really wasn't a problem for her; if not for her parents' rigid rules about dating, she'd be out every night she had free. "Yeah, thanks."

"Oh, and if your boyfriend shows up later, be sure to act surprised."

"I won't be acting."

At seven-thirty she took her break, going down to the vending machines on the ground floor since the cafeteria was closed.

The hall she walked through to get there was deserted. The doors to Radiology/Imaging and Respiratory Therapy were open, but when she looked into the departments there was not a soul in sight.

In the vending room, she dropped three quarters into the soft drink machine, and after hesitating briefly, pushed the lighted panel for a real Pepsi. Generally she drank the diet stuff, but once in a while she treated herself to a dose of sugar and caffeine.

The can dropped noisily and she leaned over to retrieve it. Her back was to the door, but she caught a glimpse of something moving behind her.

Holly felt a hand on her hip and she spun around, her mouth instantly dry.

"Scared you, didn't I?"

She had to work to swallow the lump of fear in her throat. "Fazio, you idiot."

Fazio worked as a security guard, and although he had to be thirty at an absolute minimum, most of the time he acted as imbecilic as a kid her age.

Fazio snapped his gum. "I saw you heading this way all by your female little self, and figured you might need some protection."

"Yeah," she shot back, "from you."

"Here, let me do that." He took the can from her

222

and popped the top.

Fazio had been hitting on her in not-so-subtle ways, so it wasn't that much of a shock that he'd been following her, but she didn't appreciate having the piss scared out of her. "If you don't mind? My Pepsi?"

When he handed the can back, he made sure that his fingers brushed against hers. His hand was sweaty, and in the dry Vegas air, there was no way that could be blamed on condensation on the can.

"Want me to escort you back to Admitting?"

"I'm on break," she said without thinking, and then bit her tongue, knowing he'd want to join her. The conversations she'd had with him in the past tended to be one-sided, mostly involving him making sly, suggestive comments about her love life.

But this time he merely smiled. "Well, maybe I'll catch up with you later."

"Sure, yeah, bye."

Watching him leave, she figured he must have changed his strategy and now was playing hard-to-get. Only he overlooked the main idea behind that ploy, because she didn't want him, easy or otherwise.

Men. So predictable.

Of course Fazio was waiting for her at the Emergency Department entrance when she left a few minutes after eight. He fell into step beside her, flashlight in his sweaty hand.

"Hi."

Holly gave him her best drop-dead look, but he seemed not to notice. "Don't you have *work* to do?"

"This is my job."

"I guess that explains why my locker got broken

into; you're out here fooling around."

"Not yet, but I'm ready, willing, and able."

She groaned. "Be serious. Somebody broke into my locker."

"How much did they get?"

"They didn't take any money." She glanced at a dusty van with Oregon plates parked in a doctor's space. "They didn't take anything, but—"

"How do you know, then, that anyone broke in?"

"Because the lock was hanging wide open, and it wasn't that way when I left it." She looked over her shoulder at the van and frowned. Was someone inside? She could almost make out a silhouette, but . . .

"Maybe you forgot to lock it."

"Maybe I didn't." They were approaching her car, a red Scirocco that had been her sweet sixteen birthday gift, parked almost all alone in the furthest lot. Keys in hand, she quickened her pace. "You don't have to walk all the way to the car with me."

"Yes, I do. Someone could be hiding on the floor behind the seat."

"There's not much room there . . . it'd have to be someone awfully skinny."

"A skinny man would have no trouble overpowering most women. It's better to be safe—"

"—than sorry. Yeah, I've heard." Behind her, she heard an engine start, a low *thrum* that made her stomach churn.

"A pretty girl like you has to be careful, you know." Fazio shone the light on her car, and as they came closer, directed the beam inside. "I don't mean to make you paranoid or nervous or anything, but these days there's all kinds of lowlifes skulking around."

"Uh huh." She *was* nervous though; her hand

224

was shaking when she went to insert the key.

"Let me," Fazio said.

This time she was glad for his help. For some reason — the caffeine maybe — she actually felt jumpy out here in the "back forty" of the lot.

The security guard quickly unlocked the door and opened it with a flourish, ending with a little bow. "Your chariot awaits."

Then the strangest thing happened. Holly was used to hearing her own voice in her head, but the whispery voice she was hearing now definitely wasn't hers.

Wait for him to leave and come to me.

A cold rush of panic flooded through her. Shoving Fazio aside, she got hurriedly into the car, and slammed the door, locking it and then lunging across the passenger seat to make sure that door was locked too.

Fazio rapped on the window, showing her that he still had her keys.

"Damn it." Holly rolled the window a third of the way down and stuck her hand out.

"Holly," he said, "are you okay? You look kind of pale all of a sudden."

"I'm in a hurry, Fazio. My keys?"

He took her hand in both of his, put her keys and something else in her palm, then closed her fingers around both items and squeezed. "I want you to know, I'm a man who keeps my promises."

She drew her hand inside and opened it. Beneath her key ring was a square foil packet. It took her a moment to realize that he'd given her a condom.

"I promised you protection," Fazio said, and laughed his nasty laugh.

Disgusted, Holly tried to throw it at him, but it hit the glass and bounced back into the interior, where she'd have to find it or spend the rest of her

225

life explaining to her dad. She stuck the key in the ignition and started the car.

Fazio was still laughing.

"Grow up," she said, shifting into first and short-clutching it. The Scirocco took off in fits and starts, and she waited until she was a few car lengths away before flipping him the finger.

In response, Fazio flashed the light at her on high beam, and as he swept it back and forth, the light flitted across the van, illuminating however briefly the face of the man inside.

Don't run, the voice in her head whispered. *Come with me, Holly.*

"Not on your life," she said shakily.

Looking in the rearview mirror, she saw the van back out of its space.

You can't get away from me.

"Oh yeah?" She gunned it, her tires squealing as she left the parking lot. Luckily there was no cross-traffic, because she didn't hold her lane.

Stop being foolish. There's nowhere you can hide. I'll find you wherever you go.

All the way home, she had to block out that voice, but she stuck to well-traveled, well-lit streets, and even ran a few yellow lights to keep from having the van pull up beside her. She did *not* want to look over at it, idling at an intersection; seeing the headlights in her mirror was scary enough.

At home, she sprinted inside, double-locked the door, then went up and barricaded herself in her room. She thought about telling someone, but her parents were casino-hopping, and her brother, the twerp, whom she'd glimpsed playing video games in the den, hadn't even seemed to notice that she was home.

The police weren't even an option, since everyone knew they hated teenagers, and as for her friends,

226

well, they'd make a big fuss for about two minutes, and argue over who they would most like to be stalked by — as if Tom Cruise would be interested — after which they'd decide to go out for pizza. So she put on her stereo headphones to drown the voice out.

Which seemed to work.

The thing that frightened her about all this was not the Freddy Krueger aspect — that stuff wasn't real — but that once or twice she'd wanted to obey.

Chapter Twenty-eight

Los Angeles

As surreptitiously as she could, sitting in full view of Joseph Stojanovich, the partners, and several associates, Ardath McHenry adjusted her panty girdle. Tugging carefully, she cursed the inventor of spandex, his offspring in perpetuity, and her own vanity.

At five foot seven and 110 pounds, she didn't really need the girdle to hold in her tummy, but she only owned straight, narrow skirts, and they were unforgiving of any sag or jiggle.

Thin or otherwise, when a woman reached the age of fifty-five, something, somewhere, was bound to be sagging or jiggling.

The girdle wasn't usually a problem, but Mr. Stojanovich had called an after-hours legal staff meeting, and she'd been in the torturous garment in excess of twelve hours. Her body retained water when she worked overtime, and she could feel the additional ounces.

She'd have to take a Lasix when she got home. *If* the meeting ever ended.

As the only non-attorney present, she had no control over that. Thank the Lord, no one expected her to take down this fuss in shorthand; no fewer than four tape recorders were operating, all the better to catch every brilliant legal uttering.

Her purpose was to function as a second pair of eyes for Mr. Stojanovich, who hated to miss a nuance or glance or untoward smile.

With effort, she made herself listen in.

"I don't think anyone's taken into account what taking this case will do to the firm's reputation," Eugene Kincaid was arguing. "This guy is the worst kind of sleaze. I get sick to my stomach looking at him."

"It'll *make* our reputation. Stojanovich, Kincaid, and Wheeler will become a household name. Granted, it's a *long* household name, but what the hell, who's counting?"

Samuel Wheeler had always been given to overstatement; his true calling was on the stage. In fact several of the lawyers, had they been less avaricious, might have done well as actors. The question wasn't, Ardath had often thought, whether a lawyer could act but, as the old line went, could he be real?

"What this is," Samuel went on, "is an opportunity to go for it all."

"Or lose it all. I for one don't want to be remembered as the attorney who got Ronald Jaffe off."

"Well, there's not much chance of—"

"Excuse me." Mr. Stojanovich, who'd been listening quietly, frowned at them both. "We are defense lawyers, and regardless of what we do in Jaffe's case, the standing of this firm will not be affected. So don't waste your time worrying about credit or blame."

Samuel nodded in acquiescence, while Eugene all but clicked his heels.

"Yes sir."

Ardath covered her mouth with her hand and faked a ladylike cough, hiding a smile. Eugene was no fool. He not only knew which side his bread

229

was buttered, he had an ongoing personal relationship with the cow from which the butter came.

"Reporters will be camping on our doorstep," one of the associates offered, rather ambiguously, and then gave a nod of satisfaction at his own equivocation.

Ardath made a mental note: the boy had promise. Reading over a transcript of the meeting later, no one would be able to tell whether he'd been pro or con the question at hand.

And ambiguous or not, he'd managed to perk up a few ears. "Reporters?"

"Maggots." Despite his hunger for fame, or perhaps because of it, Samuel had an unfortunate history of putting his foot in it whenever there was a journalist nearby. "But that's good. If they want a story, they'll have to park on the street. Let them have the stereos swiped from *their* cars."

That brought a snicker, no doubt political, from one of the only two first-year lawyers who'd stayed late for the meeting.

The other, Shea Novak, was absorbed in reading the file on Ronald Jaffe that his first attorney had compiled. In her first week back at work since her illness, Shea looked almost too healthy.

Ardath harbored a secret suspicion that the "cure" Shea had undergone was more a matter of misdiagnosis. As a medical aficionado, she had, of course, heard of glioblastoma multiforme, and if there ever was a killer disease, that was the one.

And while it was true that Shea's physician, Timothy Wahl, was highly regarded in his field, anyone could make a mistake, even with all the modern technology available. In this instance, Wahl's diagnosis would have to be considered a major-league mistake.

Shea glanced up just then, catching her looking,

and Ardath smiled. Belatedly, she returned her attention to the discussion.

"So we're in agreement," Mr. Stojanovich said. "We'll take the case."

Eugene nodded, his demeanor appropriately solemn. "Absolutely."

"One hundred percent," Samuel said.

There were murmurings of approval from the associates, but since they were here primarily as window dressing — and they knew it — none of them made an appreciable effort to make his voice heard.

Except for Ms. Novak.

Who stood up.

Who flung the file back-handed onto the polished oak table, where it spun in a lazy circle for a revolution or two before coming to rest.

"I think the son of a bitch should do the world a favor and step in front of a semi."

Eugene laughed, clearly startled.

Samuel's mouth dropped open so hard Ardath thought he'd dislocate his jaw.

Mr. Stojanovich looked over the top of his bifocals at her and frowned. "Ms. Novak, it appears you don't agree with our decision."

Maybe there *had* been brain damage, Ardath thought, looking on with renewed interest.

"I'm not arguing your decision, sir. Mr. Jaffe is entitled by law to the best defense he can get, and I'm certain that he'll get exactly that from Eugene or . . . I'm sorry, from Mr. Kincaid or Mr. Wheeler."

"Go on."

"I don't mean to be impertinent, but have you read the Jaffe file?"

Impertinent, indeed. Ardath had it figured, now. That doctor in Nevada had pumped her full of drugs to alleviate her symptoms while simulating recovery. The drugs must have impaired her judgment.

"I haven't read that particular file," Mr. Stojanovich said, "but I'm reasonably familiar with the man's crimes from other sources."

Shea Novak rested her hand on the folder. "Ronald Jaffe did everything he's accused of doing—"

"How can you say that?" Samuel demanded. "I *have* read the file. Jaffe hasn't confessed, there are no witnesses, no DNA evidence, no fingerprints. What are you basing your verdict on?"

"He knew every one of the victims. They all lived within a few blocks of his home."

"Not good enough." The look in Eugene's eyes was avid. Bless his tiny heart, he loved the verbal sparring, no matter that minutes ago he was arguing the other side. "It could be that he's just an aggressively friendly neighbor, who went out of his way to meet every attractive woman in the vicinity."

"His wife didn't know them." Shea sat on the edge of the table.

"So what? He's on disability—"

"Stress-related, he's emotionally disturbed."

"—so he's got a lot of time on his hands, and he likes to walk. His wife works evenings, and he meets his neighbors then."

"Not his male neighbors. Not his older, retired neighbors. Not even his homely neighbors. Only his pretty female neighbors who lived alone."

Samuel, who'd seemed content leaving it to Eugene to plead their case, snorted derisively. "That doesn't make him a killer, my friend. The guy is your typical, tight-assed, married engineer with a yen for a little outside, shall we say, romance."

"Nicely put."

"Have you *seen* the guy? He makes Wally Cox

look like the Terminator."

"But isn't it always those prissy types who can't deal with their rage?"

Ardath glanced at Mr. Stojanovich, who was stroking his chin thoughtfully. She was amazed that he hadn't put a stop to this; she couldn't recall an instance in the thirty-one years she'd spent in his employ that he'd permitted such rank insubordination.

The ink was barely dry on Shea Novak's law degree, and yet she felt qualified to argue with not one, but two of the partners? Brain malignancy or not, the young woman needed to know her place.

Mr. Stojanovich remained mute.

"—how well he fits the profile," Shea was saying. "He's white, in his thirties, reasonably intelligent, and has a problem with women."

"Don't we all?"

"Add to that proximity and opportunity, and the lack of a single alibi . . . and I'll bet if you subpoena his wife's employment records, you'll find that none of the murders occurred when she had the night off."

"But," Eugene argued, "all you have to do is look at Jaffe and you can see he's more the rampage type. Granted, he's a classic anal retentive with delusions of adequacy, but this guy is the type who takes a rifle with a scope up in a belltower."

"I don't think so." Shea shook her head. "He's so damned angry after a lifetime of not being taken seriously that it's personal with him. He has to punish them for his impotence as a man."

"Strangling is certainly personal enough, but why would he sew their eyes shut afterward?"

"You're asking me? I don't know, maybe he can't stand what he sees in their eyes when they look at him. He's such a little weasel. Have you seen that

233

smile? That smug, self-satisfied smile?"

"Sure he has," Samuel interrupted. "Every morning when he looks in the mirror, right, Eugene?"

"Excuse me."

It took a few seconds before Ardath realized that it was Mr. Stojanovich who'd spoken.

Finally, she thought, he's reached the limit of his patience.

"Ms. Novak," he said, "it occurs to me that you may be onto something here."

Or he's having a stroke, she amended.

"It's obvious you've done your homework in regard to Ronald Jaffe. And although I can't countenance your blatant disregard for Mr. Jaffe's entitlement to due process, I do think you may be exactly the person we need to help try this case."

"I'm sorry, what?"

"It seems to me that your conclusion regarding Mr. Jaffe's culpability, premature though it may be, may give us a hint of what's going on in the prosecutorial mind. Perhaps you can help us find the gaps in our defense."

"But I—"

"Of course, I know you haven't trial experience, and that's unfortunate. Even so, I can see the energy between you and Eugene, and I'd like you to work with him."

Now it was Samuel holding his hand up for attention. "I thought I—"

Mr. Stojanovich silenced him with a look. "Ardath, reassign Shea's caseload to the appropriate parties. She'll need to concentrate on Mr. Jaffe."

"Yes sir."

Unmindful of the furor he'd caused, Mr. Stojanovich stood. "Now then, I believe we're adjourned."

Ardath waited until the others had filed out before trusting herself to look at her boss.

"Well? What is it?" he asked. "I can see you're on a short fuse."

"What on earth has come over you? Don't tell me you're besotted with the young woman, too."

Joseph Stojanovich gave her a courtroom sigh, the kind that swayed juries by alerting them to the prosecutor's dirty tactics and faulty logic. "Not even remotely. She's my granddaughter's age, for heaven's sake."

"It happens."

"Not with me. Anyway, what's wrong with giving a bright young attorney a chance? At least she *has* an opinion. And Eugene will keep her in line."

"That's yet to be seen. I just hope you don't wind up a laughing stock for assigning a novice to second chair in a high profile case."

At home, ungirdled at last, lounging in her whirlpool bath, Ardath turned on the ten o'clock news, more for undemanding company than from a desire to be enlightened or, more probably, depressed.

Five minutes into the broadcast, though, her interest was caught by an account of an unidentified male pedestrian who'd walked onto the Hollywood Freeway. He'd ignored the drivers trying to wave him back across to safety, and waited patiently near the center divider until an eighteen-wheeler was bearing down on him, at which point he calmly and without hesitation stepped in front of it.

The coverage of the accident, as "breaking news," was sketchy at best, but there were a few seconds of film. The footage showed the freeway lit up like an airport runway, with flares burning in neat rows. The semi loomed like some prehistoric behemoth in the foreground, and emergency vehicles were everywhere, a coroner's van recognizable among them.

Traffic, needless to say, was congested.

Then there was a brief shot of bloodstained pavement. Even at a glance, there looked to be a lot of blood.

The victim's name was being held pending notification of next of kin. The time of death had been given as 7:11 P.M., and it was, the police spokesperson said with a completely straight face, "instantaneous."

Somehow, Ardath knew that the world had been done a favor.

Chapter Twenty-nine

Seattle

Father Edward Quincy stepped out into the damp night air and turned up his collar against the biting cold. Raining again, and summer nearly upon them.

He hurried across the spongy yard to the detached garage, which sat like an afterthought at the edge of the church's property. He yanked the doors open and fastened them back to keep the wind from slamming them shut again.

Inside the garage, he flicked a switch. The single bare bulb hanging from the wood rafters swung in whirling currents of air.

Father Quincy gave the old Chevy an affectionate if hasty pat on the rear fender. "I have serious business tonight, and I need you to start. I'll have none of your temperament, please."

He tossed the small case containing his stole, the viaticum, and anointing oils onto the passenger seat and got into the car. He was digging in his pockets when he realized that the key was where he'd thoughtlessly left it, in the ignition.

That he took as a good sign: as bad as things were in these hard days, no one was out looking to steal from the church.

He turned the key. Another good sign: the Chevy was a warm-weather transplant and usually sputtered pitifully when driven in inclement weather, but tonight the engine kicked over and purred.

With no time to waste, he backed out of the garage a shade too quickly, and narrowly avoided flattening the rose bushes that bordered the drive.

"Careful," he cautioned himself, but then sped away. He could hear the seconds ticking off in some poor soul's life.

The wet pavement reflected the red lights of the rescue vehicles as a pool of blood.

Father Quincy knew only a little about what had transpired here, only what the Communications dispatcher had told him when she called. A single-car accident, and the car's sole occupant was trapped in the wreckage.

Critically injured, the man was expected to die. He had been called to administer the sacrament of the sick, once called extreme unction or, in layman's terms, the last rites. Not a common request, but not all that rare, either.

He parked the Chevy on the soft shoulder of the road a short distance from the crash, grabbed his case, and walked toward the carnage. With each step his heart sank further; he could see inside the twisted mass of metal that a sheet had been thrown over the victim's face.

He was too late, then. He stopped in the middle of the road and crossed himself.

A fireman he knew slightly from the neighborhood saw him and started over, the reflective tape on his yellow pants winking as it caught and lost the light.

"Father Quincy."

"Anthony." MARTINO was stenciled in black letters on his slicker, and the fireman's given name came to Father Quincy, although he hadn't been sure of it until he spoke. "I'm sorry I couldn't get here sooner. The roads are so slick."

"A bad night to be out." Anthony Martino glanced over his shoulder at the mangled car. "It's gonna take us a while to remove the body. You can hardly tell what's what. Flesh and metal . . . well, you know."

He knew, but still he winced at the image that came to mind. "How long ago did he die?"

"Five minutes, maybe."

"Ah, that is too bad." There was no way he could have gotten here five minutes earlier. "Was he conscious up till then?"

"Drifting in and out, but mostly out. Nobody knows for sure he was Catholic, he was never coherent long enough to say. It was my idea to call you, to give him last rites or whatever. I hope you don't mind."

"No, no, of course not." In instances where a person's religious affiliation was unknown, a conditional absolution was often given.

They fired up the Jaws of Life, and almost instantly shut it down.

"They're having a problem," Anthony said, "finding an angle that'll work."

Another unpleasant reality. "Do you know his name?"

"No, but the police are running the tags. With any luck, it shouldn't take long to ID him. And then comes the hard part."

"The family."

"I can't tell you how grateful I am that it's not the fire department's job to notify whoever's waiting up for him tonight."

Father Quincy nodded. He'd stood in many doorways and seen far too many faces change from hope to despair on hearing tragic news. Dawn would be breaking, perhaps, when an officer knocked on someone's door.

"But," Anthony said, tugging on his suspenders as though by doing so he could uplift his spirits, "at least they'll have the comfort of knowing he's gone on to a far better place."

"Yes, they'll have that."

He stayed around for awhile, waiting to see if he could be of service in some manner, but averted his eyes when they finally removed the body.

Staring instead at the white fence posts along the roadside, he frowned. He was almost certain that this was the stretch of road where the Tanaka boys and their father had perished. Unless he was mistaken, they had slammed into the very same cement wall. He could make out the scorch marks from the fire.

Strange that he hadn't remembered that until now.

Turning slowly, he studied the curve of the road, the slight incline, the condition of the pavement. Even with the indisputable evidence of the road's treachery only a few hundred yards away, he couldn't see what it was that made it dangerous.

The rain would be a factor, of course, and it had rained the night of the accident involving Naoka Tanaka's family. But it had also rained a number of other nights in between the two tragedies.

It was probably a combination of circumstances, he decided. He knew from various accounts that Ken Tanaka had been driving faster than the posted limit. Speeding on a rainy night on a windy road

. . . yes, it was understandable that a driver could lose control.

Or even two drivers.

Fifteen minutes later, wet and chilled, he headed for the Chevy. The victim, he'd been informed, hadn't been carrying a wallet. He'd been dressed in pajamas under his overcoat, and was wearing bedroom slippers.

A five dollar bill was crumpled in his pocket, and the cops were surmising the guy had gone out for cigarettes or something of the kind.

"And bought it instead," the officer in charge had said with a shrug.

They'd found a sodden registration form in the door panel pocket, but no one had been able to decipher a name. The auto registration information was being delayed due to a system-wide computer malfunction.

Anyone waiting up for the accident victim had a long night still ahead.

And if no one was waiting, if the man died with no one to note his absence, with no one to lament his passing . . . Father Quincy wasn't sure which was the sadder outcome.

Passing the second, unneeded tow truck, he stopped abruptly. The driver was in the cab with the door open and the interior lights on. He had the radio mike in his hand as if ready to talk, but was listening instead.

"—same location as last night?"

"That's affirmative. The car hydroplaned most of the way, but what skid marks there are, match almost exactly with the ones from yesterday."

Father Quincy recognized the first, distinctive voice as that of Sgt. Wagner of the Seattle P.D., who barked—and looked—like a walrus. The other voice belonged to the officer in charge, whom he'd spoken to only moments ago. The tow truck driver was evidently listening in on one of the police radio bands.

"What do you make of it?"

"I'll be damned if I know. Maybe there's a skunk crossing nearby and they swerved to avoid hitting the damned things."

"Yeah, now there's a honey of a theory that's sure to bring a smile to the chief's face. Two fatals in a twenty-four-hour period due to rodent jaywalkers. He'll promote your ass right out of the force."

"I was making a joke, Sarge."

"Yeah, and that deafening sound you hear is nobody laughing. Now, what I want you to do is go over the scene with a—"

The tow truck driver, noticing him listening, reached over to the radio and turned the volume down. "Can I help you?" he asked.

"You have, I think," Father Quincy said, then nodded briskly and walked away.

At nine A.M. the next day, after morning prayers, he found verification of his suspicions in the newspaper. He promptly called a dozen of his most reliable volunteers to attend an urgent meeting.

"There is a serious hazard in our midst," he announced gravely, "one which has already claimed the lives of three of our church family, as well as two others in our extended community. I'm talking about Blue Spruce Road."

A murmur of interest circled the table, and all eyes were upon him.

"Five deaths within a few months' time, two in as many days. The police know about the danger, but

242

they're doing nothing, so it's up to us."

"Oh my." Iris Franklin, sitting to his right, looked distressed. "What can we do?"

Father Quincy covered her hand with his. "The very first thing is we must call on Mrs. Tanaka. We must persuade her to share her story."

"But Father, she's still in mourning."

He knew that Iris admired Naoka Tanaka for that. Iris was of a generation that believed in at least a year of respectful mourning for the departed. "I understand, Iris. But I'm sure she'd also want to do whatever she could to keep another wife and mother from going through the agony of her loss. To save one life, or many."

Chapter Thirty

Idle Springs

Jenny Purvis got out of bed, walked in a more or less straight line to the kitchen, and pushed the button on the coffee maker to BREW. Thank goodness she'd had the presence of mind yesterday, while cleaning up after dinner, to put in a fresh filter and measure out the coffee, because both tasks were beyond her, the way she felt.

She went next to the refrigerator. On top was an old-fashioned ice pack, a wedding gift — and an obvious warning — from her mother. She unscrewed the lid to the ice pack, opened the freezer, and stuffed as many cubes as it would hold inside.

Then she held the pack to her forehead. Cold permeated the canvas, and brought a promise of relief.

She'd had far too much to drink last night. She knew her limit well, but that hadn't stopped her from leaving it behind her in the dust.

Dalton was whistling in the bathroom.

The sound was like an auger, drilling into her alcohol-damaged brain.

All of this was his fault, anyway.

"Go out with the girls and have a good time," he'd said last night. "PBS has a special on the spotted owl I want to watch."

A couple of weeks ago, if Dalton had said that she'd have laughed herself sick at the notion. PBS! She doubted he even knew what the letters stood for, unless there was an adult station of that same designation. And *she* didn't want to know what *those* letters represented.

But life had changed in the past ten days.

Dalton had changed.

The sneaky son of a hyena had gotten almost civilized. He was showering every day, wearing deodorant, and changing his shorts so often she'd had to go out and buy a few new pairs, 'cause she didn't do the laundry often enough to keep up with the demand.

Any wife worth her salt knew that changes related to the hubby's hygiene usually meant one thing: another woman. But Dalton had been coming straight home from work, and once he was home, he stayed in. Things had gotten to the point where he was actually underfoot, getting in her way with offers to help with the dishes or fold the clothes from the dryer, or even cook!

There weren't any of the other usual tip-offs either. There hadn't been a single phone call with silence at the other end when she answered. And if it happened that he was on the phone when she came into the room, he didn't abruptly hang up.

And Dalton hadn't as much as hinted that he wanted a night out with "the boys" in quite some time, much less used that as an excuse for being late.

If nothing was rotten in Denmark, what was it that she smelled?

She'd told her mother about the change that had come over Dalton, and the first words out of the old lady's mouth were, "Have you done something stupid, like buying life insurance on yourself?"

Mama didn't care for Dalton, as a son-in-law or a human being.

"The man'll put you in the ground for sure," her mother had warned. "Ten thousand dollars and you're a goner. You'll be on 'Unsolved Mysteries' before you can say double indemnity."

But since Jenny *hadn't* bought insurance, she paid her mother no mind. Besides, even though he beat her on occasion, he'd always stopped himself from doing worse, and never once had he threatened to kill her.

She took heart from that.

If he'd only stop whistling. Jenny changed the ice pack from one hand to the other and held it on top of her head as she walked ploddingly down the hall to the bathroom. She rapped on the door.

"What is it, hon?" Dalton called, with revolting good cheer.

"Would you stop—"

"Oops, can't hear you." The door opened. "Good morning, beautiful."

She stared at him in disbelief. His face was completely lathered, and yet there were streaks of blood mixed in with the shaving cream. "What are you doing?"

"Shaving."

"But you're bleeding."

"Nah, a drop or two." Dalton returned his attention to the mirror and began drawing the blade of his straight razor across his face.

"Dalton Purvis, what's going on?"

"Hmm?"

Forgetting about her headache for the moment, she put her hands on her hips. "I asked you what the hell is going on here."

"Why, nothing." He used a forefinger to push his nose out of the razor's way. "I'm just shaving, like I

246

do every day."

"But you *don't* shave every day." Her left hip was cold and she put the ice pack on top of the hamper, just inside the bathroom door. "If we're picking nits, you don't always shave every *week*."

"Don't I?"

The skin in the razor tracks was an angry red, and there were dozens, maybe hundreds of tiny spots of blood beading up all over his face. "This is the second time you've shaved this morning, isn't it?"

Tilting his head back, he scraped the blade up his neck and under his chin. "The first time I didn't get close enough."

Jenny could hardly stand to look. How could he stand to talk with the razor at his throat?

"Anyway, I'm almost done." He turned to smile at her. "Then you can have the bathroom for your morning beauty routine."

"That's not funny, Dalton." She had grown up knowing she was what her daddy called pug-ugly. She'd made peace with her appearance, but she didn't like other people making fun of her.

"You know," he looked at her squint-eyed, "in this light you kind of look like Mona Charen?"

"Who?"

"You know . . . that gal who subs on 'Crossfire' and gives Mike Kinsley fits."

Jenny shook her head. "I don't know what you're talking about. Who is—"

"Never mind." He rinsed off his face, then grabbed a towel. "You know, Jenny, it wouldn't hurt if once in a while you skipped 'Geraldo' and watched a show with a little more substance to it."

"That's it! Ten days ago you were watching porno films, and now *you're* talking about substance? Something's really wrong here."

247

"I can tell you're upset," Dalton said, "but do you need to raise your voice? The neighbors—"

"The hell with you! You weren't worried about the neighbors when you were bouncing my head off the wall, and calling me every filthy name in the book."

"Jenny, I'm shocked and hurt."

"You might be both of those things, but I'll tell you what you're not." She pointed a trembling finger at him. "You're not my damned husband."

She whirled and ran down the hall, through the living room, and out the door. At first she didn't know where to go from there, but then she saw, coming down the road, an Idle Springs patrol car.

She could hear Dalton calling her name in what her mother would refer to as a "civil tone," and that set her off running toward the police car, waving her arms to draw the cop's attention. Every step reminded her of the folly of knocking back tequila shooters . . .

The cruiser slowed to a stop and she went up to the driver's-side window.

"Garrett," she said, and leaned on the car to catch her breath.

"What's the problem?"

"Him."

"What's Purvis done now?" Chief Reid removed his sunglasses and looked at her critically. "It's early in the day for a battle, isn't it?"

Jenny filled her lungs with air and let it slowly out. "He isn't beating me, it's nothing like that."

"What's he done, then?"

"Shit." She hadn't given any thought to how to explain herself. "Okay. It's this way: Dalton isn't normal."

Garrett Reid laughed. "And you're just finding this out? You could've asked me, and I'd have told you he's a bit skewed."

"No, wait. Listen." She rapped her knuckles on the car door. "Let me think a minute, here."

"I don't have all day."

"I've always liked you, Garrett Reid. Don't be making me change my mind."

He sighed, replaced his glasses, shifted the cruiser into park, and killed the motor. "Take your time."

"Thank you." Jenny took a moment to gather her thoughts, and another to steel herself against the ridicule she felt would soon be forthcoming. "That man in there is not the man I married."

"He isn't?"

"No, he isn't. And he most definitely is not the Dalton Purvis I know and love."

"I see." The chief's tone was flat but there was no challenge in it.

Reserving judgment, Jenny figured. "Wait, I have an example. You know I cuss a little."

Reid nodded.

"Well. Ever since we started dating, we had this thing. Seems like every time I get mad, I tell him, 'Kiss my ass.' And he always says, 'Make it bare' and then we laugh." She smiled, remembering. "It's kind of a funny way to let off some steam."

"Uh huh."

Jenny could see that what she was relating was foreign to Reid—which made her wonder what kind of marriage he'd had—but she persisted. "Now lately, in the past couple of weeks, when I say that to him, he goes, 'Jenny, are you upset about something?' "

"I'm sorry, but how does that make him someone other than Dalton Purvis?"

The very reasonableness with which he asked the question told her that Garrett Reid wasn't likely to

249

take the leap of faith that would allow him to believe her. She would have to show him.

"Come in the house with me. Talk to him for a couple of minutes."

"I can do that."

"Good." Stepping back so that he could open the car door, she added, "You'll see."

Inside the house, Jenny felt a stillness unlike anything she'd experienced in her life. The aroma of fresh coffee, normally a familiar smell, seemed alien.

"Dalton?"

There was no answer.

Jenny tried again, clearing her throat and raising her voice. "Dalton? Where are you?"

"Purvis?" Chief Reid called. "Purvis, you here?"

"He must be here."

A second later, they heard a muffled groan.

"The bathroom," she said. "He's in the bathroom." All at once, her legs didn't want to move. "You go."

Garrett Reid gave her a speculative look, then headed down the hall in that direction. She watched him, her hand covering her mouth.

"Purvis." The chief knocked on the bathroom door. When there was no answer, he pushed the door open. "My Lord, what the . . ."

Jenny's knees gave out and she sank to the floor. A sob worked its way up her throat. She watched, wide-eyed, as Reid stepped into the bathroom, disappearing from sight, then came back out.

His expression was bleak as he walked toward the living room. He went directly to the phone, picked up the receiver, tucked it between his shoulder and ear, and punched out what she knew must be the Police Department's number.

She saw that his other hand, the hand he deliberately wasn't using, was dripping blood.

"Oh no," she said, "oh no."

"This is Reid," he said into the phone. "I need Care Flight to take a slashing victim to the Trauma Center at St. Mary's in Reno."

From her position on the floor, Jenny noticed one of Dalton's sneakers between the couch and the wall. He'd been picking up after himself lately, almost obsessively neat, but there it was, size thirteen. Big as a boat.

"It appears," Garrett Reid said quietly, "that he cut the skin from his face . . ."

Chapter Thirty-one

Las Vegas

Morgan Lassiter walked slowly around the red Scirocco, tracing a gloved finger along its polished surface. The car was new, but already the paint was beginning to discolor from the relentless desert sun.

He was angry with Holly for running from him, angry enough to consider letting the sun have her when he was done. That hadn't been his original plan, but plans could always change.

Nothing was carved in stone.

Besides, after coming all this way for her, it irked him that she was resisting him. The girl he'd acquired and then disposed of on the drive south had yielded to his will without as much as a whimper. Of course, there wasn't a lot of satisfaction in easy pickings, but in retrospect, it seemed a fair trade-off, given the frustration he was feeling now.

He'd wanted the experience to be different with Holly, wanted it to be special and maybe even romantic. He had it in his mind that he'd be gentle with her, out of respect and admiration for her rare beauty, but his patience was running thin.

And rare beauty or not, he hadn't the time to waste playing games with her.

"Holly," he said, looking toward the school, "it'll go easier for you if you cooperate. I guarantee, you don't want me to start thinking of you as a bitch."

There was no chance, he knew, of her receiving his message, not in the babble of thoughts here. With thousands of confused young minds acting as interference, all he could hope for was that on some level, she'd be aware that he was nearby.

Waiting and watching.

For now, though, he had other things to do. With a final glance at the sprawling high school campus, he turned and headed back for his van.

When he'd first arrived back in Vegas, after reclaiming his van from the storage lot, he'd gone to the trouble of obtaining the essential medical paraphernalia to give himself treatments with Affinity. He'd left the clinic with enough of the stuff for the scheduled doses, but Kramer had intended the hospital to provide everything but the Affinity.

He'd been scheduled to return to the hospital on a weekly basis to have his treatments as an outpatient, but he hadn't kept those appointments, primarily because he didn't want someone remembering his being in the vicinity when—not *if*—Holly Caughlin disappeared. His risk would be reduced if no one could recall his face.

So he'd broken into a doctor's office at five o'clock one morning, and appropriated the necessary intravenous supplies and fluid. And he'd helped himself to a box of disposable gloves, a handful of disposable syringes, and sample packs of various and sundry drugs.

You never knew what might come in handy some day. Be prepared, that was his motto.

His long-ago training as a nurse, and the fact that he'd closely watched every move the nurses at the clinic had made, gave him confidence to run his own IVs—so much confidence that in only two weeks he'd given himself five of the six prescribed treatments, in an accelerated program of his own design.

But now he had only a single bottle of Affinity left, hidden behind a couple of six-packs of Corona beer in the "courtesy" refrigerator in the hotel room where he was staying. He'd rented the room solely for that refrigerator, since it was a monster pain in the ass trying to keep the golden liquid at the proper temperature in the van, what with ice that seemed to melt before he could pour it into the Igloo cooler.

Lassiter had wanted to hold out another couple of days before using that last bottle, but whether because of the heat, his return to poor dietary habits, or that he stayed up through too many nights playing craps, he was feeling the *need*.

If he allowed himself a treatment now, he'd be out of the stuff a few days early. Wanting it as bad as he did, that wasn't his primary concern, yet he knew he'd have to deal with the consequences of his lack of discipline, and soon, at that.

But first things first.

Lassiter parked the van a couple of streets away from the hotel so that the manager wouldn't associate it with him, should the police ever make an inquiry. He locked the doors and set off down the block.

The midday sun was intense. He took a ball cap out of a zippered pocket in his army-surplus flight pants and put it on to keep his brain from being fricasseed. Now and then, his head throbbed with a dull pain from where he'd hit it when he fell.

If he hadn't excused himself from participating

254

in society, he might be inclined to sue Dr. Alan Kramer for a few bucks, no matter that the guy had saved his life. Find a personal injury attorney and abuse the System to the full extent of the law.

Wasn't that the American way?

He stepped off the sidewalk and into the street to avoid a trio of Bermuda-shorts-clad tourists bearing down on him. Mom, Pop, and Junior, by the looks of them, plump as corn-fed beef, with that peculiar fishbelly-white skintone destined for sunburn.

The father had a glimmer in his eye, and a small plastic bucket filled with nickels through which he ran sausage-thick fingers as he walked. The coins jingled, the siren song that brought them to this oasis in the desert.

"I tell you, Gladys," the man said, "that baby was about to hit."

"That's what you always say. But I want to eat, and they've got those ninety-nine cent shrimp cocktails just up the street."

"All you think about is food," the man groused.

"And all *you* think about is money."

Their voices were soon swallowed up by traffic noise, but Lassiter heard a stray phrase to the effect that man did not live by shrimp cocktails alone.

In Vegas, man did.

Lassiter closed the drapes and used three safety pins to eliminate the gap between them. He pushed the button beside the door knob to lock it, and slid the chain into the door plate. Neither of which would prevent anyone with a pass-key and a purpose from getting in.

He turned on the television and went into the bathroom, where he retrieved the last small bag of

255

IV fluid from inside the toilet tank. After drying it with a towel, he threw it on the bed.

The needle and tubing were jammed up behind a factory-outlet-quality oil painting bolted to the wall. He wriggled his arm between the frame and the wall, dislodged the last two sealed packages, and tossed them on the bed next to the bag.

He went to the refrigerator, grabbed a bottle of beer, then pushed aside the carton and wrapped his fingers around the container of Affinity. After opening the beer and guzzling about a third of it down, he took both bottles over to the bed.

He sat down, put his Corona on the floor, scratched an annoyingly persistent itch on his upper lip, and ripped open the packages. Within a couple of minutes, he had everything prepared. He hung the IV bag from the wall lamp that swung over the bed for those who'd come to Vegas to catch up on their reading.

Now for the hard part.

For a tourniquet, Lassiter used the old standby, a belt. This particular belt was macrame with stone beads, and he'd taken it off the empty-headed little tootsie he'd picked up south of Carson City.

And dumped north of Tonopah.

Maybe the belt looked ridiculous on his sinewy arm, but it worked just fine.

After briefly contemplating the angle of penetration, he pierced his skin with the needle. A drop of blood welled from the needle shaft and trickled down his forearm. A spot appeared on the bedspread.

He was in on the first try. Could be he'd missed his calling after all; he was getting damned good at this medical crap.

* * *

After his treatment, Lassiter felt a hundred percent better. It seemed a bad omen that he'd been running on empty this soon after his previous infusion, but there was no denying that fact.

Which forced him to make a decision: he had to get his hands on more Affinity. The solution to his shortage was simple: seek out one of the others from the clinic and take his or her supply by whatever means necessary.

The question was, who and where? He was closest to Los Angeles and Shea Novak. If the little girl, Tiffany, was also in Southern California, that would give him two opportunities to score.

On the face of it, California was the logical choice. But there was an even money chance that Tiffany was out of state, at another of her family's homes. He'd overheard her tell Joshua Reid that she didn't spend much time in one place. Or even in one country.

Poor little rich girl, he thought sourly. How did she stand it?

As for Shea Novak, it was only a guess, but he had reason to believe that her supply of Affinity may have been shipped to her doctor. She'd been the first patient to leave that Sunday morning, and there'd been a flurry of activity after her departure, culminating in the arrival of a special messenger.

Lassiter hadn't recognized the Culver City address he'd heard the nurse mention to the messenger as the one he'd copied down from Ms. Novak's chart.

Which could mean he was facing a lose-lose proposition. He might wind up wasting at least twenty-four hours, and quite possibly two days, chasing phantoms.

If he nixed California, the most obvious alternative was to hightail it back to the wellspring of Af-

257

finity, the Alternative Therapy Clinic in Idle Springs. It wouldn't be difficult to get into the clinic at night when there was only one nurse on duty.

The tough part would come when he tried to get into the laboratory. For the life of him, he couldn't figure out how to get past the computer-locked door, short of incapacitating the nurse and taking an ID card. And even if that worked, he'd never been inside the lab, so he had no way of knowing what safeguards might be in use there. If he got into the lab but failed to make off with the "nutrient," there were bound to be repercussions, most likely in the form of an increased security presence in the future.

No, it would be a critical mistake to attempt the clinic without thorough, meticulous planning. And he didn't have time for that now.

Draw a line through that option, and cross off Joshua Reid as well. Aside from the petty detail that his grandpa was the chief of the Idle Springs police, there was still no reason to go breaking into that house, since Joshua would be taking his treatments at the clinic.

Which left Seattle, and Naoka Tanaka.

He knew she lived alone. He'd seen her with an Igloo container identical to his own, so she probably had the stuff.

And she was such a tiny little thing.

Seattle wasn't exactly a hop, skip, and a jump away, but he ought to be able to make the long drive before the effects of his treatment wore off. As for the return trip, who the fuck cared? He'd have what he wanted.

However, viewing his strategy even in the most positive light, he knew that it offered only a temporary solution. Even if everything went off without a hitch, if he got the four bottles Naoka Tanaka should have left, that would give him perhaps a week or ten days of comfort. Two weeks if he denied himself.

He'd have to use those two weeks wisely, and come up with a plan to crack the clinic.

As for Holly, she wasn't going anywhere. In fact, it might be better if he did delay their rendezvous. School would be out in a couple more weeks, and he'd have easier access to her then.

Satisfied that he was on the right track, Lassiter set about packing.

On the way out of town, ninety minutes later, he saw a hitchhiker alongside the road. It wasn't till he'd stopped and was looking in the rearview mirror that he realized there were two of them. Two females, one light, one dark, like negative images.

Taking a swig of Corona, he wondered if he was up to it, and then decided he was.

The passenger door opened and the blonde stuck her head in. "Where you headed?"

"Seattle." He smiled. "Get in."

Chapter Thirty-two

La Jolla

The light from the hallway spilled into the library, and Tiffany drew herself up onto the chair to avoid it. Tucking her knees under her chin, she wrapped her arms around her bare legs.

"Tiffany? What are you doing in here, all alone in the dark?" Juliet came into the room. "Tiffany? What's the matter?"

"Nothing."

"Are you ill?"

"No."

Juliet switched on the green-shaded lamp next to the chair. "You're sure?"

Ever since her leukemia diagnosis, the staff had been treating her like one of the porcelain dolls in her mother's collection. But she didn't *have* leukemia anymore. "I had a bad dream."

Juliet's uncertainty showed in the nervous way she clasped her hands, and her white-knuckled fingers. "Do you want me to call someone?"

Tiffany shook her head.

"Because I will, if that's what you want. I hate to disturb your mother—"

"That'll never work." Her mother had been in virtual seclusion since Cousin Nelson's death. The funeral had taken place days and days ago, and still her mother insisted on wearing black.

"No, I suppose not. How about something to help you sleep—"

Her mother was taking pills again, for sleep and to calm her when she was awake.

"—like a glass of warm milk?"

"No." These days, her mother never seemed to be without a glass of white wine in her hand, either. Tiffany had heard whispers among the help about that.

"Well, you can't stay up all night."

"Why not?"

"Because you need your rest. Come along, I'll take you back to your room."

Resigned to her fate, Tiffany followed her mother's social secretary, who seemed intent on nursemaiding her. After all, she didn't have much else to do these days.

Tiffany stood at the end of the bed, watching as Juliet straightened the tangled, twisted covers, and then smoothed the sheets.

"Looks like you had a running dream," Juliet said, fluffing the pillows.

"Running dream?"

"You know, where someone's chasing you and you can't get away no matter how fast you run."

"Oh. No, that wasn't it."

Juliet patted the mattress the way someone might encourage a dog to jump up on a couch. "To bed with you, young lady."

Sighing, Tiffany got into bed and lay down. "I'm not sleepy."

"You're not? Well, why don't you watch one of your movies?"

"I don't want to."

But Juliet had already crossed to the paneled wall, folding back the center doors to reveal the television, VCR, and laser disc player.

"What do you want to watch? Hmm? A Disney movie, or perhaps that one you like so much with the rabbit, what's his name? Not Bugs, the other rabbit."

"Roger." She sat up, crossing her legs Indian style. "I'm not in the mood."

Juliet laughed. "Pardon me for saying so, but you're far too young to be having moods."

"What *am* I old enough for?" Aunt Mathilde would call her question impertinent, but Tiffany was genuinely interested in an answer.

"Oh, I don't know." Juliet tilted her head, reading titles off the laser discs. "Obviously, your mother has always felt you can appreciate the wonders of international travel."

Tiffany doubted that. Naturally she had no memory of it, but she'd been told that her first trip abroad had been at the age of six months. She couldn't think of any "wonders" a little baby would appreciate.

Even at eight, international travel wasn't always wonderful. She and her mother had just returned from Cancún, where they'd gone to get away from it all. But once there, they'd spent four days in the penthouse suite and never even went to the beach.

"Look what I found!" Juliet pulled a laser disc from the shelf and held it out so Tiffany could see the jacket cover. *"Fantasia.* I remember now, someone gave this to you for Christmas—"

The someone had been Cousin Nelson.

"—and it hasn't even been opened, has it?"

262

"I was too busy," Tiffany said crossly, "traveling and appreciating."

"Well, we'll rectify that oversight."

Minutes later, alone, with the lights off, Tiffany contemplated *Fantasia*. She didn't want to be cheered up, and only smiled once, at the dancing mushrooms.

In this house, the mushrooms would *have* to dance, or the cook would slice them up and sauté them in butter, pretty as you please. Since her mother loved them on practically every single thing she ate, those cute little mushrooms would be an endangered species if they came around here.

If they *could* dance, though, maybe she'd be allowed to keep one for herself. If they could dance.

She closed her eyes for a moment, listening to the orchestra play.

If only they could . . .

Tiffany woke up. A change in the light told her that it was morning and, judging from the silence in the house, still early.

She got out of bed.

The TV screen was illuminated but blank, the speakers silent, and she realized that she'd fallen asleep during the movie. She pushed the eject button, waited as the drawer slid silently open, then removed the laser disc and put it away.

But she hesitated at turning the television off. Instead, she switched the signal from the laser disc player to the VCR, and went over to her closet. She was supposed to be tutored, these few remaining weeks until summer, but in fact the

263

household was in such turmoil that she hadn't taken her book bag off its hook in days.

Inside the book bag was the videotape she wanted to watch. She'd taken the tape from Dr. Bowman's office when she'd been left alone there while the adults had gone out into the hall to talk privately.

Or if not privately, then not within her hearing.

Tiffany withdrew the tape. It was in a padded case, and engraved in gold letters on the front and spine were the words, *Bone Marrow Transplant Program*. Below them, in red, in smaller type, it said *Donor Information*.

She went back to the VCR and put the tape in. The first time she'd tried to watch it she'd been interrupted, and it needed rewinding. As she waited, she traced her fingertips over the title.

This was the transplant program that Tiffany might have had to go through, *if* her mother had been willing to undergo the blood test to see if she could be a donor. Her mother had seen this tape at the hospital, Tiffany knew, and after that the discussion had turned to alternative methods of treating her leukemia.

Tiffany had seen the disapproval on all the doctors' faces — Dr. Langston had looked particularly grim — on hearing her mother's decision.

"With Tiffany's rare blood type," her mother had said, "I think the chances are better with a less radical form of treatment."

She pressed the play button, went over and locked her door so no one could walk in, and sat on the end of the bed to watch.

"Leukemia," the male narrator began, "is a cancer of the blood."

That much, anyone knew.

264

"The word, from the Greek, means 'white blood.' In the disease process, huge numbers of abnormal and immature white blood cells are formed."

It seemed strange now, but Tiffany remembered her teacher lecturing about leukemia during science class at her private school. Strange and funny, because most of what they taught in her classes struck her as having no connection with her life. History in particular was a puzzle to her; why did she need to know about people who'd lived and died before she was born?

But she missed school.

"Blood is produced by bone marrow within the cavities of the body's larger bones, including the pelvis, sternum, ribs, and spine."

A graphic appeared on the screen, numbers with lots of zeros behind them.

"In our blood, there are hundreds of billions of red cells, white cells, and platelets. The purpose of the white blood cells is to fight infection, but when these cells are imperfectly formed, they cannot defend the body from disease."

The screen split, showing photographs of healthy white blood cells next to sick ones.

"In leukemia," the narrator went on, "the proliferation of immature white cells means there is less room for red blood cells to carry hemoglobin, starving vital tissues of oxygen. Without adequate platelets to assure clotting, internal bleeding can occur."

Tiffany yawned. This part she'd seen before. She got up and found the VCR remote. Pointing it at the screen, she hit *Fast Forward*.

"—how bone marrow is procured for transplantation," the man was saying, when she lifted her finger and the tape slowed to normal speed.

The scene shifted to a white-tiled room, with a patient on the table, and everyone else dressed in rust-colored scrubs. Tiffany knew the pajama-like outfits were called scrubs because she'd asked.

"The donor is sedated with Sodium Pentothal and intubated. Halothane is the most commonly used anesthetic agent."

Oops, common again.

"An iodine soap solution is used to cleanse the skin over the puncture sites. Sterile surgical plastic adheres to the skin and decreases the risk of infection."

The clear plastic stuff looked like heavy-duty Saran Wrap to her. Tiffany wondered how well it would work in the microwave . . .

"Next, the donor is draped with sterile sheets."

It was hard to tell that there was a person there after that. The exposed rectangle of skin, painted orange and a bit shiny under its wrapping, kind of reminded her of E.T., the Extraterrestrial.

"Syringes are alternated during the process."

She counted eight syringes and they were huge, with wicked long needles. Tiffany gasped at the sight of one being forced into that orange skin.

"A liter of bone marrow is collected from approximately one hundred punctures along the upper ileac crest of the pelvis."

"A hundred!"

The narrator, of course, ignored her outburst. "In a glass beaker, tissue culture medium has been mixed with heparin, which will prevent the marrow and peripheral blood from clotting. The syringes are flushed with heparin between each use."

The tape showed a thick reddish fluid collecting at the bottom of the beaker.

266

"The marrow is passed through both a 200-micron and 100-micron wire mesh screen to filter out tiny particles of bone and globules of fat."

Watching a pair of gloved hands sort of twist and *screw* a syringe into the donor, Tiffany decided she'd seen enough. Unfortunately she hit the freeze frame button instead of *Stop,* and the image burned into her brain.

She ran to the set and turned it off, then pushed every control on the VCR until the tape stopped. The machine *whirr*ed and spit it out.

No wonder no one had offered to let her see the tape. No wonder.

After dressing, Tiffany snuck into Juliet's office and found a padded mailing envelope big enough for the tape. She knew any adult would recognize her handwriting as a child's, and so she searched through the desk until she found a package of blank address labels.

With two fingers, she typed Dr. Natalie Bowman's address on the label from a business card she'd rescued from the trash, where her mother had thrown it. Then she stuck the label and a couple of rows of twenty-nine cent stamps onto the padded mailer.

Hiding the mailer under the loose blouse she'd chosen deliberately for that purpose, she hurried down the back staircase, through the kitchen, out the side door, and across the lawn to the mailbox at the gate.

Tiffany didn't put up the red flag for the carrier, because they always got mail and she didn't want anyone in the house to see the flag and wonder about it. Maybe they wouldn't suspect her, but if they did, she'd have a hard time explaining what she was doing with the videotape in the first place.

Tiffany was surprised to find her mother on the patio, waiting, it seemed, for her breakfast.

A cup of coffee sat steaming on a black place mat.

Her mother also wore black, today a pleated skirt and a silk blouse. A wide-brimmed hat protected her from the sun, and a few inches of black velvet ribbon trailed down her back.

"Tiffany," she said. "You're up early."

Tiffany went to the sidebar and poured orange juice into a crystal goblet. "Not really."

"No? Well, at least you got a good night's rest. I couldn't sleep."

She glanced at her mother, who seemed pale, but said nothing. If Juliet wanted to tell about finding her in the library after her nightmare, she would.

Tiffany brought her orange juice to the table and sat down.

"The thing is," her mother said, looking off into the distance, "I know he's gone, but I keep expecting him to come through the door."

"Cousin Nelson?"

"Yes, Nelson. I can't believe that I'll never see him again. Or hear his voice."

Never could Tiffany recall her mother talking to her like this, as if she mattered. It was a most interesting development.

The maid arrived with a tray. She placed it on the table and removed the silver covers from various plates. "Is there anything else, Mrs. Gray?"

Her mother frowned, looking at her breakfast. "Yes, I believe there is. Would you be so kind as to ask the cook why she's put mushrooms on top of my strawberries?"

Before the maid could answer, though, Juliet appeared, holding a cordless telephone. Without a word of explanation, Juliet handed the phone to Tiffany's mother.

Tiffany knew that something bad had happened by the way Juliet ushered her back into the house.

Chapter Thirty-three

Los Angeles

Shea Novak used the pencil eraser to flip through the onionskin carbons of the witness depositions in the Shaw case. The tissue-thin paper tore and smudged easily, but Joseph Stojanovich preferred it, and that, pretty much, was that.

Maureen Shaw was the firm's client, and she'd been arrested and charged with the attempted murder of her former boyfriend in apparent revenge after he'd terminated their seven-year relationship.

Ms. Shaw's side of the story had some interesting elements. Yes, she had harassed her ex-lover with literally hundreds of alternately threatening and cajoling phone calls. Yes, she had broken into his apartment and trashed it once or twice. And yes, she had slashed all four of the tires on his Porsche when he had parked it overnight outside another woman's condo.

She had even, she admitted, called local mortuaries and asked them to send information on caskets, burial plots, and funeral services to his address.

But, Maureen Shaw insisted, she would never, *ever* harm a hair on his head.

She hadn't known it was him pounding on her door when she fired three .357 rounds through it. She hadn't heard him identify himself repeatedly, as each of the prosecution witnesses had. And although her door had glass panels on either side of it, in addition to being equipped with a peephole, she hadn't had the presence of mind to check and see who was outside.

As a woman living alone, Maureen Shaw stated, she was so frightened that all she could do was stand back, double-hand her new automatic, and blast the hell out of the midsection of the door and whoever was unfortunate enough to be standing behind it.

Calling 911 for police assistance had never occurred to her. Neither had calling for an ambulance afterward, when she had had a look at her handiwork.

Ms. Shaw professed amazement that the police hadn't believed her version of events. Couldn't they tell that she still loved him? Hadn't she tried repeatedly to visit him in Intensive Care?

This morning, Shea had sat in on a meeting between Eugene Kincaid and Ms. Shaw, and her gut feeling was that the case would be nearly impossible to win. Aside from the threats and vandalism, aside from the witnesses, there was the matter of Maureen Shaw herself.

The woman, an accountant in a well-known firm whose clients included the Hollywood elite, had an unfortunate hard edge to her that often manifested itself in a sneering, thin-lipped smile.

Of course they would try to soften her look, but while Shea could think of more than a few

271

male defendants who'd gotten away with an arrogant attitude, it played differently with a woman.

Selecting a jury would be tricky and—

Her train of thought was abruptly derailed by a knock on her office door. She glanced up to see the door swing open and Eugene lean in.

"It's TGIF, Shea," he said. "Want to go with us for a drink to celebrate the end of a long and truly grueling week?"

Shea put down the pencil and sat back in her chair. "Who's us?"

"Actually, me."

"I don't know, Eugene, I'm feeling a little tired." Seeing his disappointment, she added, "My first week back and all."

He came into her office and stood in front of her desk, rapping his knuckles rhythmically on the hard wood. "Are you sure? We can talk about the witch."

"Maureen Shaw?"

"None other." He pushed a stack of files to one side and sat on a corner of the desk. "I've been thinking about taking up a collection to get her lips fixed. Pump 'em full of silicone."

Shea laughed. "Come on."

"No kidding. Give her that Kim Basinger look, then load the jury with men."

"It'd never work."

"No?" He picked up her paperweight, shook it, and watched it snow. "Then we'll go the other way entirely. Have her get a razor cut and try for the butch sympathy verdict."

"Right. I can just imagine *voir dire*."

"What do you mean? A couple of subtle questions that'll go straight over the prosecutor's head, and I've got a jury that, when they look at the victim, see a scum-sucking pig who was asking for it." Eugene put the paperweight down and examined his cuticles. "It works against the victim in rape cases all the time."

"Hmm."

"Anyway, how about that drink?"

"Would you mind terribly if I asked for a rain check? It's really been a rough week for me."

Eugene's expression sobered. "You mean that Ronald Jaffe thing?"

"That's part of it."

He nodded. "They're going to scatter his ashes at sea, you know."

"I didn't know."

"On Sunday. His wife called and asked if I wanted to attend, but it's hard to get a date for that kind of a thing. Unless maybe you . . . ?"

"I couldn't, no."

The body had been smashed to pulp, beyond recognition, but Jaffe had been positively identified after they found a partial upper plate two hundred yards down the freeway from the point of impact.

She shivered, and rubbed her bare arms. "Look, I get chills when I think about it—"

"Then don't. Don't give it a second thought. What happened was a coincidence, that's all."

"Tell it to Ardath." Shea shook her head ruefully. "Evidently she thinks I'm the reincarnation of Nostradamus or something."

"No shit?"

"She keeps after me to tell her what I see in her future."

"You know," Eugene said, lowering his voice to a whisper, "she has Stojanovich's ear. You could do well to accommodate the lady."

"Except that I can't foretell the future," Shea protested.

"For her, you can. In thirty years she'll still be here, popping nitroglycerin and clocking the secretaries back from lunch."

"What a depressing thought."

"Only if we're stuck here, too." Eugene stood up. "I'll see you on Monday. And in the meantime, give some thought to that silicone idea."

The phone was ringing when Shea got home. Putting the key in the deadbolt lock, she heard her own voice on the answering machine advise the caller that she wasn't available right now, but if they'd care to leave a message after the beep . . .

"—talk to you. It's about Wilcox—"

She recognized the voice as belonging to Marcy Nolan, a member of her old study group from law school, and went to pick up the phone.

"—and you're not going to believe what—"

"Marcy? Hi, I'm here."

"Shea? Good, I'm glad I reached you. I'd feel funny leaving a message like this."

Shea sat down, a sudden sinking feeling in her stomach. Last night she'd dreamt about Professor Wilcox, a brief but violent dream that she'd woken from with her heart pounding, and drenched in sweat. "What is it?"

"You remember him, right?"

Aside from the dream, it was a silly question; Wilcox fancied himself as another Kingsfield, the gruff, exacting contracts professor in the movie *Paper Chase*. Only Wilcox had been found sadly

274

wanting in his knowledge of law. And there were nagging questions regarding his moral authority and intellectual credibility.

"Of course I remember."

"Yeah, I thought you would. Well, I heard today that he's dead."

Shea could hardly breathe. "What?"

"Dead. Do you believe it? I mean, it seems like only yesterday he was busting our chops."

"How did it . . ."

Sounding a little hysterical, Marcy laughed. "Do you remember when Payne threw all those quarters at Wilcox and told him to call his mother long distance in hell, and tell her that there was serious doubt that she'd given birth to a human?"

"Marcy, what happened to Wilcox?" she asked insistently. "How did he die?"

"Oh Jesus! He drowned."

So badly were her knees shaking, she would have collapsed if she hadn't been sitting.

The dream. A man swimming underwater in the ocean among the kelp that swayed with the tide. The water was murky and the ocean floor littered with refuse, including a large trash bag that somehow wound up tangled around the man's head and face.

A face she hadn't seen until the body washed up on the shore as human debris . . .

"—a freak accident. He must have panicked and tried to pull it off—"

"What off?"

"Only he made it worse. There was water inside the trash bag, naturally, and almost no air. Anyway, they think he drowned before he asphyxiated, but what difference does it make?

275

The man is dead."

Shea slumped back in the chair. "This isn't happening," she said under her breath.

"Is that weird or not?" Marcy demanded. "I ask you."

"Yes, it's . . . inexplicable."

"That's what I said when I first heard about it. And here Wilcox was always bragging how he swam twice a day and that's why he was in such great physical shape. Hey, wasn't it you who—"

Shea winced and closed her eyes. "Listen, I hate to cut you off, but I really have to go, there's someone at the door."

A few minutes later, Shea went into the bathroom and opened the medicine cabinet, looking for anything that might help her relax. All she had was aspirin and Alka Seltzer so old that it had probably lost its fizz.

Maybe she could call Dr. Wahl and have him prescribe something for her. Explain that a beloved teacher had tragically lost his life, and could he give her something, just enough for a day or two.

But no. She'd seen him for a few minutes this morning when she'd gone to his office for her Affinity treatment. She'd gotten the 7 A.M. appointment, primarily because he was going out of town this weekend to a medical convention in Maui.

"These guys know what they're doing, they don't hold their conventions in Lodi," he'd joked, taking her pulse.

He had a partner covering his emergencies, but she'd only seen the other doctor in passing, and she'd feel foolish trying to explain her need.

Shea closed the mirrored cabinet and looked into her own worried eyes. "Tough it out, kid."

Chapter Thirty-four

Idle Springs

"I'm going to go blind," Garrett Reid said loudly, "if somebody doesn't change the darned ribbon in the teletype machine."

"Is your arm broken?" a voice called back from the outer office.

Emily never had been easy to intimidate. "Correct me if I'm wrong, but I *am* the boss around here."

"That and a quarter'll buy you a phone call," his dispatcher retorted. "And if my work isn't satisfactory, go ahead and replace me. Go on ahead and try."

"You know I could never find anyone as obliging as you. But mark my words, there'll come a day when you'll be sorry, after I start putting dents in the furniture with my white cane."

"It's not *my* furniture."

That made him smile, and he appreciated it, since smiles weren't easy to come by these days.

Something mighty strange was happening in Idle Springs. In all his years in law enforcement, he'd never been witness to nor heard of the variety and sheer number of peculiar, scratch-your-head-in-wonder type of incidents that were befalling the town's residents.

278

Not a superstitious man by nature, he nonetheless found himself pondering about jinxes, spells, evil eyes, and whatnot that might be accountable for the series of events in recent days.

As far as he could tell, looking back on it now, the town's troubles had started innocently enough, with seemingly minor instances of personality changes. As with most small communities, Idle Springs had its share of eccentrics, each proud of his or her individuality, each staunchly resisting suggestions to tone down the more abrasive and caustic aspects of their characters.

But in the blink of an eye, practically every one of them seemed to have mellowed. No, more than that; Reid wondered if some kind of mass mutation of people's dispositions was taking place.

The Mercantile, for example, which normally carried heavy-duty, utilitarian work clothes for the men, was swamped with special orders for Bugle Boy, Dockers, and other "urban" apparel. The kind of citified finery that would normally get a fella laughed off the street, and then invited to leave town just for wearing it.

Reid couldn't recall many fashion statements being made in Idle Springs, up till the past few weeks, and he doubted he'd ever get used to seeing burly farmers prancing around in Banana Republic shirts and front-pleated chinos, accessorized with shit-kicking boots, but there was no harm to it that he could determine.

The women had likewise traded in dowdy shirtwaists or the standard T-shirts and jeans for jungle-print safari outfits, or skimpy tops and flowing skirts made out of what looked like gauze.

And Debbie Coulter, who did double duty in

279

town as a barber and beauty consultant, had a thriving concern these days. Debbie'd been working long hours creating new stylings for women whose hairdos hadn't changed since Eisenhower left office. Just today, he'd seen her rushing toward her shop with a box of those fake fingernails.

A lot else was changing besides personal appearances; vehicles were being washed and waxed every Sunday, and old crazy Lester had gone and painted his Jeep, after x number of years in basic primer.

Torn screens were being replaced, leaking roofs patched — not exactly urgent in this sixth year of drought — and the potholes in private drives were being filled. Pride of ownership had come late to Idle Springs, but when it arrived, it arrived with a vengeance.

All to the good, Reid supposed, except maybe for those sissy pleated pants.

But the stakes had altered and risen dramatically when Dalton Purvis flayed the skin off his face and neck with a straight razor. That had been the start of the injuries — and to his mind the most grisly of them — a harbinger of an ominous turn of events.

Mabel Giradot had broken her foot when the motor of her old electric Singer treadle began racing at high speed as she was sewing baby clothes for an orphanage in the Philippines. Instead of pulling the plug, she panicked and tried to brake the motor as you would a car, by pressing the pedal to the floor. Only she wasn't fast enough, and her foot got caught between the pedal and the floor.

Dennis Carney chopped his left thumb nearly

clean off while splitting and stacking a cord of wood as a favor for a neighbor with a bad back.

Luella Sandvig suffered both insult and injury. She'd been nagging her husband for years that the butane water heater setting was too low to properly heat the water from their well. Gary Sandvig finally decided to take care of the problem, but in a frenzy of chore-doing he neglected to tell Luella what he'd done.

Luella stepped into the tub, turned the hot water spigot to its limit and the cold just a nudge, which usually produced the tepid mix she was used to. Then she directed the flow to the shower head, turned so that the water was beating on her back, and waited.

In seconds, steaming hot water blasted down on her. She jumped immediately, but her fanny got a bad scalding before she could escape the tub. She was an ample woman, so that amounted to a good deal of skin.

The last Reid had heard, she was in stable condition in the Burns Unit of a California hospital, lying on her stomach and threatening to do serious bodily harm to Gary when she got out.

Then there'd been the colorful, if painful, assortment of cuts, scrapes, and bruises that had been Blue Hawley's reward for trying to rescue a kitten from a tree. Seems that Blue forgot he was allergic to cats, and when he got near it he sneezed violently, scaring the dickens out of little Fluffy and dislodging himself from the tree limb. He landed in the pyracantha bushes.

The kitten came down on its own.

Reflecting on it, Reid saw what might be the common denominator in at least some of the mishaps: most of the injuries were the result of someone trying too hard to do a good deed.

Even Dalton fit his theory, somewhat. The way he figured it, Purvis might have been trying to get a closer shave so Jenny wouldn't get a whisker burn when he kissed her before going off to work.

How did the saying go? No good deed goes unpunished? Well, that was the way he saw it. He'd almost made up his mind to court ridicule by issuing a public safety warning against good Samaritanism.

But it would have to wait until he found someone willing to change the ribbon on the teletype machine. Reid squinted at the faint print long enough to decipher that nothing new had gone down in his immediate vicinity, and tossed the advisement aside.

It was time he got back to looking through the Wanted fliers that his buddy O'Callaghan had sent along. There were an awful lot of bad guys out there, and it wasn't simple to find one face in a crowd.

"Garrett."

Reid glanced up from the fliers and looked like he swallowed his tongue. Thinking he might be hallucinating, he blinked and shook his head. "Claire? Is it you?"

Claire Elizabeth Morse stepped out of the doorway shadows. "Damn it, I can't believe it myself, but here I am."

He got up clumsily, knocking a handful of fliers to the floor. "Does Joshua know? Have you—"

"Been by the house? Not yet." Claire came further into the room and held her hand out. "Will you look at me? I'm shaking."

Reid did look at her, and felt a momentary confusion. Claire didn't much resemble the woman who'd left Joshua off all those months ago.

To start with, she was thinner, and no longer a blonde. Her wild mane of straw-colored hair had been cut to just above her shoulders, and was now a medium brown shade. He was no authority on makeup, but it didn't look to him as if she was wearing any.

What's she running from? the cop in him wondered, and then he felt ashamed. For all intents and purposes, the woman was his son's wife, and, deny it or not, Joshua regarded her as a mother.

"How've you been?" he asked.

"I'm getting by."

"That's good."

Claire nodded, as if it had just occurred to her. "And you?"

"Oh, I'm managing." Reid frowned; he was making a muddle of this. "Why don't you sit down, Claire? You want a cup of coffee?"

"If it's no bother."

"No, not at all." He started for the door—she'd stepped aside—and then hesitated. "How do you take it? Cream and one sugar?"

Her smile transformed her face. "I'm surprised you remembered. Yes, that's it."

Emily gave him a questioning raised eyebrow. "Is she who I think she is?"

Reid didn't answer, instead lifting the pot and raising it to the light, trying to judge by the color

283

of the coffee how fresh it was.

"I just made that half an hour ago," Emily said.

"Are the mugs clean?"

Emily gave an exaggerated sigh. "They truly are. Don't you think I know my job?"

"Yours *and* mine, probably." He selected two of the heavy mugs and blew in them, just to be sure dust hadn't settled since they were last rinsed.

"What are you doing? Didn't I—"

"Never mind, Emily." He put a cube of sugar in one mug, then tore open a packet of non-dairy creamer and dumped that on top.

"You didn't answer me." The dispatcher got up from the console desk, took off her headset, and came to stand beside him. "Is that her?"

"You don't give up, do you?" He poured coffee in both mugs.

"Answer me, why don't you? What if she decides to shoot you? How am I gonna be able to tell anyone who done the dastardly deed?"

"Emily . . ." He hoped the warning in his voice would suffice, although it seldom had before.

"Garrett Reid, I don't have time to keep asking you the same question. Now . . . is that Joshua's stepmother, or isn't it?"

"Where's the stirrer things?"

Emily reached up to the shelf above the coffee maker and brusquely handed him a styrofoam cup full of thin plastic straws. "I'm gonna ask politely one more time: Is that woman in your office the one who dumped Joshua on your doorstep last Thanksgiving like a charity turkey?"

"I wouldn't put it so bluntly, since she can probably hear you, but yes, she is."

"That's what I thought." Emily gave a satisfied

nod. "But I ask you, why is it so difficult for you to answer a simple question?"

"Because it isn't simple." The creamer hadn't dissolved completely and he stirred more vigorously. "It's family business, and you know I don't talk about private matters easily."

"Everyone in town knows about it," Emily said with a frown. "Why do you suppose she's come back?"

Reid tossed the stirrer in the trash and then picked up the second mug. "I don't know, but if you'll excuse me, I'm about to find out."

"How's he been?" Claire asked.

"You mean Joshua?" Before she could respond, he added: "Or Jack? I understand from him that he hasn't had a letter from you since . . . well."

"No, he hasn't." She turned her hands palm up, like a supplicant. "I meant Joshua. How is Joshua?"

Reid felt a prickle of irritation, and had to resist saying something rash. But where had she been when Joshua had been given a year to live? Where had she been when the poor boy had needed a mother to comfort him?

Of course she wasn't blood kin, but mothering wasn't one hundred percent genetics. And Claire, who'd stepped in after Bettina had died, was the only mother Joshua had ever known.

"He's doing fine," Reid answered, and couldn't resist adding, "Now."

But Claire's mind obviously wasn't focused on subtleties. "I know I said in my letter that I didn't feel anything for Joshua, but that was my pain talking. I've missed him so much."

"You hurt him." That was the least accusatory way he could think of putting it.

"I know." Her hands closed. "I wouldn't blame you if you sent me away without seeing him, after what I did, but I pray that you don't."

"Pray?" He couldn't help but be skeptical. "That's something new for you, isn't it?"

He'd expected to wound her, but evidently he hadn't. Claire lifted her chin and looked him straight in the eye. "Not really. It's how I managed to stay with Jack for all those years, when he was pulling cons and risking his son's future. It's how I put bread on the table when Jack got thrown in jail, and how I put clothes on his little boy's back. You don't know the whole story, Garrett. You don't know the half of it."

That much was true. As was so often the case with fathers and sons, Jack had rejected every value Reid held. By the time he was Joshua's age, Jack had a juvenile record a half-inch thick. He gravitated toward the people and went to the places that would land him in the most trouble in the shortest time.

It was as if the boy was determined to be his father's polar opposite. Jack had always been fond of telling a favorite joke, that one day Reid had come home and said to his son, "Hi, Jack," which the boy has taken not as a greeting, but as a command.

"We had our troubles," Reid said now. "Jack didn't want me to know what was going on in his life. How could I know . . . but I guess I should have guessed that it had to have been hard for you when he was in jail."

"He always promised me it'd be different when he got out."

Her voice was so quiet, Reid had to strain to hear. In the outer office the teletype clattered noisily, and he got up to shut the door.

"Every time, he said he'd worked through his problems, and they were behind him."

"I know." Reid had heard it too, every three or four years when Jack would call him up tearfully on the phone to, he said, fix things. But between the calls there was nothing but distant silence.

"Anyway . . . that's over. I'm not reconciling with your son. It's Joshua I care about."

Reid regarded her seriously. "So do I. It's been more than six months, Claire. The boy's hurt and angry, and most of that anger is directed at you. You were the one he counted on to be there."

The muscles of her throat worked as she visibly fought back tears. "But I came back."

He thought of Joshua, whom he'd met for lunch at Lucy's this afternoon after the boy's treatment at the clinic. Physically, Joshua was improving daily, but Reid could feel the anger still seething below the surface.

"I don't know that you *can* come back now," he said, as kindly as he could. "It may be too late."

A solitary tear dropped. "It can't be. I won't let it be."

"You might not have a choice."

"Can I see him?"

Reid nodded slowly. "All right. Come on . . . I'll take you by the house."

On the way out, Emily handed him a sheet torn off the teletype. He gave her a questioning look but her attention was focused on Claire.

"I'll be back in twenty minutes," he said.

Walking to the patrol car, he glanced at the teletype. Two female bodies had been found northeast of Tonopah, off U.S. 95, roughly midway between Las Vegas and Reno. Neither had any identification on her, and the Nye County Sheriff's Department was querying statewide in the hope that someone might have reported either girl as missing.

Reid folded the paper and put it in his shirt pocket. After he dropped Claire off, he had some calls to make.

Chapter Thirty-five

Before the front door opened, Joshua knew whose were the second set of footsteps he'd heard.

Growing up in San Francisco, he'd learned to always lock the door, so he had a few seconds to compose himself while his grandfather inserted the key. He wanted to be completely expressionless and to show not a flicker of emotion when he saw Claire.

After all, she'd come at his bidding, whether she knew it or not.

"Joshua?" the old man called as he opened the door. He had a paper grocery bag from the Mercantile in one arm. "Anyone home?"

Joshua stood up, unkinked his neck, straightened his shoulders, and waited.

"Oh, there you are. Kinda dark in here." He switched on a lamp. "What are you doing, boy? Sitting here brooding in the dark?"

In fact, that was exactly what Joshua had been doing. Sitting and staring across the road at old lady Metzger's house and wondering . . .

Claire had yet to come in from the porch.

His grandfather put the grocery bag down, then dusted off his hands as though carrying it had been a chore. "I have a little surprise for you."

Joshua felt as if Novocaine had been injected

into his facial muscles, he was so numb. "What is it?"

"We have a visitor. Someone you haven't seen for a while."

Just as he was wondering how long the buildup would go on, Claire appeared, framed in the doorway and backlit by the brighter light outdoors.

"Hello Joshua."

He sensed his grandfather's eyes on him and wondered if the old man expected him to break down, or fly into a rage. But he wouldn't give them the satisfaction of either response.

"Hi," was all he said. He was gratified to hear how nonchalant he sounded.

Claire smiled. "You look wonderful."

Joshua felt a familiar pang at her wistful tone, but blocked it out. Did she know or care that he'd been ill? Had his grandfather told her?

"You too." He surveyed the changes in her appearance, and nodded his approval. He'd never really liked her as a blond; this look was softer.

"Listen, Joshua," his grandfather said, turning his trooper hat around by the rim, "Claire's going to spend the night. She offered to fix dinner for us, and I figured after batching it for . . . uh . . . you wouldn't mind some homecooking for a change."

Joshua frowned.

"Anyway, I've got a few things I have to attend to at the department, so I'll leave you two to your own devices for a while." He glanced at Claire. "I'll be back around five-thirty."

"Thank you, Garrett, for—"

"No need for that," the old man said. "You're family. You're always welcome here."

* * *

Joshua knew that Claire expected him to help her in the kitchen while she was making dinner, but he went up to his room, closed the door, and put the chain on.

Then he opened the door a crack so he could hear the sound of pots and pans rattling, cupboard doors opening, and water running in the sink. Before long, the aroma of cooking began drifting through the house. All of which brought back so many memories . . .

He turned and went to the trunk at the end of his bed, released the brass latches, and lifted the top. His journal was in its customary place, tucked between the fabric lining and a side panel, and he reached in to pull it out.

He hadn't written his journal entry for today yet; he usually did it late at night, last thing before going to sleep. There was, however, no fooling himself that his urge to write in it now was more to distract him from the growing temptation to go downstairs than from a burning desire to document his thoughts.

His confused, fragmented thoughts.

Joshua flopped on the bed. Opening the journal, he skimmed through the entries he'd made since being discharged from the clinic, and shook his head at how naive he'd been in the beginning.

WHAT THE POWER IS & HOW I THINK IT WORKS, read one heading.

Actually, he'd figured that out within the first few days; what it was, he gathered, was some form of mind control that he had attained through his exposure to Affinity. And whatever reason Dr. Kramer might have had for so naming

291

the liquid, as far as Joshua was concerned, the name referred to the enhanced affinity or attraction of one mind for another.

Because, outrageous as it seemed, he could intentionally insert his thoughts into other people's minds. He could "suggest" things to them and by doing so, control various elements of their behavior.

The basics were pretty simple, really, even if he hadn't quite got the hang of it yet.

The first thing he had learned, while at the clinic, was that he couldn't use his abilities on anyone else who'd been treated with the stuff. But then, he supposed none of them could use influence on him, either.

He could live with that limitation, since he doubted he'd be seeing any of the others ever again.

Next, and perhaps most important, this power didn't work on everyone. His grandfather appeared to be immune — maybe their brain waves were too dissimilar or, God forbid, identical — and when he'd tried to plant a suggestion in the old man's mind, he'd ended up with an incredible headache for his efforts.

Dr. Kramer was another no-go, a mental brick wall.

Still, so far he'd found that he had access to most people. On the negative side, though, even with open channels — meaning receptive minds — it was exhausting to control more than one person at a time. And even one could be troublesome for extended periods.

Although he *had* done six at a time, if not with the best results. He hoped it proved to be a case of practice makes perfect, and that eventually, given time, he could work out the bugs.

Joshua hadn't meant for anyone to get hurt.

And recently he'd discovered another couple of details. One, the power was strongest in the early hours after a treatment, and two, his precision improved when his suggestions were directed and specific. He shouldn't just think, somebody do something. He had to focus on a specific person doing some particular thing.

As in Claire showing up in Idle Springs, although it had taken an awful long time to accomplish.

Curiosity finally drew him downstairs and into the kitchen, which smelled delectably of onions and garlic. He saw at a glance that her technique hadn't improved; there was tomato sauce splattered on the stove, countertops, and even the floor.

For some reason he didn't fully understand, he felt his resolve weakening, his anger slipping away.

"Spaghetti?" he asked, when she turned and caught him watching her.

"Yeah. It's one of the few things I can make from scratch."

"Does that matter? I mean, that you don't get it from a jar or something?"

Claire tilted her head. "It matters to me. When you put a little love into it, it tastes better."

He thought of Old Lady Metzger's apple butter, and frowned.

"Garrett tells me you've been ill." She stood holding a wooden spoon, oblivious to the fact that sauce was dripping from it.

"No big deal." He shrugged it off, but felt better now that she'd asked. "You're dripping."

"What? Oh, the spoon." She stuck it in the pot, and didn't notice that it fell all the way in. Grabbing a couple of paper towels, she bent down to wipe up the mess on the floor.

Joshua shook his head. She had stepped in the sauce, and every time she moved her foot, she smeared tomato all over the place.

"Claire, you're making it worse." He took the paper towels from her and threw them away, gently directed her over to a chair, sat her down, and took off the offending shoe. "Let me do it."

She brushed her fingertips across his cheek. "You're a good kid."

"Not so good." He dampened a towel and cleaned the sole of her shoe. "It's just that if Grandpa comes in and sees this red stuff all over the kitchen, he's gonna think one of us murdered the other."

Claire laughed. "You're probably right."

"I don't know about you, but I wouldn't want him after me if I'd done anything . . ." Joshua let the words trail off. He *had* done wrong, intentionally or not.

As promised, his grandfather returned at five-thirty and they sat down to dinner together, eating in nearly total silence.

Joshua could tell that Claire wanted to talk, but the old man clearly had his mind on other things. The creases in his forehead bore witness to the fact that he was troubled by whatever those other things were.

Joshua had grown accustomed to his grandfather's work distractions by now, but while he

294

had learned to respect the ensuing silences, he could understand how it might not be entirely comfortable for Claire. He did his best, under the circumstances, to make her feel at home, by smiling whenever their eyes met.

Grandpa Reid stood up abruptly, nearly upsetting the glass of buttermilk he had with his evening meal. "Excuse me for a minute," he said, and left the room.

"Is it the food?" Claire asked, keeping her voice low. "Too spicy?"

"No." Joshua twirled his fork in the spaghetti. "He probably just thought of something he meant to do. That's the way he is."

She leaned forward. "It's hard to believe he and Jack are father and son. I don't believe I've ever met two so thoroughly different people."

"Except for Dad and me."

"Well, maybe." Claire blinked, then gave him an odd look. "But you know, now that I see you together, you and your granddaddy are a lot alike."

"I'll take that as a compliment," his grandpa said, coming back to sit at the table. "You did a good job with the boy."

It came as no great shock when his grandfather left again after dinner.

Joshua went into the front room to watch CNN while Claire cleaned up—she'd refused his offer of help—but found his eyes wandering from the screen to the window, through which he could see the Metzger house.

The house was dark and looked abandoned. Normally well-tended, the colorful daffodils and pansies that bordered the walkway to the porch seemed to have dried up in the late spring heat.

He should have said something to his grandfather. An offhand kind of comment to the effect that he hadn't seen their neighbor lately, and didn't Grandpa think that was strange.

Every day that went by made it that much worse. It had gotten to the point that when he stepped outside, the first thing he did was sniff the air. Sooner or later, someone was bound to smell her . . .

And it had been an accident, really. At Christmas, she'd brought his grandfather a basket filled with jars of her homemade apple butter and fruit preserves. Joshua had never tasted anything as good as her apple butter, but he could hardly ask her for more, since she'd taken such a dislike to him.

So, he thought blithely, he would put the idea in her head.

And the strangest thing happened: he'd sort of flitted into her mind and was doing what he thought of as a little light housekeeping—suggesting that she be nicer to folks, maybe learn to appreciate rock and roll, that kind of thing—when all at once, his access was blocked by a dense, nearly palpable blackness.

He wasn't blessed with the ability to read anyone's mind, but somehow he knew instinctively what that absolute darkness meant. Old Lady Metzger wasn't receiving, because she was dead.

And he had killed her.

He didn't know how, but he had.

Chapter Thirty-six

Alternative Therapy Clinic

Dr. Alan Kramer flexed his gloved hand, then nodded across the stretcher to Honor.

"Don't let her move," he said, although he knew that the warning was unnecessary.

The patient, Astrid Smythe, lay on her side, legs drawn up nearly to her chest, her shoulders forward and her head bent down, as though trying to touch her nose to her knees. In this position her spine was in hyperflexion, as was necessary to perform the lumbar puncture.

The procedure tray was to his right, near the head of the stretcher. There were three syringes laid out, and he grabbed the smallest one, which held a local anesthetic, in this instance, Xylocaine.

"You'll feel a sting, Astrid."

Ms. Smythe, however, was pretty much out of it. This morning she had spiked a fever of 103.8. Her other symptoms included a slight sore throat of two days' duration, followed by the rapid onset of a dull, frontal headache, confusion, increased irritability, and drowsiness. She had vomited several times, and appeared dehydrated.

The probable diagnosis was acute bacterial meningitis, but there was a possibility of subacute aseptic meningitis or neoplastic meningitis, a not infrequent complication with metastatic carcinomas, in which the malignant cells were disseminated into the brain.

He touched her skin, already prepped with an antiseptic scrub. Using his finger as a guide, he pierced the skin with the needle and injected the anesthetic. He repeated this several times, until he was reasonably sure the surface area was numbed.

He tossed aside the small syringe and picked up the heavier-gauge needle, which he plunged deeper into the tissue surrounding the spine. Careful not to hit bone, he finished anesthetizing the area by deep injection.

Finally, he grabbed the 3-inch, 20-gauge lumbar puncture needle from the tray.

"How are you doing?" he asked.

Honor, who was bent over, holding Astrid Smythe around her shoulders and knees to keep her from moving, answered for the patient: "She's fine."

"Okay. You're going to feel pressure on your lower back and spine. You'll probably hear a crunching sound, but don't be alarmed."

Kramer palpated the spine, feeling for the depression between the third and fourth lumbar vertebrae. He positioned the needle at the midline, perpendicular to the surface of the back. Directing it at a slight upward angle, he eased the needle in.

His hand, thank God, remained rock steady.

A light touch was necessary to keep from damaging the ligaments or tearing the dura. He felt resistance on penetrating the dura, but it lessened immediately afterward as the needle entered the spinal canal.

The muscles in Ms. Smythe's lower back

spasmed briefly, but she didn't move.

Kramer withdrew the stylet from the needle. Drops of cerebrospinal fluid welled from the needle shaft. He reached for the manometer to take the CSF pressure—it was within normal limits—and then extracted samples of the spinal fluid for testing.

On gross examination the fluid appeared hazy and faintly yellow, rather than clear and colorless. There was no blood visible, nor was the spinal fluid a darker yellow, which would indicate that blood had been present for longer than four hours.

There were no clots, indicative of fibrinogen, nor did he see any of the spidery, delicate webs that were common in tuberculous meningitis.

After obtaining his samples he measured the CSF pressure again, and found it, as expected, lowered somewhat. Then he removed the needle and covered the puncture site with a thick wad of sterile gauze, which he taped securely into place.

"Finis," he said. He stripped off his gloves and discarded them, picked up the glass vials filled with spinal fluid, and headed for the door. "Make sure she stays flat on her back for awhile."

"Yes, doctor," Honor said.

He did not at all like what he found in the laboratory. As suspected, the young woman's protein count was elevated, the cell count was relatively high, just below six hundred per cubic millimeter, and the cell type was predominantly polymorphonuclear. The patient's glucose level was low, but not a matter for concern.

He performed a differential count after centrifuging a specimen, separating out the sediment, drying it, and treating it with Wright's stain. He also prepared slides for a Gram stain and methylene blue.

Finally, he prepared cultures on blood agar and chocolate plates, which he put in the anaerobic incubator for the night.

He knew, however, what the culture would probably show: acute meningitis, with the most probable causative bacteria being either Neisseria meningitidis or Hemophilus Influenzae.

Regardless of which it turned out to be, he was neither prepared, equipped, nor inclined to treat Astrid Smythe here at the clinic. He would start her on a provisional course of antibiotic therapy—in this case, intravenous penicillin—but beyond that, he needed to arrange for her transfer to a hospital in Reno.

After instructing Honor about the transfer, he went into his office and sat down to dictate his notes on the lumbar puncture, both the procedure and the laboratory findings. He would make a copy of the tape to send with the patient and CSF cultures to Reno, to be followed by a formal report by early next week.

He was troubled by Ms. Smythe's illness. Today was Friday, which meant she'd had five treatments with Affinity. It bothered him very much that she had developed meningitis while undergoing therapy.

It was the first hint that Affinity might not perform totally as expected.

They were at the end of the third week, and to date had treated fifteen patients. All fifteen had shown marked improvement in whatever diseases had brought them here, and a majority had been pronounced by their usually cautious doctors to be cured.

Astrid Smythe had been improving, too, until this morning. But if a difficulty had to arise, this was the best time for it to happen, since he'd already scheduled a week-long hiatus in treatments.

He would use those eight days—from this Sunday through next—to investigate the implications of this setback. Perhaps the bacteria responsible for her meningitis were naturally resistant to Affinity. Or possibly, Affinity did not "recognize" the bacteria as being enough of a threat to the host body to destroy them.

And there was that other matter—

The intercom buzzed, and he reached over to press the lever. "Yes?"

"Alan," Honor said, "I'm sorry to disturb you, but do you have a minute? It seems we have a problem."

"Another one?" He sighed. When it rains, he thought. "Come to the office."

Honor wore a pensive look. He'd known her long enough to tell that whatever else had gone wrong wasn't sitting well with her, on more than one level.

"Bree quit without notice," she said, and handed him an envelope.

"This just happened?" Bree worked three nights a week, Mondays through Wednesdays, and to the best of his knowledge, on her days off she stayed at her apartment in Reno. "When did she come by?"

"I gather from Judy that she was here while we were doing the spinal tap. Apparently, she came by to pack up her belongings, and left the enve-

301

lope."

Kramer opened the envelope, pulled out the note, and unfolded it. It was handwritten, and remarkably succinct: *I hereby resign my position as staff nurse at Alternative Therapy Clinic, effective this date.*

Bree had signed it, and it was dated today.

"She left her key, so I looked in her room," Honor went on. "She cleaned the place out. There's not as much as a safety pin left in a drawer."

"Do you know of any reason why she'd do this? It's rather a drastic step to take." Even in a nursing shortage, Ms. Patrick might find it difficult to secure another position without a reference from her most recent employer. Of course, with only three weeks of service, she could simply delete the clinic from her resume. "She wasn't happy with her job?"

"I guess not."

"Did she ever say so?"

"Not to me." Honor hesitated. "But I doubt that she would talk to me about it anyway; we weren't on the best of terms."

"This is the first I've heard of it."

"We had a minor personality conflict. Nothing serious, and I don't believe that it contributed to her decision to leave."

"I see. Well, obviously we'll have to replace her as soon as possible. At least we have some time to do it in. If worse comes to worst, we can change Hosfeldt's schedule so that he works the first part of the week. That would give us a few extra days . . ."

"If you want, I can call Patti Cummings."

It took him a minute to place the name. "Patti.

302

She's a good nurse, but I'd have thought you couldn't convince her to leave Boston in a million years."

"Oh, she might be receptive," Honor said, somewhat cryptically, "to the right offer."

"Uh huh. All right, I'm going to leave it up to you to decide what that offer will be. Get her here if you can, but I need a decision no later than Tuesday."

Honor's smile lit up the office. "Count on it."

"If there's nothing else, then, I'd better dictate my report."

Honor nodded smartly, and walked to the door. There she stopped and looked over her shoulder at him. "It'll be like old times with Patti here."

"Old times," he said musingly after the door closed. He didn't usually allow himself to feel nostalgic about Boston. He'd left the city, and Physician's and Surgeon's Hospital, under a dark cloud.

How long had it been, now? Nearly two years. Twenty-two months to be exact, almost to the day. At an average of approximately thirty point four days to a month, it worked out to slightly less than six hundred and sixty-nine days.

It seemed to have been both a longer *and* a shorter period of time.

Longer when he thought of the six hundred and sixty-nine days that had passed since he'd scrubbed for surgery. From that perspective, it felt like an eternity. Surgery had been his life, the center of his existence.

Could anyone but another surgeon understand the thrill that he got from holding a scalpel in his hand and taking control of a human life that

303

was, in essence, a universe of its own?

He had nearly total recall of the surgical procedures he'd performed, from simple appendectomies to resections of aortic aneurysms. Adrenaline flooded his veins at the very thought of the last such repair he'd performed, in which not one, but two pulsing, distended, membranous aneurysms had challenged his will.

Being forced to give that up had almost killed him.

That morning in O.R., when his fingers began to shake and he nicked an artery, he'd waited only a few seconds before standing aside and allowing the assistant surgeon to take over. A few ticks of the clock, but that had been too long. The patient had died on the table.

There was a maxim in surgery: sometimes the surgery was a success but the patient had a "fatal outcome." It happened to every surgeon, and had happened to him before. But because he'd been candid enough to admit to the Morbidity Committee that he'd had tremors in his fingers before, he was ostracized for going ahead with the operation "with knowledge that his impairment might result in injury or death to the patient."

That had been the end of that. He'd left Boston the same day. Within a week, he left the country and began his travels, searching for alternative forms of medicine in places that most of his former colleagues would not imagine even existed.

And a year later he'd discovered—or more properly, created—Affinity.

He would have to find out what had gone wrong, though, with Astrid Smythe. He would have to . . . have to . . .

Kramer glanced up at the desk lamp, thinking it had gone dark, but it hadn't. Rather, it was as if a dark film was falling like a curtain across his eyes.

Concerned, he waved his fingers in front of his face, and could barely make them out. Simultaneously, he felt a kind of heaviness in his facial muscles.

Was he suffering a mild TIA, a transient ischemic attack?

He stood up, and felt slightly unsteady on his feet. Better to call for assistance, he thought, than to risk injury trying to go for help. He pressed the send panel on the intercom.

"Yes?"

Judy had answered, not Honor. He opened his mouth, intending to request that she send Honor in, but all at once his brain refused to communicate.

"Dr. Kramer? Did you want something?"

Would you please . . .

The phrase repeated itself time and time again in his head, but his tongue remained inert.

Never mind . . .

He grabbed the nearest piece of paper, which turned out to be Bree Patrick's resignation, and laboriously printed the letters, *TIA,* and the word, *aphasia* on it.

Then Alan Kramer went looking for his nurse.

Chapter Thirty-seven

"Shouldn't you be sending him in the ambulance to Reno along with Astrid?" Judy Bettencourt asked in an exaggerated whisper.

Honor looked up from the treatment log in time to watch the Emergency Medical Technician and the ambulance driver—both wearing masks and gloves in deference to her meningitis diagnosis—as they hurried Ms. Smythe's stretcher past the nursing station. "He won't go."

"Is he crazy?"

The thought had occurred to her, but loyalty kept her from admitting it. "I don't think so."

Judy's eyes widened. "They always used to say back in Tennessee that doctors make the worst patients, and I swear it must be true."

"Doctors need to be in charge, and you know patients are seldom in control. Anyway, Dr. Kramer wants me to drive him home so he can rest."

"Rest? But he's had a stroke!"

"No," Honor said, "he has not."

"Honor, he all but diagnosed himself. TIA, that's what he wrote down."

"There's a big difference between a transient attack and a full-blown stroke." TIAs were of shorter duration, usually lasting only minutes and certainly no longer than a couple of hours. More significantly, they produced no residual neurological aftereffects, and weren't considered life-threat-ening.

It was the sudden, dramatic onset of an ischemic attack that was so frightening, especially to the patient, who was fully conscious throughout the episode. In this case, as a doctor, Alan had known what was happening to him, and hadn't panicked.

"I'd still ship him off," Judy muttered.

"I'll be honest with you; if the decision were mine to make, you bet I'd send him to Reno for a workup, but it isn't up to me. And he won't go."

"Some people can be so stubborn."

Honor inclined her head in agreement. "I can't force him to accept medical care, and I'm not going to try." She closed the treatment binder and returned it to its place on the counter.

"You know," Judy said, *sotto voce,* "if he'd just zone out, we could bundle him off . . ."

"Too late for that. The ambulance is gone."

"Darn."

"Listen, do you think you can handle everything while I'm gone?"

Judy shrugged. "I don't know why not. Everyone's finished with their treatments for the day. Besides, there's only the four of them now."

"All right. Call me at the house if you need to. I'm not sure how long I'll be; I want to get him settled in and make sure he's comfortable."

"Yeah, well, if I were you I'd aim that Jaguar at Reno, and haul him off."

Honor smiled faintly. "I'd better get going. See you in a while."

* * *

307

She had never been to Dr. Kramer's house before, but she had a general idea where it was — south and west of the clinic via a private road — and that, along with the crude map that Alan had painstakingly drawn, was enough to get them there. As with many homes in the area, it sat off by itself on a slight rise.

Surrounded by trees, the building was hidden from view until they were practically upon it. Concentrating on making the sharp turn into the drive, she caught only a glimpse of glass, wood, and brick.

She pulled up to the front of the house and turned off the Jaguar's powerful engine.

Alan had already opened the passenger door, so she got out and hurried around to assist him. His gait wasn't as awkward as it had been twenty minutes earlier, and she took heart from that improvement.

"The key?" she asked.

He shook his head and opened his mouth, but couldn't get the words out. Frustration was evident in his eyes, although he accepted without protest her steadying hand on his arm. They made their way slowly up the walk.

At the front door, Honor saw the digital lock, with a ten-number keyboard. She almost blundered by asking him for the code, but managed to hold her peace, standing aside and watching as he haltingly entered a five-digit code. There followed a substantial-sounding click, and she reached to open the door.

Honor stood a bit behind him, so that she could support him if the step into the house upset his balance. He made it with only slight difficulty, and she followed him in.

Because of all the windows, there was more than sufficient light, which was good, because she didn't see any switches on the walls.

"Where's your bedroom?"

Alan shook his head, pointing into the sunken living room. A white semicircular couch sat as counterpoint to a half-octagonal wall of glass that overlooked, through the canopy of trees, the dramatic desert landscape between the house and the hills to the west.

"No, you have to rest."

Again, that maddening shake of his head. He started toward the living room.

Honor caught up with him and took his arm, bringing him to a halt. "I'm not going to let you have your way, and you might as well get that straight. You are going into your bedroom, I'm going to help you undress, and you *will* get some rest, or else."

She noticed the corner of his mouth quirk before he turned his head.

Hiding a smile, she thought.

But he offered no further resistance, cooperating as much as he was able, given his temporary limitations. Within ten minutes she had gotten him into pajama bottoms, and was helping him into his king-size bed.

"The phone is right here," she said, picking up the receiver and punching in the clinic's number, then quickly depressing the switch-hook. "If you need me, call. You've got a last-number-called feature, and all you have to do is hit redial. I know you can't talk right now, but I'll know it's you."

Alan nodded, and reached for her hand as she replaced the receiver in the cradle.

"Thank you," he said, or tried to.

"Get some sleep, Alan. You'll feel better after you've had a rest."

Not completely trusting that he would stay put in bed, she waited in the hall outside his room for a few minutes. When he didn't appear, she stepped quietly to the door, which she'd left ajar, and peeked in.

He was lying on his side, facing away from her, so she couldn't tell if he was awake or not, but his respirations were slow and even.

The man was certainly intelligent enough to fake sleep, wait for her to leave, and get up. Which, in her opinion, would be the wrong thing for him to do. She had a great deal of faith in sleep as a healer, and in her years of nursing, had seen probably hundreds of patients bounce back from a TIA as if nothing had happened, without a trace of neurological deficit.

Only *they* had obeyed doctor's orders.

Other than going back into the bedroom for a closer look, which she was loathe to do, how was she to determine if Alan would follow hers?

"Wait a little longer," she whispered to herself, and backed away from the door.

After calling Judy from a phone in the living room to advise her she'd be at the house for at least thirty more minutes, Honor went to stand by the window and watched the sun sink lazily toward the mountains.

Then, feeling restless, she began to wander through the house. It was probably four or five

310

thousand square feet, and sprawling. All one level, it offered gorgeous views from every room.

The furnishings were modern, spartan, and definitely masculine. She found a study with three walls of bookcases, with leaded glass doors. The desk was oak, and roughly the size of her first apartment in Boston, back in the days when she'd been a starving student nurse. She ran her fingers across the surface, and marveled that wood could feel like silk.

She noticed a manila folder marked *Patient Clippings,* and picked it up. Then she put it back down.

She hadn't come to snoop.

But a triangle of what could only be a newspaper clipping was visible, sticking out from the bottom of the folder. It was too tempting. Turning her head to a better angle from which to read, she made out most of a sentence.

The medical examiner has . . . not released a cause of death.

Honor frowned. Whose death? she wondered. As far as she knew, the clinic patients who'd gone back to their lives were all in excellent health.

Could it be that Alan had kept the newspaper stories about the death of his final surgical patient in Boston? And was torturing himself by re-reading the clippings over and over again?

That would be terrible if it were true.

Honor rested her fingertips on the folder, still hesitant. Was it any of her business what Alan Kramer did? Did her feelings for him entitle her to intrude on the private part of his life?

No, they didn't.

Except she had to know. She opened the folder and selected an article from the top of the small

311

pile. As she did, she noticed several pages of notes in Alan's distinctive handwriting at the back of the folder.

Honor glanced at the article, which was annotated to indicate it had come from a Seattle newspaper, then back at his notes. With a practiced eye, she deciphered a line or two of his physician's scribble:

". . . is possible that there may yet prove to be a correlation between the subjects receiving therapy and otherwise seemingly random acts of violence within their spheres of influence . . ."

"What?" she said softly.

The article she held was a single column, perhaps four inches long. Last Monday's date was stamped on the top, and at the bottom there was another stamp, giving the name of a national clipping service.

The article detailed an accident that had occurred near Seattle on the previous Friday. A car had skidded out of control on wet pavement and slammed head-on into a concrete wall. The sole occupant, a man whose identity was being withheld pending notification of next of kin, had died of massive chest and abdominal injuries before he could be removed from the wreckage.

She'd read similar articles more times than she cared to remember—any waste of human life profoundly affected her—but her attention was drawn to the bottom of the column and a familiar name, underlined in red.

Naoka Tanaka.

Honor skimmed the final paragraph, which described a coalition of community organizations seeking to have a lower speed limit posted on the stretch of road where the accident had happened, and possibly force a safety study by the city. In the last sentence, a passing reference was made to the reporter's unsuccessful attempts to reach Naoka Tanaka—whose husband Kenichi and sons David and Mark had been the first to perish at the site—for a comment.

Anxiety tightened the muscles in her neck, and she massaged them absentmindedly.

She selected another article from the same clipping service, but this one was from the *Los Angeles Times*. It described the death of one Ronald Jaffe, a suspect in the murders of several women. The details of the accident that had claimed his life were given in rather gratuitously graphic terms.

At first she couldn't see what the connection was between the incident and any of the patients. Then she came upon the underlined names of Stojanovich, Kincaid and Wheeler, mentioned as the legal representatives of Ronald Jaffe. And, unless she was mistaken, that was the law firm that employed Shea Novak.

Honor shuffled through the other clippings, picking out the red-lined names. Tiffany Stratton's mother, Pamela Gray, was mentioned twice, in separate articles about the deaths of Nelson Tucker and Stuart Healy, identified respectively as Pamela's cousin and the second of her four husbands.

The sketchy account of Nelson Tucker's death was headlined, tabloid-style, *Heir To Tucker Fortune On The Rocks Again*.

Healy's death had occurred in Monaco, when he ran his Ferrari off the same winding road where Princess Grace had been killed. Healy had been a world-class race car driver in his leisure

313

time, and the article made mention of speculation in the racing world that there'd been foul play involved.

Honor began to put it together in her mind, and didn't care for the conclusion she reached: people close to, or even vaguely associated with, former clinic patients were dying at a frightening rate. It was the first week's patients, to be more specific, although she hadn't come across Morgan Lassiter's name.

Nor Joshua's. She had, however, heard rumors of strange goings-on in Idle Springs.

She put the articles aside and reluctantly picked up Alan's notes. What she read there soon sent her to the bookshelves to search for several thin black notebooks, in which he had meticulously recorded the details of his Affinity research.

The key was right where his records had indicated it would be, on a hook at the back of a utility cupboard in the kitchen pantry, where anyone coming upon it would dismiss it as unimportant. She took the key and, clasping it in the palm of her sweating hand, left the house through the back door.

The greenhouse sat perhaps fifty yards from the house. The glass walls and roof were tinted, reflecting waves of heat under the waning sun.

Dry grass crunched underfoot as she crossed to the door. Walking toward the building, she noticed that the door and door frame were reinforced with metal supports. A padlock hung from a heavy-duty hasp.

Taking a deep breath, Honor fit the key into the lock and turned it. Then, with a last glance

314

back at the house, she removed the padlock and pushed open the door.

The air was warm and moist inside. Looking up, she saw thin copper tubing along the framing, and aerating nozzles no bigger than the tip of her finger that she suspected supplied the intermittent mist the plants required.

The plants themselves were like nothing she'd ever seen before.

An other-worldly reddish-gold in color, they had large, heart-shaped leaves that grew off tall, slender stalks. The texture of the leaves was smooth and almost waxy to the touch. The leaves bore a slight resemblance to water lilies, but seemed more delicate, somehow.

The plants were not in bloom now, but from Alan's description of them, she knew that each plant produced a single star-shaped flower, which was a creamy, translucent white. The flower emerged from a pink, thinly veined, ovate pod.

Curiously, it was the plants themselves and not the flowers that gave off a scent. She could think of no other description for the smell but astringent, as illogical as that seemed.

Honor had never seen anything like these plants. Which she might have expected, since very few humans had ever come across them in the Brazilian rain forest, or what was left of it.

Alan had found the plants by chance, even as the forest was burning toward him and his native guide. He had collected ten specimens before the whirling winds of fire sent him back to the river, and safety. The rest of the plants had presumably been destroyed.

In his records, he had not specified how he'd gotten the plants into the country, but Honor knew that the borders were more porous than the federal government cared to admit, and she suspected the plants had been flown in.

Once he got them here, he had successfully cultivated the plants. He began experimenting with the substance that he extracted from pulverizing the leaves . . . a substance he named Affinity.

Honor put her fingers under a leaf and lifted it gently, wondering how anything so fragile and beautiful could do so much harm.

She had to warn them.

Chapter Thirty-eight

Naoka lifted the kettle from the burner as the water neared boiling, and turned off the gas. She poured the water into the *Tokoname* teapot that had been passed down to her from her grandmother, watching the sencha tea leaves swirl in the current for a moment before putting the lid on the pot and allowing it to steep.

From the family room came the plaintive sound of Hibari-san's song, "Kanashii-sake," in English, "Sad Sake." Hibari Misora had been the most famous Japanese singer of Naoka's childhood. Her family home in Sapporo had been filled with the singer's exquisite voice, and when Hibari-san died in 1989, she had mourned the loss of that voice, as had all of Japan.

She had come across her old but beloved collection of records while going through the closet in the bedroom she and Kenichi had shared. Theirs was the last closet in the house to be emptied, and it had held treasure.

Besides the records, she found, in a box on the very top shelf, the formal bridal kimono she had worn at their wedding. Pristine white with a red *obi* and accents on the full-cut sleeves, the kimono had been made for her by her mother.

317

Naoka had believed it was lost, mislaid or left behind during one of the frequent, disorganized moves of their early marriage. But evidently Kenichi had merely put the kimono in a different box, then had forgotten to tell her what he'd done.

It had been a very long time since she'd worn even a *yukata,* the light summer kimono. However, once taught how to properly drape the lengths of material and secure the straps, belts, and ceremonial sashes of a kimono, a young woman never forgot.

The wedding attire, of heavier fabric, usually required the assistance of at least one attendant, but tonight she had managed on her own. And looking in her mirror, she had seen the girl she once had been . . .

Kenichi's bride.

Now his widow.

The tea couldn't be allowed to steep too long or it would turn bitter. Naoka put five matching cups on the tray, picked it up, and walked carefully into the living room. There she bent down gracefully and centered the tray on the low teak table that sat, American-style, in front of the couch.

The solid wood table was too heavy for her to move, but when the men from the Salvation Army came tomorrow for the last of the un-needed furnishings, she would ask them to place the table against one of the now-bare walls, in one of the soon-to-be-empty rooms.

They could hardly refuse her request. A small charity in return for her own.

Naoka poured steaming tea into all five cups. She took her own cup from the tray and cradled it in her hand as she straightened up. Not a drop spilled.

She went next to the window and slid shut the *shoji*, the paper window coverings that she'd had installed to replace the curtains and mini-blinds. Moonlight shone softly through the thin screens.

More and more, every day, the house was being transformed into the traditional Japanese style home. Soon, it would all be in harmony.

Her guests, the dead, approved.

Naoka lowered the flame to the wick, and watched it dance for a moment. When she was certain the candle was lit, she shook the match out and placed it in a small ceramic bowl made for that purpose.

She had lit the incense earlier, and thin wisps of smoke curled up toward the ceiling. Out of respect for her mother's preference, she burned jasmine. She reached out her fingers to stir the scented smoke.

Silent faces watched her then, as she bowed her head and wept.

Outside, the trees sighed, brushing leaves against the windows. The wind had been blowing all day, and by now had found the way in, whistling among the eaves and through tiny cracks.

A night bird proclaimed its territory, warning off all potential interlopers.

"You can join us," the dead whispered.

"There is no more pain here," they lied.

Naoka understood that they wished her to share their misery, and only pretended to offer comfort for her loss. She knew this because Kenichi and her sons were not with them, and they would be

319

if what was being promised was the truth.

There were four of the dead, all related to her, and since they'd first appeared to her she had remembered their stories.

Mariko was a cousin who'd died when Naoka was in college. Mariko had been living in Newport Beach with her husband and infant daughter when she found out from a neighbor that her husband had been seen out many times with another woman.

She had gone to her husband and asked him not to shame her, but he'd laughed in her face, telling her that he would do what he pleased. And it pleased him very much to have a young and beautiful mistress.

The next morning, before the sky was light, Mariko had gone to the beach and walked into the surf, deliberately drowning herself and her child to save them from humiliation. Mariko was still holding her daughter in her arms when their bodies washed up on the shore.

The husband married his mistress, and went on as if nothing had happened. The mistress later bore a stillborn son, and after that had a baby girl whose breath was stolen from her while she slept.

Crib death, the doctors said.

Punishment, the family thought, for the wrongs done to Mariko.

Nagayo was an uncle on her father's side who had died before Naoka was even born. He had come to the United States in 1939, and he escaped internment by enlisting in the army. He never fought against Japanese troops, but he still carried the fear in him that something he had done might have led to the death of a friend.

Naoka knew his story well, having heard it told in hushed tones many, many times: after the bombing of Hiroshima and Nagasaki, he had gone quietly insane. Within a month, as the country celebrated victory around him, he had knelt in the street, doused himself in gasoline, and set himself on fire.

His self-immolation left a scorch mark on the pavement that a member of his family had photographed and sent to Japan. It was eerily reminiscent of the nuclear shadows left by the victims of Hiroshima.

Kumiko was also a cousin, the daughter of her mother's youngest sister, and thus much younger than Naoka. She lived with her parents in Tokyo, an only child who had a kind and gentle nature.

From the age of seven, Kumiko had desired nothing more than to be a musician and play the haunting melodies of *shamisen,* a three-stringed instrument, in a traditional doll theatre or tea house.

If she'd had a brother or sister, maybe her life would have turned out as she wished. But her father had not been content with such modest ambitions from his only offspring, and he demanded daily that she study hard and do well in school.

With her interests elsewhere, Kumiko had failed to meet his expectations. When she took the exams for middle school, she did so poorly that her father refused to speak to her afterward.

Her mother was torn between them, and out of fear of saying the wrong thing to either of them, said nothing at all.

Kumiko had jumped off a bridge. She was not alone, that same week, eight other students of various ages also took their own lives. *Shiken-ji-goku,* or examination hell, had claimed them all.

Finally, there was her cousin Nozomi. Nozomi had the double misfortune of being exceptionally pretty and mentally dull at the same time. A foolish girl, she had brought disgrace to herself and the family by having a child at seventeen, without the benefit of marriage. She gave the infant to her own mother to raise, then left home and promptly worsened her status by accepting a position as a bar girl. She took many foreigners as her lovers.

One of them, a German, introduced her to drugs. It wasn't long before Nozomi was concerned only with the next line of cocaine. She did so much cocaine that it ate away the mucous membranes in her nose.

Unlike the others, Nozomi hadn't deliberately killed herself, but her wanton recklessness had directly contributed to her death by overdose.

It had puzzled Naoka at first why her father, who had also brought about his own death, wasn't with Nagayo, Kumiko, and the others. But after much thought, she concluded that his love for her prevented him from enticing her to share his aimless fate.

No, the dead were not in her house because they wanted to help her. Their insistent presence only reminded her of what she'd lost. And of her weakness in allowing them to speak to her.

But she did not send them away. She didn't have the strength.

The phone was ringing again.

Kenichi had insisted on having a machine to

answer calls, and it was his voice that Naoka heard faintly from the other room, advising the caller to leave a message after the chime.

Naoka wondered who would be calling at this hour. It was nearly midnight.

Another reporter? The press had been hounding her with requests for interviews. They and Father Quincy wanted her to come forward and let everyone witness the bloody edges of her loss, let them pick at the raw wound.

The voice belonged to a woman this time, and it seemed vaguely familiar. As she turned her head to better hear what was being said, she saw a quick movement near the kitchen door.

A man, dressed in dark colors and wearing a ski mask, stepped forward.

"Mrs. Tanaka," he said, "I see you're dressed for company."

In the other room, the caller hung up.

Naoka was not afraid.

She did as the intruder requested, going with him from room to room as he checked to see that there was no one hidden in the house.

"Moving soon?" he asked, his voice echoing off the walls of David's empty room.

"No." She watched him open her son's closet and shine a flashlight in the corners.

"No? Huh. I guess you're not a pack rat, like the rest of us."

Naoka didn't understand his meaning, so she said nothing in reply. He motioned for her to go out the door before him, which she did.

"Nice house," he commented, following her along the hall to Mark's room. There he performed the same inspection, even using the toe of his shoe to lift the *tatami* and peeking behind the decorative *koinobori*—cloth fish pennants—that she'd left on the wall.

She stood with her hands clasped in front of her, waiting impassively.

"I guess you were telling the truth, Mrs. Tanaka," he said, kicking the closet door shut, "about no one else being here."

Unless he wished to count the dead, Naoka thought, but he couldn't see them.

"Back to the front room," he ordered.

It was not that she wished to identify the man, but with each word he spoke, it became more obvious. She knew that his name was Morgan Lassiter, and he had been a patient with her at the clinic in Nevada.

She didn't understand why he had come here. Certainly, it could not be a matter of chance.

But whatever his purpose was, she had no control.

In the front room, Naoka watched him count the teacups and frown. All but hers were still full, the tea cold, the leaves settled to the bottom.

His eyes, visible behind the mask, showed his lingering doubt. She could almost see him thinking that he had been through every room, looked into every corner, and found no one.

Then he turned to her abruptly. "I think this belongs to you."

She accepted the wallet he held out. Kenichi's wallet. Her fingers caressed the stained leather. She'd noticed the billfold was missing, but assumed that she'd overlooked it in the pocket of a jacket she'd given away.

"It would be polite to say thank you."

Naoka bowed. "Thank you."

"Well." His eyes scanned the room again. "I have something else for you. Naoka, is it?"

She nodded and spoke softly. "Yes."

"Uh huh." His hand went behind him to his rear pocket, and he produced what looked very much like a reclosable sandwich bag. Inside was a slender metal object, perhaps five inches long. He brought it out and showed it to her. "It's a scalpel, darlin'."

Naoka felt her heartbeat quicken.

"We asked one hundred people," Lassiter said, his voice thick with menace, "what a scalpel might be used for—"

A bit confused, Naoka frowned.

"—and the survey said—"

He was very fast, and she felt the sting as the blade sliced her across the face. Blood splattered onto her kimono, soaking into the snowy white fabric. But this was not how she wished to die, cut to pieces.

Naoka closed her eyes, took a step forward, and offered her throat.

Part Four

Late May 1992

Chapter Thirty-nine

Bree Patrick wandered through the casino, hefting and listening to the clicking of the two hundred dollars in green chips she'd built from fifty at a blackjack table. For five o'clock on a Sunday morning, there was quite a bit of heavy action going on.

These gamblers were hard core. They seemed to prefer the early morning hours, maybe because by then the rank amateurs had usually given up and gone off to bed. Mostly male, they were quiet players, and expressionless. These were not gamblers who got giddy over a win, no matter what the size of the payoff.

Neither did they appear to be interested in her as she walked by.

Bree knew that she was an attractive woman, the kind of woman who turned heads and drew whistles from the less-articulate male. It was pleasant not to be verbally harassed or hit on . . .

She stopped for a moment to watch a gray-haired lady with a thin brown cigarette dangling from her lower lip feed dollar tokens into a progressive slot. The woman had her technique perfected; a motion expert would be hard-pressed to find a single wasted movement between dropping coins, yanking the handle, and reaching for the next handful of tokens even as the barrels turned.

As Bree stood watching, single bars lined up and the woman's winnings clattered into the tray. The woman didn't blink, or even hesitate, but immediately fed more coins into the slot. The inch-long ash from her cigarette fell off onto the floor.

Bree moved along, circling back toward the gaming tables. The dealer she'd won from had gone on break, and she hadn't liked his replacement, whose sour look made her want to ask him if he was dyspeptic or just your run-of-the-mill asshole.

There was only one crap table open, the three dealers outnumbering the two players. All were intent on the game, and she guessed it might have been because one of the players was laying bets "for the boys."

They were white, hundred-dollar chips.

She watched for a few moments, saw the player win on a hard eight, then shook her head and went looking for a place to sit down. Her feet were hurting.

Wearing nurse's shoes had ruined her for heels, but she liked the way heels made her legs look. And since she was getting out of nursing, she figured she'd better get used to it.

Later today she was boarding a plane to the east coast, Washington, D.C. her ultimate destination. Bright and early Monday morning, she would begin her new career as consultant to a political action committee that represented the billion-dollar interests of the pharmaceutical industry. The position paid a cool eighty-five thousand a year, plus bonuses.

She'd already put a down payment on a townhouse, and escrow would be closing by midweek. The down payment had been a "gesture of appreciation" from the CEO at one of the industry giants for her cooperation over Alan Kramer and his discovery.

The last she'd heard, the chemical analysis on the Affinity samples she'd supplied had not yet pinpointed the origin of the substance, but they were working on it night and day.

It was simply a matter of time, from what she'd been told, before the chemists identified the compound or its components.

Dr. Kramer had made a big mistake, trying to keep his "nutrient" secret. He should have gone public with Affinity—the FDA and its restrictions be damned—then patented it, and licensed the rights. Any one of the pharmaceutical conglomerates would have eagerly agreed to whatever price he'd asked.

At any rate, it was no longer a concern of hers. She had done what she was hired to do, and in a few short hours she'd be out of here.

Which was why she was up, wandering around at this ungodly hour: she was too excited to sleep. A brand new life awaited her in Washington. At last, she'd be getting every good thing she'd ever wanted.

As for the old life, good riddance. No more playing Nancy Nurse, handmaiden and lackey to the almighty physician. She would willingly walk away from the tedious scut work that the doctors found beneath *their* dignity but rather conveniently did not consider to be beneath hers. And if she never wore a latex glove again, it would be too soon.

One of the reasons she had gone into pediatric

nursing, instead of another specialty, was that she had assumed kids would be easier to deal with. They hadn't had time to develop the chronic diseases that were so intractable in adults.

Kids tended to be acutely ill, but usually from a single ailment. The possibility of complications was very real, but they didn't *compound*. It wasn't pneumonia on top of diabetes with a side of gall bladder disease and congestive heart failure, ad infinitum.

Only there were other problems she hadn't fully considered.

Losing a patient could be a shattering experience for any nurse, but watching the little kids slip away was far, far worse. More than once, she'd been the only person at the bedside when a child passed on.

There was something about watching tiny fingers fall limp, Bree thought, that seemed to deny the existence of a benevolent God.

Beyond that came the question of parents. She couldn't count the times she'd seen a child take a cue from a mother's alarm and began wailing in fear. Left to their own devices, kids adjusted to even the most unpleasant medical procedure almost matter-of-factly.

And then there were those parents, most frequently the mothers, whose own lives were so insignificant that they co-opted their child's. Bree remembered one young mother who got a satisfied gleam in her eye every time anything went wrong with her son. It was as if she and her son were in a competition with the other kids and parents over which child would have the closest brush with death. In some perverse way, the mother felt as if her status was raised when the

332

boy, a sweet young five year old, had a setback.

Bree had come close to flattening that mother after the silly cow had accosted her in the hallway, and demanded shrilly to be told why *she* hadn't been notified that the doctors were considering transferring the boy out of the Pediatric Intensive Care Unit.

"Because he's better," was all she'd said through her clenched teeth, and then she'd shoved the noxious woman aside.

Of course she'd been reported for it, and had received the expected reprimand from the nursing supervisor within the hour.

No, Bree wasn't going to miss nursing.

At six, she cashed in her chips, walked out of the casino, and headed to the parking lot where she'd left her rented car. Her plane ticket was in her purse, the luggage was in the trunk, and she hadn't a single regret about leaving.

The night sky was beginning to lighten in the east, and she felt a sudden kinship with the sun that also shone on her new home. Very soon, she'd be airborne, perhaps in time to watch the sunrise from her first-class seat.

Bree walked faster, her heels tapping loudly on the pavement. For reasons she couldn't name, she was beginning to feel anxious to be on her way.

"Ms. Patrick?" someone said from behind her.

No one was supposed to know where she was. Irrational or not, she had a sudden fear that it was Dr. Kramer, wanting to know why she'd betrayed his trust. Except he couldn't know, yet. So she stopped and turned, after arranging her face in a smile.

He was smiling, too. "You don't remember me,

do you? From the clinic?"

In fact, she'd recognized him immediately. "If you were betting on that, I'm afraid you'd lose your money, Mr. Lassiter."

Lassiter seemed pleased. "How about that? And here I thought I had the world's most forgettable face."

Not with those eyes, she thought. "Nice seeing you. Now if you'll pardon—"

"Listen, I can tell you're in a hurry . . . do you mind if I walk along with you?"

"Suit yourself."

"Then I will." He fell into step beside her. "Besides, it might not be safe for a woman alone."

Bree glanced around and saw that he was right; they were the only people in the lot. Funny she hadn't thought of that before.

"Fancy us meeting here like this. I mean—" he grinned "—small world, eh?"

"I thought you were down in Vegas." She didn't really give a damn, but since he was acting as her escort, she thought she ought to make conversation.

"Oh, I was. Too damned hot down there, so I went up to visit a friend in Seattle. No . . . more of an acquaintance. Then I drove eighteen hours straight, coming back." He nudged her with his elbow. "But I never thought I'd run into you here."

"Hmm."

"So, did you win?"

"Win?"

"In the casino just now." He turned so that he was walking backward, his deep-set eyes surveying the casino entrance. "You were playing, weren't you?"

Bree wondered if he wasn't taking this protector business too seriously. Did he think someone was following them? "I won, but not enough that someone would tail me out to my car for it."

"You never know." His eyes burned into hers.

"Besides, isn't there a security patrol?"

"Doesn't look to be, does there? Or could be they're taking a break."

"Wouldn't that be a piss-off, if they're drinking coffee while we're out here getting robbed?"

"Or worse. Some folks don't put much value on human life."

In spite of a tingle of uneasiness, Bree couldn't stop a cynical laugh. "Tell me about it."

"It's no joke. Kids kill kids over tennis shoes, a wino will off a drinking buddy for a couple of swallows of Irish Rose, but money . . . with money you can get your throat cut over pocket change."

"I suppose you're right."

"I am."

They were nearly at her car, a sporty black Ford Probe. She began to dig in her purse for the key.

Lassiter frowned at her. "What are you doing, hunting for your keys? Don't you know any better? A woman should always have her keys in her hot little hand when she's walking out to the car."

"Thanks for the safety tip," she said dryly.

"I'm serious. The few seconds you're not paying attention to what's going on around you are all that the bad guys need."

Bree held the key up for him to see. "Got it."

"Is that your car?" he asked, indicating the Probe.

"Well, it's certainly not that ratty van." The

van, which looked as if it hadn't been washed in years, or possibly ever, was the only other vehicle parked this far back in the lot. It had been full to overflowing when she'd arrived Saturday evening.

"No," Lassiter said, revealing the shiny blade to her, "it's not that ratty van, because that ratty van is mine."

What had been a tingle of uneasiness moments ago burst into sheer panic. Bree tried not to be obvious as she looked around the lot for help. There was no one else in sight. She could try screaming, but would anyone hear? Jab him with the key? Not a good idea, she thought. If he hadn't made up his mind to hurt her, getting gouged could tip the scales against her. As for getting away, maybe she could outrun him without her heels, but then again, maybe not.

He was herding her, she realized, into the space between the van and the car.

Wanting to understand how this had happened after she'd been so careful not to tell anyone her plans, she asked, "Did you follow me here?"

"You know I did." He pulled open the sliding side door of the van. "I was out driving, killing time, and I glanced over to take a peek at the blond in the racy black car. And what do you know? Like I said, it's a small world."

Bree closed her eyes briefly. "Would you take money?"

Lassiter grinned. "I'll take anything I want."

336

Chapter Forty

Tiffany rather liked taxis. The ride wasn't as smooth as in a limousine, but there was something kind of cozy in being able to see the driver's eyes in the rearview mirror. In a limousine, the smoked glass divider kept the chauffeur distinctly separate from the passengers.

She supposed that was the idea. Not a good one, she thought.

"Bernie," she said, "how much farther?"

"Hey, great minds, or what? I was just gonna ask you the same question." His voice was raspy sounding, and made her think of the way a cat's tongue felt. "But you been here before . . . I ain't."

The cab driver leaned his head partway out the window, as if the windshield was interfering with his view, then like a turtle ducking into its shell, drew it back in. Tiffany giggled.

Bernie gave her a quick over-the-shoulder look. "Now what're you laughing at? I swear, you're a regular little giggle-puss."

"What is *that?*"

"You're kidding me, right? You never heard of a giggle-puss?"

"No," she said, and covered her mouth to hold the laughter in.

"Yeah, well, if you want to know what one

337

looks like, take a peek." The cabbie directed the rearview mirror so she could see into it.

Of course it was her own face she was looking at, and that did her in. Tiffany fell over sideways in the seat and giggled helplessly. From the front seat she heard a chuckle from Bernie.

"Whoa," he said then, "this looks like the turn. Damn, but this place you're going to is dead center in the middle of nowhere."

With an effort, Tiffany sat up. They were indeed on the private road that ended at the clinic. Looking up, she could see the building's dark windows reflecting the desert landscape outside, and even recognized a red and blue splotch moving across the glass as the cab.

"Didn't I tell you I'd get you here safe and sound?"

"I think you did," Tiffany agreed.

The cab slowed as it veered right into the circular drive, then it came to a stop exactly opposite the clinic's front entrance.

The double doors opened and, as though she'd been waiting watchfully inside, Honor Matheson appeared. Tiffany wondered at the change in Honor, who even at a glance seemed tired and . . . hurt?

She got out of the cab and shut the door carefully, as Bernie had instructed her, "because it jams like Miles Davis used to."

"Tiffany," the nurse said, "I'm glad you're here."

At the rear of the cab, Bernie lifted her overnight bag out of the trunk. "Where is here, anyway? What is this place?"

Honor's hand came to rest on Tiffany's shoulder. "This is a private medical facility."

338

"You're not sick, are you kid?" Bernie asked with a frown, as he handed her the overnight bag.

"Not anymore." Tiffany unzipped her wrist-purse and brought out a wad of money. She'd taken all her stashed allowances, and borrowed another hundred from Juliet. "How much?"

"Tiffany, I'll take care of it," Honor said. "Why don't you go inside?"

"Okay, but"—she raised her eyebrows—"don't forget I'm a generous tipper. Bye, Bernie."

"It's been fun." Bernie gave her a salute. "And when you need a ride back to Reno, don't forget to ask for me by name. Papa's got to buy a mockingbird."

It was very strange finding herself alone in the clinic. There wasn't anyone at the nurses' desk, and when she called out "Hello," her voice echoed, unanswered, along the darkened hallway.

Tiffany walked slowly to the closest of the patient rooms. It was her old room, right across from the nursing station. Funny, it seemed as if it was both only yesterday and a lifetime ago that she'd stayed here.

Footsteps sounded behind her, and she turned as Honor Matheson approached.

"Where is everybody?" she asked.

"It's Sunday," Honor said. "The clinic is closed today. Actually, it'll be closed all this week."

"Then why—"

"Did I ask you to come here?" Honor's smile turned to pain as it reached her eyes. "I'll try to explain everything, as soon as the others get here."

"Oh." She considered for a moment. "When will that be?"

"Soon. Joshua should be here any minute, and Shea Novak's flight is scheduled to arrive at ten-thirty. If there are no delays, that is; not everyone has a Lear jet at their disposal."

Tiffany did her best to look innocent, or at least, not too guilty. The jet belonged to Aunt Mathilde, and it hadn't really *been* at her disposal.

"In the meantime, why don't we put your things in your old room and get you settled?" Honor took the overnight case. "I have to say, Tiffany, I'm a little surprised you came alone . . ."

It took less than five minutes to settle into her room, since she'd packed only one change of clothes, her pajamas, and a toothbrush. Honor had said it would be like a sleep-over and not to bring too much.

She needed toothpaste, though, and didn't find any in the bathroom.

Coming into the hall, she saw that Honor was at the desk but facing the other way. She was speaking quietly into the phone.

Curious, Tiffany took a step forward, and then another. By the fourth step she could make out a few words, but one of them sent her back to her room.

With shaking hands, Tiffany opened the sliding glass door and went out on the small private patio. It was warm out, and the dry heat felt good to her after the fog she'd left in La Jolla.

Think about other things, the voice in her head advised.

340

Other things. What the weather was like in Zermatt, Switzerland, for instance. Zermatt was where her mother was supposed to have gone after Stuart Healy's funeral. She'd traveled first to Monaco, to accompany the casket when it was flown to New York for the funeral.

Tiffany wasn't sure why her mother had chosen to go to Switzerland to mourn Stuart, unless maybe Zermatt was where they had honeymooned.

No one told her anything these days. Which maybe evened things out, because she hadn't told anyone, not even Juliet, where she was going when she came here. Well, the pilot knew, because he'd flown her here, but he wasn't one to talk, and in any case there was no one to tell.

For now, anyway. When everyone came home, someone might think to ask what she had been up to while they were paying their last respects to Stuart and offering their sympathies to the Healy family, but later was later, and there was no point in worrying about that now.

Tiffany heard an engine and went to the corner of the patio that had a view of the road. An Idle Springs police car pulled up.

Joshua had arrived.

"She hasn't told you why we're here?"

"No, not yet." Tiffany sipped 7-Up from a can and then put it on the patio wall. Even though Joshua's room was next to hers, she liked the view from his patio better. "She wants to wait for the others."

"Wonderful."

She could tell by the tone of his voice that he didn't mean it was wonderful at all. "Joshua . . ."

"What?"

"Do you think . . . are we sick again?"

"Shit, I hope not." He frowned. "I sure don't feel sick. Do you?"

Tiffany shook her head. "Only I heard that kids with leukemia can fall out of remiss . . . remission."

"That won't happen."

"How do you know?"

Joshua blinked rapidly at least a dozen times. She'd seen adults do the same thing when they were asked a question they didn't like. It reminded her that Joshua would be grown up pretty soon.

"For starters," Joshua said thoughtfully, "Dr. Kramer *said* it wouldn't happen. We're supposed to be cured, all of us."

"I know he *said* that, but . . ."

"But what?"

Tiffany bit her lower lip. Having overheard what she'd overheard, she knew someone hadn't been completely honest with them. "What if one of us died?"

"Died?"

"Yes." She leaned closer. "I don't know who, but one of us is dead."

Joshua laughed nervously. "It sure isn't me. And it isn't you. Who does that leave?"

"Honor told me Shea is coming—"

"The lawyer, right?"

"Uh huh. But she didn't say anything about Mrs. Tanaka or Mr. Lassiter."

He drummed his fingers on the patio wall. "I vote for him."

"To be dead, or—"

"Dead. Definitely dead."

342

"Me too." Mrs. Tanaka had seldom spoken to her, but Tiffany felt only gentleness from her. On the other hand, sometimes Mr. Lassiter got this look in his eyes that made her want to hide. "I vote for him, too."

"Besides, maybe whoever is dead didn't die of, you know, disease. It could have been an accident."

She hadn't thought of that.

"Anyway, I feel great these days." Joshua hesitated, tilted his head, and gave her the strangest, crooked smile. "Don't you?"

Tiffany wondered if she should tell him about the dream she'd had that Cousin Nelson could fly. Or about the Stuart dream, where he was driving on a winding road when without warning, the steering wheel could only be turned to the right.

Should she tell him, or anyone, that she'd had the dreams on the very nights they had died? That she'd been angry at Nelson because her mother hadn't come home? That she'd been angry at Stuart because when he'd called to offer his belated condolences, he'd suggested that her mother join him in Monte Carlo, where just the two of them would have "a rousing good wake"?

Was Joshua waiting for her to tell him these things? Or did he already know?

Joshua was watching her closely, Tiffany realized, and she understood that what he really wanted was an answer to the question he *hadn't* asked.

"Can you do it too?"

He nodded. "Absolutely."

She was about to ask what he'd done when she turned and saw Honor standing in the shadows of his room. A glance at Joshua was enough to warn him; he did a neat about-face and smiled at the nurse.

"Is it soup yet?" he asked with an odd laugh.

"Come to the lobby," Honor said quietly. "I think it's time we had a talk."

Chapter Forty-one

Joshua brought up the rear, following Honor and Tiffany to the clinic's lobby.

He hoped this wouldn't take long, because he had other things to do. He'd missed nearly two months of school, and although he'd tried to keep up with home-study courses, if he didn't crack the books seriously, he'd be in a world of hurt come finals at the end of June.

And it was important to him that he take decent grades back with him when he and Claire returned to San Francisco. There'd be no living down bad transcripts from a little town like Idle Springs.

Boy, would he be glad to write the end to this chapter of his life! In the city, he could open his window at night and hear something other than silence.

Although he had kind of liked it in the winter, when the Canada geese flew by in V-formation, honking. He liked the way the cold crisp air smelled of wood smoke. And he very much liked how when it snowed, and the outside world faded away.

"Joshua? Did you hear me?"

He shook his head, chagrined. "Sorry, I guess I was daydreaming."

Honor motioned for him to be seated, and he

sat between Tiffany and Shea Novak, who smiled a silent greeting. For a lawyer from Frisco's arch-enemy, L.A., she looked pretty damned good in jeans.

"I'm glad you could make it here today," Honor said. "I guess there's really no need to mince words, here. I know there are some very peculiar things going on in each of your lives."

"I'm sorry to interrupt," Shea said, "but exactly how would you know?"

Joshua exchanged a glance with Tiffany.

"Of course you'd would want to know how I know," Honor said, sounding as if she were talking to herself. "Of course. All right. Please understand that this is very difficult for me, because I've worked with Alan Kramer for a long time, but . . ."

"Go on," Shea prompted.

"It appears that he has arranged to . . . well, to have you watched."

"No shit?" It was out before he could stop himself. Way to go, Reid, he thought disgustedly, what a juvenile thing to say.

"From what I've been able to find out," Honor continued, "he had two methods of tracking you. First, he hired a national clipping service to scour area newspapers for your names, or any names that he could associate with you. For example, Shea, he gave the service in Los Angeles the name of your firm and the partners, several of your neighbors, close friends, your ex-husband—"

"Steve?"

"—your doctors of course, and so on."

"Where did he get these names?" Shea asked. "How could he find out such personal information?"

"Some were right there in your medical records." Honor paused, looking down at her folded hands for a moment. Then she added, "As for the others, I believe he may have photocopied pages out of your address book while you were a patient here. Specifically, while you were undergoing your treatments."

"I don't believe this."

"Then he hired private detectives to follow up on anything he found to be of interest."

"Wait a minute, private detectives?" Joshua shook his head in disbelief. "In Idle Springs? Give me a break; the folks in town talk among themselves plenty, but they wouldn't give an outsider the time of day."

Honor smiled faintly. "You're right, not in Idle Springs. But you were close enough that he could follow your progress himself."

Shea had leaned forward, her elbows on her knees. "I'm not trying to be argumentative, but why would Dr. Kramer do something like that?"

"Because he had reason to believe that there were certain side effects of your treatment that he would need to monitor."

Tiffany had been chewing on her thumbnail as she listened to them talk, but now she gave Joshua a wide-eyed, frightened look.

"Side effects of the treatment," Shea repeated. "I assume by treatment, you mean Affinity."

"Yes."

Shea's expression was skeptical. "And these side effects you're talking about, he could monitor them by reading the newspaper? Or through private detectives? Isn't that . . . bizarre?"

"Of course it is, but that isn't the half of it." Honor turned her head. "You know what I'm talking about, don't you, Joshua?"

He touched his fingers to his chest. "Me?"

"There've been all kinds of accidents up there in Idle Springs. *I* heard rumors about them, and I wasn't even an interested party."

"Well, yeah, I suppose there have been a few mishaps, but what does that—"

"—have to do with you?"

Joshua wanted to believe it was merely suspicion in her eyes, but there was something about the careful, measuring way she looked at him that led him inescapably to another conclusion: Honor knew.

Busted!

If that wasn't a piss-off. Joshua folded his arms and slumped down on the couch. "I don't know what you're talking about."

"That isn't true. You've had a hand in Idle Springs' troubles, haven't you?"

"No." Deny, deny, deny; that had been his father's motto. I didn't do it, see it, hear about it, or think it. Of course, look where denial—also known as lying—had landed Jack Reid. "No."

Shea glanced from Joshua to Honor and quickly back again. "Just a second, Joshua, I know stonewalling when I see it. Is there any truth to what she's saying? About these accidents?"

"She hasn't *said* anything. She's implying that I know something and hoping that I'll admit to it without her having to prove she's right."

"Joshua," Tiffany said in a small voice, "don't get angry."

Honor got up, came over to Tiffany, and sat beside her. "It isn't good to get angry, is it? What happens when you get angry?"

348

"Hey, leave her alone!" he protested. "She's just a little girl."

The nurse looked at him calmly. "Not just. Did you know, Joshua, that Tiffany's cousin died tragically not long after she left the clinic?"

"Died?"

"And that less than a week later, one of her mother's former husbands was killed?"

Tiffany said nothing, but began to sniffle.

"It'll be all right," Honor said, and hugged the child to her side.

Joshua couldn't believe this was happening. "Why don't you leave her alone?"

"Because I want to help her." She stroked Tiffany's white-blond hair. "And I want to help you."

Leave us alone!

How could he have forgotten his most potent weapon? Why argue with her when he could simply suggest a different outcome?

Forget this, and we'll all go home.

"It won't work on me," Honor said patiently. "I don't know how much you've figured out about how the power works, but I have it on excellent authority that it doesn't work on everyone—"

As it hadn't on his grandfather.

"—and in any case, you can't influence another person who has been treated with Affinity. Which I have, solely as a precautionary measure."

Joshua groaned. "Damn it—"

"Hush now." Shea put her hand over his. "What power are you talking about?"

"Haven't you guessed? From the clippings I read, it would seem that the criminal justice system is being short-changed in Los Angeles these days. Felons are dropping like flies."

Awareness dawned in Shea's smoky blue

349

eyes. *"I* did that?"

"Yes, you did." For the first time, Honor appeared uncertain. "You didn't know? Really?"

Shea didn't answer immediately, but when she did, it was clear that she was bothered. "Not consciously, no. At least I don't think so."

"Regardless, what we have to do is stop it, now, before anyone else gets hurt."

"What if I don't want to stop?"

They all looked at him, and he could read the censure in their faces.

"You don't have a choice."

"Don't I? The first time in my life I've had the power to control how things went, to change things I don't like, and I'm supposed to give it up?"

Honor nodded, perfectly serious. "Yes."

"You've gotta be crazy."

"Joshua, calm down," Shea said. "Listen to what she has to say."

"I've listened, but I haven't heard anything that makes sense to me." He stood up and headed for the door. "You guys can do whatever you want, but do me a favor and forget about me, okay?"

"You're a part of this," Honor said. "Running away won't change that."

"I'm *not* running." It was a sore spot, since so many people in his life had run away from him. "I'm just leaving. There's a difference."

No one came after him. Joshua walked along the private road, his hands thrust angrily in his pockets.

It was a long way to town—three or three-and-a-half miles. In this heat, he'd be dry as a bone by the time he got to Idle Springs.

But he kept walking. With any luck, once he reached the main road someone would happen by and give him a lift into town. Then he'd go straight to the house and convince Claire that had to leave *today*.

Damn it all, anyway—why was it that something always had to happen just when he'd begun to believe he'd worked the kinks out?

It was almost as if there was someone dangling happiness in front of him, all set to pull it away the instant he reached for it.

That's what had happened this last time his father went to prison. His dad and Claire were packing up to move with Joshua into a real live house, after years of apartment-dwelling. Somehow or other, she'd scrimped and saved enough for a security deposit, plus first and last month's rent on a three-bedroom house with a yard.

Not that he didn't love living in the city, but as a white kid, he was a minority in their neighborhood, and he'd been getting pushed around a lot. The name-calling he could handle, and give back better than he got, but one of these days someone was bound to get hurt.

Him, probably.

So he'd been anticipating moving to a new house, going to a new school, maybe making some new friends . . . and then his Dad had gotten arrested for possession of stolen property and illegal possession of a firearm. Since he was a many-time loser, that penny-ante charge, coupled with repeated failures to report to his parole officer, was enough to land him a three-to-five.

Claire had had to ask their would-have-been landlord for the money back to pay for a disinterested attorney. Not that it had made any difference; the DA was unwilling to make a deal.

No wonder Claire had freaked and dumped him on Grandpa. No damn wonder.

Joshua bent down and picked up a rock, then threw it so it skipped down the asphalt. Looking into the distance, he saw a smoky haze. Something burning, somewhere.

What if, he thought, Claire decided to take off and leave him behind again? What if he did what Honor wanted, and he couldn't make Claire stay any longer? Who would that help?

He wouldn't use his abilities on anyone else. No more clumsy attempts to make silk purses out of sows' ears. He'd leave Idle Springs to the locals and concentrate on his own life.

Compromise, that was it.

Maybe he ought to go back to the clinic and listen to what Honor had to say. What Tiffany had told him about one of their number being dead worried him a little, and besides, he could probably handle the situation with Claire better if he knew his limits.

Forewarned is forearmed, he told himself.

It was uphill to the clinic, and he was out of breath by the time he made it to the driveway.

In the still air, he could hear the siren of the town's 1958 fire truck, manned by volunteers. With a final glance over his shoulder at the now billowing cloud of smoke, he reached the front door.

He took a couple of deep breaths, so he wouldn't sound winded, and then heard voices from inside.

"—asinine mistake on his part," a man said.

Dr. Kramer? But it didn't sound like him.

Joshua brought his face closer to the tinted glass, and shaded his eyes with his hand.

Morgan Lassiter stood perhaps ten feet away, facing the others, his back to Joshua.

So much for being voted dead.

"What I'm trying to tell you," Honor said evenly, "is that it isn't risk-free for any of us. There are potentially dangerous side effects—"

"Hey, life is dangerous. And I can tell you right now, side effects are the least of your worries."

Joshua saw then that Lassiter was holding a knife by his right leg. He backed away from the glass door carefully, not wanting to fall. When he was far enough away, he turned and ran.

Chapter Forty-two

From the corner of her eye, Shea watched Joshua run off, and tried to keep her expression neutral. The last thing she wanted was for Lassiter to detect a glimmer of hope on her face, and turn around to see what she might have been looking at.

She alone had seen the boy return; Tiffany was between them, and couldn't see around Honor, while Honor had been staring directly into Lassiter's eyes since he walked in on their discussion.

They had a chance, albeit a slim one, if Joshua called the cavalry in.

How far was it to Idle Springs, she wondered. How long did they have to hold out?

"—Kramer is in a hospital in Reno," Honor was saying. Honor had grown a backbone since the last time Shea had seen her.

"Now isn't that a shame?" Lassiter said nastily. "Remind me to send him a get well card."

"You're missing the point, Mr. Lassiter. The doctor had a transient ischemic attack on Friday, and yesterday he suffered a full-blown stroke. He's been treating a slight palsy he has with Affinity for—" Honor blinked "—several weeks now."

Honor was lying, Shea realized, but about what?

"Is that supposed to scare the shit out of me? Save your breath, darlin'."

"I'm only trying to warn you, it could happen to you or any of us."

Lassiter gave an exaggerated sigh. "You won't shut up, will you? Maybe I should do a quick trach, eh?" He flashed the knife.

"What do you want from us?" Shea asked, hoping to distract him.

He shrugged. "Different things. From her"—he used the tip of the knife to indicate Honor—"I want a way into the lab."

"There's nothing in there—"

"Shut up, Nightingale, or you'll be sucking air through your throat."

Catching Honor's eye, Shea shook her head. "Fine, we can get you into the lab. What then?"

"Don't worry yourself about it."

"I am worried," she said in as reasonable a tone as she could muster, "because the way you keep waving that knife around, you're frightening this child."

He grinned. "But not you?"

Always negotiate from a position of strength. Never tip your hand. "Not me."

"Brave lady," he said mockingly, then took a step closer to them. "But let's not get too far off the track. I came here to get more of the good stuff, and whatever else happens is just icing on the cake."

Shea recognized the flat look in his eyes and suppressed a shudder. He meant to kill them. If they were lucky, that was all he would do.

"First, I want to check and make sure there's no one else here." He came even closer, until the distance between them was virtually nil. "For all I know, that crap about Kramer being in the hospital is a bald-faced lie. It would be inconvenient for everyone if I was to be interrupted at a critical moment, so . . ."

Quicker than seemed possible, Lassister reached out and grabbed Tiffany by the wrist, yanking her to her feet.

Tiffany gasped, but didn't cry out.

Honor started to stand up, but Lassister might interpret that as a threat, so Shea reached over to stop her.

"What are you doing?" she asked him.

"I said I'm gonna have a look around, and Tiffany is going with me."

"I'll go."

He laughed. "Right, and *Ms*. Matheson will take off with the kid to go for help."

The man wasn't as dumb as he seemed.

"If I take Tiffany, and come back to find one or both of you gone—" almost lovingly he pressed the knife to the child's neck "—I'll kill her. Okay?"

"What are we going to do?" Honor said, when Lassister and Tiffany were out of hearing range.

"Think. And think clearly. Is there anything we could use as a weapon against him?"

"Not while he has Tiffany . . ."

"No, of course not. Later, I mean."

Honor ran a hand through her hair distractedly. "There has to be. Has to be."

"It needs to be something that'll stop him cold on the first shot." Shea stood up and began to pace slowly back and forth. "He's not going to stand there and let us have at him. Not a knife, then."

356

"I got the feeling he's good with his," Honor said.

"Me too. Or we can try and stall him." Shea glanced at her watch. "How long would it take to run to Idle Springs for help?"

"What? You heard him, if either—"

"I'm not talking about us." Shea lowered her voice. "Joshua came back. He saw Lassiter and took off running. If we can stall somehow, maybe help will get here before things get uglier."

"You mean before he kills one of us."

"Exactly." Shea felt oddly relieved that Honor didn't have to be told Lassiter's intentions. "But how much time is it gonna take?"

"It's about a quarter-mile down to the main road, and I think three miles into town."

"Damn, so far?"

"It would take at least an hour to walk, and that's at a brisk pace, so maybe add five or ten minutes," Honor said. "If he could run that far, he might make it in . . . forty-five minutes?"

"Damn. I didn't dare look at my watch when Joshua left, but I doubt it was more than ten or fifteen minutes ago. At best, that leaves us with half an hour before we can start looking for help to arrive. That is, *if* it arrives at all. Damn."

"Lassiter will be back soon," Honor said thoughtfully. "And it'll take a little while for him to get what he wants out of the laboratory. He'll want to do that next, don't you think?"

"Probably."

"I can pretend to have a problem working the locks, or something—"

"I'd think twice about that; if he catches you at it, or even suspects, he's likely to retaliate first and ask questions later."

357

"Then what do we do?"

Shea sat back down. "Improvise. Tell me about the lab. What's in there we could use?"

"Unfortunately the microscopes are bolted to the workbenches, or we could crush his skull. There are various liquid reagents that might sting his eyes if we tossed the stuff in his face, but—"

"Honor . . . could we use this power we have to get help? Like dialing a mental 911?"

Honor's expression sobered. "Actually, I've been trying to do that since the bastard walked in and announced he'd cut the phone lines. But the way it works, you have to direct your thoughts to someone specific, and I'm afraid Chief Reid isn't receiving."

"Try someone else," Shea urged.

"I would, except I don't know anyone else in Idle Springs. It would be like . . . trying to send a bouquet by throwing flower petals into the wind. And we're running out of time."

"Maybe not." Shea frowned. "I have an idea."

Lassiter returned with Tiffany a few minutes later. The child looked pale, but seemed to be all right as she came to sit between them.

"Don't make yourself too comfortable," Lassiter said. "Everybody's gonna help me in the lab. Is that understood?"

"Just tell us what you want us to do." Shea got to her feet with what she hoped Lassiter would take to be absolute resignation.

"That's good," he said approvingly. "Tiffany can hold my hand again on the way there. You two walk ahead, and go slowly so I can enjoy the view."

Shea exchanged a look with Honor, then they

358

did as they'd been told. Shea felt his eyes upon her with every step. She'd need about eight hours in the shower with Lava soap to wash the scum's stare away.

When they reached the laboratory, Honor used her ID card to open the door.

Inside, the lights came on automatically, and soft classical music began to play.

Lassiter's attention shifted immediately to the huge refrigeration unit to their left, and he didn't appear to notice that Shea remained in the doorway. Honor had told her that was the only way to keep the door from closing and locking them in.

Behind the glass were hundreds of the familiar small bottles of Affinity.

Lassiter let go of Tiffany and went to the refrigerator with the avid look of a kid in an ice cream shop. He slipped his knife into a sheath inside his boot, and then slid the glass door open.

Reaching in, he grabbed a bottle, then another. "Get me something to put these in."

Honor went to a cabinet and opened it.

Tiffany was only a few feet away from her, but Shea couldn't risk leaving her spot at the door. Despite what she understood about one Affinity user being unable to reach another, she tried to will Tiffany to turn around and look at her.

"Will this do?" Honor turned from the cabinet, a box in her hand, and as she did so, caught Tiffany's eye with a nod at the door.

Then Honor stepped between them and Lassiter.

Tiffany turned to Shea with a questioning look. Shea motioned urgently and Tiffany took a hesitant step toward her.

Leaning forward as far as she dared, she

359

grabbed Tiffany's arm. "Run and hide," she whis
pered. "Get outside if you can."

Tiffany didn't need to be told twice. She ran
lightly, hardly making a sound.

"Hold the top open," Lassiter said to Honor
who was holding the box for him.

Shea waited until Tiffany was out of sight, then
counted to ten. *"Now."*

"Catch." Honor threw the box at Lassiter, then
spun and ran for the door. Lassiter tried to grab
it, but it crashed to the floor, glass breaking and
gold liquid splattering everywhere.

"Damn you, bitch," he cried.

Shea waited a heartbeat or two, long enough to
see Lassiter's face contort into rage as he started
after Honor, then stepped out of the doorway and
into the hall.

The door began to shut.

"Come on, Honor," Shea urged, even as she
backed away. If the door closed both of them in
there, she would never forgive herself.

Honor slipped through, her face a grayish color.
"He's coming," she gasped.

They took off running, by design in different
directions so that he couldn't catch them both.
Shea felt compelled to look over her shoulder
and see what happened.

If the door closed on him, he'd be locked in
side.

"Please, please, please," she whispered.

But grunting like the pig he was, Lassiter made
it through.

Chapter Forty-three

Garrett Reid kicked at the charred earth and elt as near to cussing as he'd come in a while. But there was no use for a man to hold a principle if he couldn't abide by it. "Darn those kids."

He hadn't figured out yet which kids were prime suspects in torching Dora Metzger's garden shed, but they'd come awful close to taking the house along with it. When and if he did nab someone for it, there'd be more coming to them than the usual slap on the wrist.

That old woman would be fit to be tied when he got a look at her blackened backyard. Not that he could blame her, but she brought at least some of her troubles on herself. She ought to know that kids these days weren't going to take meekly the scoldings she dished out at every opportunity.

Oh, they might apologize when a deputy had them by the scruff of the neck, but the next time they were out to raise a ruckus, old lady Metzger's place would be right back at the top of their list.

And of course *he* would be at the top of Dora's list, because, as chief of police and as a neighbor to boot, he hadn't prevented this.

Reid shook his head. He turned around in circle again, surveying the damage. There weren many sights less appealing than scorched eart and blackened rose bushes. The smell was som what overpowering, too. An acrid, throat-cloggir smell.

"Hey, Lester," he called, spying a tendril (smoke, "there's something still smoldering there by your right foot."

Crazy Lester hopped back as if he were stanc ing on coals, and began whacking the groun with his army-surplus shovel.

"What's he doing?" Claire asked, coming u and handing him a glass of what looked like len onade. "Beating the worms senseless?"

Reid sighed. "Your guess is as good as mine He took a swallow of lemonade before he remen bered the last time Claire had made it.

"Makes you pucker, doesn't it? Do you think needs more sugar?"

"A touch." His vocal cords were seeking cove and he sounded as if he had laryngitis.

"That's what I thought." She put her hands (her hips and shook her head. "What a mess."

Luckily, his jaw hadn't quite unlocked from th tart lemonade and he had a moment to think over, during which he realized she was talkir about the yard and not her latest culinary effor

"It'll grow back," he said when he could.

"Poor old lady. What's she going to think whe she sees this?"

"Probably that her tax dollars are going waste when the police can't stop a bunch of wi kids from terrorizing a sweet old lady."

Claire laughed. "That bad, huh?"

"That bad and then some. The sad thing is,

he'd spend even a tenth as much time being friendly to her neighbors as she does tending those flowers, this wouldn't have happened."

"Tending people is important, isn't it?" Claire shaded her eyes when she looked at him.

"It surely is."

"You know, Garrett, Joshua and I have been doing a lot of talking."

"I thought you might." He reached down and plucked a slightly charred weed from the ground. "The boy wants to leave, doesn't he?"

"He does. I'm not sure I do."

Reid gave her a sideways glance. "Is that a fact?"

"I kind of like it here."

It wasn't his place to do any convincing, so he merely nodded to show he was listening.

"I thought I could get a job, maybe in Reno, and look for a place to stay."

"You're welcome in my house."

"I appreciate the offer, but Joshua . . . I think Joshua needs me to himself right now. We've got a lot to work out between us, after all."

"That's fine." But the thought of coming home to an empty house again was unsettling. Strange how after so many years of living alone he'd gotten accustomed to having Joshua around. "Whatever you want to do."

"Well, the job comes first, of course. I can't pay rent without a paycheck coming in."

Reid inclined his head in agreement at the simple logic of that. "What kind of work are you gonna be looking for? I know a lot of people, here and there. Maybe I could put a good word in for you."

Claire smiled and ducked her head. "Actually, I

don't know what I'm qualified to do. Jack alwa[y]
said maybe I'd be suited to sorting M&Ms [by]
color."

"That's a mean-spirited thing to say." Re[id]
frowned. "I hope you didn't believe him."

"There were times when I did."

"Maybe it's a good thing he's in prison," [he]
said, and meant it. "Otherwise I might have [to]
wring his fool neck for saying such things."

"They're only words."

"He has no right to put anyone down, the me[ss]
he's made of his life."

Claire smiled and turned away, but not befo[re]
he saw her eyes were wet with tears.

Feeling a little awkward, he surveyed the yard [a]
final time. Lester and Blue had gone to the fro[nt]
to fold up the canvas fire hose.

"Well, I guess I'm done here." Reid looked [at]
the glass doubtfully. He sure wasn't up to an[y]
more lemonade, but if he poured it out, nothi[ng]
might ever take root and grow on that spot agai[n.]

"I'll take that."

"It did hit the spot," he said, and hoped not [to]
be struck by lightning for his white lie. "But I'[ve]
got to get back on patrol—"

"Hey Chief!" Blue Hawley called. "Emily's [on]
the radio and she says it's urgent."

"I'll be there directly."

"Shouldn't you hurry?" Claire asked, walki[ng]
beside him. "Since it's urgent, I mean."

Reid ambled along at his normal pace. "In a[ll]
the years I've worked with Emily, there hasn[']t
been one call that she didn't say was urgent."

"Then what—"

"If it was a real emergency, most likely you[']d
hear her yelling in the microphone from here."

364

In fact, he *could* hear Emily squawking by the time he'd come around the corner of the house. He put his hand on his holster to steady his gun and took off at a trot for the cruiser.

Reaching to open the door, he had to jump out of the way to avoid being run down by Dora Metzger's red Buick Skylark. She missed the patrol car's left front bumper by a fraction of an inch and skidded to a stop.

When she got out of the Buick her expression was livid, and the first thing she did was rip off the motorcycle helmet she always wore while driving—in case an earthquake caused a bridge to collapse while she was passing beneath it—and throw it at him.

He caught it squarely in the chest. "Ouch."

"What have they done to my property?" she demanded. "What's going on here?"

"Now, Dora—"

"Don't you Dora me. Why is it I can't go and visit a friend in Gerlach for a few days without coming back to . . . to a brouhaha."

Lester, who'd stopped to watch the commotion, laughed his donkey laugh.

"If you'd give me a chance," Reid said, glaring at Lester, "I'll explain it, but right this minute I've got another call."

"Ha! Don't think you're gonna run off without an explanation." Dora waggled her finger at him. "Because I pay my taxes and I—"

Reid climbed into the patrol car and shut the door. The windows weren't soundproof, but they shaved a few decibels off the top.

"This is Reid," he said into the microphone. "What is it now?"

"There's some kind of trouble up at the clinic Emily said, a little louder than necessary. "Joshu is here at the station—"

"What on earth?"

"—and he says you'd better get on out there a hurry. He says there's a man with a knife."

"I'm on my way."

Ignoring Dora Metzger's offended expressio Reid started the engine and put the cruiser in r verse, backing into his own driveway to tu around. Then he hit the siren and floored it.

Chapter Forty-four

Lassiter stopped and listened for the sound of labored breathing.

That was what was missing in the movies: during a chase, the damned music that told you something exciting was going on—in case you couldn't tell—drowned out or covered up the ragged breathing of the pursued.

In real life, the need to fill oxygen-starved lungs was often a tip-off to a hiding place. Not too many people could breathe quietly after running even a short distance—not if their lives depended on it.

Which it sometimes did.

There weren't any lights on in the hallways or rooms, which made it difficult to see, despite it being daylight outside. But he had better than average hearing and a fair amount of experience, and he was going to find that damned Novak bitch before much longer.

And when he did, there'd be no more mistakes. He wasn't going to be made a fool of again.

He was looking forward to hearing her scream.

Lassiter walked slowly and carefully, listening. Out of habit, he ran the flat side of the blade up and down his pant leg. The fabric whispered, but wasn't loud enough to mask other sounds.

He didn't figure that he had a lot of time. H should allow for at least one of them having e caped the building. If that one happened to the little girl, he might have a couple of hou before the alarm was sounded, but only an idi would count on it.

If Novak or Matheson had gotten out, cut th time in half to an hour. Reduce it even further, thirty minutes, to allow for the unlikely possibili that whichever one it was might be able to wa down a car once she reached the main road.

Earlier today, Lassiter had spent several hou watching the road, and had counted about o vehicle per hour. The way he calculated it, t odds of that one vehicle passing by simultaneo to the bitch's arrival at the side of the road h to be astronomical.

Even so, he'd bring his safe time availat down to fifteen minutes so that if a fucking p rade was passing through when she got there, he still have a couple of minutes leeway.

Fifteen minutes.

"Not long to live," he said softly, as he push the door to Kramer's office open.

The blade whispered, too.

He'd chosen the left hallway because Sh Novak had run in this direction, but now he w beginning to wonder if he'd made the right de sion. The staff's living quarters were in this wi and most of the doors were locked, so if sh come this way she'd probably had no choice b to run out the rear exit.

Which would mean he'd wasted precious mi utes, and maybe lost them all.

"Damn." He looked further down the hall at the two doors he hadn't tried. Both were closed, and only narrow strips of light showed beneath them.

Were someone standing behind one of the doors, he would be able to see the break in the light. Of course, maybe she had thought of that. Perhaps after slipping inside, she'd gently closed the door so he wouldn't hear the click, and now was standing off to one side.

He had to go on. Down to eight minutes on his clock, he would knock her out if he found her, and take her to the van parked by the kitchen entrance. He'd get away from here ASAP and then deal with Ms. Novak at his leisure, somewhere down the road.

As for the Affinity, she had cost him that. He hadn't thought of anything but chasing them after the scheming slut threw that box at him.

Only after the laboratory door slid shut behind him did it occur to him that he couldn't get back in without an ID card. Another reason he should have gone after the nurse instead of Shea Novak.

No, he wouldn't be loading cartons of Affinity into his van, newly equipped with three Coleman coolers filled with dry—and now useless—ice. He hadn't helped himself to intravenous supplies, either.

He hadn't done any of the things he'd come here to do, and he had seven fucking minutes left. He reached the first door and listened for a few seconds before trying the knob. Locked.

Naturally, if she had gotten inside, she could've locked herself in. But he sensed that she wasn't in this room, any more than she'd been in the others, because the nursing staff who lived in

369

these rooms during the week had quite properly and responsibly locked up before leaving for their weekend in town.

Carrying his logic a step further, there was reason to believe that she wouldn't be behind the last door either, because the odds were that it was locked as well.

Except . . . except Honor Matheson hadn't gone away for the weekend. The last door could well be to her room. Would she have locked it if she'd planned to stay the night?

"The hell with it," Lassiter muttered, and walked the last ten steps to the final door without bothering to try and be quiet.

He grabbed the doorknob and nearly shit when it turned easily in his hand. "What the fuck?"

The door swung open.

He was wrong about it being Honor's room; the door opened into a linen closet, the walls lined floor to ceiling with shelves stacked high with sheets and towels and such. But he was right on another count.

"Damn," he said, and smiled. "I can't tell you how glad I am to see you, Ms. Novak. What's the matter, was the exit door locked?"

Shea remained silent.

He had to give her credit; she hadn't started to cry yet. "You know, sometimes I don't think things through. Of course you couldn't get out the exit . . . this place is closed on Sundays, and they'd want to be keeping the riffraff out, so they have to lock the doors."

"Fascinating," she said.

Lassiter laughed. "I like a woman with a sense of humor. I like you, as a matter of fact. I'm glad it's you I found."

Shea Novak stayed where she was, her back pressed against the shelves.

"But we've got to go, now. We don't have much time." He crooked a finger at her, indicating for her to come to him. She didn't obey, of course, but it pleased him very much that she didn't make any rude hand gestures in return, either.

The lady had a little class.

"Come on, Shea. Make it easy on yourself. I've got five minutes left to get out of here."

"Am I supposed to care?"

"I would if I were you. I've cooled off now, but I guarantee you wouldn't have wanted to run into me a few minutes ago." He stepped into the linen closet with her and reached quickly to grab her by the arm.

Only she startled him by spinning out of his reach. Then she ducked around him and took off running again, this time toward the front of the building.

It was the only way out, other than the sliding glass door he'd forced open in his old room.

"Shit," he snarled. He jammed the knife into the sheath in his boot and started after her.

In her running shoes she had more traction than he did in his boots, but his legs were longer and he was catching up when they reached the lobby. Seeing those double doors only a few yards away, he lunged forward and hooked his arm around her shoulder and neck.

They fell to the floor and he landed halfway on top of her, which knocked the wind out them both. He also cracked his right elbow on the floor, which made his hand go abruptly numb.

He fell over onto his back and changed his grip on her to his left hand as he tried to recover.

Dazed, he tried to estimate how much time he had left. Four minutes? Had it taken only a minute to run her down? Or could it have been longer?

Lassiter forced himself to sit up. Flexing his right hand, he got the feeling back in his fingers.

Shea's eyes were closed when he looked at her, and she was breathing heavily through her mouth. But it didn't appear that any real harm had been done.

"Come on." He stood, grabbed her under both arms, and pulled her to her feet. He glanced at the double doors, so temptingly close, but the van was parked in the back and it would be easier and faster to walk through the building than around it.

"Come on," he said again. Her legs were unsteady, though, and after a few steps he knew he couldn't spare the time. He picked her up, slung her over his shoulder, and carried her.

Down the right hall, toward his old room. He'd even left the sliding door ajar.

"Almost there," he said.

"But not quite," a voice said. Honor Matheson stepped out of the doorway to room three.

Chapter Forty-five

Honor kept her right hand behind her back, out of Lassiter's line of sight. "And the last I heard, almost doesn't count."

He grinned at her. "You know, I gave you more credit than this. How stupid can you be not to have run when you had the chance?"

"I could say the same thing about you. You could be miles away from here by now."

Lassiter put Shea down so that she was standing, facing forward but pressed against him, with his left hand spread across her abdomen. He reached down with his right hand for the knife. To Honor, Shea had the stunned-senseless look of someone who's received a blow to the head.

"But since we're both here," Lassiter said, "you can do me a favor, eh? Go to the lab and grab a few bottles of Affinity."

"Weren't you listening?" Honor thought of Alan as she'd last seen him, ashen and incoherent, being loaded into the back of an ambulance. "The stuff is dangerous. If you take too much of it—"

"Right, you said that before." He smiled and shook his head. "And then *I* said something to the effect that I don't believe you."

"Mr. Lassiter—"

"Cut the crap, lady." He showed her the knife.

"Or I will. Just shut up, do what I tell you, and I won't have to use this."

"Someone will be here, soon." Honor wasn't sure that she was doing the right thing to warn him of that, unless maybe knowing he might get caught could convince him that it would be stupid to hurt them.

"Don't waste your breath. If you're here, then it's Tiffany out there, running her little legs off for help. And there's no way a kid that age could make it into that sorry excuse for a town in less than a couple of hours. If she can make it at all."

"I wouldn't be so sure."

"There are snakes around, you know. If she wanders off the road, she could run across one. Or maybe some guy will pass by with a taste for the young stuff, and he'll take Tiffany for a ride."

Honor found it difficult to hide her disgust. How could anyone talk about something so vile and perverted in such an offhand way?

"You don't care to hear that, do you?" Lassiter asked, and laughed. "I can see it in your eyes."

"Does it surprise you? That everyone isn't as twisted as you are?"

"Twisted. I think I like the sound of that."

Honor turned her head. "Speaking of which, do you hear it? That siren?"

"I don't hear anything."

She did, though. It was far off, but coming closer. Her knees felt weak at the possibility of getting out of this alive . . .

The glee had faded from Lassiter's eyes, and she could tell that he'd heard it, too. Then she noticed that his knuckles were white from gripping the knife. He deliberately brought the blade up and touched the tip of it to Shea's face.

"Company's coming, after all," he said, and wet his lips. "I think we'd better be leaving."

"Don't!"

Lassiter ignored her. He slipped his right arm under Shea's knees and picked her up again. The knife was still in his hand and he moved it back and forth menacingly, as though to show her that he could do some damage to her if she came closer.

Desperate to stop him, Honor considered rushing him, but the sight of that six-inch blade kept her back. "Wait! I'll get the Affinity for you."

"Too late for that now." He sidled along against the wall, keeping his distance.

"Mr. Lassiter, I'm asking you, please leave her here." Honor stayed on her side of the hallway, but kept roughly abreast of him, careful to keep her hand hidden. "She'll only slow you down."

He grunted, trying to hurry and clearly feeling the strain of time. "I have to have something to show for all of this."

The siren was closing in. "In a minute, the police will be here. If you get out of the building, they'll try to cut you off, or—"

"This is a one-horse town," he said. He was opposite room five now, and he gestured to her with the knife to back away. "It's one car pulling up out there, with one old cop inside. There ain't gonna be no road blocks, and there sure as hell isn't gonna be no SWAT team storming the place."

Honor could see that Shea was finally beginning to come around, from the way she tried to hold her head up, and in the rapid blinking of her eyes.

Now's the time, she thought.

With her thumbnail she popped off the plastic needle guard, then closed her fingers around the syringe barrel and tightened her hold.

Lassiter was noticeably nervous as he crossed the hall and ducked into his former room. Honor followed quickly on his heels, but he had anticipated that and was scuttling sideways like a crab toward the open sliding glass door, watching her every move.

Shea's eyes opened and stayed open.

In the front of the building the siren died out, and was followed fifteen seconds later by the sound of footsteps running down the hall.

Honor could see the indecision in Lassiter's face. Hold on to Shea and probably get caught, or let her go and possibly get away. There was another choice—use her as a shield in making his escape—but he didn't take it.

Instead he put her down quickly and shoved her roughly away, then darted out the sliding glass door.

Honor felt adrenaline speed up her heart, and instinctively she ran after him. She hoped the cop didn't try to shoot him and accidentally hit her.

Somehow she caught up with him, just as he was about to vault over the patio wall. She grabbed onto the back of his shirt and pulled, while at the same time raising her right arm and then plunging the needle into the muscles near the right side of his neck.

Lassiter yelled and tried to pull away from her and the needle, but she had already injected him full of Pavulon. She withdrew the bloodied needle—had she hit a vein?—and stepped back to watch him fall.

Which he did, twitching, to the ground.

"I was supposed to give that to you earlier, Mr. Lassiter," she said quietly, watching his chest stop heaving as his breathing slowed. "Doctor's orders."

Epilogue

September

Shea removed the bridal veil from its box and shook it out gently. Made of fine Irish lace, it had tiny seed pearls along the crown. "This is beautiful."

"Isn't it? I found it at a boutique in Boston the last time I went home."

Shea brought it to Honor, who was sitting at the dressing table and looking slightly overwhelmed. "I would imagine Idle Springs would be home by now."

Honor smiled. "I guess it is."

"You don't sound too sure of that." Shea positioned the cap that the veil was attached to and reached around to the dressing table for the clips to hold it in place. "I haven't decided yet whether I think you've made the right choice by staying here or not. I mean, so many memories . . ."

"Sometimes I remember. Not often."

"No? I still have nightmares now and then." This morning she'd woken at daybreak, absolutely certain that *he* was standing over her, knife in hand.

Don't be silly, her inner voice had chided. *The man is dead.*

Lassiter had died from an allergic reaction to

378

the drug Honor had used to incapacitate him; there was also speculation that Affinity might have played a part, given its cumulative toxicity in Dr. Kramer.

But this wasn't the time or place for remembering.

Shea looked at Honor's reflection in the mirror and frowned. "Does that look straight to you?"

Honor turned her head slowly from side to side. "If it isn't, no one will notice. They'll be trying to figure out what the strange sound is."

Shea laughed. "And that would be?"

"My knees knocking. Why am I so nervous?"

"Well," she fluffed the lace out, "it isn't every day a woman marries the man of her dreams."

The door opened behind them, and Tiffany came in. Tiffany and her mother had arrived this morning from Lisbon, where Pamela had bought a villa to get away from it all in while Tiffany attended a nearby private school.

Coolly blond, her dark green eyes complemented by her mint green flower girl's dress, Tiffany looked very much the young heiress.

"Aren't you ready yet?" Tiffany asked. "Everyone is waiting."

Shea glanced at her watch. "We're not late."

"I remember one time when my mother got married," Tiffany said with an impish grin, "she was so late walking down the aisle that the groom got drunk and nearly passed out."

"Now there's an idea." Honor made a minor adjustment to her veil and then stood up resolutely.

Shea had to laugh. "This isn't an execution you're going to. Smile!"

Honor's smile was distinctly unconvincing.

"What are we going to do with her?" Shea asked Tiffany. "The groom is going to take one look and head straight for the hills."

"At least he won't have far to run," Tiffany said, going to the window and gazing out with a wistful expression on the desert hills. "Besides, we can always make them *think* she's smiling."

"Tiffany, hush." Months had passed, but they all had retained a hint of that . . . ability.

"All right," Honor said. "I'm ready."

Walking down the narrow aisle, Shea smiled at Garrett Reid, who'd been kind enough to offer the use of his home for Honor's wedding. He'd done a nice job, he and Joshua, with the floral arrangements, orchids accented with white satin bows.

Or had that been Claire? Shea wouldn't be surprised if one of these days she received an invitation to the wedding of Garrett and Claire. Despite the difference in their ages they made a handsome pair, he tall and straight and a little less rigid these days, and she petite and feminine in a self-assured way.

Catching Joshua's eye, Shea winked. In a few years, he'd be as handsome as his grandfather and with any luck as good a man.

Shea took her spot opposite the best "man," who oddly enough was a red-haired female nurse from Boston. Then they all turned to watch the bride make her journey down the aisle. The familiar wedding music made Shea's heart beat a little faster.

And for all her early nervousness, when she finally appeared in the arch of the door, Honor ooked absolutely radiant. In silk and lace, she seemed to almost float down the aisle.

Honor's bouquet was striking as well, featuring a dozen elegant, white, star-shaped flowers that were unlike any Shea had ever seen.

"Isn't she beautiful?" someone whispered.

Shea glanced across at Alan Kramer, who still relied on the aid of a cane after his stroke and brush with death. He had grayed at the temples since she'd seen him last, and there was a kind of ease about him.

Curious, that ease, given the storm of controversy surrounding his miracle cure, Affinity. But then he'd had a great deal of time to think while he was convalescing, and had presumably come to terms with facing the consequences of his actions.

The subsequent change in his relationship with Honor was another factor, no doubt; the transformation from doctor and nurse to friends, and then to lovers, had humanized him. When he smiled now, there was warmth in his eyes.

Eugene had been urging her to accept Alan Kramer as a client, arguing that there was no one better than she to plead his case. He'd saved her from certain death, Eugene said, and her presence in the courtroom at his side would be a potent if unspoken reminder of the good Kramer had done, even if he hadn't followed the rules.

But she'd think about that later. Right now there were other matters to attend to.

Honor had made it all the way up the aisle. Shea could see the slightest trembling in the bride's hand as she extended it to her groom. But Honor held her head up high and the doubt that Shea had seen in her eyes had vanished, now replaced by a serene contentment.

381

"—we are gathered here today," the preacher was saying, "to join this man and woman in holy matrimony . . ."

Afterward, Shea caught the bouquet.

YOU'D BETTER SLEEP WITH THE LIGHTS TURNED ON!
BONE CHILLING HORROR BY

RUBY JEAN JENSEN

NNABELLE	(2011-2, $3.95/$4.95)
ABY DOLLY	(3598-5, $4.99/$5.99)
ELIA	(3446-6, $4.50/$5.50)
HAIN LETTER	(2162-3, $3.95/$4.95)
EATH STONE	(2785-0, $3.95/$4.95)
OUSE OF ILLUSIONS	(2324-3, $4.95/$5.95)
OST AND FOUND	(3040-1, $3.95/$4.95)
AMA	(2950-0, $3.95/$4.95)
ENDULUM	(2621-8, $3.95/$4.95)
AMPIRE CHILD	(2867-9, $3.95/$4.95)
ICTORIA	(3235-8, $4.50/$5.50)

ailable wherever paperbacks are sold, or order direct from the Pub-
her. Send cover price plus 50¢ per copy for mailing and handling to:
bra Books, Dept. 3747 475 Park Avenue South, New York, NY 10016.
sidents of New York and Tennessee must include sales tax. DO NOT
ND CASH. For a free Zebra/Pinnacle Catalog with more than 1,500
oks listed, please write to the above address.

HAUTALA'S HORROR — HOLD ON TO YOUR HEAD!

MOONDEATH   (1844-4, $3.95/$4.9
Cooper Falls is a small, quiet New Hampshire town, t
kind you'd miss if you blinked an eye. But when darkne
falls and the full moon rises, an uneasy feeling filte
through the air; an unnerving foreboding that causes t
skin to prickle and the body to tense.

NIGHT STONE   (3030-4, $4.50/$5.5
Their new house was a place of darkness and shadows, b
with her secret doll, Beth was no longer afraid. For as s
stared into the eyes of the wooden doll, she heard it call
her and felt the force of its evil power. And she knew
would tell her what she had to do.

MOON WALKER   (2598-X, $4.50/$5.5
No one in Dyer, Maine ever questioned the strange disa
pearances that plagued their town. And they never d
cussed the eerie figures seen harvesting the potato fields
day . . . the slow, lumbering hulks with expressionless f
tures and a blood-chilling deadness behind their eyes.

LITTLE BROTHERS   (2276-X, $3.95/$4.9
It has been five years since Kip saw his mother horri
murdered by a blur of "little brown things." But the "lit
brothers" are about to emerge once again from their und
ground lair. Only this time there will be no escape for t
young boy who witnessed their last feast!

*Available wherever paperbacks are sold, or order direct from
Publisher. Send cover price plus 50¢ per copy for mailing a
handling to Zebra Books, Dept. 3747, 475 Park Avenue Sou
New York, N.Y. 10016. Residents of New York and Tennes
must include sales tax. DO NOT SEND CASH. For a free Zeb
Pinnacle catalog please write to the above address.*